Love at First Light

BOOKS BY STEPHANIE GRACE WHITSON

Historical Fiction
Love at First Light
Messenger by Moonlight
Daughter of the Regiment
A Captain for Laura Rose
A Basket Brigade Christmas (novella anthology)
A Patchwork Christmas (novella anthology)
Christmas Stitches (novella anthology)

The Quilt Chronicles Series (3 books)
The Message on the Quilt
The Shadow on the Quilt
The Key on the Quilt

Stand-alone Books (not part of a series)
A Most Unsuitable Match
Sixteen Brides
A Claim of Her Own
Belle of the Wild West

Pine Ridge Portraits Series (3 books)
Secrets on the Wind
Watchers on the Hill
Footprints on the Horizon

Dakota Moons Series (3 books)
Valley of the Shadow

Edge of the Wilderness
Heart of the Sandhills

Keepsake Legacies Series (3 books)
Sarah's Patchwork
Karyn's Memory Box
Nora's Ribbon of Memories

Prairie Winds Series (3 books)
Walks the Fire
Soaring Eagle
Red Bird

Contemporary Fiction *(3 books)*
Jacob's List
A Garden in Paris
A Hilltop in Tuscany

Nonfiction
How to Help a Grieving Friend: A Candid
Guide for Those Who Care
Home on the Plains: Quilts and the Sod House Experience
Ink: A Writing Life

Love at First Light

STEPHANIE GRACE WHITSON

And God said, Let there be light…
And God saw the light, that it was good.

Genesis 1:3-4

This book is a work of fiction. Names, characters, places, and incidents are either the product of the author's imagination or used fictitiously. Any resemblance to actual events, locales, or persons, living or dead, is coincidental.

Copyright 2023 by Whitson, Inc.

Scripture quotations are from the King James Version of the Bible.

All rights reserved. In accordance with the U.S. Copyright Act of 1976, the scanning, uploading, and electronic sharing of any part of this book without the permission of the publisher constitute unlawful piracy and theft of the author's intellectual property. If you would like to use material from this book (other than for review purposes), prior written permission must be obtained by contacting the copyright holder at stephanie@stephaniewhitson.com. Thank you for your support of the author's rights. www.stephaniewhitson.com

The author is represented by Books & Such Literary Management, Inc., 5926 Sunhawk Drive, Santa Rosa, CA 95409. www.booksandsuch.com.

*Dedicated to the memory of
God's extraordinary women
in every place
in every time.*

My Sincere Thanks

Sharon Campbell
for prayer support, writing retreat housing,
brainstorming, and critiques

Kristy Conrad
for prayer support, critiques, and brainstorming
(and for falling just a little bit in love with Gideon)

Gretchen Garrison
author of many fine books about Nebraska,
including *Detour Nebraska*
for critiques and eagle-eyed editing

Daniel Higgins
creative consultant extraordinaire

LoRee Peery
author of *Christmas House* and many other delightful romances
for critiques, prayer support, and eagle-eyed editing

Elizabeth Squires
for essential first-chapters critiques

Laura Steinman
Arbor Lodge Coordinator
Arbor Lodge State Historical Park & Mansion
for unfailingly generous access to historical documents and
unselfish sharing of historical expertise and knowledge

About the Author

Award-winning novelist Stephanie Grace Whitson began writing her first novel when she was inspired by the lives of pioneers laid to rest in an abandoned cemetery near her home in southeast Nebraska. What began as a hands-on history lesson for her homeschooled children became a topic of personal study that eventually evolved into a story about an 1840s woman headed west across what would become the state of Nebraska. Creating her imaginary friend Jesse King led Stephanie to learning about the Great Plains women she came to think of as sod house homemakers. Researching their stories has inspired several novels. Her writing career has spanned nearly three decades, and her idea file is still brimming with book ideas—all of them inspired by the often nameless and anonymous women who pioneered in the western United States. Stephanie is a follower of Jesus Christ and student of the Bible, a lifelong learner (she earned her master's degree in history in 2012), a lover of antique quilts who enjoys hand quilting, an avid reader, mother to five grown and married children, and grandmother to thirteen. Learn more at www.stephaniewhitson.com.

Chapter 1

Hope deferred maketh the heart sick.
Proverbs 13:12

May 2, 1868
St. Louis, Missouri

Isobel Manning stood at her bedroom window, looking down on the remnants of what should have been the happiest day of her life. The servants had spent the morning trotting here, scurrying there, all under Mother Manning's practiced eye until, at last, Isobel's stepmother declared perfection. The stage was set for the elegant launch of St. Louis's spring wedding season via the uniting in holy matrimony of Miss Isobel Manning and Mr. Alfred Sanford Warfield III "on the Manning residence lawn at four-thirty o'clock in the afternoon."

Elegant launch, indeed.

Isobel gave a low, bitter laugh. In addition to Mother's elaborate outdoor staging plans, the older woman had spent untold hours deciding on the perfect color scheme for the bridal party. Seven bridesmaids in plum-colored silk, carrying baskets spilling over with peonies and chrysanthemums as they moved slowly down the aisle to the strains of Pachelbel's "Canon in D."

What a waste.

The string quintet had departed long ago. Only the urns of flowers remained on the platform built expressly for this day. Isobel allowed a sigh. By pushing a velvet drape aside and pressing her cheek to the window glass, she could see a few of the linen-covered tables arranged off the back portico. The servants were collecting chairs, tipping them to see the names affixed to the underside of each one so they could be returned to the half dozen neighbors who'd been happy to facilitate the nuptials.

What a farce.

When voices sounded outside her bedroom door, Isobel pulled the drape closed and stepped away from the window. She glanced down at the three-carat diamond on her ring finger. If things had gone as planned, there'd be another ring beside it—the golden band especially designed to nestle against and complement the diamond. *But now...* She glanced at the watch suspended from a golden chain about her neck. *Six o'clock.* If things had gone as planned, the wedding guests would be dining on roast lamb and baked yams. Toasting the "happy couple."

Happy couple. What a—

Isobel looked down at the ring again. *What a... what, exactly? Had the entire courtship been a lie?* Had Alfred ever truly intended to keep all the promises he'd made? Why had he let it come to this? Why humiliate her in such a public fashion? Would she ever understand?

With another sigh, Isobel slipped the ring off her finger. She hesitated for a moment before crossing the room and setting it on the polished mantle above the fireplace.

A firm rap sounded at the door and Mother Manning's voice rang out. "Open the door, Isobel."

Mother had apparently recovered from the dramatic prostration she'd acted out when Isobel handed her the note Alfred had had delivered by messenger.

A messenger. The coward.

Another rap on the door. The doorknob rattled. "Isobel. Did you hear me? Please open the door."

A shiver crawled up Isobel's spine. She might be at a loss for words, but Mother Manning never suffered that affliction. Taking a deep breath, Isobel obeyed her stepmother's directive.

Mother swept in, speaking as she flung open the drapes at each of the three sets of double-hung windows. "Refusing to look at reality is no way to rise above a situation." She did not look at Isobel. Instead, she went to the bed and reached for the note lying next to the rumpled wedding gown. She read it more than once before finally looking up. "Most young ladies who've just been jilted would have collapsed in a puddle of emotion." She glared at Isobel. "Aside from keeping your drapes drawn, you seem oddly... unaffected."

Unaffected? How could Mother think that? *Just because I didn't shriek and faint doesn't mean...* Isobel looked down at the carpet. What was she feeling exactly? She wasn't sure. And so, she shrugged and said, "We weren't exactly the love story of the year." She glanced up, barely managing to stifle a shiver when she saw the expression on Mother's face. *Whether it's the truth or not, you shouldn't have said that.*

Accusation crept into Mother's tone. "You *suspected* this might happen?"

Isobel looked back down at the carpet. Had she suspected? Should she have known Alfred wouldn't follow through? She touched the now-empty ring finger, managing only a slight shrug by way of response.

Mother seemed to take the shrug as a sign of admittance. She snorted disapproval. "You might have said something. Preferably *before* I lavished so much money on a failed event."

A failed event. Money wasted. Isobel's fault, of course. It was always her fault when things didn't go the way Mother intended. Forcing herself to look up and into Mother's gray eyes, Isobel rose to her own defense. "Of course I didn't suspect. I thought we were a good match—as did everyone we know."

"Everyone except Alfred, it would seem." Mother dropped the letter back on the bed. "And little Mary Halifax." She muttered the girl's name as if it were a curse word.

The mention of curvaceous, blue-eyed, golden-haired, porcelain-skinned, eighteen-year-old Mary Halifax—who was everything slender, dark-eyed, red-headed, twenty-four-year-old Isobel Manning was not—somehow transformed Isobel's bewilderment into anger. How dare Alfred do this to her? *How dare Mother blame me?* The anger dried Isobel's threatening tears.

But Mother wasn't finished. With a deep sigh, she muttered, "First Charlie, and now this."

Isobel frowned. "What does my brother have to do—"

"Please, Isobel," Mother scolded, "you know how I hate it when you pretend ignorance. The name *Manning* has always carried weight in this city. Thanks to your father, may God rest his soul, we are leaders in commerce and culture. Certain expectations flow out of that position—among them, the creating of alliances between leading families." She extended one index finger. "One disappointment is just that—a disappointment." She waved her hand as if shooing a fly. "Every family has a black sheep. At least Charlie disappointed with a modicum of charm."

Charm. An interesting choice of words for Charlie's refusal to marry Isobel's best friend, Elizabeth Warfield. Mother had always assumed that Charlie would marry Elizabeth, and Elizabeth's brother, Alfred, would marry Isobel. When the time came, the foursome would reign over St. Louis society as had their parents before them. But Charlie had been home from the war only a few weeks when he caught a raging case of gold fever and boarded a steamboat bound for the West.

Isobel frowned. "You didn't call it *charming* when he went bust and settled in Nebraska instead of coming home."

Mother dismissed the comment with another flourish. "Men can get away with that kind of thing. Especially when they're heroes. Many of our boys were changed when they came back from the war. Restless. Unwilling to settle back into life as it had been. Besides that, Charlie wasn't the one to break things off with Elizabeth. That was her decision, and she did it in a dignified way. There was no public drama. Nothing for the gossipmongers to relish." Mother adjusted the jeweled bracelet at her wrist. "But you and Alfred? That's another matter entirely." Again, she sighed. "If he'd only stopped to consider what he was *doing.*"

Isobel reached for the letter on the bed. "I'd say he made what he's doing quite clear. He's simply doing it with Mary Halifax instead of me."

Mother turned away to peer out the window. "Can you imagine what all this means for us? How it changes things?" She recited a litany of dangers looming in the murky future—Isobel, alone, navigating a city where everywhere she went Alfred Sanford Warfield III appeared with Mary Halifax on his arm.

Dread washed over Isobel as she realized the truth of what Mother was saying. In coming days, the jilted Miss Isobel Manning would be the center of attention for the worst reason possible. The spurned lover. The former fiancée. The *spinster.* Isobel regarded her reflection in the dressing mirror positioned in one corner of the room. No man other than Alfred had ever shown the slightest interest in her as a woman. Those inclined to be kind ignored her red hair. They called her *noble, with an aristocratic nose and serious dark eyes reflecting intelligence.* But the unadorned truth was that Isobel Manning was the female reincarnation of her deceased father. As such, she was too tall. Too angular. Too everything. Her freckled skin would not bleach, no matter the claims of the endless supply of miracle creams Mother ordered. *And that red hair. Most unfortunate.*

5

"Isobel! You aren't *listening*."

With a start, Isobel apologized. "I'm sorry, Mother. I—I suppose it's finally sinking in." She stared down at Alfred's note and the six lines of beautiful script that had dismantled her future, focusing on the closing: *Fondly, even in regret.*

What unmitigated gall.

Mother crossed to where Isobel stood and snatched the note from her hand. Stepping to the fireplace, she fed it to the flames. "There," she said and swiped palm against palm.

When Mother noticed the ring on the mantle, Isobel spoke quickly. "Caesar can take it to the Warfield home tomorrow."

"Caesar will do no such thing," Mother retorted. "It was especially designed for you. It's yours."

"But—."

"After what Alfred Warfield has done, he couldn't possibly expect you to return it. Even if he did hope for that, he wouldn't dare ask."

Isobel frowned. "But I don't *want* it."

"Understood," Mother said as she pushed the ring onto her own finger. "I'll see to selling it. Discreetly, of course. To defray all the pointless expense Alfred's duplicity has caused us."

She's more concerned about the money and her social standing than she is about me. It wasn't as if Isobel hadn't known it, hadn't lived with the reality all these years since Papa's death. And yet, having Mother display the truth in such an obvious manner on such an awful day caused a new kind of hurt.

Mother pointed at the rumpled wedding gown on the bed. "I'll send Portia up for that—and Caesar to retrieve your trunks from the wharf."

She really doesn't care about me at all. Isobel clasped her hands before her in an attempt to hide their trembling. She did her best to stifle the hurt and to match Mother's businesslike attitude. "The trunks are probably already on board the *Laura Rose*."

Mother harrumphed at mention of the steamboat that was to have taken the adventurous newlyweds to Nebraska for what Alfred had called their "wilderness wedding trip." Lucinda Manning had thought the notion ridiculous. "You cannot be serious," she'd said. "You'll take the train east like every other civilized couple we know."

To his credit, Alfred had stood his ground with Mother Manning on the subject of the honeymoon. Eventually, he'd made her laugh at the idea of a buffalo rug spread before the parlor fireplace come winter. All of it, Alfred said, would be a prelude to the book he would write about the American West—with the assistance of Isobel's brother, Charlie, who'd be an excellent resource after his travels.

Thinking on it now, Isobel wondered at Alfred's sudden retreat from adventure and into the arms of Mary Halifax, who screeched at the sight of the tiniest spider and grew faint at the very idea of walking along the Mississippi, let alone floating upon the Missouri—a much more dangerous river. What would Alfred write about now, Isobel wondered.

Again the annoyed tone of voice, as Mother said, "Then Caesar will board the *Laura Rose*. He can drive the wagon down to the levee and have your trunks loaded before sunrise. There's no need to make a public spectacle of every detail of our lives." She crossed the room, giving Isobel an awkward pat as she advised, "Try to get some sleep. I'll have Cook brew some chamomile tea. And we'll all feel better in the morning. You can take the day off from making calls, of course. No one will expect you. *I*, on the other hand, will *not* have people whispering that an upstart like Mary Halifax sent the Edward Mannings into hiding." She grunted softly. "The girl's mother would love that." Opening the door, she glanced Isobel's way as she added, "We won't give her the satisfaction. I'll consult Miss Hartley's book of etiquette for guidance as to how to assure that you can

7

re-enter society with your head held high—as befits a Manning. The gossips can all go to Hades." Mother stepped into the hall, closing the door firmly behind her.

Isobel plopped down on the bed. She'd had a decade to adjust to her widowed stepmother's domineering ways, but this—this was surely the acme of the woman's insensitivity. Isobel's wedding day ruined—her future uncertain—and yet Mother's concerns were the money and her own social standing. She'd snatched up Alfred's ring to remedy the first and would consult Miss Florence Hartley's recently published *Lady's Book of Etiquette* regarding the second.

For the next few moments, Isobel sat motionless in the fading light, staring at the closed bedroom door and wishing with all her heart that Papa was still alive. She retreated even further into the past to long for the mother she barely remembered. How would Mama have reacted to today's fiasco? There was no way to know, for Isobel barely remembered Mama. She was, however, confident that Papa's only concern would have been that his "busy Izzy" be all right.

Busy Izzy. She'd earned the nickname as a child and done everything in her power to live up to it as she grew. Papa had always approved of her boundless energy and found ways to soften the disapproval of the woman he married after Mama died. Sadly, the second Mrs. E. L. Manning seemed to think Isobel a rival for Papa's affections. While she didn't exactly belittle Isobel's accomplishments, she never praised them. Isobel had always loved poetry, and when a local newspaper published one of her poems, Papa beamed with pride. Mother Manning said very little. When Isobel learned to play a difficult etude on the piano, Papa applauded. But Mother Manning began finding excuses to leave the room when Isobel played.

The stepmother-stepchildren relationship grew even more complex when Papa died, leaving Isobel and Charlie at the mercy of the woman who barely tolerated them. With the outbreak of war, Charlie enlisted. Isobel poured her energies into volunteerism—something Mother deemed acceptable "under the circumstances." She joined the Ladies Aid, serving as treasurer of her small circle and writing anonymous promotional pieces for the upcoming St. Louis Sanitary Fair. She worked in various booths during the fair and was gone from early morning until late at night during the month-long event. Eventually, however, even that resulted in Mother's disapproval. The St. Louis paper praised Isobel by name, mentioning her "tireless efforts and excellent journalistic contributions." Mother was horrified. It was unseemly for a young lady to be "called out" in such a public way. Thinking back on it now, Isobel realized the older woman's criticism still smarted.

Alfred Warfield's proposal was the first thing in Isobel's life to win Mother Manning's unabashed approval. After all, a Warfield-Manning union would guarantee the Manning family's standing in St. Louis society. And now—now Mother's position was at risk. Of course, Isobel was to blame. After all, she had failed to keep Alfred's interest.

Isobel was still resisting tears when a soft rap sounded at the door. It opened a few inches. "It's Portia, Miss Izzy. Brought you a tray of comforts."

Isobel rose, opening the door to admit the wizened housekeeper who was carrying a tray laden with all manner of goodies. Noting the aroma of bergamot, a grateful Isobel allowed a little smile. "I thought Mother mentioned chamomile."

Portia sniffed. "And why'd I bring chamomile when I know you don't cotton to it?" She settled the tray on a marble-topped side table. "Brought a couple slices of fresh bread. Butter. That cheese you like. A couple nice apples. That-a-way you need some time to yourself, you don't need to be worrying about something to eat." She paused. "Way I figure, a woman what's been mistreated by a low-down varmint of a man probably needs a little time to herself." She looked Isobel in the eye. "And a man who don't know what a prize you are, Miss Izzy, be a low-down varmint if there ever was one. And that is the truth, so help me God."

Kindness did what disappointment could not. For the first time since Papa's funeral, Isobel Victoria Manning allowed the tears to flow. And Portia Jefferson did what Mother Manning never would. She took Isobel in her arms and let her cry.

Chapter 2

And where is now my hope?
Job 17:15

Isobel thought she'd convinced Caesar to help her escape, but when the time came to board the *Laura Rose*, the old man hesitated. "I don't know, Miss Izzy. Miz Manning ain't gonna like it. Not one bit."

"Maybe not at first," Isobel agreed. "But when she really thinks about it, she'll be relieved. And if *you* really think about it, you'll know I'm right." She reached into the bag at her wrist for the note she'd labored over the night before and held it up. "You won't need to say a word. Just hand her this. I've explained about visiting Mr. Wilder at the bank and how he helped me with the details of the trip. I even mentioned his convincing the ticket agent to honor Alfred's reservation—absent Alfred. And to assign me a smaller berth and refund the difference in cost. Mother will understand it's all for the best." The truth was that Mother Manning would be *relieved* to be rid of her stepdaughter for a while, but Isobel wasn't about to say that aloud.

When Caesar finally accepted the note, Isobel tapped it with a gloved finger. "Please be certain to wait until *after* the *Laura Rose* has pulled away from the landing before delivering that." The last thing she needed was Mother Manning causing another scene to impress onlookers with her "touching concern" for her stepdaughter.

Caesar tucked the note away, but still didn't move toward the gangplank. Isobel grabbed the carpetbag he'd been carrying. "If you aren't going to escort me aboard, then please step aside." She glanced pointedly at a couple making their way toward the steamboat. "We're blocking the way for other passengers."

With a grumbled protest, Caesar took back the carpetbag. He followed Isobel up the gangplank, across the steamboat's freight deck, and toward the wide stairs leading up to the main deck. Finally, they located Cabin 3, so designated by an elegant ironwork number affixed to the center of a narrow door. Opening the door, Isobel stepped into the cabin.

Caesar remained outside as he handed in the carpet bag. He motioned toward the door set in the cabin's opposite wall. "That one opens into the social hall. Dining room come mealtime." He hesitated. "You sure I can't talk you out of this? I got to be able to tell Miz Manning I tried."

"You did try," Isobel said, "and I listened. But now I'm going to visit my brother." She might not have been thrilled by the prospect of traveling in the West when it was Alfred's idea for their wedding trip, but now she was—well, determined if not exactly thrilled. Going to Nebraska meant she wouldn't have to see Alfred squire a younger, prettier woman about town. She wouldn't have to see her friends pretending not to watch her. And best of all, she wouldn't have to endure Mother Manning's moods day in and day out. Embarking on this journey offered an escape she could not resist.

"Folks talk bad about ladies that go off by theyselves without a escort."

Isobel took a deep breath. "Folks are going to be talking about me anyway." She forced a smile. "Once I'm with Charlie in Nebraska, I'll write. Even if she's upset with me, Mother will love having news of Charlie. We both know she has always favored him over me."

Caesar raised another concern. "You never had to worry over money, Miss Izzy. You going all the way up that river, how you gonna get by? They got a telegraph in New-braska? They got banks and such?"

Isobel reassured him that Papa's own banker had confidence in her financial abilities. "In the past, Mr. Wilder praised the balance sheet I kept for the Ladies Aid funds." She patted the carpet bag as she continued. "He set out a reasonable budget for me to follow. I have funds for the trip itself, and thanks to Papa's making provision for me in his will, I don't need to worry over money—as long as I live sensibly. And I will."

Caesar still shook his head. "Miz Manning gonna be terrible upset."

Isobel let her frustration sound in her voice as she snapped, "When *isn't* 'Miz Manning' upset about something I've done or haven't done?" She plopped the carpet bag down at the foot of the cot, forcing calm into her voice as she said, "I always wondered what it would feel like to run away from home. Now I'll know." At the blast of a whistle, she exited the narrow berth, brushing past Caesar and crossing to the railing to watch the packet next to the *Laura Rose* back away from the levee.

Caesar followed, muttering about having her trunks brought up from the lower deck.

"You can set them on the cot opposite mine." Isobel pointed to the place another passenger might have occupied, had Isobel not requested—and paid for—privacy. While Caesar was gone, she concentrated on watching the activity on the wharf. A thrill of excitement coursed through her mid-section. Or was it dread?

Isobel wasn't entirely certain which. Not that it mattered. She was leaving.

※

Sunday, May 10, 1868
Midnight
Nebraska City, Nebraska
Attracted to the river by a steamboat's shrill arrival signal, Gideon Long peered out from beneath a canopy of sumac crowding the banks of the Missouri River. When the packet's whitewashed corbels and railings glinted in the moonlight, he muttered to the dog at his side. "That's the *Laura Rose*." He remembered seeing it laid by at this same spot seven years ago when he and the rest of the First Nebraska had steamed past aboard the *West Wind* bound for... glory.

"Glory." He spat the word out as a curse as he reached up to trace one of the scars forming a hideous map across his face. The dog whined and touched a cold nose to the palm of Gideon's hand. He patted the animal's head as he muttered, "I was a fool, thinking bullets and cannon were little more than pieces in a game of heroes." He watched as the steamboat's boom lifted a plank, dropping it in the perfect spot to facilitate the transfer of passengers and freight from the packet to the landing. *Passenger,* Gideon noted. Only one. A woman, from the shape of the shadow silhouetted against the moonlit surface of the water. He drew back a bit farther, watching. There hadn't been much freight to unload. A few crates and two trunks, the latter probably hers.

A wide swath of earth between the landing and the top of the hill leading into Nebraska City had been worn bare. As the whistle announced the *Laura Rose's* departure, Gideon looked toward town, watching for Ezra Carter, who'd be leading his mule, Jezebel, the latter pulling a two-wheeled cart.

Something about the waiting woman seemed uncertain. She kept turning this way and that, first facing town and then looking back toward the river as the *Laura Rose* departed. Almost as if she regretted disembarking. Why was she alone? Ladies didn't travel alone these days. He grunted. Maybe she wasn't a lady. Maybe she'd answered one of those newspaper ads promising young ladies employment in "reputable establishments" that were anything but. Maybe those trunks held ruffles and lace and—*never mind*. The Good Book said to keep one's mind on things above.

"Good advice," he muttered. "Good to keep your mouth shut, too. Only crazy people talk to themselves as much as you— or to their dogs, for that matter." Probably true. Quiet now, fingers clutching the bandana that served as the dog's collar, Gideon lurked in the shadows. Watching.

❦

Alone in the dark, Isobel watched the *Laura Rose* head upriver. As the paddlewheel churned the water, it shattered the reflected moonlight into countless pieces of shimmering silver. She watched until the steamboat was out of sight, then glanced in the direction of what was supposed to be a growing town. Where was Charlie? Alfred had telegraphed their expected arrival date— hadn't he? *Or maybe he hadn't. Maybe he'd decided there wouldn't be a wedding trip long before the day of the ceremony.* Again, his betrayal clawed at her midsection.

Locusts and frogs had always been friendly night sounds at home. Here, with shadows looming and a dense overgrowth of trees and scrub along the river, every sound seemed ominous. The town itself was obscured from view by what must be a steep incline. The soft glow from a couple of windows downriver indicated buildings, but it was impossible to know whether they were dwellings or warehouses. A rim of pale light at the top of the hill was the only other indication of civilization. When an owl hooted, Isobel startled.

Finally, a jangle and a steady creaking sounded from the direction of the city. *Thank heavens.* A circle of yellow light appeared at the top of the hill, and a flaming torch came into view. It was held aloft by a giant of a man with a shock of white hair.

"Sorry I made you wait, ma'am," the giant boomed. He jangled the mule's halter. "Jezebel, here, was especially reluctant to make the trip to the river tonight." He dropped the torch into a hollow iron pipe jutting out of the earth, then gestured toward the crates and her trunks. "All this yours?"

Isobel shook her head. "Just the trunks."

The mule brayed. Its owner ordered it to quiet down before introducing himself. "Name's Ezra, ma'am. Ezra Carter." He spoke to the mule again. "We're helping a *lady* tonight, Jezebel, so you mind your manners. She done give you a light load, too. That's another reason to be nice." The man kept a running one-sided conversation going with the mule as he guided her into place. Once the back of the two-wheeled cart was in position for him to load Isobel's trunks, he did so with ease and then asked, "Hotel or house?"

"My fiancé made reservations at the Morrill House some time ago. He—uh—he couldn't make the trip. But we'd already made the plans, so I decided to come alone. To visit my brother. Perhaps you know him? Charles Manning, editor of the *Register.*"

The man cocked his head. "Yes'm, I know Charlie." Retrieving the torch, he held it aloft and nodded toward the back of the cart. "You inclined to hop aboard for a ride up the hill?"

Isobel shook her head. "I'll walk."

"You sure? A long wagon train climbed this hill right about sunset last evening. Plenty of calling cards along the way, if you know what I mean."

"Calling cards?"

The man chuckled. "The soft, steaming kind that'll ruin a lady's slippers if she doesn't take notice."

"I'll be careful," Isobel said.

Carter retrieved the torch, grasped the mule's halter with his free hand, and they set off.

Isobel followed, wishing the moonlight were brighter. Happy to be leaving the dark river and its shadowy banks behind.

※

Crouched low, his back braced against the trunk of a burr oak tree, Gideon waited until Carter and Nebraska City's lone new arrival were at the top of the hill and out of sight before he moved. It was good of the old man to warn the lady about the numerous piles of manure dotting the rutted trail. Also good of him to avoid saying too much about Charlie Manning. Did Charlie's sister know about her brother's troubles? Not Gideon's business, but he couldn't help but wonder. Then again, maybe the sister had troubles of her own. He'd suspected something sad behind that pause just before she mentioned the missing fiancé. Almost as if she were rearranging reality.

As the creaking of Ezra's cart faded into the night, Gideon rose. "Better get to it," he said aloud and released Trouble, who waited for Gideon to stretch his legs before moving away from the river. Together, the two trotted past the crates left waiting on the levee and into the undergrowth on the other side, past the place where John Boulware moored his ferry, and, finally, up a hill. Gideon slowed only when he reached a familiar creek bank a couple of miles past the town burial ground.

The creekbank was steep. While it might have posed a danger to someone else moving about in the dark, Gideon knew this land almost better than he knew the contours of his own ravaged face. Ordering the dog to *stay,* he stepped off into inky space and what might seem a canyon to someone else. He was only taking a step onto a ledge that ran parallel to the rim of the earth—a ledge that gradually descended toward a thread of water silvered by moonlight.

He paused at the water's edge, closing his eyes to listen. When a twig snapped on the opposite bank, his mouth watered in anticipation of venison steak. If the sound indicated what Gideon suspected, the massive buck he'd been watching for days had bedded down. Tonight would be its last. With a single click of his tongue against the roof of his mouth, he summoned the dog to his side. The animal slipped down the creek bank and settled next to him to wait.

As he listened to crickets and toads, Gideon pondered the odd truth that he'd learned to love the night. As a boy, he'd loved the light—loved to lay back in the grass and close his eyes, savoring the warmth of the sun on his face. Until Pa scolded that it was time to get back to work and harness wouldn't mend itself, and he'd yet to hear of a crop that would plant itself, either.

Back then, a young Gideon had resented Pa—some days with an emotion bordering on hate. The cantankerous old man demanded too much. He never thanked a boy for his hard work. Never seemed to think it was good enough, no matter what a boy did.

"You must understand," Ma would say. "Your father's worried the cholera that took the Inskeep's pigs will spread to ours."

Gideon never talked back to Ma—not aloud, anyway. But he thought plenty. Thought of how if it wasn't the pigs causing Pa to worry, it was the lame horse or the dry cow or the broody hens. And the hens weren't even his concern. Ma tended the chickens. No matter. Pa always had a reason to worry, and too often the worry landed about Gideon's shoulders or across his backside—according to Pa's particular mood and what was handy when it came time to dole out the worry.

Pa was the reason Gideon had signed on with the First Nebraska, bent on showing the man a thing or two—marching home with brothers in arms, all of them with stories about Gideon Long's bravery that would, once and for all, make Pa realize his boy was capable of more than shoveling manure and mending fences. Now, waiting in the dark seven years later, Gideon's thoughts turned once again toward the burying ground.

Any hope of proving anything to Pa was gone forever, for Pa had died while Gideon and the First Nebraska were encamped at Benton Barracks north of St. Louis. When Ma wrote to tell him, Gideon had been hard pressed to grieve the loss. He'd worried plenty about Ma alone on the homestead, but he didn't think he'd miss Pa. Whenever he thought about it, Gideon wondered if his failure to honor his father was the reason for this life in the shadows. Sometimes he wished he could ask Reverend Moody about that—and about why God had let Ma die before he got home.

He hadn't known about Ma until he sneaked back unannounced, a full two years after the war was over, his fate likely unknown by the men he'd been with at Shiloh, his only companion the dog he'd encountered on the long walk home. When he reached the cabin built into a hillside near the river, the place was obviously deserted. Debris littered the front porch Ma had always swept daily, the windows were clouded with filth, and there wasn't an animal on the place. What had happened? Who'd put padlocks on both doors? Where was Ma?

He had to find her. Henry and Birdie Tanner would know where she was. He'd simply have to take a chance on their keeping his secrets. Breaking into the house, he retrieved a crockery bowl and pumped water for Trouble. Setting the bowl by the hearth, he climbed the ladder to the loft and yanked a dusty coverlet off the bed he'd once shared with his twin brother. Back on the main floor, he folded the coverlet in fourths, then summoned Trouble and ordered him to lie down. "That's your bed, now. You stay." When he opened the door, Trouble rose and whined a protest.

"No," Gideon insisted. "You *stay*. I'll be back." Slowly, the dog lowered himself onto the coverlet. Gideon nodded. "Good dog."

First, he'd stop at the cemetery between the home place and town. Ma would ask if he'd paid his respects, and he wanted to be able to say *yes*. If he spoke to Pa's grave, he could say the words he'd kept back as a boy. Maybe that would lay to rest some of the bitterness. But it didn't work out the way he'd planned.

He'd come looking for Pa's stone, and there it was, shining in the moonlight, right next to Gabriel's. It wasn't all that surprising to see his own name on another stone set next to Gabe's. After all, he'd been listed as missing after Shiloh, and he'd been gone a long while. Bless Ma's heart, she'd made sure he wouldn't be forgotten. But then—*Grace Evelyn Long.*

The shock felled him like a tree. He dropped to his knees, tracing the carved letters with trembling fingers. *December 29, 1864*. Gideon was no stranger to agony, but this was a different kind of pain. His heart pounded and he clutched at his chest, groaning and gasping for breath. Instead of speaking his piece to Pa, he stumbled back to the deserted home place. Hunkered beneath one of Ma's patchwork quilts, he wallowed in grief for days, wondering what to do now. If he wasn't needed to help take care of Ma, then why was he still alive? There didn't seem to be a point. Fresh bitterness flooded in, flowing around the small bits of resentment he'd harbored against Pa and swelling them up like a festered wound.

If Pa's old shotgun had been in working order, Gideon would have ended his story right then and there. But the shotgun didn't work. Besides that, Ma's presence lingered inside the remote little cabin by way of a quilt folded over the back of her rocking chair and the dusty Bible atop the table beneath a south-facing window.

Gideon didn't open the Bible, but he couldn't get rid of it either, out of respect for Ma. He finally came out from under the patchwork quilt on the bed. He braved making contact with Henry and Birdie Tanner, convincing them to provide coffee and sugar in exchange for pelts or meat.

Eventually, Gideon pulled a golden thread out of the web of staggering loss that fate had woven around his life. He decided Ma's death had been a mercy. She'd never have to see what war had done to her only child. What made him love the night.

Chapter 3

...how can one be warm alone?
Ecclesiastes 4:11

Grateful for the moonlight that enabled her to avoid the "calling cards" Mr. Carter had warned her about, Isobel followed the mule-drawn cart upwards on a trail that ran virtually parallel to the river below. She'd begun to regret her insistence on walking when, finally, they reached the top of the hill. Turning west, they continued on what proved to be a surprisingly broad and very dusty street.

Carter halted his mule. "It's still a good distance to the hotel, ma'am. You sure you don't want to ride?" He lifted a small wooden box off the cart. "Got a step right here."

Grateful for the man's thoughtfulness, Isobel accepted the offer and was soon perched on the back of the cart next to the smallest of her two trunks. As they creaked along, she realized that the reality of Nebraska City had very little in common with Alfred's faulty assumptions. The main street might not be paved, but it was far removed from a narrow trail leading past primitive shacks. The expected number of drinking establishments clustered near the river, but by block four, faint lamplight shining from windows illuminated signs for tobacconists and druggists, milliners and cafes. When she expressed her surprise to Mr. Carter, the older man chuckled.

"Well, ma'am, I reckon we are smallish compared to Kansas City and St. Louis. But we're holding our own. Growing, too, even though most folks who venture upriver are on their way to somewhere else. Still, I'd guess there's a couple thousand who've put roots down in Nebraska City."

Isobel nodded even as she smiled at the number. St. Louis boasted probably ten times as many people. What was it about this place that kept Charlie here? She twisted about, peering into the distance. "How much farther to Morrill House?"

"We crossed Fourth Street. The hotel is right up ahead on the corner—southwest corner of Main and Fifth."

"And how many more blocks of businesses after Fourth Street?"

Carter pondered for a moment, then said, "All the way to Fourteenth, at least. But it's not solid buildings all that way. There's vacant lots as you get away from the river. After Fourteenth, there's still more city, but streets tend to run every which way farther west."

"I take it the city fathers didn't do a lot of planning?"

"Way I heard it," Carter replied, "*three* towns started up on the river hereabouts. Nebraska City won out over Prairie City and Kearney City for naming rights." He paused. "Mind you, I wasn't here when it happened. We didn't come 'til after. Followed the First Nebraska Cavalry up from Arkansas."

Surprised, Isobel peered at the white-haired giant. "You fought in the war?"

Carter shook his head. "Didn't fight. Enlisted as an undercook. The First was good to me, so my Pearl and I decided we'd see it for ourselves once the shooting was done."

We. Pearl and I. Isobel's mind swirled with questions. Who was included in that word? Had they been slaves in Arkansas?

Were they happy they'd come to Nebraska? But Carter had brought the cart to a halt before a substantial three-story brick building, and so Isobel squelched her curiosity. Hopping down before Mr. Carter could retrieve the step, she took in the generous porch roof stretching out over a boardwalk above which a half-dozen shuttered windows looked down on Main Street. Large bay windows graced the main floor. Through the beveled glass set into the two heavy entry doors, Isobel could see a large, dimly lit lobby.

Glancing toward the check-in desk and the wide stairs leading up, she nodded with satisfaction. Alfred had reserved a suite, and she hadn't changed that. It would be wonderful to wallow in a comfortable bed instead of tossing and turning on the narrow cot she'd endured aboard the steamboat. Wonderful to have a maid to clean her muddy shoes and the hem of her traveling ensemble before she visited Charlie's office in the morning. Assuming he didn't come looking for her. Where was he, anyway? She turned in a circle, wondering which of the buildings along Main Street housed the *Register*, with offices below and Charlie's apartment above.

Isobel stepped up on the boardwalk, then hesitated, searching the shadows around the doors. "Will the door be locked?" she asked in a low voice. "Is there a bell I should ring?"

"No ma'am. The sisters that run the hotel knew there was a packet due about midnight. They would have been listening for the whistle. Don't know which of the ladies will be on duty tonight, but they'll be ready for business." He proved his point by opening the door for Isobel to enter, then retreated to the cart to shoulder the smaller of her two trunks.

The hotel lobby would never be called opulent, but Isobel supposed it was nice enough, especially assuming Alfred's warnings about their accommodations being substantially more rustic than any of the St. Louis hotels. A wide, carpeted staircase rose from the middle of the lobby toward a broad balcony on the second floor. The registration desk spanned the space between the right stair railing and the wall, and a lamp cast a soft glow over the pages of an open registry. Isobel rang the brass bell beside the lamp. As she waited, Mr. Carter stepped inside with the smaller of her two trunks. Setting it down, he retreated outside for the second.

A thump and a low voice beyond the door behind the desk signaled that the bell had been heard. Presently, a rail thin woman dressed in black stepped into view. Shifting a cane from one hand to the other, she thumped her way to the desk.

Isobel signed the registry. "You've a reservation for the Alfred Warfields."

The woman looked pointedly past Isobel toward the street. "And Mr. Warfield is...?"

"Not coming."

The woman turned the registry book around and peered down at Isobel's signature. She looked back up. "The reservation was made in the name *Warfield*. Might I inquire as to who you are?"

"I am—was—Mr. Warfield's fiancé." Isobel felt her cheeks warm as she blushed with embarrassment. "He elected to stay behind. I've come alone. To visit my brother." She swallowed. "Perhaps you know Charles Manning of the *Register*? He's expecting us—um—me." *Although he didn't meet the steamboat, and I have no idea why.*

With a little shrug, the woman stepped back from the desk and retrieved a key from a niche behind her. She motioned for Mr. Carter to follow them and led the way up the grand staircase, across the wide mezzanine, and down the hallway to the left. Unlocking the very last door, the prim little woman gestured for Isobel to enter. She finally spoke a welcome as she tapped her way past the foot of the bed and lit a lamp mounted between two tall, double-hung windows. "You'll have the advantage of the morning breeze from the east."

Mr. Carter set Isobel's trunk down inside the door and left to fetch the second. Isobel hesitated, looking about the space. A small sitting area with two armless chairs and a low table was tucked into the corner to her right. On the left, a wardrobe occupied the part of the wall not taken up by the door. The bed faced the door from its position between two windows on the opposite wall. Isobel assumed the odd arrangement was intended to take advantage of the aforementioned morning breeze. Still, the space was nothing like what she'd expected. She protested mildly. "We—that is, my fiancé—paid for a suite."

The desk clerk stiffened visibly, shoulders back, chin lifted. "You have the largest room in the finest establishment in the city, Miss Manning. Your fiancé assured me you would make do. I apologize if our accommodations do not meet with your approval." Her tone was anything but apologetic.

Isobel felt her cheeks warm again. *Fabulous. I've barely set foot in town and I'm already offending people.* "Of course. I didn't realize. He—Alfred—didn't tell me." Just then, Mr. Carter returned with the second trunk. Isobel took a few coins from the bag at her wrist and pressed them into his hand.

Carter looked down at the money. With furrowed brow, he handed two coins back. "Fair is fair." He touched the brim of his hat and took his leave.

The desk clerk moved to follow, then paused at the door. "Do you require anything else tonight?"

Isobel spoke as she untied her bonnet. "Perhaps the maid could come for my skirt and see that it's cleaned?" She lifted the hem to show her boots. "And my boots need attention."

One side of the woman's mouth curled as she said, "I suppose you're accustomed to having someone do your unpacking as well."

"That would be lovely."

"I imagine so." The woman gave a dramatic sigh. "Alas, it seems Morrill House is destined to disappoint. The girl who sees to the rooms will be up early in the morning with fresh water. She's an enterprising sort. No doubt she'll be able to make suggestions as to the hiring of a personal attendant since you obviously require one." She opened the door and hesitated on the threshold long enough to say that breakfast was served beginning at five o'clock in the morning. "There isn't much remaining for those who linger past six-thirty." She closed the door firmly behind her without waiting for a response.

In the wake of the woman's unspoken judgment, Isobel hurried to lock the door. She might have regretted giving offense over the size of the room, but she most certainly did not appreciate the thinly veiled disapproval. She gazed about her in the dim light. Could this possibly be the largest hotel room in Nebraska City? That seemed unlikely. Who'd ever heard of a fine hotel that didn't offer help with the endless tasks required to maintain a lady's wardrobe? As to the comment about *lingering* in bed past six-thirty in the morning—well. The prim little busybody might as well have called Isobel *lazy*. That stung.

Removing her gloves and laying them atop the smaller of her two trunks, Isobel crossed the room and perched on the edge of the bed, sighing with pleasure over the soft mattress. The bed itself boasted a curved canopy and blue and white toile drapes secured at the four bedposts with white bows. Quaint elegance from days gone by. From where she sat, Isobel inspected the room more closely. Maybe it wasn't so bad, after all. She'd think of the sitting area as *cozy*. As for the shaving stand next to the marble-topped dresser, she would have that taken out. Doing so would not only gain her a little more space but also dispense with a looming reminder of Alfred's absence.

Crossing to a window, Isobel looked out on the deserted street, wondering anew about the location of Charlie's newspaper. She would rise early, do her best to freshen her own skirt hem and boots, and go there at once—without soliciting help from whoever brought up the water and most definitely without asking directions of the crochety desk clerk.

Stepping away from the window, she began to unpin her hair. Depositing hairpins atop the marble surface of the dresser, she opened the largest trunk and retrieved her hairbrush from the tray perched atop the substantial packing space below. Returning to the window, she pondered the light glimmering in a window above one of the businesses between the hotel and the river. The street itself was a straight bit of dark ribbon.

Thoughts of Alfred with Mary Halifax on his arm, the two of them navigating all the spring events together came unbidden. She stepped away from the window and laid the hairbrush aside. How long would it be before thoughts of Alfred stopped invading her life? *Think about tomorrow. Finding Charlie. Seeing his office.*

Unbuckling the belt that cinched the overdress about her waist, Isobel let it fall to the floor. Next, she unbuttoned the long row of buttons marching down the front of the underdress and stepped out of it. She untied the tape holding her petticoat in place. It landed atop the dress. Next came the corset. With a sigh of relief, she stepped over the pile of clothing to retrieve a buttonhook before perching on one of the chairs to unfasten her boots.

When she'd kicked the boots off, Isobel dropped the button hook on the table and extinguished the lamp. Weariness settled in, and she decided to forego changing into a nightgown. Instead, she slipped into bed wearing chemise and bloomers. The bed linens smelled of... *could that be lavender?* A nice touch.

Aware of the empty space that should be occupied by Alfred, she grabbed the unused pillow, pounded it a couple of times, and clutched it to her midsection. *Take that, you cowardly cad.* Outside her door, a harsh male voice cursed. Something about a card game gone wrong. *Thin walls.* Isobel hunkered farther beneath the bedcovers.

Imagining her brother's scathing reaction to Alfred's betrayal brought a smile to her lips. Charlie would undoubtedly disapprove of Alfred's choice of accommodations. He wouldn't be able to invite her to share his apartment—which was, in Charlie's words, suitable only for a "lonely bachelor." But he would probably insist that she move from Morrill House to a better hotel. It would be grand to see him. To finally be in the company of someone who genuinely cared for her. To see the look on the desk clerk's face when she realized her rudeness had resulted in the loss of business.

Chapter 4

*A friend loveth at all times,
and a brother is born for adversity.*
Proverbs 17:17

Awakened when a herd of boot-clad men clomped down the hall outside her door, Isobel grunted a protest. She peered from beneath the bedcovers. No glimmer of morning light filtered through the lace curtains. What time was it, anyway? Was that coffee she smelled? *Yes. Coffee. And bacon or sausage.* Her stomach growled. What had the desk clerk said about breakfast? *Ah. Breakfast is served beginning at five o'clock.* She threw back the covers and sat up. Now that her eyes had adjusted to the dark, she realized she could discern gray shadows in the room. The days of lingering in bed, waiting for Portia to deliver a breakfast tray were no more. *Welcome to the West, m'dear. The only breakfast you're getting is the one you get for yourself.*

More stomping sounded in the hall—this time accompanied by men's voices. Isobel rose from bed. Intending to light the lamp on the opposite wall, she nearly tripped over the pile of clothing she'd dropped on the floor. She'd just gathered them up and laid them atop the unmade bed when a faint knock sounded at the door.

"Fresh water for Miss Manning."

The voice was that of a young girl. Isobel fumbled about in the smallest of her two trunks and pulled a wrapper out, donning it as she hurried to open the door.

"Sorry to bother you so early, ma'am," the girl said as she swept past with a bucket of water, "but Miz Oliver wouldn't hear of anything but me coming up the minute I stepped in the back door." She hoisted the bucket and filled the pitcher on the washstand.

"I was awake." *Barely.*

"I reckon so," the girl replied. "You probably thought there was a herd of elephants out in the hall. You want me to light the lamps?"

Isobel thanked her. "Mrs. Oliver didn't leave me any matches."

"Oh, that wasn't Miz Oliver last night," the girl said. "That was Miss Bennet. They're sisters." The girl kept talking as she circled the room lighting each of the three lamps, one each in the brackets on two opposite walls and the third atop the dresser. "Miss Bennet wouldn't have left matches in the room. She's careful that way since the fire. I was too little to remember it much, but sixty buildings burnt some years back. Practically the whole town. Must have been awful. Still, Miz Oliver doesn't see hoarding matches as being *careful.* She calls it *stingy.*" The girl laid a small box of matches atop the dresser. "Miz Oliver was widowed when the mister took the fever in camp. He wasn't a soldier like my daddy. He was a chaplain—but a good one, to hear my daddy tell it. Anyway, Miz Oliver is real nice. Miss Bennet isn't quite so positive-minded, her being a spinster and all. Folks say they look alike. I suppose they do, but they're as different as night and day. You'll see what I mean if you stay here long." The girl looked over at the garments piled on the bed. "Are you? Staying long?"

Her mind spinning from the nonstop commentary, Isobel hesitated to answer. In the space of a couple of minutes, the girl had divulged the personal history of the irascible desk clerk and her sister. The last thing Isobel needed was someone talking about her with similar abandon. "The length of my stay isn't really your concern, Miss...?"

The gentle scolding didn't faze the girl. "*Simmons*. But call me Molly. And I don't mean to pry, if that's what you're thinking. I'm only asking how long you'll stay so I know how maybe I could help you out." She pointed to the blue traveling ensemble atop the bed. "Those are some fine duds. You want me to get 'em clean and pressed before you wear 'em again? Wouldn't cost much. My Ma does laundry for lots of folks. When she takes on something fine like that skirt, she sends me over to Miz Hall—she's a first-rate dressmaker—and gets advice on the best way to clean it. And she's never ruined a single thing, fine laces and all."

Isobel frowned. "Am I to understand that the hotel doesn't provide laundry services?" What had Arthur been thinking, reserving rooms—a room—in this place?

"Not officially," the girl said. "But I do all kinds of things—unofficial like. Ma wants the work, and Miz Oliver don't mind 'cause she knows I'm saving up."

"Saving," Isobel repeated. "For what are you saving?"

The girl shrugged. "Can't say, exactly. But when it shows itself, I'll know it, and I want to be ready. Don't want to be a water-carrier-chamber-pot-emptier the rest of my life."

Isobel suppressed a smile. The girl had spunk, one had to give her that. "How old are you, Miss Simmons—if you don't mind my asking?"

"I'll be fifteen this summer."

Isobel nodded. "And what does your mother think of your plan to leave home?"

Molly shrugged again. "Haven't exactly told her. My older brother's the only one that knows. He says it's all right for me to make plans, as long as I don't leave Ma and the others in the lurch."

"Others?"

Molly counted off on her fingers as she recited names. "Edgar's sixteen, then comes me. After that, Elvin, Eben and Earl—they're twins—then Ethan, then Grace." She barely took a breath before continuing. "Ma takes in laundry, like I said. She makes first-rate butter and jam, and there's eggs to trade at the mercantile. We got a big garden. I told Edgar he and Ma can count on me at least 'til I'm seventeen. By then the twins and Ethan will be old enough to work and Ma won't have to depend on me so much."

The girl's matter-of-fact recitation of her family's dire situation landed like a stone in Isobel's midsection. *Seven children, their mother a widow. Taking in laundry. Making butter. Keeping chickens. Gardening.* She couldn't imagine being trapped in such a life. Her current difficulties paled by comparison. Isobel cleared her throat. "I'm so sorry."

"'Bout what?" The girl honestly seemed surprised.

"About your father. How hard it must be."

Molly shrugged. "Ma says it doesn't pay to dwell on the bad, that we just got to pull together and trust the Lord." She offered a faint smile. "Pa's a kind of hero, him dying in the war and all. Folks around here've been real good to help us out. Miz Oliver took me on here at the hotel, even when Miss Bennet said I was too young. But I showed her I wasn't. Showed her I can pull my weight." Mention of hard work seemed to remind the girl about the task at hand. She grabbed the empty bucket from near the washstand and asked about the skirt again. "Usually I charge twenty-five cents, but seeing as how you're new to town, I'll give you my special price. Ten cents and I'll bring it back today."

When Isobel hesitated, the girl nodded toward the boots. "And for another nickel, I'll have Elvin polish those up for you good as new. He's a first-rate shoe polisher."

"I'll remember that," Isobel said, "but I think I can manage for now." It was time she learned to take care of things for herself. Boots and skirt hems were as good a place to start as any.

Molly took the refusal in stride, hesitating only long enough to say, "You need help with anything else, you let me know. Dressmakers, millinery, any of that—I know the best places. We've got good churches, too. Methodist, Presbyterian, Lutheran. I'm Baptist, myself."

Isobel nodded. "Thank you, Miss—Molly. I'll be sure to ask for help, should the need arise." She moved toward the door, barely managing to suppress a yawn, in spite of the fact the sun was up and light streamed in the window on the east side of the room.

"Those wagon masters woke you, didn't they? Like I said, a herd of elephants wouldn't make any more noise. Be glad you weren't in the dining room while they ate. It was enough to make a lady like you lose her appetite, and that's the truth. Reaching and pawing and slurping like they were starving. Which they wasn't—weren't. Not a one." She shook her head. "They're all in a tizzy, though, racing to see who can be the first to sign up a bunch of travelers and get on the trail. They all want to be first this time of year—get the best grass before the worst of the heat sets in. That kind of thing." An animal in the street below bellowed. Molly sighed. "You'll hear a lot of that, at least for the next couple of hours. And plenty of swearing to go along with it."

Isobel nodded but said nothing, hoping the girl would take the hint and depart. But she didn't.

"Last thing, you might want to avoid the grits this morning. That's what I ate when I came in, and they ain't creamy one bit.

Grits are supposed to be creamy. These are more like—well, nigh on ready to be sliced up and fried like mush." The girl shuddered.

"Thank you for warning me." Isobel said. "I'll avoid the grits."

A harsh rap on the door made both her and Molly jump. Molly opened the door a crack.

It was the same disapproving voice from the night before. "Precisely how long does it take to deliver one pitcher of fresh water to one room?"

Isobel wasn't about to be the cause of Molly Simmons receiving an unwarranted scolding, and so she hurried to the door. Mindful of her state of undress, she positioned herself behind the door and called out, "I've been peppering Molly with questions about Nebraska City, and she's been very kind and patient with me. I apologize for detaining her. It won't happen again."

With an appreciative glance in Isobel's direction, the girl slipped out of the room and hurried away. Isobel sensed Miss Bennet lingering just across the threshold, but she closed the door anyway. She did her best to attend to her skirt and scuffed boots, then dressed and descended to the dining room—where she heeded Molly's warning about the grits. And wished the girl had given a similar one about the dark sludge that passed for coffee.

Isobel hesitated on the boardwalk outside the hotel's double doors, amazed by the transformation daylight had affected on the town. Last night's deserted road was now a bustling thoroughfare. Wagons jammed the right of way. Oxen bellowed, horses stomped, and unshaven men shouted and swore. The only female in sight was a young, poorly clad, round-shouldered waif

35

perched on a wagon seat at the end of the block. Something in the child's demeanor elicited a pang of... sympathy? Despair? Isobel wasn't sure which. Whatever it was, it made her thankful for the smiling face in her not-too-distant future. *Charlie. I'm here. Can you believe it?*

Opening her parasol, Isobel turned her back on the river and proceeded west along Main Street. At the first corner, she stepped into the street and navigated around several fresh piles of manure before landing safely at the beginning of the next block. No overhangs provided shade in front of the first few businesses, and Isobel was thankful for the parasol that shaded her face. Finally, she caught sight of a white board sign above a window identifying the *Nebraska City Register*. Her heart pounding, Isobel hurried across the street. She wanted to burst in with a shouted greeting, but the door was locked. Someone had scrawled *closed due to illness* on a bit of paper taped on the window.

Charlie was ill? Isobel glanced up toward the second story and the two windows overlooking Main Street. That had to be Charlie's apartment. Both windows were closed, curtains drawn. Her heart racing, Isobel scurried around the corner and past the two windows at the side of the building. At the back, a narrow flight of stairs led up to what had to be the door to Charlie's apartment. Isobel hurried up the stairs. She was nearly at the apartment door when a voice sounded from below.

"Can I help you, miss?"

Isobel glanced down at the speaker, noting a shopkeeper's apron and neatly trimmed gray hair. "It's my brother—there's a note at the front. It says he's ill. I just need—" she took a couple of steps and peered through the window, horrified at the sight of two boot-clad feet protruding from around a corner. "Charlie!" She rattled the doorknob, surprised when it gave way. Snapping her parasol closed, she called to the man below. "Please get a doctor!"

The second Isobel stepped across the threshold, she staggered back, raising one gloved hand to her nostrils in a vain attempt to mitigate the stench of filth and vomit. Empty liquor bottles littered the bare wood floor. Leaning her closed parasol against a wall, Isobel picked her way to where Charlie had collapsed at the foot of a rumpled bed tucked into an alcove off the main room. When she tried to rouse him, he groaned and pushed her away, muttering curses and demanding to be left alone. His clothes were filthy, his scraggly dark beard caked with dried vomit. Charlie wasn't ill. He was drunk.

A voice sounded from the doorway, and Isobel glanced up. "You must be Isobel. Charlie said you'd be visiting. On your wedding trip, he said."

Charlie moaned again. Knowing he was in no danger of expiring, Isobel rose and pushed past the stranger and back outside, sucking in fresh air as she clutched the railing with both hands, trying to control concern and disappointment, uncertainty and rage.

The stranger followed her, leaving the apartment door standing open behind them. "I'm Henry Tanner," he said. "My wife, Birdie, and I run the mercantile next door." He sighed. "I'm sorry you had to see him this way."

"Henry? Is everything all right?"

Isobel looked down at the lovely white-haired woman who peered up at them, her hands on her hips, her brow wrinkled.

Mr. Tanner leaned over the railing and answered in a stage whisper. "Charlie's indisposed." He nodded toward Isobel. "Just when his sister's arrived."

The woman's scowl transformed. With a sad smile, she called up to Isobel. "Oh, dear. Such an unhappy welcome." She indicated her husband. "You've met Henry. I'm Birdie." She gestured for Isobel to descend the stairs. "Why don't you have a cup of tea with me while Henry tends to Charlie?"

A cup of tea? As if that would resolve anything. Isobel glanced back toward Charlie, frowning.

Mrs. Tanner stepped off the board platform that formed a rustic porch at the back of the mercantile. She came to the foot of the stairs before speaking again. "Please, dear. Let Henry see to the boy. Charlie told us about your impending visit. We've been looking forward to meeting you and your husband." She paused. "Speaking of your husband, should we send word to the hotel? Mr.—Warfield, was it? Yes, that was it. Warfield. He could join you and me while Henry sees to Charlie."

Surprised that the little woman knew and remembered Alfred's name, Isobel managed a response. "That won't be necessary. There's no—what I mean is, Alfred didn't—" She cleared her throat. "I came alone."

The Tanners exchanged a look. "Well, then," Mrs. Tanner said, "it'll be just the two of us. And if you prefer coffee to tea, I'm happy to brew some."

Mr. Tanner muttered encouragement, ending with, "Let me get things to rights with Charlie."

Again, Isobel looked toward the inert figure lying on the bare wooden floor. For a moment no one spoke. Isobel relented and retrieved her parasol and started down the stairs. Mr. Tanner moved toward Charlie. It was a dream. A bad dream. She would awaken and—

Mrs. Tanner put a hand on Isobel's shoulder. "I am so sorry you had to see him this way." Her blue eyes shone with compassion. "Now which will it be, tea or coffee?" She guided Isobel toward the mercantile.

"Tea," Isobel said, and followed the older woman into what proved to be a well-stocked storeroom.

Mrs. Tanner waved Isobel toward a small table crowded into the far corner. "Please sit down, dear. I'd already put the kettle on to boil when I heard you call to Henry for help, so it won't take but a moment." She took two tins down from a shelf and asked, "Earl Grey or English Breakfast?"

Surprised that she had a choice, Isobel replied, "Earl Grey."

"My favorite," Mrs. Tanner said. Setting the tin atop the table, she excused herself and hurried up the stairs along the far wall. She returned almost immediately bearing a footed silver tray atop which sat an elegant blue and white transferware tea set and a tin of English biscuits. "When Henry suggested we open a store in the wilderness, I told him I had no intention of giving up either a decent cup of tea or my favorite biscuits." She set the tray down, removed the teapot lid, and retreated to the stove for the steaming kettle. "I keep the tea tray at the ready in the center of my dining table upstairs." As she poured hot water over the tea leaves, the aroma of bergamot wafted upward. She closed her eyes and inhaled. "Doesn't that smell divine?" The kettle returned to the stove, she sat down opposite Isobel. "Your brother will be very happy to see you—once he's overcome the embarrassment of your finding him so indisposed. He's spoken of you in the fondest of terms."

Charlie had talked about her? Then why the scene she'd just witnessed? Disappointment simmered. Presently, Mrs. Tanner poured the tea, which Isobel sipped before saying, "Thank you for going to the trouble of making tea. Again, I apologize for the inconvenience."

"It isn't an inconvenience, my dear. We've been looking forward to meeting you. It's a joy—or, it would be if it weren't for Charlie's trouble."

Isobel glanced toward the door. "Mr. Tanner was very kind to take Charlie on just now. I'm grateful, and I'm certain Charlie will feel the same—once he recovers."

Mrs. Tanner opened the biscuit tin, encouraging Isobel to take one while she said, "It isn't difficult to be kind to Charlie. If Henry and I'd had a son survive to adulthood, we'd have prayed he would grow up to be as caring as your brother."

Isobel nibbled a biscuit. *Caring.* That was the Charlie she remembered. The war seemed to have erased his ability to smile much, but he'd still been thoughtful and caring. At least until he left for the West. After that—Isobel couldn't say. What on earth was going on with him now?

Mrs. Tanner continued. "Recent difficulties notwithstanding, Henry and I are both quite fond of Charlie. It's—" She sighed and shook her head. "It's been hard on him, losing them both the way he did."

Isobel cocked her head. "Losing—who?"

"Why, Vera, of course. And the baby."

Chapter 5

*It is good that a man should both hope
and quietly wait for the salvation of the Lord.*
Lamentations 3:26

Gideon hunkered down behind the ridge overlooking the block of Nebraska City buildings that included Charlie Manning's newspaper office and Tanner Mercantile. He absently fingered the key in his pocket—the key to the mercantile storeroom. He didn't usually come to town after dawn, but he was completely out of coffee and sugar and low on lamp oil. Hence, after field dressing the massive buck, he'd taken a chance—leaving Trouble in the cabin happily gnawing on a hoof.

As it turned out, he'd almost been spotted by the same woman he'd watched disembark from a steamboat last night. He'd just topped the ridge when she staggered out of Charlie Manning's apartment and called down to Henry for help. He hadn't seen her face last night, but he'd heard her rich, warm voice as she spoke with Ezra Carter. He might not have been able to make out exactly what she was saying, but hers was not a voice easily forgotten. From the way she'd held the back of her hand to her nose a few moments ago, Gideon could imagine what she'd found inside. Charlie Manning was drunk. Again. Henry would help out. He always did.

How would she know Charlie Manning? He muttered a scolding reply. "That's none of your business." His only business in town this morning was to drop a shank of venison inside Tanner Mercantile's storeroom door, gather provisions, and note what he'd taken in the ledger Henry kept. But it was broad daylight now, and drama was unfolding between the Tanners, Charlie Manning, and the woman whose blue outfit shimmered in the morning light.

He watched as Henry retreated into Manning's apartment and the woman followed Birdie inside the mercantile. A wagon rounded a corner and stopped behind the livery at the far end of the row of buildings. Gideon pushed himself away from the top of the ridge. Today was not the day to brave the light. Hunkering down, he slung the burlap bag over his shoulder. The meat would keep, sunk into the pit behind the house where a cold spring bubbled up from the earth. As for the list of things he needed—he'd simply have to go without.

It wasn't as if he didn't know how to do that.

Mrs. Tanner reached across the table and squeezed one of Isobel's hands. "I am so sorry. Obviously, you didn't know." She clucked regret.

Isobel stared down at the steaming liquid in her blue and white teacup as she tried to absorb the news of Charlie, *married,* Charlie, *anticipating fatherhood* and then, suddenly a widower who'd lost not only his wife but also their baby.

A sharp rap sounded from the front door of the mercantile. A muffled voice called out, "Open up! Ma's run clean out of her snuff, and you know how she gets."

"Oh, dear." Mrs. Tanner rose from the table. "That's Jack Jessen. He won't give up."

"Don't apologize," Isobel replied. "You have a business to run." She grabbed up the gloves she'd laid on the table and reached for the parasol leaning against the wall. "I'll just see how things are with Charlie. Perhaps I can assist Mr. Tanner in some way."

Mrs. Tanner held one hand out to stay Isobel's departure even as she called toward the door. "Jack, I'm here. Wait a minute." To Isobel, she said, "Please call me *Birdie*. And trust Henry to see to things. Have another cup of tea. I'll see to Jack and then—then we can talk. You surely have questions, and it might help both you and Charlie if I answer at least some of them."

The boy pounded on the door again. "Miz Tanner, please! She's nigh onto a tizzy fit. You got to open up!"

Isobel settled. Mrs. Tanner swept through the curtains hanging in the doorway and into the store. From where she sat, Isobel heard the resulting exchange.

"I'll add it to your account, Jack. Give your mother my best."

"You feeling poorly, Miz Tanner? It ain't like you not to open on time."

"Mr. Tanner and I are in fine fettle, but we have some private business to attend to."

"I seen the sign at the newspaper. Charlie drunk again? I bet that's it. *Whoo-ee*, must be a real humdinger if it takes the both of ya to clean it up this time."

Mrs. Tanner's tone sharpened. "What part of the phrase *private business* did you not hear, Jack?"

"Aww, Miz Tanner. Don't get all riled up. I don't mean nothin' by it. I was just askin'. I *like* Charlie."

"Then stop mining for gossip."

Isobel heard the door close firmly and Mrs. Tanner's footsteps as she hurried back to the storeroom. She stirred up the fire in the little stove and put more water on to boil before sitting down.

"I suppose I should apologize for Jack. He isn't a bad sort."

Isobel grimaced. "Does the entire town know about Charlie's problems?"

"I don't know as the 'entire town' knows, but—" Mrs. Tanner gave a deep sigh. "The *Register* was doing well before Charlie and Vera met. He's the kind of man who's easy to like. He had many friends. People tried to help after Vera died, but Charlie—" Mrs. Tanner shook her head.

"How long has he been like this?"

"Vera died the end of January. Childbed fever."

Over three months ago. "And the baby?"

"A little boy. Not strong enough for this world."

Why hadn't Charlie written? Whatever closeness they'd once enjoyed, it obviously didn't exist anymore—not if he hadn't even told her he was getting married. She shook her head. She'd been a fool to think Charlie might help her deal with the wedding debacle.

Mrs. Tanner reached across the table to squeeze her hand. "It's good you're here."

Again, Isobel shook her head. She allowed a low, sad, laugh. "I'm here because I thought Charlie would help *me.*" *Now what?* Unable to hold the tears back, she let them fall—along with a litany of her own troubles. Alfred's abandonment, Mother Manning's reaction, her dread of facing a social season as a jilted spinster—all of it. "But it's nothing compared to what Charlie's endured." She took a wavering breath. "I never should have come."

When Mrs. Tanner finally responded, she said, "I disagree. You and Charlie can help one another." She offered a faint smile. "I got the impression you two were once very close."

"You did?"

Mrs. Tanner nodded. "Charlie told us a little about your shared past. He mentioned that you two depended upon one another a great deal after your mother died. Especially when your father remarried."

Charlie had talked about all of that? He and the Tanners must be very close, indeed. Isobel gave a little shrug. "Our stepmother didn't entirely embrace the idea of raising another woman's children. Charlie and I took refuge in one another."

"It must have been especially difficult for you after he left home."

Isobel blurted out a response. "It wasn't *difficult*. It was *terrible*. I'd never felt so alone." Startled that she'd made the admission aloud to a stranger, Isobel quickly added, "But Charlie wrote almost every day. Alfred's sister, Elizabeth, and I got very involved in the Ladies Aid and the Sanitary Commission. That helped me feel closer to my brother."

Mrs. Tanner nodded. "He told us a little about that."

"He did?"

Again, Mrs. Tanner nodded. "He was very proud of what you'd accomplished."

"And then, after the war, he wasn't home but a few weeks when he left again—this time for Colorado. That time, he didn't write. Not once." *And so I spent more and more time with Elizabeth and, eventually, with Alfred, whose attentions earned Mother Manning's approval, which was nice.* She frowned. "When I finally did hear from him again, he was settling here in Nebraska. He seemed happy, but he didn't mention a woman." Again, she wondered aloud, "Why wouldn't he tell me he was married?"

Mrs. Tanner took a sip of tea before answering. "Charlie and Vera's courtship was—unusual. Something of a whirlwind. There were special circumstances. Perhaps he wanted you to meet Vera and the baby before he shared that part of their story."

Special circumstances. What on earth did that mean? "To have welcomed a son in January, he had to have been married over a year. How long was he going to wait?" Again, hurt rose up. "It doesn't make any sense."

Mrs. Tanner cleared her throat. "They hadn't actually been married that long."

Isobel frowned. "What?"

"As I said, there were special circumstances." The older woman only smiled, but those blue eyes communicated—something.

Ah. Isobel understood. Plenty of babies arrived long before the parents had been married for nine months. Her cheeks warmed with a blush. She lifted her chin. "He still should have told me. He's my brother. I would have understood."

"Once you hear the entire story," Mrs. Tanner said, "I'm confident you'll agree it's a beautiful one. And you'll admire Charlie more than you ever have."

Isobel snorted softly. He might have done the honorable thing and married the girl, but the behavior that led to a rushed wedding was hardly *admirable*.

Mrs. Tanner leaned forward a bit. "Trust what I'm saying, dear. You'll be proud of him."

"Why won't you tell me? I *will* try to understand."

"Charlie needs the healing that comes from telling you in his own way."

Isobel shook her head. If Charlie didn't write to confide his indiscretions, what made Mrs. Tanner think he would ever talk about it? And how could she attach that word *admirable* to it all? Isobel stared out the window toward the horizon as she said, "I'm in no position to help anyone. I only came to Nebraska because—" She croaked, "Because I don't have anywhere else to go." Bowing her head, Isobel dabbed at tears.

Mrs. Tanner moved her chair close and put one arm about Isobel's shoulders. The gesture opened the floodgates. When Isobel's tears finally subsided, the older woman gave her a warm hug. "I believe the Lord has an abundance of good things in store for both you and our dear Charlie. You were right to come."

Isobel gave a little shake of her head. She closed her eyes. It seemed eons since she'd left St. Louis. Hours since she'd exited the hotel, excited to see Charlie. Now, everything was muddled. And as for Mrs. Tanner's "good Lord," life was already complicated enough without bringing the Almighty into it.

Chapter 6

What is my strength, that I should hope?
And what is mine end, that I should prolong my life?
Job 6:11

"Why won't you *listen*?!" Charlie moaned. He flopped over on his back and peered through half-closed eyes at the figure looming over him. He waved a hand in the direction of the open door. "I said *leave me alone.*"

"Can't do it."

Charlie opened one eye a little further. *Henry.* His mouth felt like someone had stuffed cotton in. And that smell. Was that him? He grimaced.

Henry bent down and extended a hand. "Get off the floor, Charlie. I'll fetch water so you can clean up. Your sister's here."

"Wh-what?!" He opened both eyes, squinting against the bright light pouring in through the open back door. "Izzy—here?" He lifted his head and looked around the apartment.

"Birdie took her to the store to settle her down."

Charlie frowned. "Settle her?" He remembered. *That was her?* He groaned and pushed himself to a sitting position, then leaned against the foot of the bed.

"Be back in a minute," Henry said. He grabbed the white pitcher off the washstand. "You might see if you can find some cleaner clothes."

Charlie peeled his vest and shirt off and tossed them into a corner atop a pile of unwashed clothes and linens. His stomach roiled. With another groan, he hoisted himself onto the bed just as Henry returned and poured water into the bowl on the washstand.

"You got any clean... anything?"

Charlie scratched his neck as he looked around the apartment. He shrugged. "I doubt it."

"I'll get you something from the store," Henry said. He headed for the door again. "While I'm gone, why don't you put all your clothes in a pile on the bed. I'll wrap 'em in that sheet and have Edgar haul the bundle to his ma."

Charlie protested with a mild curse. "Wait a gol-durned minute. Isobel's wedding is May 2. She won't get here until the eleventh—at the earliest."

"And today's May 11. She got here last night. Checked in at Morrill House and rushed right over this morning. Couldn't wait to see you."

There was a hint of disapproval in the man's tone as he moved about the apartment, picking up bottles. And making noise. So much noise. The floor creaked, the bottles clanked.

Charlie pressed his palms to the sides of his head. "Please. Stop."

Henry grunted. "I promised your sister I'd see to you."

Again, a tone of—judgment? Charlie half snarled a response. "Well, thank you, Saint Henry of Nebraska." Pushing himself to a standing position, he did his best to ignore the pounding in his head as he shuffled to the washstand. He peered into the mirror, shocked by the scraggly beard, the long hair, the dark circles beneath his bloodshot eyes. Smoothing his hair with a trembling hand, he backed away from the washstand and sat on the bed again.

Henry had set the empty bottles on the table and opened the front windows to let in fresh air. "Do you want me to bring you clean clothes or not?"

Charlie sighed. "I shouldn't have said that. You're only trying to help." He wrapped his arms about himself, feeling ashamed. "But I can't see them now." He paused, his sluggish mind trying to formulate a plan. "Can you—can you ask them to wait—tell them I'll meet them at Morrill House for supper." The thought of food made his stomach heave again. He swallowed. "This evening. Seven o'clock." He scrubbed his face with his palms. "Tell Izzy I'm sorry." He paused. "Be sure to say *Izzy*. It's what our father and I used to call her. Maybe—maybe that'll help somehow. And—yes to the clothes. Please. Something suitable for Morrill House, in case Mrs. Simmons can't get my laundry done before this evening."

"I don't think you should make your sister wait to see you. Not after the shock you've given her."

Charlie sighed. "If it was just Izzy I might agree, but that husband of hers—"

"She was alone," Henry said. "I assume the husband is still at the hotel."

Charlie scowled. *What was Alfred thinking, letting his new wife walk the streets of Nebraska City alone?* Another reason not to like the man. On the other hand, if he could see Izzy without Warfield—

Henry spoke up. "How about I bring a pot of coffee up along with the clothes? Birdie can keep your sister busy for a little while longer, you can get cleaned up, and then—"

Charlie gestured about him. "This place is in no condition—"

"Once you're decent, come next door. Talk to your sister over coffee in the storeroom."

Charlie considered for a moment before agreeing. "All right. Ask her to wait."

Henry nodded. "Back in a few minutes." He stepped outside, leaving the door open so the apartment could air out.

As Henry descended the back stairs, Charlie returned to the washstand. Leaning down, he plunged his face into the cool water, then stood up, sputtering. His head was pounding, but the dunking had helped clear the cobwebs out of his muddled brain. By the time Henry returned, Charlie had opened all the windows in the little apartment, sucked in some fresh air, and was feeling a little more clear-headed. He chugged strong coffee at intervals while donning pants and shirt. He glanced in the mirror again. "I need a haircut and a shave."

Henry agreed. "But you need to see your sister first."

The man was right, but the thought of it filled him with dread. "What will I say?"

"Don't I remember you saying the two of you were close growing up?"

"That was a long time ago."

"Even so, she's come a long way to see you. I'd say tell her the truth. The *whole* truth."

It was good advice, if only he had the courage to take it. As he dragged a comb through his tangled hair, he said, "I don't deserve your friendship." His voice choked with unexpected emotion.

Henry waved the words away. "Credit Birdie. In case you haven't noticed, she's more or less adopted you."

"I don't deserve that, either."

Henry smiled. "Lucky for you and me both, Birdie doesn't consider whether a body deserves her love or not. She just loves."

Charlie swallowed the knot in his throat and concentrated on finishing combing through his hair.

※

Isobel rose to her feet when Charlie stepped through the back door of the mercantile. He looked worse than she expected, even from the brief glimpse she'd had earlier. His once raven hair was peppered with gray. He needed a shave, and while he'd always been thin, he looked undernourished now. Worse than his appearance was the fact that he couldn't seem to look her in the eye.

Mr. Tanner spoke into the awkward silence between them. Glancing Charlie's way, he asked, "I see Birdie made tea for the ladies, but I'm thinking you'd appreciate more coffee?" When Charlie nodded, the older man took a coffee grinder off a shelf and handed it over. "Make yourself at home. I'll send word for Edgar to fetch your laundry." Motioning for Birdie to precede him, he stepped through the doorway into the store and drew the heavy curtain across the opening.

Grateful for the Tanners' tactful exit, Isobel sat back down while Charlie busied himself making coffee. Uneasy silence reigned until he finally had a steaming mug in hand. Out in the store, a tinkling bell announced a customer. Scuffles and voices—a woman and a child. Charlie plopped onto the chair opposite her. "Henry said you were alone this morning. Should we send word to Alfred?"

Isobel shook her head. "Alfred stayed in St. Louis."

Charlie frowned. "Why?"

She spit out the name. "Mary Halifax." She allowed a note of bitterness to sound as she added, "He sent a note on our wedding day. About an hour before Reverend Miller arrived." Beyond muttering surprise, Charlie had nothing to say about it. Did he even care? Isobel blinked tears away, grateful for the interruption when someone rapped on the storeroom door.

Charlie rose and opened the door far enough to reveal a boy with startlingly red hair. "I got the laundry," he said, turning a bit so Charlie could see the bundle tied up in a sheet. "Ma doesn't have much going by the way of laundry today. Between her and Molly, I should be able to return it all first thing tomorrow morning. Does that suit?" He didn't try to hide his curiosity as he strained to see past Charlie.

"That suits," Charlie said and abruptly closed the door.

Silence again. Isobel did her best to fill it. "The chambermaid at the hotel is named Molly. She mentioned a brother named Edgar. Is that him?"

Charlie nodded as he sat down, silently sipping his coffee.

"It sounds like a large family. Seven children, I believe?"

Again, Charlie nodded. "Their father died at Shiloh. They've had a hard time of it. Molly went to work for the sisters at Morrill House. Edgar's a jack-of-all trades. Most recently, he's learning to set type for the *Register*."

Still no reaction to my arrival. To Alfred's betrayal. No mention of what just happened upstairs. All right, then... Isobel related her interactions with Molly at the hotel. "She seems an enterprising sort. She offered to assist me with everything from finding a church to locating the best milliner in town."

"That'd be Molly," Charlie said. "Fourteen going on twenty-four." He paused. "They've all had to grow up fast."

Isobel tried to nudge him toward a more personal topic. "As did you and I when Papa died."

Charlie shrugged. "We had it easy compared to Edgar's family."

Isobel reached up to fiddle with the gold watch dangling from the chain about her neck. She glanced down at the time. *Only eight-thirty in the morning.* The tea was cold. She could almost hear the minutes ticking by as the two of them sat together—and yet miles apart. Charlie wasn't interested in talking about anything that mattered. She finished the cold tea. When she finally huffed audibly, rose, and reached for her parasol in preparation for leaving, Charlie held out a hand.

"Wait."

She left the parasol leaning against the wall.

"Please." He pointed at her chair.

Isobel sat, backbone straight, chin lifted, emotions a tangle of disappointment and frustration, anger and hurt, pressing in on her and threatening to produce more tears. *Do not cry. Do not cry. Do not cry.*

"You're at the Morrill House?"

Yet another topic of no consequence. "Only until you recommend something better. I find Miss Bennet truly unlikeable."

"You can't do better than Morrill House."

"Really?" Isobel turned her head to look out the window.

"Warfield telegraphed me for a recommendation," Charlie said. "If you don't like Morrill House, blame me."

"It's not actually the hotel itself. It's that it's run by one of the most unpleasant people I've had the misfortune to encounter in the recent past."

"You've obviously met Miss Bennet. Her sister, Mrs. Oliver, is the complete opposite."

Isobel shrugged. If all he was going to talk about was hotels and desk clerks—

"I'm surprised you still came. Alone, I mean."

She looked back at him. He still wasn't meeting her gaze. His right index finger was tracing the rim of the coffee mug cupped in his left palm. "The prospect of staying for the season was highly—unattractive." She paused. "You remember what it was like, don't you? All the flirting and pairing off. The expectations. After what Alfred did—" She broke off. Cleared her throat. "To be honest, I couldn't bear the thought of watching him and his new lady love. Let alone staying in that house beneath the cloud of Mother Manning's disapproval." She took a deep breath. "Visiting you was a way to escape all that. It seemed a good idea *at the time.*"

Charlie looked up. He met her gaze long enough to say, "I should have been at the landing to meet you."

Isobel waited for the apology, but it didn't come. When Charlie asked if her room at Morrill House was suitable—in spite of the disappointment she'd expressed—she shrugged.

"It's hardly the suite Alfred described, but it will be adequate for no longer than I'll be here." *Since there doesn't seem to be much point in my staying on.*

Charlie set his coffee cup down. He took a deep breath and blew it out slowly before saying, "I'm sorry for the way Warfield treated you. Sorry, too, that you escaped that debacle only to step into mine." He raked both hands through his once-raven hair before rubbing his forehead and abruptly leaping out of his chair, flinging open the storeroom door, and stepping outside.

He'd left the door open, and Isobel could hear him retching. The tea was cold, but it would be easier on his stomach than coffee. Refilling her cup, she followed him outside and offered the tea. When he tried to wave her away, she persisted. "At least rinse your mouth out."

He obeyed and then handed the cup back. Leaning back against the building, he muttered yet another apology.

"I should go," Isobel said. "We can talk another time." She headed back inside to get her parasol.

Charlie followed her, but he left the storeroom door standing open. "Don't go. Just—wait." He tossed the coffee out of his mug and onto the ground outside. "Sit," he said. "Please." When Isobel obeyed, he settled opposite her and asked, "What has Birdie told you about my—situation?"

She didn't mince words when she replied. "That you lost your wife and child in January." She paused. "But, Charlie, we didn't even know you'd married."

He didn't look up. "I didn't know what to say. How to explain."

"How hard could it be to say you'd met a girl and fallen in love?"

"It's not that simple."

"Is anything ever simple?" Isobel bit back her own hurt and forced warmth into her tone. "I would have been happy for you. I would have understood."

Charlie had opened his mouth to speak when Mrs. Tanner drew a curtain aside and, with a quick apology stepped into the storeroom. She looked up at the top shelf behind her and then over at Charlie. "Would you mind reaching that top box for me? It's a special order and the customer's come from quite a distance to retrieve it."

Charlie pulled the box down.

"Perfect," the storekeeper said. "Thank you." She looked from Charlie to Isobel and back again. "I'll bet your sister would love to see the newspaper office." She smiled at Isobel. "I remember Charlie touting your involvement with the press at the St. Louis Sanitary Fair."

Isobel looked at Charlie as she said, "He did?"

"Oh, yes," Mrs. Tanner said. "He was especially proud that you'd gotten your name into print. He even showed Henry and me a couple of those articles you wrote."

Isobel stared at Charlie. "You kept them?"

"He did," Mrs. Tanner said, looking at Charlie. "You should give her a tour."

Charlie looked doubtful, but finally relented and rose from his chair. "I guess I could. If you're interested."

"Of course she's interested. What sister wouldn't be?" Mrs. Tanner practically lifted Isobel out of the chair. Taking up both Isobel's gloves and parasol, the older woman handed them over and then motioned toward the open door. As Isobel and Charlie stepped into the sunshine, Mrs. Tanner spoke from the doorway. "Come back this evening for supper." She looked at Isobel and warned, "Trust me, dear, you don't want to eat too often at that hotel. Shall we say six o'clock?" She closed the door without waiting for a response. It sounded more like an order than an invitation, but Isobel was grateful for something to do this evening that didn't involve sitting across the table from the stranger her brother had become.

"I'll have to get the key to the office," Charlie said and shuffled up the stairs.

He looks like an old man. Isobel's heart sank as she watched him move, shoulders bowed, hand on the rail. Sadness descended. Whatever closeness had once existed between them was gone. She didn't know this Charlie at all. He clearly had no ability to help her through her own difficulties, and what was worse—she had no idea how to help him.

I should never have come.

Chapter 7

I am weary with my groaning; all the night make I my bed to swim;
I water my couch with my tears.
Psalm 6:6

As he mounted the steps toward the stink in his apartment, Charlie sensed Izzy watching him. She'd had a hard time of it and for that he was sorry, but the fact that they had once been close didn't mean he would talk with her about Vera and the baby. He didn't even want to show her the newspaper office, let alone confide in her. When it came right down to it, he didn't want her in Nebraska.

Taking the *Register* office key off the nail inside the apartment door, Charlie lingered, trying to collect his thoughts and wishing the hangover would release its hold on him. He stared down at the key. The last thing on earth he needed right now was a sister looking over his shoulder, making sure he was all right. He wasn't all right, and Izzy couldn't do a thing about it. He wanted to be left alone, and the sooner she accepted that, the better. The sooner she left Nebraska the better, too. He was a lost cause and whatever happened next shouldn't be witnessed by the only Manning who cared about him. Somehow, he had to convince her to go home.

Back down the stairs, he fumbled the first attempt to unlock the *Register* door. To her credit, Izzy pretended not to notice.

Finally, the lock released and he pushed the door open. As his sister stepped across the threshold, Charlie raised the shade on the window next to the door. Dust motes danced in the light. He moved on, raising window shades around the room. All except for the ones on Main. Best to leave those down, lest someone think he was open for business.

To keep Izzy from broaching a personal topic, he launched into a description of how he'd gotten set up here in Nebraska City. "There was a bigger space available, but I liked the idea of windows on three sides of the space. Extra light."

Izzy crossed the room to stand by the printing press. Putting her hand to the wheel that, once cranked, would lower paper over platen to create a printed page, she asked, "Where on earth did you learn to run a printing press?"

Charlie relaxed a little. That, he could talk about. "His name was Royal Alcott, and he was running a newspaper out of a tent pitched along Clear Creek in Colorado."

"Out of a tent?" Izzy glanced back at the press. "Surely not with this beast."

Charlie pointed to a second, smaller press just beyond his desk on the wall separating his space from the mercantile next door. "That's the one Royal used. It comes in handy for small jobs—invitations, memorial cards, things like that." He pointed at the larger press. "I had the beast brought up from Kansas City late last year."

"Why'd you leave Colorado?"

"It only took about six weeks for me to lose interest in gold mining," Charlie said. "I was having a drink at a saloon one day when Royal ambled in with a stack of news. 'Hot off the press,' he said. One thing led to another, and before long, he'd roped me into visiting the camps, both to collect news and to sell papers. When he decided to sell out and move on, I took things over. Not long after that, my enthusiasm for life in a mining camp hit bottom. I took up with a teamster who agreed to haul the smaller press back east for me."

"You were coming home?"

Charlie shrugged. "I didn't really know where I'd land—only that it'd be somewhere that needed a newspaper. I'm not the only paper in town here, but I've managed to carve out a niche."

"You should be proud of this," Izzy said, gesturing about them.

Charlie looked down at his ink-stained fingers. It was a nice thing to say, but he didn't feel proud. He didn't feel anything much these days.

Izzy pointed at his hands. "Papa would say that ink is a badge of honor. He always said honest work is honorable work."

Charlie felt his cheeks flush. It was embarrassing, the way she was ignoring his troubles in favor of touting what was essentially a failure. After all, the *Register* was only a weekly, and it hadn't been issued regularly since January. Probably wouldn't survive. Feeling queasy again, he slumped onto the stool near the cabinet that held trays of type.

Izzy continued her inspection of the office. Walking closer to the large desk, she laughed as she perused the advertisement pinned above it. She read the sign aloud, whispering the fine print.

Every Lady Guaranteed a
Happy
Husband Who Purchases
Tobacco, Pomade, and other Gentleman's Sundries
at Tanner's Mercantile.

"That's very clever."

"Not my idea."

"Then whose?"

"Believe it or not, the boy who hauled my laundry away a little while ago."

Izzy glanced at him. "Molly's brother came up with that?"

Charlie nodded. "He begged me to let him set type one day. Truth be told, I was surprised he could read, what with the size of his family and the two oldest farmed out to work. As it turns out, Mrs. Simmons is determined to give her children a future. Somehow, she manages to teach them to read at an early age. And Edgar has a knack for language." He pointed to the type drawers. "Of course, only being able to read doesn't make a good typesetter. You create a mirror image, so—"

Izzy interrupted. "I know. Typesetters have to read—and spell—backwards." She pointed to the narrow drawers. "Not to mention remembering what's where." She returned to the press and looked down at the plate waiting to be printed. "What's 'General Order No. 11'?"

"It came down from the Headquarters of the Grand Army of the Republic a week ago. I've mostly steered clear of politics with the *Register*, but I knew I had to run that. Read it and you'll see why."

The 30th day of May, 1868, is designated for the purpose of strewing with flowers or otherwise decorating the graves of comrads who died in defense of their country during the late rebellion, and whose bodies now lie in almost every city, village, and hamlet churchyard in the land. In this observance no form or ceremony is prescribed, but posts will in their own way arrange such fitting services and testimonials of respect as circumstances may permit.

It is the purpose of the Commander-in-Chief to inaugurate this observance with the hope it will be kept up from year to year, while a survivor of the war remains to honor the memory of his departed comrads. He earnestly desires the public press to call attention to this Order, and lend its friendly aid in bringing it to the notice of comrads in all parts of the country in time for simultaneous compliance therewith.

Izzy pointed to a word. "Edgar left an *e* off all three uses of the word *comrades.*" She kept reading. Again, she pointed at a line of type. "And he inserted an unnecessary comma."

"Doesn't matter. I never printed it."

Izzy whirled about to face him. "Why on earth not? You're one of the survivors mentioned. Don't you think it's a good cause?"

"I suppose it is." He shrugged. "But I was too drunk to operate the press."

Izzy grasped a lever. "Come over here and show me how it's done."

He didn't move. "You know how it's done. You saw it every day in the office at your fair in St. Louis."

"But I've never seen a press this size in operation. Do you need fresh ink?"

She wasn't going to give up. Might as well do what she wanted. Maybe then she'd go back to the hotel. With a sigh, Charlie got up and prepared an ink tray. Retrieving a roller, he inked the type. Finally, he positioned a clean sheet of paper over the type, flipped a few levers, and deftly transferred the inked image to the paper. He lifted the printed page carefully and hung it from the clothesline that spanned the office, front to back. "It has to dry before distribution."

"How many copies would you have printed the day you wanted this to circulate?"

"A couple hundred. I was hoping to win some new subscribers. 'Rally 'round the flag' and all that. It doesn't matter now."

"Of course it matters."

"Decoration Day will hardly be big news here in Nebraska City. Our cemetery consists of only about two hundred graves.

Edgar and Molly's father isn't even buried here. As far as I know, there are only two casualties of the Rebellion who are—unless you count the deserting coward I've heard about. No one's going to be decorating his grave."

"Is there a G.A.R. Post here?"

Charlie looked surprised. "How do you know about the G.A.R.?"

Izzy huffed. "Because I know wives, mothers, and sisters of men who served in the Grand Army of the Republic. I remember the first St. Louis chapter being formed. Our newspapers were rife with political controversy every step of the way." She paused. "So—back to the question at hand. Is there a chapter here? If so, I'd assume the members would be in charge of services."

"Yes, there is a chapter, mustered in a few weeks ago. I'm sure they'll do something. But I don't know what, and I don't want to be involved." Thankfully, Izzy didn't pressure him to bare his soul about his lack of enthusiasm for celebrating the war.

"Maybe Decoration Day doesn't have to be *only* about the war," Izzy said. "Don't you remember going with Papa to put flowers on Mama's grave? It was sad, but it was comforting, too. We held hands and—somehow it wasn't so awful because we did it together. Community observances can be a comfort. They can bring people together." She paused. "I'm sure you've been back to lay flowers at Vera and the baby's graves."

Her voice was gentle, but the words felt like barbs scraping at the place where he'd locked his grief. He didn't want to talk about graves and flowers. Didn't want to think about a community gathering. Grief was a private thing, and he wanted to keep it that way. He pointed at the printed page. "Whatever Nebraska City—or the *Register* does— shouldn't really matter to you. After all, won't you be gone by May 30?"

Izzy's expression changed from interest to hurt. "I suppose I will," she said. "Since it's obvious you don't want me here." She headed for the door.

Charlie called after her, stammering a lie. "I-It's not that. It's—you'll be bored to tears after a week or so. There's precious little going on in Nebraska City compared to what you're accustomed to back home." When she hesitated at the door, he added, "I'm not fit company," Charlie said. "Not for anyone."

"Let me help you."

"You can't. No one can."

"Let me try," she pleaded.

He shook his head. She had no idea what she was saying.

"Then maybe *you* can help *me*."

Again, he shook his head.

Her voice wavered. "I can't go back to St. Louis, Charlie. Not for a while, anyway. If I go back now, Mother Manning will make it her goal in life to make certain I never forget how I ruined everything for her."

What was she talking about? "You didn't ruin anything," Charlie protested. "Warfield's the one who backed out. And if you ask me, you're better off without him."

Izzy sighed. "Try convincing Mother Manning of that. The only thing I've ever done that earned her complete approval was to become engaged to a Warfield. But then I failed to complete the deal. She'll make life miserable for me."

"Surely it can't be as bad as that."

"It's not just about Mother's reaction," Izzy said. She looked away. "I cannot *bear* the thought of watching Alfred dandy about with Mary Halifax on his arm. It would be so—humiliating." Again, she pleaded with him. "Please don't send me away." She motioned toward the pile of papers atop Charlie's desk. "I'll make myself useful. I can organize things for you. I did that for the Ladies Aid. I was good at it."

Charlie gazed at the desktop piled with papers. Izzy took it as a sign of his weakening. She plunged ahead.

"Let's print the notice about Decoration Day."

"Now?" He shook his head. "I can't run the press now." Truth was, he did feel a little better, but—he didn't want to do it. What was the point?

"I bet folks all up and down Main would agree to put it up in their windows. It'll be good for the town. Good for the *Register,* too, to be seen supporting something worthwhile—and it *is* worthwhile, whether you think so or not."

"Printing is dirty work. You're hardly dressed for it."

Izzy set her parasol down. "I'm not offering to *print* it, Charlie. I said I'd help." Removing her gloves, she reached for the apron draped across the typesetting desk. She motioned for Charlie to get up. "Come on. Show me how to fix the errors in the type. Then run the press. I'll hang the pages to dry and we'll be finished before we're expected at the Tanners. Tomorrow, I'll help distribute flyers."

With a sigh of surrender, Charlie stood. She wasn't going to give up. Might as well go along. "Edgar can distribute the flyers," he said. "He'll be glad for the work." As he donned his own apron, he muttered, "Just don't say I didn't warn you. I'm not fit company."

Chapter 8

And be ye kind to one another, tenderhearted, forgiving one another, even as God for Christ's sake hath forgiven you.
Ephesians 4:32

The sky was still an inky backdrop to the stars when Gideon hoisted a chunk of venison out of the vat in the spring house and put it in a clean flour sack. Shouldering the bag, he summoned Trouble and headed up the trail toward town. A pang of regret coursed through him as he passed the burial ground. The Tanners had assured him that Ma passed away before rumors began to circulate about him. He wished he knew for certain.

Lost in thought, Gideon stumbled a bit when his boot encountered a rut in the road. A lone figure lay prone in the trail. He heard something up ahead. *Road agents!* His heart pounding, he ran for the edge of the woods. Lowering the sack to the earth he crouched down, one hand on the hilt of the hunting knife at his waist. Were the lone traveler's attackers nearby? He tilted his head, listening for a twig to snap—a horse to stomp—anything to signal evil lurking.

Trouble didn't seem concerned about anything beyond the prone figure lying on the trail. After a few moments, that figure moved. *Not dead.* That was good. When the hapless victim muttered something, Gideon strained to make out the words.

Gibberish finally resolved into discernible words. *Not road agents. Just Charlie Manning. Drunk again.*

Ordering Trouble to stay by the venison and *guard it,* the implication being that he'd better not help himself to the meat, Gideon rose to his feet. Back on the trail, he hoisted Manning over one shoulder, lugged him up the hill, deposited him in the shade of the oak tree, and hurried away. To his surprise, Trouble had obeyed the order regarding the venison. Gideon praised him as he slung the sack over his shoulder and continued the trek toward town.

※

With a low curse, Charlie swiped at his cheek, then scratched the bump where he'd been bitten by some infernal insect. He'd been lying on his stomach. Now he rolled over and opened his eyes. *Leaves. Blue sky.* And the all too familiar sensation that several tiny critters were hammering tacks in place along his hairline.

Bleary-eyed, he sat up and looked about him. He could have sworn he remembered staggering back into town last night. Was he so far gone he'd begun hallucinating? *No.* He distinctly remembered finishing a bottle, tossing it into the tall grass that rimmed the burial ground, and making his way to the road. He cranked his head around and searched the prairie until he located the empty bottle. *Not hallucinating. At least not entirely.*

For a moment, he sat quietly, listening to birdsong. A cardinal, he thought. He craned his neck to peer into the branches above him. That made his head hurt worse, so he gave up locating the bird. Wincing, he massaged his temples in a vain attempt to relieve the headache. The sun was high in the sky. He groaned. Whatever the present hour, by the time he walked the mile and a quarter back to town and got cleaned up, he'd have missed lunch with Izzy—and this only her second day in Nebraska. How had it come to this?

You know exactly how. In the fog of fresh grief, he'd come out to the graveyard every day this past January. To pay his respects, he told himself. In the frigid weather, an occasional swig from a small flask warmed him up. But then the occasional swig became half the flask. When the flask was no longer enough, he brought a bottle.

By the time winter passed into spring, whiskey had become more than just a way to keep warm. It was a way to numb hopelessness. And he didn't simply want a drink. He needed it. He began to miss important meetings and contented himself with reprinting news that had already appeared in other papers. He stopped seeking subscriptions. By the time he faced the truth about being trapped in a downward spiral, he couldn't seem to help himself. He'd become like so many of the men he'd known during the war. Men he'd criticized as "too weak to cope without a liquid crutch."

With a low grunt, he forced himself to stand up. *You turned your nose up at them. Remember? And look at you now—a drunkard like them.* What would he say to Izzy? Only yesterday, Henry had encouraged him to "tell the truth." It was good advice—except Izzy had come to Nebraska to escape her own unhappy truth. She was counting on his newspaper to occupy her time and him to help her get over the humiliation of being left at the altar. What would she do when she realized how far he'd sunk?

Hoofbeats sounded from the direction of town. A buggy came into view. Charlie recognized the horse. It was Birdie Tanner's strawberry roan, Rosie. And next to Birdie, a red-headed woman dressed in blue. Dread washed over him. *Oh, Izzy.*

His head pounded when he bent to retrieve his hat. With a low groan, he slapped it against one thigh, then flicked a few stubborn fragments of grass off the brim. He put it on carefully, watching as the buggy turned off the road to ascend the hill. *Tell her the truth. You're a lost cause. The paper will fold. And staying in Nebraska City is the worst idea she's had since she agreed to marry Alfred Warfield.*

He steeled himself for the inevitable lecture. Izzy would be furious, and rightly so. At least he didn't reek of vomit this time. But instead of heading for where he was waiting in the shade of the one mature tree on the hilltop, Birdie pulled up just off the road. When Izzy alighted, the older woman gave a little wave in Charlie's direction and then guided Rosie in a tight circle and back toward town.

Charlie frowned. What to make of that? He looked back to Izzy. She was walking up the hill, taking her time and inspecting first one gravestone and then another as she moved away from Charlie toward the south. When she reached the far boundary of the cemetery grounds, she turned about. Along the row where some graves were marked with little more than a large rock, some not at all, she crouched down to inspect a homemade marker. Charlie knew the story behind that one. Ezra Carter had fashioned it, embedding the concrete cross with bits of colored glass to create a unique memorial stone for his wife, Pearl. Carter and his daughter left flowers at the grave on a regular basis. Almost as often as Charlie brought flowers to Vera. *But Carter doesn't come up here to drink.* Then again, he had a daughter. *Maybe if our baby had lived*—Charlie gave a little shudder. It made his head hurt worse.

When Izzy finally made her way to where he waited, she didn't speak. Instead, she inspected the four-foot-tall obelisk bearing Vera and the baby's names.

Sacred to the Memory of
Vera Manning
Aged 19 yrs. 7 das.

Infant son Charles
Aged 1 day
Died
January 22, 1868

"It's a fine marker," she said and looked out over the graveyard. "The tallest one in the cemetery."

"I had it brought from Kansas City," Charlie said. He'd waited weeks for the stone mason's work to arrive. It had caused quite a stir in town, being the first grave marker to require a crane to offload it and a specially outfitted freighter's wagon to get it to its spot here in the cemetery. All that effort hadn't done a thing to relieve his pain.

Izzy looked up at the tree branches above them, then toward the road. "It's a lovely spot."

Charlie nodded.

"Birdie was sure you'd be here. She offered to drive me out."

Birdie. Of course it would be *Birdie*, not *Mrs. Tanner*. Already. It didn't take the older woman long to draw those needing shelter under her wing. She'd done it with Vera and now Izzy. Birdie knew all about Charlie's habit of cemetery visits and liquid comfort.

"She offered to wait, but I told her we'd walk back. That we've taken quite enough of her time in the last couple of days."

Bristling at the accusatory tone, Charlie flung yesterday's conversation back at her. "I *told* you I'm not fit company. I said you can't help me." He motioned toward Vera's marker. "Not with this, anyway. You should have believed me. For that matter, so should Birdie and Henry. You should all leave me alone."

"I can't leave you alone, Charlie. I *won't*."

He pushed off from the tree and moved away from her, muttering, "Then you're a fool."

※

Isobel watched as Charlie shuffled away. What to do? What to say? Did the brother she'd always loved even exist anymore? She launched a desperate plea heavenward: *Help me. Please.* Then hurried after him. When she tucked a hand beneath his arm and gave a little tug, he paused. "Tell me about Vera," she said.

He grunted. "I expected Birdie would have done that on the way out here."

"As it happens, she spent the drive out here telling me about her committee."

"Which committee would that be? Birdie has a finger in a lot of pies around town."

"The one she's organizing to care for the cemetery." She paused. "She invited me to join the effort."

"I'm not surprised," Charlie said. "Birdie's a crusader. She'd probably run for mayor if women were allowed. And Henry would vote for her." He grunted. "For that matter, so would I."

The tension between them relaxed a little. "From what I've seen of Mrs. Tanner, Nebraska City could do worse," Isobel said. "She's organizing a clean-up day out here for this coming Saturday. I didn't commit to joining the committee, but I did say I'd help with that."

"If you stay long, one clean-up day will be only the beginning. Don't say I didn't warn you." Charlie led the way toward the road.

Halfway down the hill, they passed a plot with four similar markers all in a row. The family name was *Long,* Isobel pointed at the seedling tree planted near the father's marker. "Someone besides Birdie cares about this place." She glanced behind them toward Vera's grave. "Did Vera have a favorite flower?"

Charlie frowned. "Why?"

Isobel shrugged. "You already have a tree—and a mature one at that—shading the marker. Something that blooms every spring might be nice, too. Peonies, maybe?"

"Too fancy. She liked wildflowers."

When they reached the road, Isobel pointed at the sign nailed to a single fence post. *Wyuka Cemetery est. 1854.* "Birdie said this land belonged to the Otoe Indians until a few years ago, and *Wyuka* means—"

"*Here I rest,* according to some old-timers."

"It's a nice sentiment," Isobel offered.

"*Nice?*"

"You know what I mean." For a few moments, they walked in silence, down a hill to a narrow bridge that crossed a creek and then up again toward town. Finally, Isobel said, "Sometimes it's impossible to find the right words for tragedy. There's nothing *nice* about having to say goodbye to the ones we love."

At first she thought her awkward attempt at an apology had made things worse between them. But then, Charlie began to talk about Vera. How, one night when he was riding back from a dance west of town, a terrified young woman darted out of a plum thicket and onto the trail. When a bellowing ox of a man charged after her, Charlie intervened, surprising even himself by his fury against the drunkard, who retreated into the night shouting threats. He dismounted and convinced the girl to let him help her mount the hired horse, which he then led into town.

"All I could think to do was take her to Birdie. Early the next morning, I heard a ruckus over at the mercantile. When I got there, the man I'd seen chasing the girl was demanding

Henry return her—in language that reduced her to little more than a piece of livestock. Claimed he was her father." He paused. "I went for the sheriff."

Isobel shuddered. "How horrible."

"It was worse than any of us imagined."

Something in Charlie's tone made Isobel look over at him, but his face was a mask. She waited, trudging alongside him wordlessly.

"The sheriff threatened to jail the man for what he'd done." Charlie cleared his throat. "He left town. Vera stayed with Birdie and Henry, and she blossomed. She worked in the store, and everyone who knew her learned to love her. Including me."

They could just see the courthouse rooftop up ahead. Isobel squeezed his arm. "Birdie said I'd be proud of you when I knew the story. She was right. I am."

"It took some doing to convince her to marry me and stay in Nebraska City. People had been kind, but she was afraid all of that would change as soon as the baby arrived."

Ah. The baby. "But you loved her," Isobel said gently, "and you did the honorable thing. You married her."

"Vera never doubted my love for her. But she wasn't sure I could love a baby I hadn't created. Convincing her of that took a while."

A baby he hadn't created? Isobel took in a sharp breath as the truth came clear. An abused young girl. A violent father. *Oh... Vera.* As they walked along, she looked over at her brother. "You're a good man, Charlie Manning."

"Not that good," he said. "Truth be told, I had my doubts, even if I never voiced them. But the moment the little guy was born, I loved him." He paused. Gave a cough that was half sob. "And then—I lost them." They had reached the stairway leading up to his apartment. Charlie looked up toward the door. "The drinking started innocently enough on those cold January days when I visited the grave. A little nip to warm up. But now I can't seem to stop."

Oh, Charlie. What could she possibly say? She squeezed his arm again.

For a long few minutes, Charlie didn't move. Finally, though, he looked her way and croaked, "I'm sorry you walked into my mess. I think you'll regret staying, but I guess—if you really want to—I wouldn't mind."

Chapter 9

A man's heart deviseth his way: but the Lord directeth his steps.
Proverbs 16:9

MAY 15, 1868
MRS. E. L. MANNING
ST. LOUIS, MISSOURI

YOUR TELEGRAM RECEIVED. STOP. WELL SITUATED IN NEBRASKA CITY. STOP. ENJOYING TIME WITH CHARLIE AND NEW FRIENDS. STOP. RETURN DATE UNKNOWN. STOP. WILL WRITE—

Standing at the counter just inside the Nebraska City telegraph office door, Isobel lifted her pen from the paper and stared down at the words *will write*. Why was she promising to do that? What could she possibly say that Mother Manning would want to read? She'd be appalled that Charlie had married without telling his family. She would understand neither his struggle to overcome the loss nor his terrifying fondness for alcohol. She would disapprove of Isobel's befriending a couple who were "mere shopkeepers" and openly sneer at the notion of Isobel helping in the newspaper office. As for Isobel's volunteering to help clean up the local cemetery—Mother would be horrified. Pulling weeds?

Trimming grass? *Ladies* hired such work done. Isobel could almost hear the older woman clucking her tongue with derision.

Re-reading Mother's telegram, Isobel carried on an imaginary conversation with its imperious author.

ST. LOUIS FRIENDS AGHAST AT YOUR BEHAVIOR.

My behavior? What about Alfred's behavior?

GOSSIP ABOUNDS.

A good reason to stay away.

WASTING INHERITANCE IN THIS MANNER ILL-ADVISED.

According to Mr. Wilder, my inheritance will last for the rest of my life—as long as I live reasonably. I am doing just that. Incidentally, why didn't you ever tell me I had access to funds that had nothing to do with your household budget?

CHARLIE AGREES.

That's a lie. Charlie has introduced me to his banker and helped me open an account. He said he's glad I'm here.

That last part was a bit of an exaggeration, but at least Charlie seemed to be warming to the idea of having her around.

PLEASE ADVISE AS TO EXPECTED DATE OF RETURN.

Isobel scratched a one-word response directly on Mother Manning's telegram.

No.

She looked down at the two-letter word and smiled. Even a rebellion staged from hundreds of miles away provided a new sense of independence. It felt wonderful.

On the telegram she'd been composing, Isobel drew a line through the words *will write*. There was no reason to write. At least not immediately. Her response to Mother's message provided all the information courtesy demanded. For now, courtesy was all Isobel was prepared to offer.

Affixing her name to the bottom of the form, she tucked Mother Manning's telegram into the silk bag at her wrist. Handing her response across the counter, she paid the fee, pulled on her gloves, and stepped out into the May sunshine. Now to rectify the mistakes she'd made when packing for the trip—too many ball gowns. Nothing fit for everyday life in Nebraska City.

Molly Simmons had been true to the promise she'd made the morning of Isobel's arrival. Asked to recommend a dressmaker, the girl had mentioned a Mrs. Hall. Then, while Isobel had breakfast, Molly handed over an edition of the *Morning Chronicle*, folded to reveal an advertisement spread across two columns of the five-column page.

"That's her," she said, pointing to the ad, "and you can't do better."

> Mrs. Warren Hall would inform the citizens of Nebraska City
> that she is prepared to receive orders for HAIR JEWELRY
> of every description and style.
> HAIR, FLOWER, TAMBOUR, EMBROIDERY,
> SILK CHENILLE and WORSTED EMBROIDERY
> stamping, braiding, china painting.
> Particular attention to DRESS MAKING.
> Patterns of the latest style constantly on hand
> at the residence at Fifth and Pleasant.

Isobel looked up in surprise. "One woman does all that?" It was hard to believe.

Molly sounded hurt. "I wouldn't steer you wrong, ma'am. Mrs. Hall sews for all the fine ladies hereabouts. But if you don't believe me, ask Mrs. Tanner."

Isobel asked, and now she was walking along Pleasant Street toward a white gingerbread-trimmed cottage, identified as a business only by the name *Mrs. Warren Hall* in gilt letters on a black sign above the front door. A broad, low porch shaded both the front and east side of the cottage. The narrow path from the street to the front steps wound through an inviting wilderness of grasses and flowers, the latter blooming as if an artist had spattered the yard with paint. A second smaller cottage sat at the rear of the property just beyond a path wide enough to accommodate a buggy. The entire property exuded welcome, well-being, and peace.

The slim young woman who answered Isobel's knock on the front door sported a starched white apron and a yellow headscarf that reminded Isobel of Portia, who always kept her abundant mop of tight curls expertly wrapped in vibrant color. The girl was, Isobel thought, about the same age as Molly Simmons.

"Good day, ma'am," she said. "How may I help you?"

Isobel introduced herself. "I'm newly arrived in Nebraska City and have discovered that I didn't pack appropriately. Mrs. Hall came highly recommended by both the chambermaid at my hotel and Mrs. Tanner of Tanner Mercantile."

With a nod, the girl stepped back to admit Isobel into a large room with an impressive array of goods. To the left, a tall glass-fronted display boasted several shelves of hats in the latest style. To the right of the front door, a long, low case housed row upon row of wooden compartments overflowing with trims and laces, buttons and feathers. Straight ahead, a short hall led to what was obviously a work room. From where Isobel stood, she could see a dress form and part of a sewing machine.

Birdie had mentioned that Mrs. Hall was a war widow. But the raven-haired woman who glided into view from the direction of the work room was probably not over thirty years old—not at all what Isobel had envisioned. Offering a warm smile, Mrs. Hall introduced Sarah Carter, the young woman who'd answered the door. "Miss Carter is my combination apprentice, housekeeper, cook, and, when the situation calls for it, my rescuer. In truth, she is the one who makes all that I do possible."

Miss Carter grinned. "You keep that up, and I'll be asking for a raise."

"Which I would give, so please don't ask," the dressmaker said with a wink before turning to Isobel. "Shall we ask Miss Carter to make tea? Or is this a preliminary visit? I can see by the ensemble you're wearing that you are accustomed to expert service. I'd understand if you want to interview more than one dressmaker before committing. There's a Miss Sparks over on Laramie who does excellent work."

Miss Carter spoke up. "Mrs. Tanner sent Miss Manning to you, ma'am."

"You know Birdie?" the dressmaker asked.

Isobel nodded. "The Tanners are friends of my brother, Charlie. Charles Manning, of the *Register*."

Mrs. Hall clasped her hands before her and exclaimed, "Thank goodness you've come! Birdie's been so worried about Charlie. We've all been worried. Losing Vera and the baby was a terrible blow."

We've all? Did the entire city know about Charlie's trouble?

"Vera was the sweetest girl," Mrs. Hall continued. "It's a shame you didn't have a chance to know her." She asked Miss Carter to proceed with making tea and motioned Isobel forward. "Allow me to show you my workroom." As she led the way toward the back of the house, Mrs. Hall said, "I do hope you'll forget I mentioned Miss Sparks."

As she looked about the workroom, Isobel thought she probably would. To the left, a pair of wide screen doors not only offered a view of the abundant blossoms in the yard but also admitted bright light and fresh air. On the far wall, not one but two sewing machines sat beneath a framed bulletin board covered with Godey's fashion plates, bits of trim, measuring tapes, and bins holding scissors and all manner of tools. Above the board, a painted slogan declared, *It is a woman's duty to be as attractive as possible.* Two dress forms occupied space in opposite corners of the room. One awaited a garment, but the other displayed a coffee-colored silk dress trimmed with plaited ruffles and bands of scarlet silk.

Isobel recognized the gown immediately. It was a stunning realization of the hand-colored fashion plate affixed to the bulletin board right behind it, which featured four women, a young boy, and a bride. The bride modeled the very gown Mother Manning had declared perfect for Isobel. Turning her back on the fashion plate, Isobel surveyed the last wall in the room. Floor-to-ceiling shelves displayed dozens of bolts of cloth. "I've never seen so much fabric in one place," she exclaimed. "To find it here is more than a little surprising."

Mrs. Hall tilted her head. "Here in the wilderness, you mean?"

Quickly, Isobel said, "I didn't mean to offend."

"Oh, you haven't. Not at all. It's no secret that people think of Nebraska City as the place they are forced to pass through on their way to where they want to be." Mrs. Hall smiled. "Fortunately, the same steamboats spilling out emigrants also bring me the latest fashion news, fabrics, and trims."

Miss Carter arrived with a tea tray and set it down before seating herself at the opposite end of the table. While she went to work applying trim to a straw hat, Mrs. Hall slid open a drawer and withdrew a pile of pattern pieces, which Isobel instantly recognized.

"You're familiar with Powell and Kohler?"

"More familiar than I care to be," Mrs. Hall chuckled. "Be glad you weren't a mouse in the corner when I was learning their system."

"Anyone who's deciphered the complexities of Powell and Kohler," Isobel said, "has my confidence. If you can work me in, I'd like you to make a few things." She took a quick sip of tea before explaining, "I've convinced my brother to let me help out at the *Register*. Nothing I brought with me is suitable for a day in a newspaper office."

Mrs. Hall didn't seem at all shocked by the notion of Isobel's working in a newspaper office. She merely nodded and crossed to the wall of fabric. "I'd suggest skirts and shirtwaists, easily laundered and easily pressed."

Isobel agreed.

The dressmaker pulled down a bolt of rich brown crepeline and an ivory batiste, suggesting the brown for a skirt and the warm white for a shirtwaist. "A jabot of the brown would be a nice touch." She looked over at Isobel. "The warm tones will complement that glorious red hair of yours."

Glorious? Isobel gave a nervous laugh. "That's a very kind way to reference the bane of my existence. My stepmother has spent hours scouring ladies' magazines to find a cure for this abominable color."

"A *cure?*" Mrs. Hall sputtered. "She actually used that word?" When Isobel nodded, Mrs. Hall took both bolts of cloth in hand and marched over to the worktable to plop them down. "What a notion! Your hair is lovely. A woman should capitalize on the things that make her unique."

Unique was another word for it. Isobel surveyed the wall of fabric. "I'll want at least two more outfits."

"Blue suits you nicely," Mrs. Hall said as she reached for a blue plaid cotton. "What about a shirtwaist and skirt to match?"

Isobel reached up to touch the blue bonnet on her head. "Excellent. I'll still be able to wear my favorite bonnet."

"Perhaps you'd like to stay with blue, then," Mrs. Hall said and took down an indigo calico. "I'm not trying to pressure you at all, but I will say that Miss Carter is an excellent milliner. In fact, she made all the pieces on display in the case out front."

Isobel looked over, admiring Miss Carter's work. The young woman was doing a lovely job of trimming a straw bonnet. "I probably will need something else once summer arrives," Isobel said with a little shrug. "We—" she broke off. "*I* didn't pack with staying in mind."

"No one has claimed that piece yet," Mrs. Hall said, indicating the hat on the work room form. "Miss Carter could easily trim it in blue—if you're interested."

Isobel was, and in a short while she'd also ordered three new ensembles.

While Mrs. Hall took measurements, jotting them on a sturdy brown card, she suggested a few changes in overall styling, not the least of which eliminated hoops. "If you ask me," she said, "it makes a great deal of sense—especially for a businesswoman."

A *businesswoman.* Isobel rather liked the term. While she might not be quite ready to think of her red hair as *glorious,* she very much appreciated Mrs. Hall's belief that a woman should capitalize on what made her *unique.* Isobel Manning wasn't curvaceous or blue-eyed or golden-haired or porcelain-skinned. Nor was she eighteen years old, like the girl who'd lured Alfred away. When it came down to it, Isobel could list any number of things about herself that would fall under the heading *unique.* Including the fact that she was about to take a job in a newspaper office. Mother Manning would be appalled. Isobel was both surprised and pleased to realize she didn't really care.

Chapter 10

Whatsoever thy hand findeth to do, do it with thy might.
Ecclesiastes 9:10

Isobel lay awake, worrying her way toward dawn. Would Charlie keep his promise to help with the cemetery clean-up today? What if he failed to appear? What if today was only a repeat of this past Monday and Tuesday? He'd said he didn't mind her being here. He'd even helped her open a bank account and shown her the town. But things still weren't right between them. Birdie said Isobel shouldn't take it personally and that any difficulty was because Charlie wasn't "right." Isobel thought that was probably true, but still—

Slipping out of bed, she went to the window, watching as the first of the day's wagon trains began to line up in the darkness fading toward dawn. The scene was a visible reminder of how far she was from everything familiar. Beyond whispered gossip, she knew precious little about the power of alcohol to lure seemingly strong men into the abyss. *You knew Geoffrey Tate.* The name landed like a stone in her midsection. Why hadn't she realized Geoffrey's real problem? A friend of Alfred's, Geoffrey had been shipped off to somewhere in the east "for health reasons" only a week before the wedding. Informed that he wouldn't be in attendance, Isobel had expressed surprise. She hadn't realized the man was ill, she said. Alfred muttered something obscure and changed the subject. Thinking back, Isobel realized the truth. The family had couched Geoffrey's problems in an acceptable phrase. *Ill health* was acceptable. *Drunkenness* was not. How could she have been so naïve?

She wished she knew more. Where had Geoffrey gone? What treatment did he receive? Was it successful? Should Charlie go away to a place like that? Was resisting the temptation to drink a matter of the will, or were darker forces at play? What if Charlie couldn't help himself? What if, even now, he was lying in his apartment with another collection of empty bottles strewn across the floor? *What if everything I try comes to naught?*

The sound of boot-clad feet out in the hall stamped out the swirl of worry. Isobel turned away from the window and grabbed her wrapper, donning it just as a knock at the door announced the chambermaid's arrival with fresh water. Isobel yanked the door open and greeted Molly Simmons with a thanks for recommending Mrs. Hall, the dressmaker. "She is, indeed, a wonder."

While the girl poured fresh water into the pitcher on the washstand, Isobel blathered on about her visit to Mrs. Hall's, her surprise at the woman's obvious skill, and the three new ensembles, ending with, "Now that I'll have clothing that requires regular laundering, I expect to take advantage of your mother's service. If she'll accept a new client, of course."

"Ma don't turn away work. Too many mouths to feed for that." When Isobel retrieved the blue walking dress—again—and laid it on the bed in preparation for dressing, Molly chuckled. "I reckon you'll be glad when Mrs. Hall finishes the new duds."

"You're right about that," Isobel agreed.

The sun came up while Isobel was having breakfast in the hotel dining room. Lingering over the bitter coffee, she perused the *Morning Chronicle's* announcement concerning Nebraska

City's "Exemplary Tribute to the Grand Army of the Republic. Not to be Missed." A flag-raising and speeches at the courthouse would begin the day and be followed by a wreath-laying at the cemetery. In the afternoon, the Episcopal Church would host a special service. In the evening, the Nebraska City Cornet Band would offer a program at Hawke's Hall. Isobel smiled. Had the flyers she and Charlie printed and she and Edgar Simmons distributed inspired the lavish celebration? She hoped so. She hoped Charlie was pleased.

Returning the newspaper to the front desk, Isobel exited the hotel, opened her parasol, and marched toward Charlie's. Shouts and curses rang out, thanks to the assembly of teams and wagons, freighters, and emigrants lined up along Main. Assaulted by the smell of animals, tobacco, sweat, and manure, Isobel regretted the hearty breakfast she'd eaten. And she worried.

What if Charlie isn't there? What if he's there, but he's drunk again? What if he doesn't recover? What if I can't help him? What if—as Isobel rounded the corner, intent on reaching the stairs to Charlie's apartment, a ragged stranger exited the back door of Tanner's Mercantile. Scraggly shoulder-length hair trickled from beneath a black hat and over the collar of a long black coat. The scarf wrapped about the stranger's neck obscured the lower half of his face. He carried a large sack over one shoulder. *He'd broken in!*

Her heart pounding, Isobel took a step back. Intending to flee, she hesitated when a wagon appeared from the opposite direction. Henry and Birdie! Isobel opened her mouth to cry a warning, but then Henry raised a hand in greeting, and the stranger hurried toward the wagon. Birdie leaned down to speak to the man. He nodded before glancing behind him, then hesitated an instant before loping off toward the south.

Isobel watched until he disappeared from view. By that time, Henry had pulled the wagon up to the storeroom door, helped

Birdie down, and disappeared inside. And Charlie—God be praised—Charlie was descending the stairs from his apartment. He was dressed in bib overalls, a blue work shirt, and a wide-brimmed hat that had definitely seen better days. He looked ridiculous and wonderful at the same time, for he was clear-eyed when he reached the bottom step and called a greeting. He even *smiled*.

"You're overdressed, fair sister."

"Obviously." Isobel replied. "But it's the best I could do until Mrs. Hall fills my order for more sensible clothing. I have a fitting early next week."

"Just don't think that get-up is going to get you out of actually working today."

He was teasing her. *Hallelujah!* Isobel tossed her head. "I have every intention of proving myself a worthy, if temporary, member of the Cemetery Improvement Society."

"The—what?"

Isobel repeated it. "The Cemetery Improvement Society. It has a nice ring to it, don't you think? I just this moment made it up."

"It's perfect," Birdie called as she stepped back outside, a picnic basket in each hand. She handed one to Isobel. "Help me stow these under the seat while Charlie and Henry collect the tools we'll be needing today."

Isobel took a picnic basket in hand, nodding toward the south. "Who was that?"

"That's the Charlie we all know and love," Birdie said. "And isn't it wonderful he's decided to make an appearance." She settled another picnic basket beneath the wagon seat.

"I was asking about the stranger." Isobel lifted the other basket into place. "When I saw him come out of the storeroom with that sack over his shoulder, I thought you were being robbed."

"Oh—him? A customer. Something of a hermit. He and Henry have an arrangement." Birdie directed Isobel's attention to a full water barrel and a bunch of seedling trees in the wagon bed. "Unless we can persuade our city board to fund on-site improvements including a well, we'll be hauling water all summer to keep those trees alive. There's need for a fence, too—and a decent gate with a better sign. If we can get a well dug, I'd like to encourage folks to plant even more trees—and flowering shrubs." She looked over at Isobel. "Do you think a Cemetery Improvement Society could manage all that?"

"Probably—if it existed."

"I hope it will after today," Birdie said. She looked pointedly at Isobel. "It's a pity we don't know anyone with experience raising money for a good cause. Someone who was involved in, say, a successful sanitary fair like the one they had in St. Louis. I remember it made an impressive amount of money. You don't happen to know anyone like that, do you?"

Obviously, Charlie had at some point mentioned Isobel's enthusiastic involvement in St. Louis's successful fair. She held up a hand in protest. "Projects like that require a community to have faith in the organizers' abilities. This community has never heard of me."

"At least half a dozen of my friends are coming today," Birdie said, "most with husbands in tow. All have a vested interest in keeping the wilderness from swallowing up their loved ones' final resting places." She paused. "Do think about getting involved. Please."

Henry and Charlie exited the mercantile with the last of the needed tools. While Henry helped Birdie up onto the wagon seat, Charlie lowered the tailgate, lifted Isobel up, and then jumped up beside her. She began to open her parasol, but decided it would look ridiculous—or pretentious, which was worse. She laid the closed parasol beside her.

As the wagon rolled along, Charlie asked, "What's Birdie want you to think about?"

Isobel glanced over her shoulder before saying in a low voice, "She overheard me joking about a 'cemetery improvement society.' Only she didn't take it as a joke."

"And?"

"She seems to think I should get involved in fundraising for the improvements she'd like to see out there."

"I warned you about Birdie. Fingers in pies and all that." When Isobel nodded agreement, he nudged her shoulder. "And?"

"I'm hardly the ideal person, and I told her as much. In St. Louis, I was working with people who'd known the Manning name for decades. Here, I'm not even a newcomer. I'm a *visitor.*"

"How did Birdie react to that?"

"Swatted the facts away like so many flies." After a moment or two of companionable silence, she murmured, "It *is* a worthwhile cause, though." When Charlie snickered, Isobel looked over at him. "I didn't commit to anything."

"Yet."

Isobel lifted her chin. "What if I did?"

Charlie shrugged. "If you're going to stay for a while, you might as well have something worthwhile to occupy your time—besides a failing newspaper."

Chapter 11

One generation passeth away, and another generation cometh...
Ecclesiastes 1:4

As soon as Henry pulled the wagon to a halt beneath the lone mature tree at the cemetery, Isobel and Charlie jumped down, assisting in the placing of seedling trees in the spots Birdie indicated. The older woman introduced Isobel as other volunteers arrived. Eventually, teams spread out to the four corners of the cemetery. They would move toward the center of the grounds, with ladies trimming around the bases of markers and men planting trees and mowing the tall grass. Henry would watch the time and announce lunch. Isobel worked with Birdie, who shared bits of information about those in attendance.

"You already know Teddy Hall," Birdie said. "America Payne's parents were among the first to cross the Missouri into Nebraska Territory back in the '50s. She can always be counted on to support anything connected to honoring the old settlers."

Birdie nodded across the hill toward a young widow dressed in half-mourning, who was trimming about the base of an obelisk while the much older woman she'd accompanied to the cemetery looked on. "That's Electa Bishop and Jennie Wilcox. They'll see to Freddie's grave first. Jennie is Freddie's widow. He was Electa's only child."

Isobel frowned. "*Wilcox? Bishop?*"

Birdie explained. "Freddie's father, James Wilcox, was Electa's first husband. Sadly, Mr. Wilcox died when Freddie was quite young. I believe Freddie was about six years old when Electa married Julian Bishop. The Bishops never had children of their own, and they were understandably devastated when Freddie succumbed to lung fever in camp in Tennessee. Not a battlefield casualty, but still a tragic loss." She went on. "Freddie and Jennie hadn't been married even a year." Pausing, Birdie looked over at Isobel. "Jennie doesn't have other family. She's stayed on with her in-laws, but she doesn't have many friends her own age. I think the two of you would get along quite well."

Isobel offered a noncommittal response and concentrated on pulling a particularly stubborn weed. She wasn't planning on being in Nebraska long enough to cultivate friendships.

Birdie nodded toward another couple working near four marble lambs at the end of one row. "That's Helen and Dutch Shook. Helen tends those graves for the mothers forced to leave them behind when they moved west. I remarked on how kind it was of her one day, and she told me she was happy to do it, that she'd left four little graves behind in Ohio. She hoped someone there was tending her little lambs."

Four? Isobel took a quick breath. "I cannot imagine surviving that kind of heartbreak."

Birdie nodded agreement. "There's no denying the sad stories represented here, but there are also stories of courage and admirable testimonies to deep faith." She ran her fingers across the epitaph inscribed on the stone where she knelt. "Henry and I knew this couple. The husband, Willis, ordered this marker after losing his young wife." She read aloud.

Lord she was Thine,
And not mine own,

Thou hast not
done me wrong;
I thank Thee for
the precious loan
Afforded me so long.

Isobel didn't know what to say. She couldn't imagine anyone being so accepting of a beloved spouse's death. And yet—how different things would be for Charlie if he could find his way to that kind of peace. How different for everyone who knew him.

When Henry announced a lunch break, several volunteers retrieved patchwork quilts from their buggies and wagons and spread them beneath the towering oak tree growing near the northern edge of the cemetery grounds.

As the ladies settled with their baskets, Birdie exclaimed, "Jennie Wilcox, you've brought enough food to feed an army!"

The young widow blushed and waved the compliment away. "I was expecting a bigger turnout."

Lunchtime conversation centered on plans for the upcoming Decoration Day. When Mrs. Wilcox's father-in-law, Mr. Bishop, began to share the local G.A.R. chapter plans, his wife interrupted. "Julian. Let's not give away too much too soon. We don't want the editor of the *Chronicle* to think we're speaking out of turn." She spoke to Charlie. "Your competitor plans to publish a detailed calendar of events." She looked about at the group. "And you'll all want to be certain to buy that edition, whether you subscribe or not."

Isobel bristled. Was Mrs. Bishop's promoting a rival newspaper a deliberate snub? She looked Charlie's way. He shrugged and gave a quick little shake of his head. *Don't say anything.* Isobel didn't. *But really. How rude.*

Birdie broke in with what she called a "wish list" when it came to cemetery improvements—first, a well and a fence. After that, more plantings, a flagpole, and—

Mrs. Bishop interrupted. "While I don't disagree with the general idea of improving things out here, I don't think we should expect people to fund anything quite so *extreme* as what you're suggesting." She gestured about them. "A fence is a good idea to keep cattle out, but we would do well to remember that it's *prairie*, not the Garden of Eden."

America Payne disagreed. She thought Decoration Day was a good start, but only the beginning when it came to honoring the past. "An Old Settlers Association has been established for Otoe County. We should do something to honor them, too."

Mrs. Bishop smirked. After all, she said, some of those "old settlers" had crossed the Missouri River before it was even *legal* for them to settle in Indian Territory. "I'm not certain we'd want to 'honor' behaviors that were, technically, against the law."

Isobel thought Mrs. Payne showed admirable self-control, glowering but saying nothing more about her ancestors even as she adamantly agreed with Birdie about more plantings. She glanced at her husband as she said, "Once there's a fence, Buck and I will donate flowering shrubs to line the road. I'd suggest forsythia and something complementary to carry the bloom past summer. Perhaps asters for fall color. But we can decide when the time comes." She looked around the circle of ladies before focusing on Mrs. Bishop as she said, "Teddy's lawn is proof that with a little planning, a 'square of prairie' can be transformed into a beautiful garden."

Mrs. Hall nodded toward the road as she said, "I always collect seeds as the season progresses. I'd be happy to broadcast this year's supply inside the cemetery boundary."

Mrs. Bishop punctuated everyone else's agreeable murmurs with a snort. "You'd be wasting both the seeds and your time—unless we can convince someone to turn the earth first. And if anything did grow, installing a fence would crush it." She took the last cookie off a plate and popped it in her mouth.

"Well," Mrs. Hall retorted, "as it's *my* time to waste and *my* seed, you needn't concern yourself."

Jennie Wilcox spoke into the tense silence. "I'd plant daisies if I thought they'd have a chance." Her voice took on a wistful tone as she murmured, "Freddie always brought me daisies, soon as they started blooming."

"Daisies are very hardy," Mrs. Hall said. She suggested a memorial garden at the base of the flagpole Birdie had mentioned. "We could preserve the names of donors on a plaque."

Mrs. Bishop clicked her tongue. "Ladies, ladies. We are getting ahead of ourselves. Let us stick to the business at hand, which is preparing for Decoration Day, 1868."

America Payne spoke up. "What about wreaths at our veterans' graves?"

"I like that." Mrs. Wilcox looked over the hillside. "Do we know who they all are?"

"That might be a challenge," Birdie offered. "From what I know, the earliest records were lost, long before our current sexton took over. Sadly, the cemetery hasn't received much attention in recent years."

Mrs. Bishop opined that public servants who didn't perform their duties should be replaced.

"Let's not be too hard on Mr. Riley," Birdie said. "He's been in poor health." She looked about the circle. "It seems to me that we've just demonstrated a need for a more organized approach to cemetery improvement."

When one of the husbands raised the issue of water for the trees they'd planted, Birdie proposed a solution. "The wagon we're using today belongs to the Simmons family. Nettie wanted to be involved somehow, but as we know, she's a very busy woman. At any rate, she loaned the wagon Henry and I drove out, along with the water barrels." She looked about the group. "What would everyone think of hiring the twins and Ethan to keep the trees watered? I know they'd be both reliable and grateful for the opportunity to bring a little extra money home."

Again, Mrs. Bishop had an objection. "You're proposing we spend money that hasn't been raised by an organization that doesn't really exist." She pursed her lips and shook her head like a schoolteacher scolding a naughty child.

"I was *going* to ask for donations from the people who came today," Birdie said. Annoyance tinged the words.

Mrs. Hall spoke up. "I'd be happy to donate toward having the Simmons boys tend the trees." She added, "I'll also offer my home for an organizational meeting. How about this coming Thursday evening? Shall we say six o'clock?"

Birdie thanked her. "Those interested in joining the Ladies Cemetery Improvement Society" she winked at Isobel— "are invited to meet at Teddy's, this coming Thursday evening at six o'clock." She guided the conversation back to the topic of memorial wreaths. Repeating the question about identifying veterans' final resting places, Birdie offered to speak with the sextant before Thursday's meeting.

"I already told you," Mrs. Bishop muttered, "that he won't know anything."

Charlie spoke up. "What if I put an announcement in the next edition of the *Register*, asking readers to come forth with any knowledge of military service represented among the burials here at Wyuka." He glanced at Isobel. "We could also print flyers to post about town."

"That's a wonderful idea," Birdie said. "Thank you, Charlie."

"I'll ask Miss Carter to make half a dozen wreaths," Teddy said. "She's a wonder with floral anything. I'm certain she can have a sample ready in time for our meeting."

Birdie nodded. "We already know we'll need at least four." She listed the names. "Warren Hall, Chaplain Oliver, Freddie Wilcox, and Gideon Long."

"Don't forget Mr. Dorsey," Mrs. Bishop said, pointing toward a nearby monument that indicated John W. Dorsey had been a private in the Indiana Militia during the War of 1812. She frowned. "As to Gideon Long—I hardly think we want to decorate the grave of a *deserter*."

Isobel looked at Charlie in disbelief. Did the woman ever say anything positive? Charlie just shrugged.

Birdie retorted, "Surely you would agree that *rumor* should never dictate who is remembered on Decoration Day."

"It isn't rumor. There were witnesses."

With a decided snap of her napkin, Birdie sent breadcrumbs flying. She folded the napkin and thrust it into her picnic basket as she said, "Not *witnesses*, plural. One person claimed to see something in the thick of a horrific battle. And everyone knows there was no love lost between the Inskeep family and the Longs."

"I hardly think—" Mrs. Bishop began.

Birdie interrupted. "Grace Long was a dear friend of mine. There *will* be a wreath at her son's grave." She snatched up her picnic basket and marched toward the rear of the farm wagon, from where she proclaimed, "I will pay for it, and *no one* had better try to remove it."

"For heaven's sake, Birdie," Mrs. Bishop said, "if I'd known you'd feel so strongly about it—"

"Now you know." Birdie looked about the circle of women. "If anyone wishes to give a little toward hiring the Simmons boys to water trees, please see Henry before you leave today.

I'll hope to see some of you at Teddy's Thursday evening. Until then, shall we get back to work?" Grabbing a pair of shears, she marched off.

Mrs. Bishop said something about having business to attend to in town. Her daughter-in-law hesitated, clearly not wanting to leave. Mrs. Payne offered the young widow a ride, and an unhappy Mrs. Bishop summoned her husband and departed.

Returning to Birdie's side, Isobel worked quietly, wondering over markers that were little more than large rocks. Did any represent the final resting places of a veteran? Unless someone in the community came forward, they might never know. She remembered the worn stones near Papa's monument in St. Louis, each one crowned with the figure of a lamb. The names were illegible, but every spring blue forget-me-nots carpeted the earth around them. Isobel had never really thought much about those illegible names or the lives they represented.

Forget me not. It was inevitable that names be forgotten and records lost—a sad reality about which nothing could be done.

Or could it?

Chapter 12

Mine enemies speak evil of me...
Psalm 41:5

Crouched at the bottom of a gash in the earth carved out by a meandering creek, Gideon listened to the sounds emanating from Wyuka Cemetery a short distance away—shovels digging, harness rattling, women and men calling out to one another. The occasional laughter seemed out of place, but then, it wasn't a funeral.

He detected Birdie's light trill and smiled. A good organizer, Birdie was likely directing the production. Of course, Henry was there, too. He always supported Birdie's projects. Charlie Manning was in attendance, as was his sister, who'd startled Gideon this morning when she rounded the corner at the far end of the block just as he exited the mercantile storeroom. He'd glanced her way, and she stopped short, poised like a wary doe about to take flight. He would have run off, but then he saw Birdie and Henry approaching from the opposite direction. He spoke to them briefly, and they told him about cemetery cleanup.

A group of us will be working out at Wyuka today. Getting ready for Decoration Day. Birdie mentioned a flyer explaining it all, but Gideon hadn't wanted to wait for her to retrieve a copy—especially not after being seen by the woman in blue. Birdie's warning was enough. He should avoid going near the cemetery. Oddly enough, instead of warding him off, her words had lured him back. He'd left an unhappy Trouble locked in the cabin and now, hidden from view, he lapped up the sounds of humanity like a thirsty dog snuffling at a trickle of moisture.

Decoration Day. He'd read something about that in the *Morning Chronicle,* the other Nebraska City newspaper Henry often tucked into his bag when he made supply runs. Obviously, the citizens of Nebraska City were embracing the idea of what a general order out of Washington City had designated a "day for honoring the war dead." He wondered if there'd be a parade and thought probably, seeing as how Nebraska City had its own G.A.R. chapter now. He'd had his share of parades as a soldier, beginning right here in Nebraska City when the First Nebraska left for Missouri and ending with the Grand Review of the Armies in Washington City. He'd been in good company there at the end, marching with men who'd followed him into battle—men who saw scars as their own kind of medal. Men who didn't look away.

But then came the long journey home. He was finished with trains after the first one, when he realized he was frightening two children staring wide-eyed from the shelter of their mother's skirts. Adults were more polite, although more than a few crossed to the other side of the streets he walked before daring horrified second glances. Folks might have become accustomed to empty sleeves and wooden legs, but there was no getting used to the likes of him. And so he ended up walking home, taking remote roads and wooded trails, avoiding people as much as possible.

Remembering, he reached up to trace the jagged scars that ran from his hairline, across the thickened flesh that stretched across his forehead, through the partially missing eyebrow, and down the bridge of his nose. Scar tissue formed something of a cheek, continuing down his neck and disappearing beneath his collar. He'd never intended to come home at all. The only purpose he could think of for God letting him live was so that he could take care of Ma. And now, weeks after learning of Ma's death, here he was in hiding near the cemetery, wondering why he was still alive.

Birdie's voice called him back to the moment. He strained to hear what had happened to upset her, but he couldn't make out the words. It had to have been something pretty bad. Next to Ma, Birdie Tanner was the kindest gentlest woman he'd ever known. She'd proven that the night loneliness and wanting to know exactly what had happened to Ma drove him out of the desolate cabin and to the storeroom door at the rear of the Tanner's mercantile.

His neck and face swathed in a scarf, a wide-brimmed hat pulled down to his brow, Gideon rapped on the door. He was trembling with dread by the time he heard someone clomping down the stairs from the apartment above the mercantile. When Henry opened the door a crack, Gideon took a step back and croaked, "It's me, Henry. Gideon Long. Come to ask about Ma. About what happened."

Henry snorted disbelief, "I don't know what you think you're pulling, but both Gideon Long and his mother were dear friends of ours, and I don't appreciate—"

"I saw the grave markers," Gideon said. "Ma wrote me about the quinsy taking Pa, but—what happened to her?"

Birdie had descended the stairs and come to stand at her husband's shoulder. When Gideon mentioned the illness that had taken his father's life, she brushed past Henry. "Praise be, the reports were wrong! Oh, if only Grace had known—" She latched onto the arm of Gideon's coat and tried to draw him inside.

Gideon resisted. He reached up to adjust the scarf. Pulled it higher. "I don't need to come in. Only—tell me about Ma. Please."

"Of course you'll come in," Birdie insisted. "I just took an apple pie out of the oven. You remember my apple pie, don't you? First prize in the territorial fair when you were a boy."

Gideon remembered. He could smell the aroma wafting down the stairs from up above. His stomach growled.

Henry must have heard it, for he put a hand on Gideon's shoulder and gave a tug. "Come in, son. You know how Birdie is. She won't take 'no' for an answer."

Hunger for more than pie won out over the dread of unwrapping the scarf. *It's Henry and Birdie. You can trust them to keep your secrets.* He stepped inside and Henry closed the door. Gideon took off his coat and hung it on a hook. Next, came the hat. And then... "I—uh—I was hurt. Bad. Didn't know who or where I was for a long time." He unwrapped the scarf and hung it with the coat. Even though he did his best to keep the worst side of his face turned away, Birdie still saw enough to make her gasp. "The doctors did what they could," he said and shrugged.

Birdie pulled him into a hug. Her voice wavered. "Oh, you beautiful boy. What have they done to you?" She was still for a moment, and then she grasped Gideon's hand and led the way upstairs. She ordered him to sit at the table and Henry to make coffee. As she retrieved plates from a cupboard and served generous slices of pie, she talked. "You'll take the rest of this pie home. And one of the loaves of bread I made this morning. We'll get some of Nettie Simmons's eggs and butter from the store downstairs before you leave and—" She sat down opposite him and touched the frayed edge of his sleeve. "—and you'll take a new shirt, too."

Birdie's kindness almost did him in. He took a bite of pie to keep from having to talk. Henry poured coffee and sat down. When the pie was gone, Gideon sat back. Still looking down at the crumbs of pie crust left on the plate, he croaked, "It doesn't hurt anymore." *Physically.*

Birdie reached over to squeeze his hand. "How I wish Grace were here to welcome you home. It would have made her so happy. No matter what anyone said."

He nodded. Ma would have loved him, regardless of the poor outcome of surgeries and months in hospitals. She wouldn't have liked the idea that he was ashamed to come home, but she'd have been proud when she heard he'd mustered back in with the First Rhode Island and kept right on fighting. She'd have been especially impressed when she saw the medals, and when he told her the whole story, she would have forgiven him for letting her think he was dead. But Henry and Birdie didn't need to hear about any of that. He'd knocked on their door for one thing: news of Ma.

"How'd she—pass?" He couldn't bring himself to say the word *die*.

"In the same way she lived," Birdie replied. "Gently and with grace."

Henry explained. "It was last fall. She'd come into town like always, trading butter and eggs for a few supplies. She was feeling poorly. Coughing and pale. Birdie convinced her to stay with us."

Last fall? Gideon frowned. *She's been gone for months.* He should have written. Could have, so many times. But the truth was he didn't think he'd ever want to show his face in Nebraska. Literally. Every time he thought to write, he talked himself out of it. Ma had probably come to terms with the idea he'd been lost to the war. Plenty of men were. Best to let it be. Except for the fact that he couldn't "let it be" and finally, finally, he made his way back. To nothing.

"She seemed to be getting better," Birdie said. "In fact, Henry was planning to take the cow and the chickens home in a couple of days." She explained that during Grace's illness, Henry and Edgar Simmons had fetched the cow and the chickens to the Simmons place so that Nettie and the children could tend them.

Again, Gideon nodded. He liked the idea that Tom and his family could benefit.

Birdie continued. "She passed in the afternoon. She'd come upstairs to rest. I was going to join her for tea a little later." She allowed a sad smile. "She looked as if she'd simply fallen asleep."

"She didn't suffer, then?"

"Only from thinking she'd lost you at Shiloh."

Gideon looked over at Henry. "You say you gave the livestock to the Simmonses. How's Tom faring since the war?"

Henry and Birdie exchanged a look—confusion, Gideon thought. Henry shook his head.

Gideon's stomach knotted around the pie he'd eaten. He took a sip of coffee to steady himself. "I was hoping—I mean, I didn't see a grave marker. And I looked." He shook his head as he muttered, "I shouldn't have run off. Maybe if I'd stayed—"

Birdie leaned forward. "It had to be terrifying. Anyone's first instinct would be to protect himself. You mustn't wallow in guilt."

Protect himself? Wallow in guilt? What was Birdie saying?

"You'd seen your friend horribly wounded," she continued. "Blinding fear is a normal reaction to something like that. I know men don't like to admit it, but certainly you aren't the only Union soldier to panic and seek escape."

Dumbfounded, Gideon blurted out, "Y-You think I *ran*? That I ran and left Tom to die?"

Birdie cast a pleading look in Henry's direction. "We understand how it could happen."

Both hands fisted, Gideon leaned forward. "Who's saying I ran?"

Henry held a hand up. "Now, son, calm down. We're not judging you. Goodness, we can see you've paid a terrible price."

Gideon swept a hand across his scarred brow as he choked out the words, "Did Ma think—?"

"No!" Birdie spoke quickly.

Henry added his reassurance. "You were reported missing. As time wore on—" He shrugged. "Your Ma was in heaven before any of that began to surface. It was after the boys were mustered out. We only heard bits and pieces, here and there."

"From who?"

Henry looked at Birdie as he said, "I think it was Wade Inskeep who first said something about seeing you running toward the rear. I did what I could to hush it up, but you know how people are."

"Always quick to believe the worst," Birdie added.

Inskeep. There'd been bad blood between Pa and the Inskeeps ever since Gideon was a little boy. Something to do with Pa's beating out Wade's father for a better piece of land. But for Wade to lie like that? Gideon shook his head. "Tom was shot in the thigh. It was bleeding pretty bad, but I thought it missed the bone. I thought maybe, if I could get a doctor fast enough, maybe Tom wouldn't lose his leg. I put a tourniquet on and told him to hang on, that I'd be back with help." He looked from Henry to Birdie. "I *did* run, all right. For *help*. As fast as I could. Jumping over bodies. Stumbling. Running on, until—an explosion. A flash of light." He raked his hand across his face as he said, "An iron claw came out of that light and then—darkness." Weariness washed over him. He hung his head and choked out the words. "I was running for help. Trying to save Tom."

He told them about all the hospitals. The last surgery. The dismal results and his decision to reenlist. The belief that it was best for Ma to think the worst, since dying wasn't really the worst thing war could do to a man. Not in his view, anyway.

"I never planned to come back, so I didn't write. But then, when I mustered out, I thought maybe, since I'd lived through the rest of the war, maybe God meant for me to take care of Ma."

Henry and Birdie nodded. They seemed to believe him. Birdie's expression brightened. "We could write to the War Department and get proof."

Gideon shook his head. He didn't want that. He knew what Birdie Tanner would do if she learned everything. The last thing he wanted was to draw attention to himself. "Don't. Please. I just want to be left in peace."

Birdie protested. "You can't go on living like a hermit. It isn't right. Grace was so proud of you, Gideon. She told us how the boys had started calling you *Preacher Long*."

Gideon winced when she said it. He shook his head. "That was before—" He swept a hand across his scarred face. "—before this."

"But you can't give up on that—not if it's a true calling."

"You know any preachers who look like me? It's obvious I was wrong about all of that."

"But, Gideon—"

Thankfully, Henry interrupted, reaching out and putting his hand on Birdie's arm. "Let it go, Birdie. The boy doesn't want to talk about that right now."

Gideon pushed himself away from the table. Henry was partially right. He didn't want to talk about it right now. He *never* wanted to talk about it. Muttering thanks for the pie, he rose to leave. Birdie grabbed a basket off a shelf and ordered him to wait. She settled the remaining pie in the bottom of the basket and covered it with a towel. Gideon protested. "You don't need—"

Birdie shushed him. "Don't tell me what I need to do." She added a small loaf of bread and then led the way downstairs. While Gideon donned coat and hat and re-wrapped the scarf, Birdie ducked into the store. Returning with the basket in which she'd nestled a dozen eggs along with a pound of butter wrapped in brown paper, she handed him the carrier.

Gideon thanked her as he took the basket. As he was stepping outside, Henry asked what else they could do for him. Gideon hesitated for a moment before saying, "Let me barter with you. Game for eggs, butter, coffee, and sugar."

"Done," Henry said.

"And—don't tell anyone I'm alive."

After that, Gideon had thought about leaving the area, but where would he go? The cabin was secluded. If he didn't build fires during the day, if he kept Trouble from wandering, it should be possible to keep from being found out. He'd give it a try. He cut firewood and cleaned the interior of the cabin. He left the exterior looking a mess—*just in case someone comes snooping around, Ma.* He hung a quilt over the windows when he read by lamplight. Together, he and Trouble hunted and trapped. It worked. Eventually, Gideon convinced himself he didn't mind living alone. Except here he was, hunkered against a creek bank, eavesdropping on conversation in a cemetery.

Stupid. Pathetic.

Taking care not to be detected, Gideon scuttled away. Away from the cemetery. Away from the voices. Back to the shadows where he belonged.

Chapter 13

*To everything there is a season,
and a time to every purpose under the heaven.*
Ecclesiastes 3:1

Oh, Charlie. Isobel stood at the edge of the lawn surrounding the First Baptist Church, doing her best to calm the fears clutching at her midsection. *You promised. Where are you?* The assumed answer set her heart to pounding.

The service had dismissed some time ago. She'd been genuinely encouraged by the minister's message and decided that less formal church services weren't anything to be dreaded. In fact, she'd determined to return on the following Sunday. The people were welcoming. She liked the atmosphere of the place. The singing was less than professional in quality and the congregation a bit—*spirited*—for Isobel's taste. Yet these Baptists had a kind of faith that was oddly compelling. Overall, the morning had gone well. Until now.

Oh, Charlie.

Birdie and Henry, who knew Charlie had promised to fetch Isobel after church, came to stand beside her. Henry asked how they could help.

Dismay sounded in her voice when Isobel replied. "I don't know."

"Come with us," Birdie said as she tucked a hand beneath Isobel's arm. "His apartment is a good place to start the search. Henry can check it for you."

Isobel nodded and followed the Tanners for the short walk home. With every step, the cloud of dread over her darkened. Henry hastened up the stairs to Charlie's apartment, but there was no sign of him. The cemetery was the next logical place to check. Simmering anger fueled Isobel's insistence that she would go alone. "There's no reason for Manning troubles to ruin your day of rest."

"It won't ruin anything," Birdie said. "We'd just sit here and worry."

"Then pray," Isobel said abruptly, surprising even herself with the request. "Pastor Duncan reminded his congregation that God would help if people asked for wisdom. You can pray *I* have wisdom—especially if Charlie's intoxicated again." *Because if he is, I'm going to want to throttle him.* "And—perhaps allow the loan of Rosie and your buggy in the event walking back to town isn't...ideal?"

"You'd be welcome to it," Henry said, "but Rosie threw a shoe yesterday and the blacksmith can't see to it until tomorrow."

"Not to worry," Isobel said. "I can hire a rig," *Although I haven't driven myself anywhere in a good long while.*

"You're certain you wouldn't rather I drive you?" Henry asked.

"I'm certain." Pretending confidence she didn't feel, Isobel opened her parasol and hurried toward the livery in the next block. Confidence waned when the only buggy horse not already reserved for a Sunday drive proved to be a wild-eyed gray gelding. When the creature nearly kicked the livery owner as he hitched it to a rundown buggy, Isobel almost backed out. But how would she get an intoxicated Charlie home without a buggy? Besides, how hard could it be to drive a country road for a couple of miles? It wasn't as if she had to navigate the crowded streets of St. Louis.

"Now, Bud," the owner drawled as he fastened the final buckle, "you settle down. You'll be scaring this fine lady and we both know you aren't half the hellion you're pretending to be."

Bud. Surely a horse with such a homely name couldn't be all that much trouble. The horse *did* settle after the livery owner's scolding. As Isobel gathered the reins, it turned its head as if to study her. Urged to *giddap*, it trudged up the street, more like an ox pulling a freight wagon than a horse hitched to a light buggy. Isobel relaxed enough to think about what she would say to Charlie when she finally caught up with him.

As the buggy passed Teddy Hall's place, the horse lowered its head still further and snatched a mouthful of wildflowers, then seemed to wave the resulting mouthful of blue blossoms in the air. Isobel chuckled. Her amusement lasted until they reached the edge of town. Suddenly, the complacent nag content to plod along munching wildflowers transformed.

Head up, ears erect, the horse moved into a trot. "Hey, now," Isobel called. "Not so fast." She tugged on the reins. Instead of slowing, the horse tossed its head and quickened its pace. It moved into a lope. The buggy lurched. Terrified of being thrown from the seat, Isobel hauled back on the reins with all her strength, yelling at the top of her lungs for the horse to *whoa*. The gray responded by going still faster, its hooves pounding along the trail. Again, the buggy hit a rut. This time it didn't just bounce. It seemed to fly for a brief second before crashing back to the earth.

The buggy clattered across the narrow bridge spanning the creek north of the cemetery. By the time the cemetery came into view, Isobel was yelling. "Whoa! Stop! Charlie! Help! Whoa!" The buggy careened over onto one wheel, then the other. Isobel's terrified screams only served to urge the horse onward.

They streaked past the cemetery gate, past the furthermost row of grave markers and, finally, past the post marking the edge of the cemetery property.

A low spot loomed ahead. A dry creek bed? A clod of earth flew up and hit Isobel square in the jaw. She hauled on the reins, frantically trying to turn the horse into a field. It didn't work. She screamed again.

A dark shadow lurched onto the road. The gray snorted. The shadow loomed larger and a deep, throaty voice boomed out a commanding *WHOA. WHOA. WHOA.* Hands raised above his head, the man stood his ground. There was a dog at his side. They were going to be run over! The man called out again. *WHOA WHOA WHOA.* The horse whinnied and kept running. The foolish stranger still didn't move. WHOA, THERE. HOLD, BOY, WHOA, THERE. HOLD ON.

Miraculously, the gray slowed. For a moment, Isobel thought she was safe. But then, a wheel caught the edge of a rut. Isobel dropped a rein. Trying to grab it, she leaned forward, lost her balance, and barely avoided pitching out headfirst. Somehow, she managed to right herself, but only for a brief second. Again, a wheel dropped into a deep rut. With a hideous sound, it shattered. The buggy began to come apart. One second Isobel was in the buggy and the next she was airborne. Flying. Landing. Enveloped by a dark cloud. Lost in darkness.

※

Gideon had just set a rabbit snare in brush south of the cemetery when he heard a woman screaming. Pounding hooves and the unmistakable clatter of a buggy moving fast. Crouching, he peered through the brush as the rig came into view. Trouble tore off in pursuit, and Gideon reacted on instinct, calling for the dog as he charged toward the road. Once there, he planted his feet and waited. Lifting his arms, he called out in a vain attempt to slow the runaway. A flash of color identified the driver. *The woman in blue.*

His heart pounding, Gideon called out again. *Pointless.* Flecks of foam flew from the wild-eyed creature's mouth, even as it threw up its head and shied away. And then it was as if the world slowed as the sounds of splintering wood and whinnies, screams and pounding hooves combined. A wheel spun away, the buggy lurched, and the woman flew.

Arms outstretched, Gideon launched himself toward the blue blur. Too late to catch her, he threw himself between her and the earth. She landed atop him with a grunt. The force of the impact drove the air out of his lungs. For a fraction of an instant, the world dimmed. He heard a whine and felt moisture as Trouble licked his face. He gasped for breath, but the woman was silent and unmoving.

God in heaven... no.

Fearing the worst, Gideon sat up—slowly, ever so slowly, until he was cradling her in his arms, willing her to breathe. Trouble whined. Warding the dog off with a raised hand, Gideon leaned close. Relief flooded through him as a puff of air caressed his unscarred cheek. *Alive.* He looked up at the sky. *Thank you.* Reassured, he laid the woman down as gently as possible, watching for any grimace, any sign of pain that might hint at a broken bone. When there was none, he got to his feet. Trouble lowered himself to the earth and waited, nose on paws, ears alert, as Gideon looked about for the horse and what might be left of the rig.

What was she doing out this way alone? *Ah. Probably looking for her brother up on the hill.* Charlie Manning had been there earlier and laid flowers at the grave. Gideon knew that because he'd seen it happen. But Manning hadn't lingered this time. Instead, he'd hurried back toward town on foot. Wherever he'd gone, he'd apparently failed to notify his sister.

Gideon looked down at her, at first gratified to see the blush of color on her cheeks. He checked her pulse in the same way he'd seen countless nurses do when he was in the hospital. *Strong.* That was good, but he needed to go for help. First, though, he had to get her off the road and into the shade. Bending down, he lifted her back into his arms. Her head dropped onto his shoulder.

Cradling her like a sleeping child, he hurried into the cemetery and up the hill to the tree that shaded Vera Manning's grave. Trouble followed. When Gideon put the woman down, she groaned a bit. Trouble whined and moved to lick her face. Gideon warded him off. *No.* If she came to, she'd be newly terrified at sight of a huge dog and a monster standing over her.

Again, he checked her pulse. Strong. He looked toward town. *Get help. Get it now.* Pulling a blue bandana from his pocket, he moistened it with water from the canteen slung over his shoulder and knelt beside her.

"You're going to be all right," he said, as he brushed her russet hair off her forehead and laid the cool compress in place. "I don't like leaving you alone, but I've got to get help. Someone will come. I promise." He rose to go. The woman's eyelashes fluttered. Quickly, he shrugged out of the canteen strap and set it beside her. "Water in the canteen." She took in a deep breath and sighed. He stepped away. "Someone will come. I promise."

Patting his thigh to signal Trouble to follow, he ran for town.

With a low groan, Isobel reached up to touch the cool cloth. *Who'd put it in place?* Frowning, she opened her eyes. *Leaves. Blue sky.* She lifted her head and looked about. *The cemetery?* It all came back. The runaway, the terror, and some fool standing in the middle of the road. A booming voice trying to get the gray gelding to slow down. And then...flying. She was flying through the air.

Taking the cloth off her forehead, Isobel pushed herself to a sitting position and looked around. She saw the canteen at her side and picked it up, staring at the letters *U.S.* stenciled on the canvas cover. Whoever he was, her rescuer must have been in the war. There was no sign of him now. Where was he? And how had she gotten off the road and up the hill? She grimaced. Had there been a dog? A whine?

Removing the cork from the canteen, she dribbled more water onto the cloth, which proved to be a dark blue bandana. The bandana moistened, she pressed it to the back of her neck, slowly tilting her head, first this way and then that. Her head pounded. With a shudder, she remembered the horrible sound of splintering wood and the sensation of flying as she was thrown from the buggy. What had happened then? Where was the rig now?

Someone will come.

Was she imagining a low voice saying those words? Promising to go for help?

I don't like leaving you alone.

She looked toward town. No, she hadn't imagined that. Someone had been here. Taking a deep breath, she scooted back until she could lean against the tree trunk. She took a sip of water. Hoping to shade her eyes, she reached up to reposition her bonnet. *No bonnet.* Her hair had to be a mess. Hoping to locate the bonnet, she looked about and saw the flowers at Vera's grave. Charlie had been here, after all. *But that wasn't Charlie on the road. And it wasn't him promising to go for help.* Again, she examined the canteen and the bandana, looking in vain for a laundry mark...a name...initials...anything.

After a moment, she rose slowly to her feet. The world tilted. She put out a hand to steady herself, bracing against the tree.

After her airborne departure from the buggy seat, she supposed it was something of a miracle that nothing was broken, nothing sprained. The only issues were a bit of dizziness, a raging headache, and a lost bonnet. It was probably down by the road. She'd look for it later. She examined her dress for damage, finding a small tear on one sleeve and a good amount of debris scattered here and there.

The sound of pounding hooves from the direction of town drew her attention back to the road. An unfamiliar team...a wagon...someone standing behind the wagon seat. She put one hand to her brow and squinted into the distance. *Henry. Birdie. And Charlie standing in the wagon bed, clinging to the back of the wagon seat.*

Clutching the blue bandana in her hand, Isobel took a few uncertain steps toward the gate. The moment Henry slowed the team, Charlie bounded out of the still-moving wagon, and raced up the hill. Throwing his arms around her, he choked out a string of words that combined thanksgiving and questions.

Isobel gasped and put both hands on Charlie's shoulders to push him away. "Sore ribs."

"Sorry. I'm so sorry." He released her, but still held her arm. "What happened? Are you truly all right? Sore ribs—I can only imagine. But is that all? I can't believe it! We thought—" he broke off with a half sob and called out to Henry and Birdie. "She's all right. Thank God, she's all right."

Birdie echoed Charlie's thanksgiving as she alighted. Coming to Isobel's side, she took her free arm. "We'll still have Doctor Donovan check you over."

Isobel frowned at Charlie. "Where were you? I thought—"

"I know what you thought," Charlie interrupted. "You thought I was drunk again—out here, at Vera's grave." He motioned toward the wagon. "I'll explain later. We need to get you to the doctor."

Isobel nodded a reply and allowed herself to be led to the wagon. Halfway there, a wave of nausea hit. The world began to spin again. She swayed and nearly fell. Charlie caught her. Henry lowered the tail gate and Charlie lifted her into the wagon bed and then climbed up beside her. When he put his arm about her, she leaned into him and closed her eyes.

"Someone was here," she murmured. "I need to find out who. I need to thank him. I—I think he had a dog."

"Sshh," Charlie said. "Don't talk. Rest."

Chapter 14

And thine ears shall hear a word behind thee, saying,
This is the way, walk ye in it,
when ye turn to the right hand, and when ye turn to the left.
Isaiah 30:21

As the church bells of Nebraska City rang out, Gideon sat at the low table beneath a south-facing cabin window, Ma's Bible open before him. For the most part, he just turned pages, seeking comfort from reading the verses Ma had underlined. He'd always been amazed and humbled by her ability to live with the angry, profane man Pa became after Gideon's five-year-old twin brother, Gabriel, died. Ma spoke of Gabe's death as one of angels carrying her child to heaven. Pa described it as an unknown illness "putting him in the ground." Ma remained gentle—even when Pa forbade her to go to church out of what Gideon thought of as pure meanness.

He wished he could respond to the sound of church bells as Ma had. She said they were a reminder that God's Word was going forth to some of her dearest and kindest friends. Although she couldn't be part of the congregation, she would be thankful for their sake—thankful, too, that she had her very own copy of God's Word and the blessing of being able to read it. Thus far, Gideon hadn't managed to follow Ma's example. For him,

Nebraska City's church bells were a reminder of all he'd lost. And yet, he still spent time with Ma's open Bible before him, hoping the words that had spoken to her would seep into his life.

Sometimes he'd leave off Bible reading and turn his attention to the letters he'd penned while sitting by campfires in Missouri or Tennessee. Ma had saved them all, and Gideon found comfort in knowing that, while his parents were gone, they'd died knowing some good things about their son. The First Nebraska had been proven in battle and praised by none other than General Lew Wallace. Above all, though, Gideon was drawn to the letters that reminded him that yes, it really had happened. He had had a personal encounter with God. He might have misinterpreted what God wanted from him, but his conversion was real.

Bored with the monotony of camp after the Battle of Fort Donelson, Gideon had wandered over to a religious service led by an evangelist named D. L. Moody. Something about the man's words gripped Gideon's heart. When Moody looked out over the gathering of soldiers and asked, "What will you do with Jesus who is called the Christ? Will you take your stand on the Rock of Ages?" Gideon answered *yes*.

In the following weeks, he spent hours reading the little Bible the Christian Commission had given him, reveling in the words and excited to share them with others. The men began to call him *Preacher Long*. Some didn't mean it as a compliment. Gideon didn't care. When he looked into the future, he no longer envisioned farming. Instead, he dreamed of a pulpit ministry, harvesting souls instead of crops—until a flash of light erased the dream.

The time since he'd been home had dulled the pain of unanswered questions a bit, but the sound of sabbath church bells still beckoned a strange brew of memory and longing seasoned with—fight it as he would—bitterness. Whatever he'd once thought God wanted from him, he'd obviously been wrong. He wasn't even needed to take care of Ma, so why was he still here?

This morning, though, theological musings hadn't taken center stage, thanks to a distraction sitting at the edge of the very table where Ma's Bible lay open. *The woman in blue's bonnet.* He should have noticed it was missing when he carried her into the shade of the oak tree, but he didn't. Apparently, she hadn't missed it, either. Trouble called attention to it once the Tanners' wagon headed back into town and Gideon and the dog were returning to the cabin.

He should have let it be, but he picked it up, and now he couldn't stop looking at it. Couldn't stop wondering how Miss Manning was. There was nothing he could do—certainly nothing he should do, beyond minding his own business. He'd made certain she had no broken bones. *But what if she'd cracked some? Entirely possible. Potentially dangerous.* He'd checked for cuts and bumps beneath that mane of red hair. *But what if they leave her alone in that hotel room? She could die if there's a head injury.* Birdie wouldn't let that happen. *It's the Sabbath. You're supposed to be thinking about God.*

He turned a page in Ma's Bible and read a Psalm aloud. He thought about the woman. With a sigh, he sat back, staring at the bonnet. Charlie Manning's sister was a woman of means. Nothing that stylish had ever been inside this cabin. A feather was broken off and a small bunch of delicate flowers crushed. The little flowers were probably silk—like the blue dress that had rustled when he picked up the unconscious Miss Manning. He knew that sound. He'd heard it before when women in mourning visited the hospital wards, doing their best to minister to others. Mrs. Lincoln herself had visited more than once.

He reached for the bonnet. Whoever shaped it and made those tiny flowers was quite the artist. There was netting, too— the kind fine ladies pulled down over their faces to create a kind of veil, although it seemed mostly for effect. Nothing like the war widows' black veils. He'd seen enough of those to last a lifetime.

Rising to his feet, he stepped outside. Trouble darted past him, bounding away toward the river. Birdsong drew his eyes toward the treetops. A flash of blue confirmed his suspicions. A bluebird in the vicinity. *Ironic.*

The unmistakable rap-rap-rap of a woodpecker redirected his attention. Again, he searched the trees until he located the source. Black and white body, a wide red brushstroke at the back of its head. He allowed a faint smile. Better to stand here enjoying birdsong than to drown in regret when church bells rang. Better, too, than hunkering in a creek listening to voices in a cemetery. Better than wishing for what he could never have.

Trouble came loping back and plopped down by the open door. When a breeze wafted the sweet aroma of blossoms his way, Gideon reached up to touch his crooked nose. *You still have a nose. Things could be much worse.* He inhaled deeply. The moist earth smelled good, but the aroma brought new regret as he thought of all the acres of farmland he wouldn't be plowing, the crops he wouldn't be planting, the harvest he would not reap.

He looked about at the ramshackle hen house, the broken gate that once kept Pa's mules and Ma's milk cow in a nearby pen. He regretted having to leave the place looking deserted. Then again, there was no reason to mend either the hen house or the gate. Even if he announced his presence, he'd never take the animals back from Nettie Simmons. She needed them far more than he.

The realization brought him up short. How was Tom's family faring? Henry said the oldest, Edgar, was setting type for the *Register*. Now that spring had come, would he try to farm, too? The twins and Ethan weren't old enough to plow, were they? Maybe Nettie had rented out the place. Why hadn't he wondered about that until now? *Because you've been stewing about yourself. Only and always about yourself.*

Goosebumps crawled up his arms as he thought about the buck he'd dressed a couple of nights ago. Even after trading at the mercantile, he still had plenty of venison left. He'd have to be clever about it, but he knew Tom's place as well as he knew his own. It wasn't even that far away. He could make it work. All he had to do was wait for the sun to go down. After leaving venison for Tom's family, he would go to the mercantile. Birdie would have news of Miss Manning. Knowing Birdie, he wouldn't even have to ask.

It would be a long night, but a good one.

※

Henry opened the storeroom door the moment Gideon knocked. "Thought you might check in. I've been—" Looking down at Trouble, Henry took a step back.

"Trouble, sit," Gideon said. The dog obeyed, looking up at Henry and thumping his tail. "You have a dog," Henry said.

"He has a small bear." Birdie spoke from the landing halfway up the stairs to the apartment.

At sight of Birdie, Trouble started to get up, but Gideon held out his hand, palm up, and the dog relented. "I was going to be gone longer than usual this evening," Gideon said. "I didn't have the heart to leave him behind." He paused. "This is Trouble."

"I certainly hope not," Birdie said.

"He's not really—not trouble, I mean. He's not much to look at, but he's actually a pretty good dog."

Hearing the phrase *good dog*, Trouble thumped his tail again and shifted his weight from one paw to the other.

Birdie spoke to the dog. "Is that right, Trouble? Are you a good dog?"

Trouble rose to all fours, but he didn't leave Gideon's side.

Henry looked up at Birdie, as he said, "Unfortunately, Birdie has a very firm *no dogs* policy."

As if he understood what Henry had said, Trouble sank to the floor with a sigh and put his head on his paws.

"We don't need to stay," Gideon said. "I just—I wondered about the woman."

Birdie smiled. "So it *was* you."

Henry admonished his wife. "I told you I recognized the canteen." He looked over at Gideon. "I shoved it behind the tree with my foot. Figured you'd be back for it."

Gideon nodded. He'd retrieved it before finding the bonnet. "You didn't—"

"—tell anyone we knew you?" Henry asked. "Of course not."

Birdie interrupted, looking at Trouble as she said, "Will the beast eat cornbread and beef stew?"

"I imagine," Gideon replied.

Birdie started up the stairs. "Then come along." When Gideon hesitated, she clarified. "Both of you. And Henry, do not think this means there's going to be a change to my *no dogs* policy. As I said earlier, that's not a dog. It's a lop-eared bear." She paused on a stair and spoke directly to the dog. "Don't expect pie."

Over supper, Gideon told the Tanners a brief version of how he'd encountered an injured dog on the long journey back to Nebraska. "He needed me." He glanced at the dog, who was sound asleep at the top of the stairs. "And then, when he healed up and didn't really need me anymore, he stayed around." He took a sip of coffee and changed the subject. "She's all right, then?"

Birdie answered. "Doctor Donovan assured us that she'll be fine after a day or two of rest. Charlie insisted on staying with her at first, but I'm going to relieve him soon."

Henry added to Birdie's report. "She didn't seem to remember a lot about what happened after the buggy began to come apart."

Gideon nodded and took a swig of coffee. "I felt bad about moving her, but I had to go for help. At least up on the hill, she had some shade."

"To hear her tell it, you probably saved her life," Birdie said.

Gideon stopped mid-chew. Frowned at Henry. "I thought you said she didn't remember much."

"She didn't," Henry said, "past seeing a crazy person plant himself in the middle of the road."

"After that," Birdie said, "a cool cloth on her forehead and a kind voice talking about going for help." She paused. "And she thought there might have been a dog." She glanced at Trouble before asking, "What *did* happen, exactly?"

Gideon shrugged. "You know everything that matters."

Birdie snorted. "I'll wager a second piece of rhubarb pie that I don't." She rose to dish up more pie and to refill his coffee cup.

With a sigh, Gideon relented. "I was setting a line of rabbit snares in amongst the wild plums and elderberry south of the graveyard. First, I heard a rig rattling along. Then a scream, so I crouched low and looked toward the road. All I saw was a flash of blue, but it was clear the woman driving the buggy had lost control." He glanced at the dog. "Trouble dashed out and I followed. I didn't really think. Just reacted. Tried to stop the horse. Failed. A wheel dropped into a rut, and she went flying." He paused. "The way she landed knocked the air out of us both."

Birdie perked up. "*Both* of you?"

"No time to do much but dive under, hoping to break her fall."

Birdie clasped her hands together and beamed at him. "You really *did* save her life."

Feeling uncomfortable, Gideon spoke to Henry. "Trouble and I were partway to town when I saw you all racing toward the cemetery. I assume you knew about the accident because the runaway ended up back at the livery?"

Henry nodded. "Charlie was supposed to take Isobel for a drive after church. He was running late—something about a meeting with the cemetery sexton. At any rate, he'd arrived at the livery to rent a rig when the horse limped back into town, dragging what was left of the buggy. Poor Charlie was beside himself when he came pounding on our door."

"Glad it all worked out," Gideon muttered. Miss Manning was going to be all right. Relief washed over him. He rose to go, looking from Henry to Birdie and thanking them for the good news and the food.

Birdie stood as well. "If you can use more eggs and butter, Nettie's hens are laying and the cow has a newborn calf. Charlie's doing better, too, since his sister arrived, so Edgar will be back to typesetting this week."

"I meant to ask about the farm," Gideon said. "It's good ground. She could rent it out."

"She tried," Henry said, "but—" he looked to Birdie. "You know more about it than me."

"There was interest," Birdie said, "just not the kind of interest Nettie wanted. It's a long story. Last I heard, she plans to let the fields lie fallow until the boys are ready to take it on. Shouldn't be more than a couple more years." She pulled the shawl off the back of her chair as she said, "I'll follow you downstairs. It's time I was getting over to the hotel to give Charlie a break."

Downstairs in the storeroom, Gideon gathered up a few supplies. As Henry entered them in the ledger, Birdie pulled a tin off a shelf and extracted a strip of what looked like beef jerky. She asked Gideon to have "the bear" sit. Trouble heard *sit* and did so.

Birdie chuckled. "Charmer." She cautiously held out the treat. Trouble lifted his nose and took the jerky with surprising care. Birdie patted the dog's head. "You still don't get pie."

<p style="text-align:center">~~~</p>

Back at the cabin, as Gideon stirred up the fire and set a chunk of venison to roasting, his thoughts turned to Tom's family. He wondered about the "long story" Birdie had mentioned in regard to Nettie's renting out the farm. Things would be easier if she remarried. She was still young—and pretty, Gideon remembered. Plenty of men might be interested in a pretty widow with a good amount of rich farmland. Sadly, not many would be equally interested in taking on seven children.

He wondered what the Simmons page in the mercantile ledger book would reveal about Nettie's situation. It was safe to assume there would be far too few credits, and the number at the bottom of the debit column would be daunting. But Henry and Birdie Tanner were good people who'd do everything in their power to keep from pressuring Tom's widow about money. They'd never let those kids go hungry.

Good people. Faithful friends. A flood of memories washed in. Birdie's hug that first night back when he knocked on their door. Henry's handing over a key to the storeroom. Their reluctant promise to protect his privacy. Careful warnings that helped Gideon avoid being seen near the cemetery. All of it without expecting anything in return. All of it when they clearly disagreed with his decision to stay to himself.

Stepping outside, Gideon leaned against the door jamb, thinking. Birdie said the past winter had been a long, lean one for Tom's family. His throat constricted. He'd spent the winter feasting on venison, with plenty to spare for a dog. Wallowing in his own disappointments. Mourning the loss of some mythical

"Preacher Long." Lurking in the night without once thinking about anyone but himself. His cheeks burned with shame. An owl hooted. He peered up at the night sky. Instead of the vastness of the dark canopy of night, he noticed the stars. Something stirred inside him. Pinpricks of light. *Light.*

Forgive me for choosing the darkness. For failing to look for the light.

Chapter 15

*Charity ... believeth all things, hopeth all things,
endureth all things. Charity never faileth ...*
1 Corinthians 13:7-8

When Birdie insisted on staying with Izzy overnight, Charlie feigned reluctance. But then the older woman said it was probably better for Izzy to have a female nurse, and a relieved Charlie acquiesced. He had no stomach for nursing. Not since Vera.

As it turned out, though, avoiding keeping watch over his ailing sister didn't reap a peaceful harvest. He couldn't escape the feelings of guilt when it came to his part in a scenario that could have killed his sister. If only he hadn't been late meeting her after church. If only she hadn't assumed he was drinking again. What if some stranger hadn't been crazy enough to try and stop the runaway? He shuddered to think what might have happened.

When he finally went to bed, nightmares punctuated his sleep, all of them with one thing in common—Izzy's presence. She was the soldier next to him who lost an arm at Shiloh; the goldminer stooped down in a cold stream panning for gold and later dying of pneumonia; the freighter dead on the prairie, his body pierced with so many arrows he resembled a porcupine. In every dream all night long, Izzy perished. In every death,

Charlie was culpable. Every single one. And when he woke, the guilt didn't go away. *She could have died. She was looking for me, and she could have died.*

The first time Charlie woke, he turned over and fell back to sleep. The next time, he sat up for a moment, reminding himself that Izzy was safe and Birdie was with her. He got up and drank a glass of water. But the nightmares kept coming and finally, a new battle began. He knew how to stop nightmares, but he didn't have the required tonic. Henry had removed every single bottle from the apartment.

Good thing Henry did that. You can't face Izzy if you've been drinking. He knew it to be true, but he still wanted a drink. Just a little something to help him sleep.

Dawn finally came. Birdie wouldn't expect to see him at the hotel this early, but trying to sleep was pointless. He splashed water in his face, combed his hair, and made coffee. Maybe he'd go downstairs to the office. He could write a first draft of the announcement about the newly formed Ladies Cemetery Improvement Society for the *Register*. After the second cup of coffee, he got dressed.

He still wanted a real drink.

Pulling on his jacket, he stepped outside. Clouds obscured the sunrise. Distant thunder sounded, and the scent of rain wafted in on a gust of wind. He sighed. It was going to be a gloomy day.

He wanted a drink.

Write the announcement. Forget about drinking. Closing his eyes, he took in a few deep breaths to clear the cobwebs before descending the stairs and unlocking the back door to the newspaper office. Up the street, the livery owner was sliding open one of the barn doors. The screeching grated his nerves.

He wanted a drink.

Lightning flashed in the western sky. More thunder rolled across the landscape.

Opening the newspaper office door, Charlie stepped inside. He remembered the bottle hidden at the back of one of his desk drawers. He looked around at the dimly lit space, trying to imagine sharing it with Izzy in coming days. What would it be like to work side-by-side with her? They'd been close once, but that was a long time ago. The idea of her looking to him for some kind of help in the midst of her own life dilemma? What a ridiculous notion. Charlie Manning was the last person on earth to help anyone.

One drink wouldn't hurt. If it came to it, he could buy some rose water at the emporium—on pretense of making it a gift for Izzy. Surely gargling rose water would mask evidence of one little drink. Bending down, he opened the bottom desk drawer and retrieved the bottle.

She could have died because of you. She came to Nebraska City thinking you could help her recover from Alfred's betrayal, and she could have died.

Pulling the desk chair out, he sat down, bottle in hand. Shouldn't it feel good to be needed? It didn't. It made him feel panicky—a lot like he'd felt when he got back home from the war and realized he simply could not return to his old life. Too much had changed. Discovering a talent for the newspaper business had given him new hope. Falling in love with Vera had brought new light into his life. And then it all fell away, and the loss wrung every flicker of light and hope out of him.

Izzy could have died because of you.

He set the bottle down and went back to stand in the open door, looking out as a gentle rain began to fall. He loved Izzy, but he had little to offer her beyond the distraction of Birdie's cemetery project and the drudgery of working in the filthy office of a failing newspaper. Of course she didn't realize it would be drudgery—yet. Now that she'd escaped both Mother Manning and the gossip circulating back in St. Louis, Izzy was basking in her own romantic notion of what it meant to be independent. She'd already ordered a new wardrobe. If he encouraged her the least little bit, she'd stay in Nebraska for good. Admitting he didn't want that—even to himself—made him feel guilty. He retreated from the doorway and sank down onto his desk chair. How long was she planning on staying, anyway? What would happen when she was once and for all confronted with the unvarnished reality that her brother was a lost cause?

He reached for the whiskey bottle and looked down at it, studying the label. Old Overholt Rye, said to be General—now *President* Grant's favorite whiskey, *distilled in Pennsylvania, production undisturbed during the rebellion.* If he uncorked it, he wouldn't be visiting Izzy today. He'd be working his way to the bottom of... not just this bottle, but the bottom of the barrel. Which was probably where he belonged.

He'd been going through the motions in recent days, helping with cemetery cleanup and even visiting with the sexton while Izzy was at church yesterday morning. None of it plugged the black hole once filled with hopes and dreams involving a wife, a baby, and the *Register*. None of it made him want to resurrect the newspaper—the one thing he could actually do something about. Not really. But Izzy seemed excited about helping out in the newspaper office. He needed to pretend a little longer. Until she finally gave up and went back to St. Louis where she belonged.

Pretending required courage. Whiskey didn't provide true courage, and Charlie knew that, but it would do for today. He opened the bottle. *Just a nip. Not even a real drink.*

"Don't, Mr. Manning. Please. Don't."

Startled by the pleading feminine voice sounding from the open doorway, a frowning Charlie looked toward the figure silhouetted against the gray landscape. Before he could respond, Jennie Wilcox stepped across the threshold and reached for the bottle.

"You don't really want that," she said.

What could Jennie Wilcox possibly know about what he wanted? He licked his lips. "Oh, but I do."

"No," she said firmly. "You want the pain to go away." She waited for him to meet her gaze. "That's not the way. The pain always comes back." She paused. "Trust me on that. I know."

He grunted denial. "Sweet Jennie Wilcox" didn't know anything. He tipped the bottle to take a drink, but when Jennie didn't lower her outstretched arm, he hesitated. She took another step forward. The scent of rain wafted in—rain and something else pleasant. Flowers?

"Please hand it over," she said. "I'll pour it out, and you can go over to Morrill House and see how your sister fared overnight—without having to camouflage the scent of alcohol on your breath."

How did she know about that? Charlie looked up at her, but he didn't offer up the bottle. For a moment there was a standoff. Jennie's cheeks took on a rosy glow. She was blushing, but she wasn't giving up. *Fine.* There was no harm in letting her feel good about helping him. After she left—and what was she doing, anyway, lurking in the back alley—after she left, he'd close the door and get the one from the bottom drawer of the filing cabinet. With a sigh, Charlie handed the bottle over. Ignoring the rain, Jennie—he could not bring himself to think of her as a stodgy Mrs. anything—emptied it outside the back door.

As she deposited the empty bottle in the waste can beside his desk, she said, "I didn't mean to disturb you. I was actually headed for the mercantile. But as I walked past the alley, I noticed your door open and thought I'd ask after Miss Manning. It must have been a horrific experience."

"How'd you hear about it?"

She recounted how the story had traveled from her father-in-law, who'd rented a rig from the livery, to her mother-in-law, who "caught up with" Henry Tanner first and then "just happened" to run into Dr. Donovan before bringing home news of the accident. As she talked, she was circling the office and raising the blinds, seemingly impervious to the dust. "I can only imagine how terrified you must have been until Doctor Donovan said your sister was going to be all right." She paused by the front door and surveyed the room. "It's going to be wonderful to read the *Register* again. I've missed it. I imagine all your subscribers have. I especially enjoy reading over the sermons you print on occasion. With Miss Manning helping, you might even be able to issue more frequently than once a week. Or attract more job printing." She paused. "It's only logical that ladies would enjoy ordering calling cards and the like from one of their own. Especially from someone like your sister, who knows what's in fashion when it comes to that sort of thing."

When was she going to leave? He hadn't stood when she invited herself in, but she hadn't seemed to notice his rude lack of decorum. Unable to take a hint, she was actually reaching for the broom propped in the corner by the front door.

"You dust, I'll sweep." She gestured about the office. "But first, how about we empty all the other bottles?"

That brought Charlie to his feet as he stuttered, "Wh-what makes you think there are others?"

She moved toward the filing cabinet. "Probably at the back of one of these drawers." She started with the top drawer, obviously intending to search them all. Charlie intervened.

"I'll get it." He hurried to open the bottom drawer and withdrew the unopened bottle. When she reached for it, he resisted. This wasn't Overholt's. It was, in fact, imported from Scotland. "This is an expensive bottle of the finest—"

She interrupted him. "Ah, yes. The 'finest.'" She smiled her sweet smile, accompanied by an arched eyebrow. "I preferred the 'finest,' too—peach brandy, in my case."

He glared at her. "I don't believe that. Not for a minute. People would know. I would have heard. *Everyone always knows.*"

She shrugged. "*Everyone* doesn't have a mother-in-law determined to keep 'the shame of it all' from becoming common knowledge." Taking up the broom, she began to sweep, talking as she moved away from him, progressing along the front wall and toward the far corner. "I think you'd just opened the newspaper office when Freddie's parents shipped me off—all the way to Saratoga Springs in New York. Complete with a private escort to ensure I'd arrive." She reached the corner and turned to face him. "They called her a *nurse*, but she was more of a *keeper* for the first few weeks." She swept along the west wall.

Again, he blustered, "I don't believe it!"

It was an exclamation of surprise rather than actual disbelief, but Jennie took it literally. She looked back at him. "Ask Birdie. She knew all about it. Prayed for me every day I was gone." When she reached for the dustpan hanging on a nail, Charlie protested.

"Please, Jennie—Mrs. Wilcox. Stop."

Instead of obeying, the young widow crossed to the back door and made another circuit with the broom, this time sweeping along the back wall until she'd reached the pile of dirt waiting in that corner. "I was gone for nearly three months. I got back after New Year's. And you were happily married." She looked over at him, smiling. "I knew I was going to be all right after seeing you and Vera in church together—seeing another happy couple about the same age as Freddie and me—didn't make me seek out the peach brandy again." Leaning the broom against the corner, she crossed back to the filing cabinet and snatched the bottle away from Charlie. "It felt like a miracle when I realized I could be happy for someone else—that every single thing didn't have to send me spiraling back down into the pit of despair about my own loss." She marched to the back door and emptied the bottle of Charlie's finest.

Newly aware of the sweet aroma that lingered in the woman's wake—was it honeysuckle?—he wondered at her resolve. Jennie Wilcox had always been given to blushing and second-guessing most things she said. Although now that Charlie thought about it, he'd rarely seen her without her overbearing mother-in-law alongside.

"I suppose I've made you angry," she said. "I didn't mean to barge in, but when I saw you with that bottle..."

Charlie looked away. He shrugged. "I never guessed about you. Obviously, I knew you were widowed, but I didn't give much thought—" He broke off. The truth was, he hadn't given thought to anyone else for a long while. Not until Izzy arrived and forced the issue. He cleared his throat. "How'd you get—better?"

One corner of Jennie's mouth curved up in a sardonic smile. "Me? I learned to bake."

Charlie snorted disbelief.

"I know it sounds simplistic, but idleness was not allowed where the Bishops sent me. Every moment of every day was planned out. I was assigned tasks that contributed to the running of the facility, and I did them—begrudgingly. But one of the cooks said I had a knack for baking and took me under her wing. She'd had her own difficulties, and she understood how to give *meaningful* comfort—not platitudes. We talked while we kneaded bread or made pie crust. Over time, I began to walk the path that led to sobriety." She gestured about them. "Fortunately, you don't have to *discover* a talent. You're an excellent newspaper editor."

"It doesn't help. The walls close in on me. I can't focus."

"That's the whiskey," Jennie said abruptly.

Charlie met her gaze. She didn't look away. Finally, he said, "Even if you're right, I can't simply tell myself to stop wanting a drink. Believe me, I've tried."

Her voice was gentle when she responded. "Conquering the desire to drink might be the hardest thing you've ever done." She paused. "I'll help you—if you'll let me."

Jennie Wilcox help me? The very idea was laughable. He attempted to soften his refusal with a joke. A bad one. "Thank you, but I don't cook."

Jennie pursed her lips. "Do you walk?"

"Do I—what?"

"Walk." She moved toward the back door. "Don't let the walls close in on you. The minute that starts, get up and walk out this door."

"I can't simply get up and leave when the mood strikes me. That's already nearly ruined the *Register*'s chances at surviving."

Jennie nodded understanding. "At the clinic, we were assigned a companion—someone to help us on the days when the required activities weren't quite enough. We could call on that person at any time, day or night. Perhaps your sister could be your 'someone.'" Jennie smiled. "Perhaps that's the real reason she's here in Nebraska."

"She came so that *I* could help *her*." Had he really just said that? Isobel would be angry—or hurt—or both, if she ever learned that he'd referenced—but Jennie interrupted him.

"Maybe you could help each other." She glanced outside. "The rain's let up, and I really must be going. Mother Bishop has circle meeting tonight and that means I have baking to do." She nodded toward the two empty bottles in the waste can. "Before I leave, though, let's finish what we started."

"Finish?"

She gestured about the office. "I always hid at least three."

Chapter 16

And be ye kind one to another, tenderhearted, forgiving one another,
even as God for Christ's sake hath forgiven you.
Ephesians 4:32

With Trouble at his side, Gideon made his way along the shelterbelt of osage orange and Russian olive trees bordering one of Tom Simmons's unplanted fields. He hadn't slept well, worrying that the venison he'd left the previous evening might not be enough for a meal. He'd decided to return with more. A storm was blowing in, but he was determined to make the delivery. Sneaking to the rear of the house, he hung the day's offering from a tree growing between the house and the privy.

Someone set a lighted lamp in a back window. His heart pounding, Gideon darted off, pausing only when he reached a stand of trees. From there, he watched as a small figure emerged from the house. *Too short to be Edgar or Molly. One of the twins. Elvin or Eben.* Too young to remember Gideon, even if they caught a glimpse. Now that he thought about it, none of them would recognize him now. Not even Nettie.

Intent on the privy, the child hurried past the sack dangling from the tree limb, but the moment he emerged from the necessary, he trotted back to the house. A girl came back outside with the child—a girl tall enough to take the sack down. It had to be

Molly. Sack in hand, she paused to peer about before stepping inside and closing the door behind her.

Gideon waited a while longer, studying the house, taking in the peeling paint, the broken front porch railing, the spot on the roof that would need repair to prevent a leak. He glanced toward the dark clouds building in the west. What if the roof was already leaking? He blew out a frustrated breath. *If only.*

Finally convinced that he wouldn't be seen, he hurried away. The familiar scent of wet earth and spring rain ushered in the first raindrops. Rain began to fall in earnest as he reached his cabin. He ducked inside but lingered in the open doorway to watch the storm. He'd expected to feel happier. Instead, he felt burdened by a weight of guilt. *If you hadn't wasted so much time feeling sorry for yourself, you could have been doing this for months.*

Isobel woke to the sound of soft whispers. Without moving, she opened her eyes and blinked just enough to bring the figures of Birdie and Charlie into focus. When Birdie slipped out of the room, Charlie closed the door softly, took off his jacket, and settled in the chair Birdie had occupied for most of the night. Isobel sat up, grimacing as she put her open palm to her rib cage.

"Doctor Donovan said the bruised ribs would take a while to heal," Charlie said. He rose from the chair and tucked an extra pillow behind her.

Isobel thanked him as she adjusted the bedcovers, wincing with the effort.

"Birdie said you slept well."

"Like a log," Isobel said, "except when I had to turn over."

"You didn't hear the rain?"

"It's raining?"

"Storming is more like it," Charlie said. He strode across to open the drapes. "I'm afraid it's going to be a gloomy day." He turned back to look at her. "Headache gone?"

Before answering, Isobel tilted her head from side to side. "Yes, actually," she said. "Gone."

A key turned in the hotel room door and it opened a few inches. A husky whisper announced, "Breakfast for Miss Manning."

Charlie opened the door and admitted Molly Simmons bearing a tray laden with food.

"Mrs. Oliver said I'm to bring your meals up as long as you need," the girl said as she slid the tray onto Isobel's lap. She pointed at the huge cinnamon roll on the tray. "That's Miss Bennet's way of saying she hopes you feel better real soon."

"Miss Bennet made this?" Isobel took a bite. Closing her eyes to savor the perfect balance of spices, she smiled, then looked over at Charlie to report. "That's almost as good as Cook's." She glanced at Molly. "Our cook at home prided herself on her pastries, so it's a true compliment."

"I'll tell Miss Bennet you liked it," Molly said.

"You might skip the mention of a cook in St. Louis," Charlie interjected. "Miss Bennett doesn't seem the type to appreciate hearing that her efforts *almost* measure up."

Molly grinned. "She wouldn't, and I won't mention that part." She paused before adding, "As she was leaving a bit ago, Mrs. Tanner asked me to report in, soon as you were fully awake. What should I tell her?"

"That my headache is gone and I'll stop in later."

Charlie intervened. "You will not. Doctor Donovan said you should take it easy today. 'Taking it easy' does *not* allow for gallivanting about town. Besides, Birdie is bringing you a late lunch. She'll see how you are for herself."

"Going to see Birdie is hardly 'gallivanting,'" Isobel protested.

Charlie turned to Molly. "Please tell Mrs. Tanner the patient is feeling well enough to threaten rebellion, and her brother has quelled the notion."

A grinning Molly excused herself. Sitting back down, Charlie took his watch from his vest pocket and glanced at it before tucking it back in place.

"You really don't have to babysit me," Isobel said. "Aren't you eager to get to the office and get to work on the announcement for the cemetery society?"

"As it happens, I've already been to the office. Edgar's hard at work setting type for the next issue. I didn't have time to work on the announcement, but I'm hoping to have something for Birdie to bring with her when she visits later today." He paused. "Before I leave, though, there's something I need to say."

Was he tearing up? He was. *Oh, Charlie.*

"I hardly slept last night for going over and over what happened to you. I couldn't shake the feeling of guilt."

"Guilt? For what?"

"For my bad behavior creating the scenario that put you at risk. When I didn't show up at church, you had good reason to suspect the worst." His voice wavered. "You could have been killed because of me."

"A crazy horse and my own stupid pride put me at risk, not you."

"But I—"

Isobel interrupted him. "Let me finish. First of all, when the Tanner's horse and buggy weren't available, Henry was more than willing to drive me out to Wyuka in a rented rig. I refused his help, even though I've never been a confident driver. Then, the only thing available was that gelding. The minute he tried to kick the livery owner, I should have opted for either walking out to Wyuka or checking another livery. But I was upset, and I didn't stop to think. Instead, I forged ahead. None of those bad decisions are your fault."

"But it *is* my fault that you had good reason for suspecting the worst." Charlie blathered on for a moment or two, recounting a litany of failures. He hadn't met the *Laura Rose*. He'd subjected her to a horrible scene at his apartment that first morning. He hadn't made her feel welcome at all. He was a terrible brother.

Finally, Isobel held up a hand in protest. "Stop. Just—stop. You're sorry. I forgive you. *I'm* sorry I assumed the worst yesterday morning. Will you forgive me for that?"

"I don't think there's anything to—"

"Will you forgive me?"

Finally, he nodded.

"All right, then. That's quite enough regret for one day." On impulse, Isobel took a slice of bacon off a plate of eggs, bacon, and biscuits and offered him the rest. When he accepted it she smiled. "Eat and be at peace, dear brother. Just don't expect me to share Miss Bennet's cinnamon roll."

Chapter 17

A prudent man concealeth knowledge...
Proverbs 12:23

Charlie was gone and Isobel had fallen back to sleep when an unusually loud crack of thunder roused her. She sat up carefully. Slipping out of bed, she padded barefoot across the room to stand at the window and watch, as pouring rain transformed the street below from rutted dirt to mire. Nervous teams tossed their heads in protest as they trudged through the ever-deepening mud. On the opposite side of the street, three ladies hovered beneath the stationery store awning, obviously hesitant to brave the rain and mud.

Turning away from the window, Isobel shrugged into her wrapper. When she reached up to remove whatever hairpins might still linger in the matted mess of curls, pain shot across her mid-section. Maybe her hair could wait. Crossing to the dresser, she looked in the mirror, horrified by the vision she'd presented to Henry... Birdie... Charlie... Doctor Donovan... Molly Simmons. They'd all seen her like this.

So did <u>he</u>. What else had her rescuer seen as she flew through the air? She'd awakened beneath the lone shade tree on the cemetery grounds. He'd carried her—and probably regretted it. She was, after all, not a small woman. Warmth crept up her neck and onto her cheeks as she contemplated the possibilities.

Taking a slow breath, she reached up, carefully, ever so carefully. With a low grunt and a few grimaces, she managed to remove five hairpins. Retrieving her brush, she sat down and worked at the tangles, occasionally leaning back and closing her eyes to rest.

The storm calmed. She lay down, the hairbrush still in hand, and was drawn into a dream world populated by hoop-skirted widows beside uniformed men at a grave. The cemetery disappeared, and she was standing in a Sanitary Fair booth—dressed in her wedding gown. Alfred was her customer, and he was purchasing a nosegay for a blushing Mary Halifax, whose worshipful gaze never left his face. The scene dissolved, and Isobel was standing beneath the awning outside Tanner Mercantile as a parade passed. A small group of elderly men towed a cannon. Ezra Carter came next, his mule, Jezebel, bedecked with bunting and bows. Jennie Wilcox marched alone, sporting a gown made of daisies and beckoning to an inebriated Charlie, who stumbled before falling face first into a puddle. Finally, a soldier with shaggy hair held a regimental flag aloft, setting the pace for a dozen drummers. She couldn't see his face.

Isobel stirred. *Not drums... not a dream... knocking.* Someone was knocking on the door to her room. Feeling groggy, she opened her eyes. Could it be time for lunch? Already? She called out for whoever it was to wait and rose carefully, grateful when little more than a slight twinge reminded her of yesterday's events. Laying the brush on the dresser, she glanced in the mirror. The rat's nest was gone, although with her hair trailing down her back, she was hardly in any condition to receive company.

"It's just me," Birdie called.

Isobel opened the door. Apologizing for her state of undress, she admitted the older woman.

"Don't think of me as company," Birdie said, indicating the basket over one arm. "Think of me as a friend bearing gifts." She stepped across the threshold and set the basket on the low table to the right of the door. "I hope I didn't keep you waiting. It's well past lunchtime, but I couldn't get away until now."

"In truth," Isobel said, "I fell back to sleep not long after breakfast. What time is it, anyway?"

"Early afternoon. I'm glad you were able to rest. Both Charlie and Molly gave a good report this morning, but it's nice to see for myself that you're doing well. When Charlie told me the sisters sent up a veritable breakfast banquet, I opted to bring a light lunch. I hope that's all right."

"It is." Isobel closed the door and eased toward a chair.

Birdie sat down, took a few sheets of paper out of the basket, and set them aside. She then unpacked sandwiches and apples along with two canning jars filled with tea. "Did I hear correctly that you were treated to an Ophelia Bennet cinnamon roll this morning?"

Isobel nodded. "Molly seemed to think it the equivalent of a peace offering."

Birdie chuckled. "I suppose Molly would know." She withdrew a package wrapped in brown paper and tied with ribbon. "Jennie Wilcox stopped in at the mercantile just as I was about to leave. She sends her good wishes for a speedy recovery."

"How did she know about the accident?"

"Apparently, Mr. Bishop had rented from the same livery for a Sunday drive. The story traveled from him to his wife, who learned more from Dr. Donovan and then carried the news home to Jennie." She handed the package across to Isobel. "If it's what I think it is, we are in for a treat—assuming you share." She winked.

Isobel unwrapped the package to the aromas of ginger, cinnamon, and nutmeg. *Spice cake.* She smiled. "If it is a Nebraska custom to invite friendship by way of cinnamon rolls and cake, I heartily approve."

Birdie chuckled. "While it might be premature to think Ophelia Bennet is actually inviting *friendship*, I do think that's exactly Jennie's intent. Since Freddie's death, she's tended to associate with her mother-in-law's set, which is mostly older women. I imagine she'd be grateful for a friend more her own age."

It was a shame for someone as nice as Jennie Wilcox to be lonely. But hearing how Electa Bishop had nosed into the details of Isobel's accident made her hesitant. "Surely Jennie and Freddie had young friends."

Birdie gave a little shrug. "I'm sure they would have in time, but they met in Omaha, where Jennie was a housekeeper for a wealthy family. Distance alone would have made it difficult for Jennie to stay in touch with Omaha friends—even if the Bishops had approved after she came to live with them. But I suspect they didn't."

"Why on earth not?"

Birdie hesitated a moment before saying, "Electa is very— shall we say—socially aware." She paused. "Freddie convinced his parents to take Jennie in when he left for the war. Once she was under Electa's roof, she would have been expected to adjust to what Electa would have considered her 'new station in life.' That being the case, Electa would have been disinclined to help her daughter-in-law maintain contact with Omaha friends."

Because they were housekeepers and cooks. Birdie didn't have to say the words for Isobel to understand. She frowned. "Freddie Bishop insisted his wife move into a situation like that? He had to know she'd be terribly lonely. Why would he do such a thing?"

"I can't say for certain, but I do know that *Mr.* Bishop— Julian—very quickly became fond of his new daughter-in-law. I wouldn't be surprised if the two men in the family had an understanding that made Freddie feel good about the situation."

She paused. "Sadly, Freddie contracted camp fever not long after his regiment departed Nebraska City."

"Poor Mrs. Wilcox," Isobel said. "And yet, she's stayed here."

Birdie nodded. "I don't know the whole story—I'm hardly a confidante of Electa Bishop's—but as I said, *Mr.* Bishop is devoted to his daughter-in-law. I think it probably took a bit longer for Electa to come around, but she's been able to take advantage of Jennie's baking skills—"

"Wait," Isobel interrupted, frowning. "They've made her their *cook*? That's awful."

"No, no," Birdie said quickly. "Jennie loves it. Her prowess is very much appreciated here in Nebraska City." She paused. "I once saw two men nearly come to blows over the last piece of a lemon meringue pie Electa brought to a church supper. I think Electa enjoys the reflected glory."

Isobel had finished her sandwich. Ignoring the apple, she reached for the spice cake, which she cut into two pieces. With the first bite she murmured appreciation. "Everything's just right. It's moist, the texture's perfect—" She broke off with a low laugh. "I sound like a judge awarding a blue ribbon at the county fair."

Birdie took her own bite of cake, then said, "Life has not always been kind to Jennie Wilcox, but she's managed to rise above it all. In my opinion, she is one of the hidden gems of our fair city. I think you'll see what I mean as time goes on."

Isobel gave a noncommital nod. There was obviously more to Jennie Wilcox than met the eye. Still, Isobel didn't want to spend a lot of time with someone living in Electa Bishop's shadow. She'd traveled a long way to escape Mother Manning, and she was disinclined to associate with anyone remotely like her.

Birdie seemed to sense Isobel's hesitance. She changed the subject. "Are you up to discussing society business before I leave? If you need to rest, please don't hesitate to say so."

"I've slept most of the day. What is it?"

Birdie reached for the papers she'd set aside and held them out. "Charlie brought these to me a bit ago. I thought you and I might look them over together in preparation for our society meeting later this week. Read the top one, first. I think it's excellent, but I'd like a second opinion before presenting it to the group."

Isobel recognized Charlie's handwriting.

The *Register* is pleased to announce its support of a new project embraced by the newly formed and forward-thinking Ladies Cemetery Improvement Society. Participants in last Saturday's clean-up efforts at Wyuka Cemetery are sincerely thanked for their support of this fledgling body of concerned citizens. Plans for upcoming Decoration Day festivities are underway with the society's full endorsement. Citizens are asked to assist in identifying graves known to be the final resting place of men who served in any of the wars since our nation's founding. The ladies wish to honor their service by placing wreaths at their graves as part of Decoration Day observances. Further plans for cemetery improvement will be announced at a future date. Comments may be submitted to the committee in care of Mr. Charles Manning at the offices of the *Register*.

Isobel read the announcement twice. She smiled at the notion of Charlie volunteering to assist Birdie's committee—especially in light of his somewhat sarcastic commentary about "fingers in pies." She pronounced the announcement *excellent* as she set it aside to peruse the rest of the papers. There was a plot map of the cemetery grounds and a long list of names. A letter and a number appeared after each name. Isobel assumed they referred to a specific location in the cemetery.

Birdie verified that was, indeed, the case. "Charlie convinced Mr. Riley to lend the originals long enough for him and Edgar to make copies. They spent most of the day at it, and the originals are already back with Mr. Riley, as promised."

Isobel studied the list. After a moment, she looked up. "I didn't count gravestones the day we were out there, but if memory serves, this list of names should be significantly longer."

"I'm afraid you're right," Birdie said. "Mr. Riley told Charlie that he had every intention of completing a survey this spring, locating each tombstone on the plot map and transcribing names and dates. Sadly, his health hasn't allowed it. He seemed very pleased to learn of the society's plans to improve things out there."

"Does that mean he'll support our—*your*—efforts moving forward?"

"It does," Birdie said, "and they are *our* efforts—for as long as you wish to be a part of them."

Isobel wasn't ready to commit to the organization. Still, she said, "The logical first step is to complete Mr. Riley's records."

"I agree."

"Someone needs to do what he intended. They need to walk the grounds and record what they see on the gravestones—names, dates, maybe even epitaphs. On Saturday, I noticed that several are nearly worn away. Those inscriptions should be preserved before time erases them."

"I'm so pleased to hear you say that," Birdie said. "I intend to propose that on Thursday evening." She took a breath and then, with a bright smile, said, "I'm hoping you might volunteer to organize it. And before you refuse, please consider: it's a short-term commitment with a definable conclusion—a perfect project that doesn't require you to make a permanent decision about staying in Nebraska. Although of course I hope you'll do just that."

Isobel suppressed a knowing smile. Charlie was right about Birdie Tanner's "fingers in pies." In this case, though, Isobel didn't mind the older woman's essentially assigning her a task. In fact, she rather appreciated the implied trust in her capabilities. On the other hand, if she'd learned anything from her involvement in the St. Louis Ladies Aid, it was that one should tread lightly when women like Electa Bishop were members. And so, instead of immediately accepting Birdie's proposal, Isobel said, "I'm not saying *no*, but I'd feel more comfortable waiting to see if someone who's a current resident wants to take it on. Before I barge in."

Birdie agreed as she began to pack up the remains of lunch.

"Before you go," Isobel said, "there's something I'd like to ask you about."

"Of course. What is it?"

"My rescuer. I'd like to thank him for what he did. He really did display extraordinary bravery."

Birdie tucked the announcement for the *Register* and the cemetery papers atop the things in the basket before answering. "I'm not certain that's possible. Whoever it was had departed long before we arrived on the scene."

"But—surely you have some idea who would have been out that way on Sunday afternoon."

Birdie rose from her chair and took up the basket. "Dozens of townspeople take drives on Sunday afternoon. It could have been anyone."

Isobel frowned. "I remember he said he was going for help, but I don't remember hearing a buggy leave. As far as I recollect, he was on foot." She paused. "And I'm fairly certain there was a dog." When Birdie was still silent, she asked, "What about landowners in the area?"

Her hand on the door handle, Birdie gave a little shrug. "Let me ask Henry. Maybe he'll have some ideas." She opened the door. "Right now, though, I need to be getting back to the store—and you probably need a nap. Charlie said he's bringing supper up. You rest until he arrives. And be certain to lock the door behind me, dear." Without waiting for Isobel to reply, Birdie pulled the door closed.

Isobel locked the door and leaned against it, thinking. *Interesting.* One little question about a supposedly unknown man, and Birdie was in a hurry to leave. She was, in fact, visibly flustered.

Very un-Birdie-like.

Chapter 18

God is our refuge and strength, a very present help in trouble.
Psalm 46:1

Commanded to rest and recover, Isobel reluctantly stayed in her hotel room for a few days. Molly brought breakfast and Birdie delivered lunch. Charlie arrived about supper time and lingered for a couple of hours. While they ate the meal he brought up from the hotel dining room, he filled the time with stories about prominent citizens, his competitors in the newspaper business, and local lore.

He mentioned Mr. and Mrs. J. Sterling Morton and their farm west of town. "I've heard the place is over a thousand acres now. As soon as you're up to it, we'll drive out that way. They have an expansive orchard with all kinds of fruit trees—pear, plum, peach, and apple. They should all be in bloom about now. I imagine it's quite a sight."

Isobel put her hand to her rib cage. She didn't think she'd be ready to be jostled in a buggy any time soon.

Charlie went on to tell her about a few more of the town leaders, among them Daniel Gantt, who'd been U. S. Attorney under President Lincoln. Alexander Majors was not only a partner in the Pony Express but also the head of a freighting empire. The latter had resulted in improvements to Nebraska City's landing that had provided jobs for hundreds of men. "He actually left last year," Charlie said, "but he's generally thought of as one of the most influential and highly respected men in the town's history. In fact, local dignitaries presented him with a gold watch at a ceremony last November."

"And did the *Register* report on the event?"

"Of course. Vera and I—" Charlie's face clouded briefly. "It was a nice evening."

"I'm sorry," Isobel said. "I didn't mean to stir up bad memories."

For a moment, Charlie was quiet. Finally, he said, "You know... you didn't. That's a good memory." He nodded. "I need to be reminded of those."

Over the course of their few evenings together, Isobel caught glimpses of the brother she'd always known. It gave her reason to be hopeful about his future and, by association, her own. Every evening after he departed, Isobel's thoughts inevitably returned to the same topic—the man who'd rescued her. She remembered strong arms. A cool cloth to her forehead. A soothing voice murmuring comfort and promising that help was coming. He'd been brave. So brave to step into the road—into the path of a runaway horse and carriage.

As the days went by and Isobel replayed the memory, she decided her rescuer was tall. She thought he had blue eyes. Had she simply imagined that? She didn't think so. As for the dog, she couldn't recall much beyond dark fur, but she didn't remember being frightened by the animal. That had to mean something, didn't it? His canteen indicated he'd served in the Union army. And yet, Birdie continued to avoid discussing possible identities. And the more Birdie obfuscated, the more determined Isobel became to find him.

※

By Thursday, Isobel had had her fill of resting and recovering. She might still be a bit sore, but she would keep her afternoon dress fitting appointment with Mrs. Hall. It would be a joy to lay aside the blue silk traveling ensemble in favor of more practical clothing. The outing would also be a welcome distraction from her fruitless wonderings about the man the Tanners didn't want to talk about.

The sun was shining when she stepped outside the hotel. As she opened her parasol, she smiled to herself, realizing that the snorting and bawling emerging from the teams lining the street no longer seemed out of the ordinary. The strutting wagon masters and tobacco-chewing freighters no longer intimidated her. As for the less-than-pleasant aromas of the street—well. A freighting business necessitated thousands of oxen, many of them kept nearby at an outfitting area that included a warehouse and various shops needed to keep wagons rolling and oxen hauling. Nebraska City residents had learned to live with it. She could, too.

Making her way up Main Street, Isobel stopped at Charlie's office to greet her brother. Pleased to find him hard at work selecting copy for the next edition of the *Register*, she was delighted when he invited her to have an early supper with him before this evening's cemetery society meeting. For the first time since arriving in Nebraska, she felt confident about what lay ahead—at least for today. It was a welcome feeling. As she neared Mrs. Hall's house, the dressmaker hailed her from the side porch just off the workroom.

"I can't tell you how good it is to see you up and about," she said, the moment Isobel was within earshot. Inside the workroom, one dress form displayed the ivory batiste shirtwaist and dark brown skirt Isobel had ordered. The other sported the blue plaid ensemble. Isobel's third outfit, the indigo calico, lay draped across a chair.

"They're wonderful," she exclaimed.

Mrs. Hall picked up the new indigo ensemble and directed Isobel to change behind the dressing screen positioned in one corner. "Birdie said you'd injured your ribs. Don't hesitate to ask for help if you need it."

Isobel spoke from behind the screen, moving carefully as she disrobed and draped each piece of the blue silk traveling ensemble atop the dressing screen. "It could have been much worse if it hadn't been for a brave soul who stepped into the path of the runaway." She stepped into the new skirt.

"I heard."

Tucking the shirtwaist into the skirt, Isobel stepped out from behind the screen. "I want to find out who it was so I can thank him, but Birdie seems to think it's impossible. But really, how many lone farmers could have been out that way on Sunday afternoon?"

"I wish you well in solving the mystery," Mrs. Hall said, directing Isobel to step up on the small platform positioned before a dressing mirror.

Isobel obeyed, turning this way and that as she looked in the mirror. "I'm glad you suggested I do away with hoops. The overall line makes so much more sense when I think of navigating around the machinery at the *Register*. And the fit is perfect." She pointed at the blue silk draped over the dressing screen. "After today, I may never wear that again."

"If you mean that, the Ladies Aid at church is collecting clothing that can be remade for the less fortunate. I can think of more than one young lady in Nebraska City who'd be delighted to own something as richly appointed as that."

"Really?"

Mrs. Hall nodded. "In fact, I have just the candidate. She's not nearly as slender as you, but she's shorter. With a little creative altering, I could make it work. And you'd be making a late spring bride very happy."

Making a bride happy. How ironic. "Consider it done. In fact, if I had anything to wear back to the hotel, I'd leave it with you today."

The dressmaker knelt and began to pin the hem. "Ankle length is more practical, if you're comfortable with that."

Isobel looked down. She could see the tips of her boots. She peered into the mirror. *And my ankles.*

"If that's too short—"

"No," Isobel said. "You're right. It is more practical. I like it."

"I've already made the buttonholes in two of your shirtwaists. If you really want to leave the blue silk behind and if you have time to wait, I could sew the buttons on one and hem a skirt."

"I'd love that," Isobel said. "The blue plaid, I think."

"Consider it done—as long as I don't have to make any major adjustments. Try it on next so we'll know."

As Isobel changed, she thought about the ball gowns back in her hotel room and spoke from behind the screen. "You have a way to use the traveling suit. What about ball gowns? I brought an entire trunk full, and I've no use for them."

Mrs. Hall sounded doubtful. "I'm not sure you should be eager to part with those. Your brother's been on more than one guest list for elegant affairs in the past. He'll want you on his arm when the next opportunity arises."

Isobel wasn't certain about that, but there was another reason to rid herself of her ball gowns. As she stepped out to have the blue plaid hem pinned up, she said, "Even if that were to happen, I'd want something different. Something that wasn't part of my trousseau."

"*Trousseau?*" Surprise showed in the dressmaker's eyes when she met Isobel's gaze in the dressing mirror.

Isobel nodded.

"I am so sorry. I didn't know."

"Birdie didn't tell you?"

Mrs. Hall shook her head. "Birdie would never repeat something so personal. Nor would I." She smiled. "It's very bad business for a dressmaker to become known as a gossip. Not to mention the fact that I'm hoping you and I become friends. To that end—I'd like it very much if you'd call me Teddy." Finished with pinning up the hem for the blue plaid skirt, Mrs. Hall rose. "Let's see if you can find some buttons you like," she said and then led Isobel into the front room. Once there, she stepped behind the large display case, withdrew a couple of bins, and set them before Isobel.

Impressed by the assortment of porcelain and brass, black jet and pearl, Isobel finally pointed to a set with a delicate openwork brass design backed with a mirror. "Too flashy for the blue plaid?" she asked.

"Perfectly flashy." The dressmaker counted out the dozen required for the shirtwaist. "And now for the indigo calico—although I should mention I could make fabric-covered if you like that idea." When Isobel nodded, Mrs. Hall returned the trays to the display case. "If you'll excuse me for a moment, I'm going to ask Miss Carter to bring us tea and something to snack on while I stitch."

Isobel retreated to the work room. When the dressmaker returned, Isobel pointed to the black sign hanging on the wall above the double screen doors. Gilt letters proclaimed *Hall Dressmaking & Millinery, est. 1865.* "Has it really been only three years you've been in business? I assumed much longer." She followed Mrs. Hall onto the side porch, where the two women settled at a small table.

Mrs. Hall opened the sewing box she'd brought outside with her. Threading a needle, she took up the first button before saying, "Mr. Hall was a lovely man, but he believed in maintaining strong boundaries between a man's world in business and a lady's world in the home. He ran a hardware store in the space occupied by Tanner Mercantile now. That was his world, and our home was mine."

Isobel nodded. She'd known from the start that Alfred would never invite her into certain parts of his world, even after they married. His men's club and his business would forever remain out of bounds to her, and she didn't question it. That was simply the way the world operated.

"Of course, Mr. Hall didn't expect to leave me alone with a hardware store to manage, either." Mrs. Hall gave a little shudder. "I was completely overwhelmed when he passed away."

"You? Overwhelmed? That's hard to believe." Isobel gestured about them. "You obviously know how to run a business."

"I learned. But before I learned, I had many terrible days. Eventually, I gave them a name. I called them my 'face down days', because I spent them quite literally face down on my bed, sobbing and telling God I couldn't possibly go on."

"But you did go on," Isobel said.

The dressmaker nodded. "I've had three good business years—thanks to the good Lord sending Henry and Birdie Tanner west." She smiled. "They were new to Nebraska City when they just happened to visit my church. It was not long after Mr. Hall passed away, but I'd already had my fill of face-down days. Under my direction, the hardware business was a fiasco, and I knew it. Imagine my relief when I learned the Tanners intended to open a mercantile. Instead of purchasing an empty space, they bought my business and my inventory. And they've transformed it." She snipped a thread and took up another button. "Birdie encouraged me to turn my many hobbies into my own business. I resisted at first—because I knew what Mr. Hall thought about ladies in business."

"But then?"

Mrs. Hall chuckled. "Then Birdie pointed out that I'd actually *been* in business for some time before Mr. Hall died. We just didn't call it that."

"What did you call it?"

The dressmaker thought for a moment before responding. "The price of calico inflated horribly during the war. In response to that, I began to experiment with ways to update my own dresses—adding contrasting cuffs or collars, creating decorative motifs at hemlines—that kind of thing. When my friends complimented my efforts, I offered to do the same for them." She chuckled. "Mr. Hall would never have allowed me to accept *money* for such work, but if a friend brought a cake or biscuits or cookies as a thanks?" She smiled. "He did love sweets." After a brief pause, she continued. "After Mr. Hall passed away, word of mouth brought me my first paying customers. In time, some of our city's well-to-do citizens found me." She paused. "You were impressed with my fabric selection. I have the Tanners to thank for that. Early on, they invited me to combine my fabric orders with theirs for the mercantile. That opened the world of wholesale goods to me. My costs went down and *voilà*. A successful business born."

When Miss Carter appeared with the tea tray, Mrs. Hall laid the shirtwaist aside. She ate two petite sandwiches before beginning to stitch the hem of the blue plaid skirt. She didn't look up as she said quietly, "The good Lord had a rescue plan for me after Warren died, and He has one for you, Miss Manning—and for your brother. Trust *Him*. You'll find your way."

Isobel nodded and sipped her tea. It would be good to believe in the future, but right now the past hovered over both her and Charlie like a dark cloud. Mrs. Hall meant well, but, like Birdie, she assumed Isobel had a far more developed relationship with the Almighty than she did. Mrs. Hall saw God's hand in things like the Tanners' visiting her church when she needed help with the hardware store. Isobel preferred to think of things like that as *benevolent coincidence*. She felt great relief when the dressmaker's next words weren't about religion. Instead, she mentioned the wreaths Miss Carter was making to show the ladies at the society meeting. That led to a discussion of the fundraising needed to support the society's future plans.

Isobel's sojourn at the dressmaker's ended with the donning of her new blue plaid ensemble. She departed with her head held high. Forgoing hoops and shortening her skirts had been wise decisions. *Mother Manning would never approve of the new style.* But Isobel realized she didn't care.

I approve. That's what matters.

Chapter 19

...let me alone, for my days are vanity.
Job 7:16

By the time Isobel and Birdie arrived for Thursday evening's meeting, a dozen ladies were gathered in Teddy Hall's parlor. Isobel had just taken a seat when Birdie raised her voice above the hum of conversation.

"Without gavel and without having been formally elected to do so, I hereby call the first meeting of the Ladies Cemetery Improvement Society to order." Birdie smiled at Jennie Wilcox. "I've asked Mrs. Wilcox to be our recording secretary until we've elected one."

The ladies in attendance moved to occupy the circle of chairs in the room. In a matter of moments, they had frustrated Electa Bishop's obvious plan to grasp control of the committee. They elected Birdie Tanner president, America Payne vice president, and Jennie Wilcox recording secretary.

A unanimous vote established dues at fifty cents per annum, required of those who wished to cast votes at meetings. Once the ground rules were established, Birdie called on Isobel to tell the group about Charlie's Sunday morning meeting with the cemetery sextant. Before Isobel had a chance to speak, Electa Bishop rose to her feet.

"If you'll forgive the intrusion," she said, looking about the room, "I promised Mr. Bishop I would remind the society that the cemetery grounds are owned by the city. Any and all improvements must be pre-approved by the city council." She gave a little smile. "As a member of said council, Mr. Bishop has graciously volunteered to introduce our proposals as the need arises."

The mood in the room shifted. Isobel was reminded of Mother Manning, who had always dominated Ladies Aid meetings like a queen reminding her subjects of their station in life. Teddy Hall exchanged a frustrated glance with America Payne. Jennie Wilcox concentrated on taking notes. Slowly.

"Thank you for bringing that up," Birdie said. "As it happens, my Henry took the liberty of speaking with Harlan James and Colby Ritter. Both were very supportive of what we're proposing and have promised to address the council on our behalf—as soon as we present cost estimates for our proposed improvements."

Mrs. Bishop harrumphed. "It's lovely that Mr. Tanner has taken it upon himself to draw Mr. Ritter and Mr. James into the matter, but the meeting minutes should note our understanding that only *two* members of the council do not have the authority to spend city funds."

"I think we all understand that," Birdie said. Everyone nodded and she looked over at Isobel. "I yield the floor to Miss Isobel Manning, who has a progress report."

Mrs. Bishop sat, her hands clasped in her lap, her back straight, her head held high.

Isobel spread both copies of the cemetery map and the list of names on the low table in the center of the room. "These are copies. Mr. Riley retains the originals, and he's verified that there are more tombstones at the cemetery than we see noted here." She paused. "It seems to me that a good first step would be to establish a solid foundation for future improvements by completing the extant records." When the ladies murmured assent, Isobel continued. "That means walking the grounds and noting the gravestones not included on the diagram. Mr. Riley not only agrees, but also suggests the transcribing of the information on every stone, so the tributes are preserved long after time and weather obscure them." Again the ladies murmured agreement.

Teddy Hall spoke up. "I suggest the society appoint Miss Isobel Manning to oversee the creation of a complete record of burials at Wyuka."

"I'm flattered to be trusted with the task," Isobel said, "but someone from Nebraska City might be a better choice."

Birdie looked about the room. "Anyone?" No one volunteered. When Birdie asked those who supported having Isobel oversee the project to raise their hand, every hand went up.

Isobel cocked an eyebrow and glowered at Birdie. *You had that planned, didn't you?*

Birdie fluttered her eyelashes. *Who...me?*

Jennie Wilcox spoke up. "If you need help, I'd be pleased to assist."

Isobel thanked her and, remembering Birdie's comment about Jennie's needing a friend her own age, once again glanced at the older woman. Again, Birdie batted her eyelashes.

Perfect. Just what I'd hoped for.

Isobel barely managed to stifle her laughter.

"Moving on," Birdie said, "we have a draft of the announcement Charlie Manning has offered to put in the *Register*—at no cost to us, I am pleased to report. He also proposes distributing flyers about town to encourage people to provide information about military service represented at Wyuka." She went on to read the announcement aloud.

Mrs. Bishop joined in the general approval of the announcement and the idea of distributing flyers, but then she turned a compliment into thinly veiled criticism of Charlie. It was good of Mr. Manning to donate printing. His additional offer to compile public comments for the committee was welcome. She only hoped that if residents of Nebraska City responded with information, they wouldn't be disappointed when they called at the newspaper office. "I only bring it up as a matter of concern, since we all know the *Register's* business hours have been *erratic* for some time now."

Isobel pressed her lips together. *Calm down. You do not want to make an enemy of Electa Bishop.* Finally, she said, "As it happens, my brother has invited me to assist in the office. I can assure you all that if he isn't available at the office, I will be." Charlie hadn't exactly invited Isobel's assistance, but really—the woman needed to be silenced.

Birdie moved on to the matter of wreaths for graves. Thankfully, even Mrs. Bishop admired Miss Carter's creations. The members quickly approved the purchase of half a dozen—the expense to be paid out of society coffers.

When asked what she would charge, the young woman said, "Daddy and I already gathered more grapevines, and he has plenty of scrap wood for the crosses. Twenty-five cents each should more than cover the cost of ribbon for the flowers and streamers."

Jennie Wilcox spoke up. "Everything we want to do is going to cost money. If there's one thing the ladies of Nebraska know how to do, it's how to raise money for a cause they believe in." She glanced at Isobel. "I don't recall how much we contributed to your fair in St. Louis, but the cash and goods we sent for the 1865 fair in Chicago came to $25,000." She looked about the room. "Why couldn't we do something similar right here in Otoe County—on behalf of the pioneers laid to rest at Wyuka Cemetery? Why not set the example for the rest of the state when it comes to honoring the departed?"

"We are already doing that," Mrs. Bishop said, "with wreaths and bunting and speeches."

"All good things," Mrs. Wilcox agreed, "but Charlie—I mean, Mr. Manning's—announcement for the *Register* makes it clear that the society has a broader purpose."

"It's getting late," Mrs. Bishop said. "Please get to the point, Jennie."

The young widow's cheeks reddened. "I was thinking—I mean—you all know how much I love to cook, and I don't mean to boast, but my pies and cakes have always been popular at fundraisers. What if we set up a lunch counter on Decoration Day, with all proceeds going to cemetery improvements?"

Enthusiastic conversation ensued. Birdie suggested the committee set up in front of the mercantile. "Beneath the awning," she said, "so there's shelter from the sun."

A beaming Mrs. Wilcox took notes as the ladies promised pies, cakes, and sandwiches. In a few moments, the plan had come together, with several members also volunteering to research costs of a new gate, a fence, a well, and even a flagpole.

As soon as the meeting adjourned, Isobel noticed Mrs. Wilcox speaking earnestly with her mother-in-law. The two women lingered on Mrs. Hall's front porch while Birdie and Isobel took the garden path toward the street. They'd just gone through the gate when Mrs. Wilcox caught up.

"Mother Bishop's agreed to let me borrow the rig on Monday," she said. "I can drive us out to the cemetery. What time would you like me to pick you up? I'm awfully pleased to be helping."

Mrs. Bishop spoke as she brushed past. "I doubt you'll still feel that way after a day spent recording the names of the dead." She turned around. "It's simply not wise for you to participate so directly. Not with your tendency to melancholy."

The young widow ducked her head. Isobel rushed to say something—anything to save the poor girl further embarrassment. "I'm hoping the project will spur Nebraskans to remember *good* things. The people may have passed on, but their stories shouldn't die."

Mrs. Bishop cleared her throat again. "Some stories should."

"Perhaps," Birdie countered, "but many others should be preserved for posterity. In fact—" she looked from Isobel to Jennie— "depending on how things go with your recording, you've given me an idea."

"Why am I not surprised," Mrs. Bishop grumped.

The four ladies walked on, parting ways at the corner of Pleasant and Main.

"I will never understand that woman," Isobel said. She's like a dark cloud looming on every horizon." She looked over at Birdie. "Does Jennie Wilcox really have a tendency to melancholy? And even if that's true, why would her mother-in-law say such a thing in front of you and me?"

Birdie muttered something vague about Electa Bishop's not being the most tactful of women before changing the subject and remarking on Isobel's new ensemble, which she declared *fetching*. "You look like a woman who knows what she's about."

Fetching. Ha. "Mother Manning will be outraged when she next sees me."

"That won't be anytime soon, I hope."

"I promised to complete the cemetery survey, and I will."

"Good. I'll count on your giving a full report at the next society meeting."

"That's not until next month. I don't know that I can commit to staying that long. Besides, Jennie is perfectly capable of giving an excellent report."

"Of course she is," Birdie agreed. They turned a corner and passed the back door of the *Register* office. "But Charlie needs you here. At the newspaper—and in his life. In fact, he's already beginning to appreciate having you here."

"Really?" What did Birdie know that Isobel didn't?

They reached the mercantile. Opening the back door, Birdie led the way inside and called up the stairs to where Charlie and Henry had spent the evening playing checkers.

"Thank goodness you're back," Charlie said when he came into view. He nodded at Henry, just visible over his shoulder. "I've let Henry win so many matches, he's beginning to be suspicious."

Henry clapped a hand on Charlie's shoulder and gave him a little shake. "Is it pleasant in that dream world of yours?" He winked at Isobel. "Fond as I am of the boy, I have to say he's worse at checkers than Birdie."

Birdie waggled a finger at her husband. "Leave me out of your remonstrations and exaggerations."

As Charlie descended the stairs, Isobel called up to Henry, asking if he minded coming down, too. The moment he did so, she said, "I'd really like to thank my rescuer for what he did. In person." Something passed between Birdie and Henry. Isobel couldn't tell if it was fear or caution. When neither spoke, she persisted. "What is it? I don't understand why a simple request makes you two so ill-at-ease. Why all the secrecy?"

Henry shrugged. "It's not so much *secrecy* as respecting a man's privacy. If a man wants to be a hermit, then—"

Hermit? That word again. *Long hair. Collar turned up.* But there hadn't been a dog—had there? Isobel looked over at Birdie. "You called the man I saw coming out of the storeroom last Saturday morning a hermit. I thought he'd robbed the store, but you said no, that he was a customer." She turned back to Henry. "Is that who rescued me?"

Finally, Birdie spoke up. "Yes. It was him."

A shiver ran up Isobel's spine. "Can he read? Could I at least write a note?"

Birdie made a noise that sounded more like a stifled laugh than anything. "He can read. If you write a note, I'll see that he gets it the next time he comes in for supplies."

"Do you know when that will be?"

"Unpredictable," Henry said quickly. "He said he was well stocked when he came into town last Sunday night."

Sunday night? Isobel looked over at Birdie.

"He wanted to make sure you were all right."

"He sounds kind," Isobel said. Birdie seemed about to say something more, but when Henry cleared his throat, she was silent. Isobel relented. "All right. No more questions. I'll drop a note by on my way into the newspaper office in the morning. Along with the bandana."

Both Birdie and Henry spoke at once. "Bandana?"

Isobel nodded. "I tucked it in my waist before Charlie helped me into the wagon Sunday. I didn't even remember it until later in the day when I was changing. And there it was—a dark blue bandana." She glanced at Birdie. "I told you about that. He moistened it with water from his canteen." She looked over at Henry. "Your hermit was a Union soldier. Did you know that about him?"

"What makes you say that?"

"He left his canteen with me when he went for help. It had *U.S.* stamped on one side." She glanced at her brother and then back at Henry. "Charlie had one like it when he mustered out."

Henry shrugged. "There are lots of those around." He glanced at Charlie. "I bet you still have yours."

"I do," Charlie said. He offered Isobel his arm. "Shall I walk milady home?"

As they crossed Main Street, Isobel said, "I don't understand why they are so loathe to let me thank the man in person."

As they stepped up on the boardwalk leading to the hotel entrance, Charlie said, "The man doesn't want to socialize.

Write the note, and let it go, Izzy." When Isobel didn't react, he asked, "Can I expect you at the office in the morning?"

Isobel hesitated. "I don't want to get in the way."

"You won't be in the way. Edgar will be setting type for the flyers first thing. We'll get them printed. After that, you can either help him with distribution or help me plan the next edition of the *Register*. Either way, there's quite enough to keep both of us busy all day." He paused. "And on Saturday, I'll teach you to drive. Henry said we can borrow Rosie."

"Alfred taught me how to drive," Isobel said, "although he skipped the lesson on 'how to stop a runaway.'"

"Then my lesson won't take long, and we can take a nice drive. You can see the orchards I mentioned the other day." He wished her a good night and kissed her cheek as he left.

Once back in her room, Isobel changed into her nightgown before perching on the edge of the bed to brush her hair. Henry and Birdie had undoubtedly said all they would about the hermit who scuttled into town for supplies and left just as quickly.

Scraggly hair. Battered hat.

Blue eyes. Kind voice.

Rising from the bed and laying the brush aside, Isobel crossed to the window and looked out. He was out there somewhere, alone. *Except for the dog.*

What kind of man sought such a life?

Chapter 20

A talebearer revealeth secrets:
but he that is of a faithful spirit concealeth the matter.
Proverbs 11:13

The moment Izzy arrived at the newspaper office Friday morning, Charlie handed her two recent editions of the *Register*. "Look these over. While you read, Edgar and I will print the flyers. Once you've familiarized yourself with the kind of things I like to reprint for my readers—" he pointed to the Kansas City, St. Louis, and Denver newspapers atop his desk "—peruse those and circle what you'd suggest I use." He offered a pencil.

Izzy didn't say the word *plagiarism*, but she looked concerned about the assignment, and so he explained.

"It's common practice in the newspaper business. Subscribers want to read about what's going on elsewhere. The only way I can tell them is to seek out sources that have either more staff or first-hand knowledge of events." That seemed to convince her, and Izzy retreated to his desk and began to read.

He expected it to be an exercise in futility. He hadn't expected her to be any good at it. But later that morning, when Izzy left to help Edgar distribute flyers and he reviewed her work, he was amazed. She might actually have a knack for the news business. She'd passed over the same articles he would have ignored and circled several his readers would enjoy. In fact, except for one inane poem she'd selected, he agreed with her every choice. He sat back for a moment, thinking.

The bell affixed to the front door jangled just as Charlie finalized his plan for the *Register's* front page. He looked up at the visitor, who was brandishing one of the newly printed flyers.

"Says here there's a committee that wants to set the record straight on folks buried at Wyuka."

Set the record straight? What did he mean by that? Charlie rose from his chair. The man closed the door behind him. As he came closer, Charlie smelled whiskey. What should have been off-putting wasn't. It made him want a drink.

"I got a story." The man looked around the office. "Or maybe I should wait and tell yer sister about it? When she gave me the paper, she seemed real interested in our little town—*little* compared to where she come from, anyhow."

Izzy had engaged an ill-kempt, almost-drunk man in conversation? Not a good idea. He would have to make that point when she returned. "I'll be glad to take down what you have to say," Charlie said abruptly. He reached for a sheet of paper and sat down again. Dipping a pen in the brass inkwell atop his desk, he asked for the man's name.

"Wade Inskeep. I-n-s-k-e-e-p." He watched Charlie write the name before continuing. "It's about the Longs. All five buried up at Wyuka. My Pa knowed the old man. He was no good, just like the boy that growed up, name of Gideon. Guess the wife was all right. And the young-un took by the ague. Got nothing to say about them."

Charlie swallowed. The aroma of whiskey wafted about with the man's every word. This was not at all what Birdie and her committee had in mind when they invited people to provide information about the cemetery. He tried to explain. "The project isn't so much about stories as it is about verifying burials, Mr.

Inskeep. The hope is that people will come forward to help create a more accurate plot map—to correct mistakes in the record concerning names or dates. That kind of thing."

Inskeep glared over Charlie's head and out the south window for a moment. "They're puttin' wreaths on graves, ain't they? Wantin' to know who served?"

"Yes."

He narrowed his gaze as he stared down at Charlie. "Did you? Serve?"

It was none of the man's business, but Charlie answered him. "I did. With the 24th Missouri."

"See fighting?"

That's prying. "I don't see what my service has to do with—"

"You said they're wantin' to correct mistakes. Says on Long's stone he went 'missing in action.' I'm here to tell you he might be missing but he wasn't in any action that deserves notice. He turned tail and ran, and I come to tell those ladies they don't want to be putting a wreath at the grave his mama marked for a deserting coward." Inskeep sniffed and wiped his nose on his sleeve. "For all anyone knows he took a new name and is living high on the hog someplace far away from here. Plenty did just that."

Charlie swallowed, almost wishing he could get a taste of the whiskey-laden vapor spewing from the man's mouth. He cleared his throat. "As I said, Mr. Inskeep, the ladies weren't exactly—"

The man tapped the top of Charlie's desk with a tobacco-stained finger. "You don't want to write it out, that's fine. But you tell that committee 'no Decoration Day wreath for Gideon Long. Or else.'"

Or else. Charlie put the fountain pen back in the inkwell and rose to his feet. "All right, Mr. Inskeep. I'll pass your story—your information—on." He motioned toward the front door.

"And now, if you'll excuse me, I'm supposed to meet my sister for a late lunch."

Inskeep allowed Charlie to herd him toward the front door. "You'll tell her?"

"My sister isn't in charge of the project. I will inform the person who is."

"Bet you mean Birdie Tanner." Inskeep spoke the word like a curse. "Got her fingers in too many pies, you ask me. You tell her it happened like I told ya."

Inskeep looked past Charlie toward the back door, which had just opened. Charlie looked around in time to see Edgar hang his cap on a hook.

Inskeep lowered his voice. "Left Tom to die and now all them kids goin' hungry and his widow workin' her fingers to the bone. It ain't right. You tell Birdie what I said, now. I let it go these years, but I ain't lettin' it go no more. Not if they decorate that grave. No, sir."

Charlie opened the front door. "I'll pass the message along."

"You better." Inskeep stepped outside, clamped his hat on his head, and trudged away.

Edgar spoke as Charlie pulled the sign down announcing *Out to Lunch Back Soon*. "Who was that? Did I hear my Pa's name?"

"Said his name was Wade Inskeep."

"What's he got to do with my Pa?"

"Apparently he was in the First Nebraska." Charlie paused. "He was—um—*concerned* about your family."

Edgar marched to the front door and stepped outside, staring first up and then down the street. When he re-entered the office, he was fuming. "What business has he got talking about my family?"

"He probably meant well."

Edgar snorted. "Somebody who means well wouldn't be talking about us behind our backs. Wouldn't hurry off without so much as saying hello to me."

"I suppose you make a good point."

But Edgar's pride clearly had been wounded. "We do all right. Molly and I have good jobs. Mr. Tanner's going to let Ethan start sweeping the store for him. The twins are going to keep the trees at the cemetery watered, and they're getting paid to do it. Yesterday, Mr. Carter said they're so strong, if they want to help haul freight, all they have to do is meet him and Jezebel at the levy when they hear a steamboat coming." He paused. "If Mr. Inskeep cares so much, he might talk to Ma about planting a field instead of spreading lies about Uncle Gideon."

Uncle Gideon?

Edgar must have noticed Charlie's reaction to the term.

"That's what we called him and always will. Whatever happened to him, he didn't run off and leave our Pa to die."

Charlie nodded. "If Mr. Inskeep comes back, I'll tell him what you said. Or as much of it as I can remember. That was quite a mouthful." He forced a smile, hoping to defuse Edgar's rage.

Edgar forced a low grunt, and then he allowed a little smile. "Guess I did carry on a bit. Sorry. But I don't want folks thinking Ma isn't caring for us, because she is. She works hard and we manage." He plopped down at the typesetting station. "And like I said, if that busybody is so all-fired worried about us, he's welcome to patch the privy roof or fix the porch railing any time." He broke off. "I wasn't complaining about things needing fixing."

"I understand," Charlie said quickly. "Too often, people jaw about problems, but they aren't willing to be part of the solutions."

Edgar nodded. "And the folks who solve problems don't always talk about it. They just take care of things." He positioned the article Charlie wanted typeset atop his workbench. "Anyway, you have a nice lunch with Miss Manning."

"Would you like to join us?"

Edgar reached down and lifted up a tin pail from which he extracted an apple. "Thank you, but Ma packed me a lunch."

Charlie departed by way of the back door. As he made his way up the street toward Lila's Café, he pondered Edgar's reaction to Wade Inskeep's comments about the Simmons family. Poverty had not robbed the boy of familial pride and the instinct to defend his mother. But the family had needs Edgar shouldn't have to meet, even if he could—among them, a leaking roof. Carpentry was not a skill Charlie possessed, but Henry would know men who did. Perhaps a few such men could be gathered for a workday at the Simmons residence. When it came down to it, Charlie decided there was no better way to mark Decoration Day than to help a soldier's family.

It was a shame he couldn't ignore Inskeep's comment about disrupting Decoration Day. The Cemetery Improvement Society shouldn't have to deal with such things. Still, Birdie deserved to know about the man's threat.

※

Gideon looked down at the note centered in the circle of lamplight atop Ma's table. Birdie had given both it and his blue bandana to him earlier in the evening, when he'd stopped in for a few supplies.

"Isobel wanted to thank you personally," Birdie said. "Henry and I convinced her that wasn't necessary. But she insisted I give you this." She waggled both note and bandana back and forth until Gideon took them.

He'd been back at the cabin for a while now, trying to read Ma's Bible—without success. Fidgeting with the bandana, he stared from the note to the bonnet he had yet to return. *The bonnet.* Why hadn't he taken it to town and left it hanging on the back doorknob of the newspaper office? And why was he treating the note like it might hurt if he touched it?

Because it might.

He'd barely started down the path of helping Tom's family. Barely begun to hope he could see a reason he'd survived. Barely grasped at some version of contentment. The bonnet was a problem, for it made him think of the mass of Titian red curls that had spilled out when it came off. Maybe he'd take it back yet tonight.

The bandana was a problem because it carried a faint scent of—what, he didn't know, but it sure didn't smell like Trouble anymore, and it had been around the dog's neck before it served as a cold compress.

Get it over with.

Tossing the bandana aside with an impatient huff, he leaned forward, opened the envelope, and spread the note in the pool of lamplight.

> *Kind Sir,*
>
> *Your bravery in stepping into the path of a runaway and your subsequent ministrations will be forever remembered as the kindest of deeds, all the more appreciated because they were performed for the benefit of one unknown to you. Could I deliver my thanks in person, be assured that I would do so. However, your loyal and trustworthy friends, the Tanners, have convinced me that I must be content with this mode of communication. I therefore take this opportunity to offer my sincerest gratitude, even as I acknowledge its inadequacy to express the depth of my appreciation. Since I cannot possibly repay you, I shall hope the Almighty will reward you for the selfless heroism that saved the life of a stranger.*
>
> *With my utmost thanks,*
> *Miss Isobel Manning*

Resting his folded arms on the edge of the table, Gideon reread the note before rising from the table to make coffee. Once again seated, he perused the flyer Henry had tucked in with Gideon's supplies. A *Ladies Cemetery Improvement Society*. Birdie had told him all about it. Miss Manning and Freddie Wilcox's widow would be tromping about the cemetery for the next few days, hoping to complete the sexton's inadequate record. The public's assistance was requested with that part of the project. Wreaths were to be placed at soldier's graves on Decoration Day. Comments were invited.

He would need to move the rabbit snares and avoid the cemetery until after Decoration Day. He could only imagine what kind of comments might be forthcoming in regard to Private Gideon Long. It was actually *Sergeant* Long by the end of the war, but no one knew about that. No one knew about the medal, either. And no one ever would.

Laying the flyer aside, Gideon read Miss Manning's note again. Beautiful handwriting and a lofty vocabulary. Neither should come as a surprise, based on the quality of the silk traveling suit she'd been wearing and the artfully trimmed bonnet. He reached for it.

Birdie had never approved of Gideon's decision to remain on the fringes of society. *Defend yourself,* she'd said more than once. *Don't let people go on thinking you left your dearest friend that way.* When she'd given him the bandana and Miss Manning's note earlier this evening, there'd been something in her expression that made him uneasy. He sat back, thinking it through as he finished his coffee. Eventually, he came up with a plan. And he wrote his own note.

Chapter 21

*Two are better than one;
because they have a good reward for their labour.
Ecclesiastes 4:9*

Early Monday morning, Isobel responded to a knock at her hotel room door. It was Molly, who handed over a note.

"Mrs. Wilcox was mightily flustered when she dropped that off," Molly said.

Isobel frowned as she read. The mother-in-law was demanding that Jennie finish baking for a Tuesday evening event before leaving for the cemetery. *How Mother Manning of you.* Isobel huffed frustration.

"You want me to take a note back?"

Isobel shook her head. "It'll get you in trouble with Miss Bennet."

"Mrs. Oliver's on duty this morning. She won't mind."

Isobel hesitated, then waved Molly into the room and closed the door. Hurrying to the small writing desk, she wrote. *Dear Mrs. Wilcox, Charlie gave me a driving lesson after church yesterday. I shall rent a rig and begin. Join me as you are able.* With only a moment's hesitation, she signed the note *Your friend.*

Dressing as soon as Molly departed, Isobel gathered her travel desk and writing supplies and descended to the dining room. She was eating breakfast when Molly returned.

"She nigh on to cried with relief," Molly said. "Two pies are done and she has two more and then a batch of ginger snaps. She said to tell you she'll bring lunch with her."

Isobel finished breakfast and exited the hotel. Her heart sank when she passed the *Register* office on her way to the livery. The shades were still drawn on all the windows. Hurrying around to the back, she stood at the base of the stairs, peering up at Charlie's apartment.

Charlie's voice sounded from behind her. "No, he isn't up there in a drunken stupor."

Isobel wheeled about, denial on her lips.

"Don't deny it," Charlie said. "I could hear worry percolating the minute I stepped outside from next door. I wanted to talk to Henry about recruiting some men to help with repairs out at the Simmonses'." He brushed past her to unlock the newspaper office door, then paused before entering. "I thought you and Jennie—uh, Mrs. Wilcox—were driving out to Wyuka this morning."

Isobel explained what had happened, and he offered to drive her out. "Just let me leave a note for Edgar."

"Were you going out there anyway?"

Charlie lifted one shoulder in a half-shrug. "Those daily visits haven't been particularly healing. I thought I might try a different way to cope." He nodded toward the office interior. "Work, for example."

Isobel nodded. "Then that's what you should do. As long as the chestnut mare we drove yesterday is available, I'll be fine." Hope surged through her as she took her leave. Maybe Charlie was going to be all right, after all.

Gideon strode to the top of the cemetery hill, Miss Manning's blue bonnet in one hand and a good-sized rock in the other. Inverting the bonnet as he set it down, he took the note he'd written out of his coat pocket and weighted it in place in the crown. Positioned as it was at the base of Vera Manning's grave marker, the bonnet would surely catch her attention. Movement on the road made him look up. He hurried away, dropping out of sight below a slight ridge. But then, he stayed put. The blue bonnet was an expensive bit of millinery. It couldn't hurt to make sure she saw it. After all, it would be a shame for it to go unnoticed, only to be ruined by a spring storm.

He drew Trouble to his side. When he heard the buggy slow, he raised up a bit and separated the grass just enough to satisfy his suspicion—no, his hope—that the early morning visitor was, indeed, Miss Manning. Alighting from the buggy, she went to the horse's head. The animal almost leaned into her, and she rubbed its ears and spoke to it in a voice that was, from this distance, little more than a murmur.

Gideon smiled. One harrowing experience hadn't made her too frightened to drive again. That was good. After a moment, she led the animal toward the blackberry bramble at the far edge of the cemetery, probably intending to hitch the horse. On her way to do that, she paused. Gideon raised up a bit more to get a better view. She was bending down to pick up the bonnet. He lowered himself to the earth. When things were quiet, he peered through the grass again. She set the bonnet on the buggy seat and then proceeded to the edge of the grounds to hitch the buggy. Finally, she withdrew the note. He watched as she read it and ducked down when, note in hand, she looked about her.

Raising her voice, she called out, "If you can hear me, thank you for returning my bonnet. It's very kind of you." She paused. "You're correct in what you write. I've suffered no lasting ill effects. I owe you thanks for that, as well."

Trouble strained to get away. Knowing he'd bound toward the woman, Gideon clutched at the bandana about the dog's neck. He waited, not daring to move.

"I think I know who you are. I mean—not really, but—I think I saw you leaving the mercantile the morning we all came out here to Wyuka to clean things up. I would much prefer to thank you in person, but both Henry and Birdie say you wouldn't want that."

Gideon's heart pounded. The mere thought of someone knowing about him—someone wanting to talk with him—

"At any rate, thank you."

She paused and then he heard laughter, soft and low.

"I suppose it's absurd for me to stand here talking to the air. But maybe I'm not. Maybe you *can* hear me." Another pause. "Jennie Wilcox and I are going to be here at the cemetery for a few days. We're trying to make a more accurate plot map. And we're transcribing the information on the tombstones."

She paused, and when next she spoke her voice was brighter.

"When we've finished, I'll tie a bandana where I've hitched my buggy. A red one. In the blackberry bramble. I hope you can hear me. When you see the bandana, you'll know we've finished." She paused. "So thank you again for everything. And for returning my bonnet. And—goodbye."

Gideon waited for a long while before easing away. He'd been right about any kind of contact threatening his newfound sense of—what? Peace? Contentment? Neither, yet. But the regret he felt about not being able to answer Miss Manning—he had to avoid a repeat of that. He ran his fingers over his scars. He had to come to peace with the way things were. The way they always would be.

Feeling foolish for speaking aloud to empty air, Isobel lingered for a moment with the hermit's note in her hand. It wasn't much of a note. One line. No signature. *I am pleased to know you suffer no ill effects from your accident.*

Both the handwriting and the syntax hinted at someone who was far from being any kind of hermit. She looked toward the spot beneath the tree where he'd left her that day when he went for help. Finally, she gazed toward the spot to the south where she'd nearly died.

Don't be so dramatic. You didn't nearly die. You weren't even badly hurt. Looking about her, she wondered where her rescuer might live. Miles away in a dugout? In a cave near the river? *Surely not a cave.* How silly to have called out—as if a man determined to remain anonymous would care to hear a word she said. That rustle in the grass a moment ago was only the wind. And yet—Isobel shivered. She'd had an uncanny sense of someone listening. *That's absurd.*

Taking herself in hand, Isobel retrieved the blanket she'd brought with her and spread it beneath the tree. Gathering supplies, she settled down to review the plot map and the sextant's records. Wyuka Cemetery wasn't laid out in neat rows. Grave sites weren't of equal size, and family plots could be either squares or rectangles. Curved, winding paths led up from the road, making for uneven section lines. Isobel looked up from the papers. Doing this alone was going to be difficult.

Rising to her feet with both map and list in hand, she located the first grave.

John W. Dorsey,
Pvt. Ind. Militia

War of 1812
1785 –1861

Indiana? What had brought Private Dorsey to Nebraska, and what had Nebraska City looked like when he arrived?

Isobel gazed westward and then back toward the river. The stark contrast between the verdant canopy along the water and the treeless prairie made it seem that the Creator had tired of planting hickory and walnut, oak and hackberry, and simply flung grass seed across the earth toward the west. She thought back to the glowing accounts Alfred read aloud when they were planning their wedding trip. He'd been enamored with what he called "the true West," but words on the printed page paled in the face of reality. Going west might sound adventurous and romantic, but now that she was here, the notion of heading onto that treeless plain made her shudder with dread.

Once again, she scanned the dozens of stones. She wished she knew more than the names. More than birth dates and death dates. More than whatever hints a poignant epitaph could provide. She moved to the next stone in the current row, startled by the epitaph.

Remember me as you pass by.
As you are now, so once was I.
As I am now, soon you will be.
Prepare for death and follow me.

How odd. Eerie, even. But then, as she copied the words, Isobel realized they didn't have to be eerie. Perhaps they were simply meant as a reminder to the living. *Face reality. Everybody dies. Be prepared.* It would be interesting to meet whoever had selected that epitaph and ask them what they had intended.

Isobel finished writing, newly aware of the inadequacy of a few lines to represent a lifetime. She remembered the mention of an Old Settlers Association at last Thursday's meeting. Was that group preserving people's stories? *Were they writing them down?* Slowly, she made her way down the row, frowning when she realized that a couple of the names on the sextant's list were not represented by a corresponding grave marker. In another case, a child's name carved on a small marker was missing from the list of names.

The chestnut mare whinnied. Afraid she'd lose her place in the process of labeling the plot map, Isobel stayed where she was as a buggy came into view from the direction of town. *Mrs. Wilcox.* Once she'd hitched her buggy, the flustered young woman joined Isobel next to a small stone featuring a beautiful bas relief of a robed figure standing next to an urn.

"I am so sorry," she babbled. "Mother Bishop insisted I—" She paused and took in a gulp of air. "I couldn't—"

"It's all right," Isobel said. "Believe me, I know what it's like to live under the same roof with a difficult and demanding woman. I'm not in the least upset with you, but I am glad you're here." She held out a sheet of paper to show the young widow what she'd been doing.

"I may be recording secretary for the society," Mrs. Wilcox said, "but your handwriting is much better than mine. How about I dictate and you continue to do the writing?"

Isobel nodded, and they made their way down another row. When she commented on the artistry and symbolism represented in memorials for two children who'd died only four days apart, she murmured, "How awful to endure such a loss."

Mrs. Wilcox nodded. "It was. Their poor mother was never the same. Eventually, the family left Nebraska."

Startled, Isobel said, "You knew the family?" When the young widow nodded, Mrs. Bishop's comment about her daughter-in-law's *tendency to melancholy* came to mind. "I'm so sorry." She paused. "I didn't think about your knowing many of the families represented here. If this proves too difficult—"

"It isn't. It won't. I want to help."

"If you change your mind—"

"Thank you," Mrs. Wilcox said, and then suggested they break for lunch.

Isobel agreed, exclaiming over the amount of food in the huge basket the young widow hauled to the blanket spread beneath the tree.

"I thought you and Charlie might enjoy a home cooked meal for a change."

"You made a special supper, too?"

"Not really. I just made extra." She produced two plates onto which she loaded sliced ham and pickled beets, fresh bread and potato salad before retreating to the buggy for what proved to be a peach pie.

"That's not a pie," Isobel exclaimed. "That's a work of art." And it was, with a lattice top adorned with flower buds and leaves, all of them created from pastry. "I've never seen anything like it."

Mrs. Wilcox shrugged. "I don't bother with such fancy crust when something's going to be cut up immediately and served as individual pieces—like for a church supper. But it was fun doing this one for Char—for you and Charlie." As it turned out, the young widow had brought two individual pieces of pie for the two of them to eat, so as not to cut into the one that had impressed Isobel.

And now it can impress Charlie.

Isobel smiled to herself.

Chapter 22

Submit yourselves therefore to God.
Resist the devil, and he will flee from you.
James 4:7

Sleepless nights were nothing new, but Charlie didn't want to reach for the usual remedy. Drinking couldn't fix the real problem and would unavoidably create others. He hadn't needed to hear that from Jennie Wilcox—although the shock he'd felt when she said it might have served a purpose. As did having a sister in town. Taking a deep breath, he threw back the covers and slid to the edge of the bed where he planted his feet on the floor and stared into the darkness. *Get up. Get out. Move. Walk. Pray.*

Pray? Where'd that come from? With a low grunt, he stood up and stretched. Actually, he knew where the idea to pray had originated. Something the preacher had said on Sunday. He allowed a little smile as he dressed, remembering the look on Izzy's face when he slid into the pew next to her. He didn't think he'd listened all that well to the sermon, but apparently at least part of it had stuck with him. Something about "letting requests be made known to God" when a person needed help.

Finally dressed, he reached for the glass of water he'd left on the nearby table and padded across the room to light a lamp. His shadow flickered on the wall as he guzzled the water. Next, he opened a window to let fresh air in. Faint strains of piano music drifted up from one of the saloons near the river. Charlie ran his hands through his hair, battling the siren that beckoned him to quench his thirst with something besides water—something that would also dull the pain of loss.

He'd never heard anyone mention the fact that grief could hurt physically, and it surprised him when Vera died. On the worst days, very real pain throbbed in his gut, obliterating his appetite for anything but whiskey. People said time would heal the wound, and maybe it had dulled the pain—a little. But there were still nights like this when he battled a monster so real it seemed that he could hear the creature breathe, sense it crouching in the corner of the apartment, spewing its fetid breath into the air, waiting for him to give in.

Bending down, he braced his palms on the windowsill and sucked in fresh air. As he did, other words Pastor Duncan had read this past Sunday came to mind. Something about fleeing the devil. *People who tell you to be a man and face the enemy aren't always right. Sometimes running is exactly what we should do.* Charlie swallowed and turned away from the window. He was going to have to run this time. Out of the apartment. Away from the music.

Dressing quickly, he splashed water on his face and swiped a comb through his hair. When he yanked the apartment door open, moonlight spilled inside and illuminated the basket Izzy had brought with her from the cemetery. The two of them had shared its bountiful contents with Henry and Birdie last evening, but one piece of peach pie remained. His stomach rumbled. Pie before dawn? Why not?

Pie tin in one hand and a fork in the other, Charlie stepped out the back door. He listened to the music from up the street while he ate. Once finished, he settled the empty tin back in Jennie Wilcox's basket. Leaving the dirty dish and fork for later, he exited the apartment, scooped up the basket, and descended the stairs. He paused for a moment, looking toward the river. Listening. Moistening his lips as he imagined the welcome sensation of whiskey burning its way down his throat. He set the basket on the bottom step.

Flee temptation.

Closing his eyes, Charlie flung a desperate prayer heavenward. *Help me. Please. Help me.* The preacher's words melded with Jennie's, almost as if they were speaking with one voice. *Flee temptation! You know the pain always comes back.*

He did know. But he also knew the desire for a good drink always came back, too. What was the point of fighting for sobriety when relief, however brief, was only a short walk away?

Vera would want you to fight. Izzy and Jennie want you to fight. So fight. The voice of conscience was gaining strength, but it still couldn't drown out the other one. *Just one drink. It'll help.* He took a step toward the music, but then a skittering sounded near Jennie Wilcox's basket. He stopped short. Blast Jennie Wilcox, anyway. He could almost hear her pleading. *Don't, Charlie. Please don't. The pain always comes back. Trust me. I know.*

She did know, and pondering that surprising fact made him hesitate. With a low curse directed at the creature skittering about in the dirt—or maybe at himself and his weakness—Charlie snatched up the basket. It was too early for anyone at the Bishops' to be up, but he could set the basket outside the kitchen door. He could walk out to the cemetery. Come sunrise, he could share this first victory—however thin said victory might be—with Vera. He could come back into town and buy Izzy breakfast at Lila Ritchie's café. And for today, he and Izzy would engage in the newspaper business. It might not be much, but it was something. Something good. If he could put a string of days together like that, life might be better than good.

As expected, the tall windows across the front of the Bishops' two-story brick manse were all dark. But to Charlie's surprise, light spilled onto the side lawn from the kitchen wing at the back. At this hour? He walked around the corner, wrinkling his nose as he approached the kitchen. Something was burnt to a crisp. He wasn't the only one whose day had gotten off to a bad start. Intending to set the basket at the door and make a hasty exit, he hesitated when he recognized Mrs. Bishop's voice.

"What on earth did you think you were doing?!"

Poor Cook.

"I was hoping to get a head start on—"

Not Cook. Mrs. Wilcox. Jennie.

Mrs. Bishop interrupted. "Get a head start on *what*? Burning down the house?"

Ignoring the twinge of guilt over eavesdropping, Charlie lingered.

"I'm sorry if I woke you," Jennie soothed.

"*If* you woke me? *If*? Of course you woke us! Heavens above, I'm surprised someone didn't call out the fire company."

"M-Mrs. Simmons brought some beautiful rhubarb into Birdie's yesterday," Jennie stammered. "When Isobel and I stopped in to report on our progress at Wyuka, I bought enough for two pies. I couldn't sleep last night, and so I decided to bake. I'm sorry for disrupting your sleep."

"And *I'm* sorry you refused to listen to me about spending so much time in that cemetery," Mrs. Bishop retorted. "Insomnia was one of the reasons your health failed when Freddie died. I *told* you it wouldn't be good for you to stir up painful memories. If you ask me, *two* charred pies prove I was right. You really must resign from Birdie's little project. It simply won't do for you to backslide."

Jennie didn't speak. Charlie willed her to reply. *Defend yourself. Don't let her bully you.* Finally, she did.

"With respect, Mother Bishop, I'm not backsliding. In fact, I talked about Freddie yesterday when Isobel and I came to his marker. She's a good listener, and I realized that something has changed for me—in a good way. It was *comforting* to talk about Freddie." She paused before adding, "And after spending the day together, Isobel and I have all manner of ideas for funding the cemetery improvements. I love being involved in the project. As for the burned pies, all they prove is that I should monitor the oven more carefully."

Apparently, Mrs. Bishop wasn't convinced. Charlie didn't really listen to much beyond her tone of voice, for he was pondering Jennie's comment about Izzy being a good listener. That surprised him. If Izzy was a good listener, why hadn't he noticed? Mrs. Bishop continued her harangue. A mention of Jennie's "illness" drew his attention back to what she was saying.

Jennie's tone changed to impatience. "I wasn't *ill*, and we both know it. I was numbing my grief with enormous amounts of peach brandy. Had it gone on much longer, there's a distinct possibility I would have killed myself." Her tone softened. "I can only imagine the pain I caused you and Pa Bishop. But really, Mother Bishop, you don't need to fear a return of those dark days. The reason I couldn't sleep was I couldn't stop thinking about the ideas Isobel and I discussed yesterday. And baking isn't a symptom of trouble. On the contrary, it makes me happy. I tried something different when I made those two pies. It didn't work. Please don't make it out to be something more than it is."

In the ensuing silence, Charlie imagined the two women staring each other down. Amazingly enough, when Mrs. Bishop broke the silence, she seemed to be giving Jennie the benefit of the doubt.

"Well, there's no time for more pies now. Try to get this mess cleaned up before Cook arrives. The last thing I need is trouble with her." When Mrs. Bishop next spoke, her voice was further away. She must have retreated to the doorway leading into the main house. "I am still very concerned about your level of involvement with Birdie's new project, but as I can see you have determined not to listen to what I have to say, we'll let the matter rest. For now." She paused. "I suppose one good thing about your involvement is that you are in a position to keep your father-in-law informed about the society's plans. I'm not certain Birdie Tanner can be trusted in that regard. Everyone knows she tends to act first and seek approval after the fact."

"I'll tell you both all about the ideas Isobel and I discussed," Jennie said. "This very morning, if you like. And I think you'll *both* be pleased."

Charlie frowned. Jennie sounded so enthusiastic. Why hadn't Izzy said anything? *Because you, Charles Manning, are about as far from being a good listener as a man can get.* Not only was he not a good listener, he was biding his time until Busy Izzy decided to go home.

Jennie was humming to herself as she moved about the kitchen. It was time to complete his errand and be gone. He stepped to the open door. She was standing with her back to the door, scraping burnt pie into a wastebasket. He rapped softly on the door frame and said, "Just returning your pie tin and the basket." As he stepped inside and set her luncheon basket on a nearby counter, he said, "It doesn't appear you've had a good start to your day."

Jennie smiled and began to empty the second pie tin. "In truth, it's been something of a triumph."

"But you burnt your rhubarb pies." Even as the young widow arched an eyebrow, Charlie scolded himself. *Rhubarb? How would you know it's rhubarb? You dolt. You've given yourself away.* He cleared his throat. "I mean—it's clearly pie that's failed, and there's a reddish tint to what you're throwing out, so I assumed—"

Jennie chuckled. "I saw you sneak up on the porch."

"I did not sneak." The eyebrow arched again. "Well, all right—I did." He lifted his chin. "I thought you might need rescuing."

"On any other day, you would be right." Jennie looked toward the door leading into the main house. "I can't quite believe I spoke up that way." She smiled at him. "I'm glad you walked this way, instead of toward the river."

He felt his cheeks flush with embarrassment, then nodded. "I hope to make it a habit—walking in the opposite direction of the saloons, that is. Not the lurking outside your kitchen door."

Jennie set the pie tins in the sink, shrugged out of her apron, and moved to hang it on a hook by the door. "You needn't lurk, Mr. Manning. You are welcome in my kitchen any time." She waggled another apron hanging beside hers. "Just be prepared to help."

"You can't intimidate me with the threat of an apron," Charlie said. "I wear one every day at the *Register*." He looked over at her. "Although if I'm to work in your kitchen, you'll have to call me *Charlie*."

"Then I suppose you'll need to call me *Jennie*."

Charlie gave an odd little salute and departed. The sun was up by the time he returned home—by way of the mercantile, where he delivered a message from Jennie about her needing enough rhubarb for two pies and would Birdie save some back.

Jennie, not *Mrs. Wilcox*.

Charlie instead of *Mr. Manning*.

How about that.

Chapter 23

*Put on therefore, as the elect of God ... kindness,
humbleness of mind, meekness, longsuffering; forbearing
one another, and forgiving one another ...*
Colossians 3:12-13

As work at the cemetery progressed, Isobel and Jennie discovered more than a few discrepancies between what they saw before them and what had been recorded by former sextants. Triangular and even trapezoidal grave plots added to the challenge. Inevitably, when Isobel was most frustrated, Jennie came to the rescue by deciphering the plot map or helping to discern faded names or dates.

Jennie knew quite a bit about those laid to rest on the hillside. When Isobel noted that Andrew Jessen had died just the previous year, Jennie mentioned his surviving wife, Margaret, who'd been Nebraska City's first schoolteacher. Widowed, she now operated the family farm. Cynthia A. French was foster mother to Caroline Morton, wife of the well-known J. Sterling Morton.

"Foster mother." Isobel said, inviting more information, but Jennie didn't know more. "Mrs. Morton's name seems to come up a good deal in conversation about civic projects."

"She's always been a quiet, but generous benefactor of many good causes."

"Do you think she'd be interested in supporting our efforts here at Wyuka?"

"I wouldn't be surprised," Jennie said, "if the right person raised the subject in the right way."

"Meaning?"

"Birdie should make the appeal. And don't mention it in Mother Bishop's hearing."

"Why not?"

Jennie shook her head. "Just don't. Old wounds."

Clearly, Jennie was not going to say any more. Which Isobel supposed was to her credit. "Charlie intended to drive me past their home yesterday after church, but we didn't end up going that far."

"The orchards are blooming. It's a sight to behold."

Isobel filed away what she'd learned about Mrs. Morton. She and Jennie made good progress on the project, and soon, by mutual consent, they were *Isobel* and *Jennie* instead of *Miss Manning* and *Mrs. Wilcox*. At midday, as Isobel wrote *Calvin Chapman – Second Nebraska Cavalry,* Jennie mentioned that before the war, Mr. Chapman was rumored to have escorted runaway slaves from Nebraska to Iowa back in the 1850s.

"Runaway slaves?" Isobel looked up in surprise. "From Nebraska? I didn't think—"

"At least two of the early settlers brought slaves with them," Jennie said. "Freddie told me about it. I honestly don't know much beyond that. Mr. Chapman was helping runaways from Missouri. They'd cross over into Nebraska, and Mr. Chapman and other abolitionists—like the Mayhews, who donated the land for this cemetery—helped, either by hiding them or by transporting them on to Iowa."

"Is anyone making a record of such things?" Isobel asked. "I mean a written record."

"I've no idea," Jennie said. "Mother Bishop says the part about helping runaways is all rumors, but I'm inclined to think it may well be true. Mrs. Mayhew's brother was one of the supporters of John Brown who died at Harper's Ferry."

"Someone should be writing down all of this before everyone who knows the truth passes away. Before people forget."

Jennie gazed toward her husband's grave marker. "It'd be nice to think people wouldn't forget—not just family, but others, too. My Freddie wasn't important compared to abolitionists and war heroes, but he was a good husband."

"And he always brought you daisies," Isobel said.

"You remembered!" Jennie's voice wavered. "I wish there was a way we could remember only the good."

Isobel put a hand on the young widow's arm.

"I'll be all right," Jennie said. "I was just remembering—well, some things I wish could be different. Things I wish I'd done better."

"Regret seems to be part of being human, doesn't it."

Jennie nodded. "And some of us have more to regret than others."

"I can't imagine you have too much of that," Isobel said, trying to cheer her up. "You're one of the kindest people I've ever met."

Jennie shook her head. "You wouldn't say that if you knew how I was after Freddie passed. Still am, sometimes—especially with Mother Bishop."

Still trying to help Jennie feel better, Isobel said, "It's hard living in a house ruled by a difficult older woman. Your mother-in-law reminds me a lot of my stepmother. Truth be told, when it comes to interacting, I suspect you're an angel compared to me." Isobel began to talk about Mother Manning. "I suppose she was a good enough wife to our father, but Charlie and I always felt like we were in the way. He escaped by enlisting in a local regiment. I eventually found activities that created a truce of sorts between us, but I never really felt I belonged in that house. To be honest, I think the only thing I ever did that Mother Manning approved of was getting engaged to the son of a prominent family. She was delighted by that bit of news and planned a lavish wedding. But then my fiancé failed to materialize on the wedding day and—"

"He—w-what?"

With a wry smile and a nod, Isobel explained. She even mentioned Mary Halifax. "And so here I am. I left St. Louis to avoid hearing the gossip. But it was more than that. I was desperate to escape Mother Manning's disapproval." She paused. "Never once did I think about *her*—about how I was leaving her alone to deal with the aftermath of that awful day." She took a deep breath. "So whatever failings you're blaming yourself for, Jennie, you haven't run away. What's more, I've never heard *you* say a negative word about your mother-in-law—even when she practically labeled you a lunatic at our first society meeting." *Lunatic.* Had she really just said that? She hurried to apologize. "Oh, Jennie, I am *so* sorry I didn't mean—"

Jennie held up a hand to stay Isobel's apology. "It's all right. Some might say that Mother Bishop had a point when she said those things."

The acceptance rankled. Isobel stood firm. "There is nothing lunatic about suffering melancholy after a terrible loss. But here you are again, making my point. Defending your mother-in-law when all I've done is complain about Mother Manning."

Jennie looked down at the list of names in her hand as she murmured, almost as if to herself, "All this time, I assumed you were visiting Charlie because *he* needed *you*." She looked up at Isobel. "We have more in common than I imagined." She paused, and then said, "Mother Bishop *is* difficult—even harsh with me at times. But she has her reasons." And then it was Jennie's turn to tell an incredible tale.

Isobel listened in stunned disbelief. *Peach brandy. A private nurse. A sanitarium.*

Jennie's voice trembled as she finished her story. "Not only did I fail to grieve *with* them, I created even more heartache. They could have cast me out, but they didn't. They gave me a home, and when I needed help, they saw that I received it." She paused. "No amount of baking for church suppers will ever repay what Mother and Pa Bishop have done for me. So if—*when*—Mother Bishop has moments when she's—*outspoken*—I give grace—with God's help."

For a long moment, Isobel was silent.

Jennie sighed. "I h-hope knowing all of that about me doesn't ruin any chance of our being friends." She lifted her chin and met Isobel's gaze. "I don't drink anymore. *Ever.* I don't even cook with wine, and I would never do anything to lure Charlie—or anyone—back to—"

"Goodness," Isobel interrupted, "that concern never entered my mind. Truth be told, you might be in a unique position to help Charlie." She paused. "But I suppose it would be unfair to expect it—I mean, for it to work, he'd have to know about *your* past, and I don't suppose you'd want that. Not after the Bishops have gone to such lengths to protect your reputation." *Wonderful. First you use the word* lunatic *and now you mention how her past could ruin her reputation. Sadly, that was a possibility. Drinking too much might be glossed over in a man, but a woman having the problem was entirely another matter.*

"It's a relief to hear you say you won't hold my past against me."

"Hold it against you? If anything, it makes me admire you. It also gives me hope for Charlie."

Jennie smiled. "We all have hope for Charlie." She blushed furiously and returned to the subject at hand. "If you decide to do more than simply transcribe what's on the tombstones, I'd like to contribute something about Freddie. It would please Mother and Pa Bishop so much."

Isobel looked over the hillside, contemplating the dozens of markers, each one witness to a life that played a role in the scheme of history here on the banks of the Missouri River. This, she realized, was the true West. Alfred never would have discovered it, because he was too caught up in stories of fame and fortune. *The true West. True history. Witnesses. Write it down before it's forgotten.* "You know, Jennie," Isobel murmured, "you may have hit on something that could make our cemetery project even more meaningful to people—and garner more support for improvement." She paused. "What if we invited stories about everyday life—how people lived before Nebraska became a state? After all, that was only last year."

"What would you do with them?"

"Publish them." Isobel's mind whirred with possibilities. "Sell subscriptions to the collection. Use the proceeds to fund a fence or to have a well dug, for example. Wouldn't it be wonderful if sales supported everything the society has proposed?"

"Publish a book?" Jennie sounded incredulous.

"Why not? We already know a printer. I doubt it would take much convincing to get Charlie to do it."

"But can he? I mean—I've seen the presses, but isn't more equipment required to produce a book?"

"I don't know. But it'll be easy to find out. Assuming the ladies think it's a good idea."

Jennie grinned. "Are you quite certain you aren't related to Birdie Tanner?"

Isobel didn't mind the comparison. "So what do you think? Is it a good idea?"

"Better than good. Brilliant. I'm quite certain Birdie will want you to bring it up at the next society meeting. But first—" Jennie pointed at the next gravestone to be transcribed.

Isobel nodded and dipped her pen in the crystal inkwell that was part of her travel desk. "Ready."

Jennie read. "'Sacred to the memory of Gabriel Long...'"

Chapter 24

For thus saith the Lord God;
Behold, I, even I, will both search my sheep, and seek them out.
Ezekiel 34:11

A red bandana. Today? It's only Thursday. Gideon and Trouble had been trotting along the creek, making their way back home after a fruitless hunting expedition, when a flash of red drew Gideon's attention to the blackberry bramble at the edge of the cemetery. He hesitated for a moment. Wasn't a red bandana supposed to signal the conclusion of the cemetery project? Miss Manning couldn't have finished yet. He'd caught a glimpse of her and her helper late yesterday, and they were only halfway down the hill to the road. The red bandana made no sense.

Slowly, he climbed the creek bank. It was late in the day, but he still took care to keep the blackberry thicket between himself and the cemetery until he was certain Miss Manning and her helper had departed. Even so, he was quick about snatching the bandana away and sliding back down the steep embankment. When Trouble took it for a game and tried to grab the bandana away, Gideon scolded the dog.

"Leave it! It's not a game. There's something inside." He untied the knot. *A letter.* His heartbeat ratcheted up as he skimmed the first few lines. *I called out... Logic argues against the notion...*

He looked toward town. *I was there. I heard you.* For a moment he stood motionless, remembering how he'd hunkered down, peering through the tall grass, listening as she spoke aloud. What had inspired her to do such a thing?

He startled when a steamboat whistle drifted up from the river. Trouble whimpered and thrust a wet nose into Gideon's palm. Gideon nodded. "You're right. We need to get moving." Stuffing the bandana in one pocket and the letter in another, he and the dog trotted toward home.

Back at the cabin, Gideon tossed Trouble a bone. Daylight was fading, and so Gideon lit a lamp before sitting down to read.

You were very kind to return my bonnet. I had considered it lost—trampled into oblivion or blown away by a prairie zephyr. But there it was, waiting to be discovered yesterday morning, when I arrived to begin the Ladies Cemetery Improvement Society project. We are creating as accurate a record as we can of the cemetery. Perhaps you know this.

I do.

I can imagine Birdie and Henry might have mentioned it.

They did.

On the subject of privacy—I believe I know who you are. Not your name, of course—but I think I saw you leaving the mercantile last Saturday. It was the morning my brother and I joined Henry and Birdie and a few others here at the cemetery in preparation for the upcoming Decoration Day. I don't think you saw me, but later, something Henry said led me to think that the mercantile customer and my rescuer were one and the same.

Something Henry said? Gideon wanted to believe that whatever it was, it was unintentional. After all, Henry had given his word. Carefully, Gideon reread what she'd said. She hadn't realized that *he* saw *her* Saturday morning. He continued reading.

Yesterday morning, when I found the bonnet, I called out to you—imagining you just out of sight, listening.

I was there. I heard every word.

I promised that, on the day Jennie and I finish, I would tie a red bandana on the bushes where I hitch my rig. For some reason, I thought you'd appreciate knowing there wouldn't be people in the cemetery after a certain point—excepting for Decoration Day, of course. Do you know about the plans for this Saturday?

I am aware.

It is the impetus for the activity at Wyuka. If you are reading this unorthodox communication, please know that I placed the red bandana early. We have not quite finished, but I decided to try and contact you this way. If the bandana is gone when I return tomorrow, I will know it has been found and that this mode of communication will be a satisfactory signal that our transcribing has been completed. Even as I write this, I realize that I could simply send a message via Birdie Tanner. But you did not return my bonnet in that most logical manner, and so I follow your example, even though I am not quite certain as to why.

Should you determine to assign a descriptor to the author of this missive, I beg you to reject <u>eccentric</u> and settle for a gentler word... <u>grateful</u>. As indeed I am, both for your kindness and bravery to me individually and for the sacrifice you made in the name of freedom during the rebellion.

I remain in your debt,
Miss Isobel Manning

P.S. I wish I knew your name.

Gideon looked up from the missive. *If you knew my name, you wouldn't want to have anything to do with me. Especially if you've heard from Wade Inskeep.* Perhaps others believed the lie as well. It was impossible to know how many people had heard Inskeep's version of things.

An owl hooted. Trouble gnawed his bone. And Gideon sat quietly, trying to decide how he felt about it all.

❦

Isobel admitted defeat on Friday morning when she met Charlie at Lila's Café for breakfast. "We've worked hard, but Jennie and I aren't going to be able to finish the cemetery survey before tomorrow."

"No one's going to fault you," Charlie said. "You took on more than originally planned when you decided to transcribe the information on the tombstones."

"I know, but it seemed necessary if—"

Charlie held up a hand to interrupt. "I'm not criticizing. Your reasons are sound and the community will benefit." He took a sip of coffee just as Lila's son, Sam, slid a stack of pancakes before him. Charlie asked for elderberry syrup, and Sam went to fetch it.

"We might have come close," Isobel said, "but Jennie's up to her ears in baking for tomorrow's luncheon counter, so I'll be on my own today. Although she was kind enough to promise a picnic lunch if I'd drop by on my way out of town and pick it up." Sam brought the syrup and for a brief moment, Isobel and Charlie concentrated on spreading butter and pouring syrup.

The boy had refilled their coffee cups and stepped away when Charlie said, "It's too bad you don't have anyone else to step in."

Isobel nodded agreement. "Birdie would, but she and Henry still have a great deal to do at the mercantile. The awning needs repairs before they can even set up the lunch counter. Birdie wants to make a poster listing the things the society would like to accomplish at Wyuka. Teddy's helping Sarah put the finishing touches on wreaths. Everyone has something much more important to do today."

Charlie popped a forkful of pancakes in his mouth and pointed to himself while he chewed. "What about me?"

"Y-you?" Isobel faltered. "What about the *Register?*"

"I'm saving the front page to report on Nebraska City's Decoration Day festivities. It'll take Edgar the better part of the day to typeset the middle pages we've planned. He can mind the office while he does that. I don't need to be there until it's ready for proofreading. Plus, it'll give us the opportunity to talk about an idea I've been mulling over." He took a sip of coffee.

"What idea?"

"All in good time, Busy Izzy," Charlie teased, "all in good time."

Charlie had not yet arrived at the livery when Isobel learned the chestnut mare was already loaned out. "But I told you I'd want her every day this week," she protested. "I need a rig for the day, and after my first experience with that gray gelding—"

Roy Daniels, the livery owner, raised both hands in protest. "Now hold on. I didn't know that horse was crazy when I let you have him. And I said I was sorry about what happened. You'll be glad to know the son of a ... gun ... is long gone. Probably turned into a nice, tanned hide by now."

Tanned hide? Isobel just stared at the man. *He wouldn't really do such a thing, would he?*

Daniels must have noted the look of horror on her face. "Now don't get the epizootics, miss. I didn't mean it. Fact is, I don't know what happened to him exactly, but I knew I couldn't trust him, so I moved him out. There's half a dozen other well-broke horses waiting for something to do today. You can have your pick." He led the way to the back of the lot.

Isobel hurried after him. "*My* pick? I'll be expecting a little more guidance than that, Mr. Daniels." At the sound of a low whicker, she looked toward the horses. A sway-backed, spotted gray standing alone had lifted its head and looked her way.

The livery owner began to laugh. "Guess the 'ugly duckling' wants a job."

Ugly was certainly the right word. Irregular gray and black splotches on a pale ground made the poor thing look like she'd wandered under a painter's ladder and been bombarded with random spills. Her head was too big, her neck too thin. Her mane and straggly tail were little more than random hanks of white, black, and gray. No ribs showed, so the mare wasn't underfed, but her hip bones protruded from her flanks. And she was swaybacked. When the poor creature reached the fence, she thrust her head over the top pole and snuffled at the traveling desk in Isobel's arms. Isobel took a step back. The horse whickered and pressed against the pole, as if trying to follow her.

Daniels cleared his throat. "There's no chance in he—um—no chance this old gal will give you any trouble. Haven't seen her show a lick of spirit since the folks that owned her moved out two days ago. Said she was too old to walk to Oregon. Wanted to sell her, but I wasn't going to throw good money away. Then a gal with 'em set to carrying on something terrible about leavin' 'her Elsie' behind. The pa slipped me a dollar. Guess I'm just soft-hearted. After that, what could I do? Don't mean to keep her, but if you want her for the day, I can guarantee she won't give you any trouble."

Charlie appeared in the doorway that led into the stable. Frowning, he said to Daniels, "Don't tell me you're trying to rent my sister that nag."

"The horse heard the lady's voice, lifted her head and hustled across the corral to say hello." Daniels scratched his ear. "Now that I think on it, could be Miss Manning, here, sounds a bit like the girl who was cryin' about leavin' her." He shrugged. "Anyway, the horse started it."

Charlie spoke to Isobel. "You had a horse reserved."

"Yes, and Mr. Daniels, here, rented it to someone else." Again, the horse whickered. Isobel shifted her travel desk, freeing one hand. She held it out, palm flat. The horse snuffled it, clearly expecting a treat. Isobel wished she had one. "Poor thing," she murmured, reaching up to pat the light splotch between the mare's dark eyes.

Daniels focused on Charlie. "We're looking over the rest of 'em to pick the best." He pointed at a gigantic black horse. "Personally, I'd say the Shire. He'll plod along like what he is—a plow horse." He waved the coiled rope in his hand at the ugly mare. "You git, now."

When the horse refused to budge, Daniels ducked into the corral. When he waved both hands at the horse, she rolled her eyes at him but didn't move. Pushing against the mare's side and flank, the impatient livery owner launched into a stream of language that made Isobel blush. Again, he mentioned the tanning of hides.

Isobel protested. "You wouldn't, would you?"

"Wouldn't what?"

"Do away with her." The mare lowered her head. Isobel stroked the velvety muzzle as she murmured, "No one deserves to be rejected just because she isn't beautiful." She looked over at the livery owner. "You said the girl's father gave you a dollar to take the horse?"

The man nodded. "That's right."

"I'll give you two."

Chapter 25

*Yea, mine own familiar friend, in whom I trusted,
which did eat of my bread, hath lifted up his heel against me.*
Psalm 41:9

Charlie didn't protest when the owner of Brown's Livery quoted the cost of boarding Izzy's two-dollar mare in a box stall. But while Brown retrieved harness to hitch the mare to a rented buggy, he just had to say something. "Are you sure about this?" He gestured about them. "Granted, it's nicer than the other livery, but—"

"You saw the way Mr. Daniels treated Elsie," Izzy said, "an animal he knew had been abandoned by someone she loved. All because Elsie's—"

She refused to say the word they were both thinking. Poor Elsie was *ugly*.

Izzy held one hand up to keep him from arguing. "And before you make the obvious reference to someone else who was abandoned because she wasn't beautiful—don't."

"I have no idea what you're talking about," Charlie said with overplayed sincerity. "If you want to rescue a horse and board it in luxury, that's entirely your business."

Izzy nodded. "Exactly. I'm happy to hear you say it."

When the ugly mare once again thrust her head at her and whickered, Charlie teased, "Well, at least she has good manners. She knows when to say thank you."

Izzy stroked the mare's scrawny neck. "Of course she does. She's a sweetheart." She directed the next comment to the horse. "Aren't you?"

When the mare bobbed its head, Charlie laughed. In moments, Elsie the Ugly Mare was hitched and Charlie was driving toward Wyuka. Rescuing the horse had put Izzy in a good mood. As they crossed the bridge over Table Creek, she waxed poetic about the endless sky and the sea of grass stretching away toward the horizon.

"It does put a man in his place," Charlie said.

"I keep wondering about the women who climb aboard those wagons heading west. Are they frightened? Do they want to go?" Izzy shook her head. "Albert droned on and on for hours about 'finding the true West' and writing about it. If he ever *had* found it, I don't think he would have known what to do with it. Unless, of course, he had servants to make camp, cook for him, and clean his boots every night." She shuddered. "You couldn't pay me enough to take on that journey."

"Free land is a powerful promise. Remember hearing about the Homestead Act a few years back?"

"Yes but benefitting from it means leaving behind everything familiar." Izzy shuddered.

Charlie glanced over at her. "*You* left everything familiar to come west."

She sputtered denial. "*I* came to visit my brother. Outfitted with a trunk full of ball gowns if you can imagine that." She gave a low laugh. "You should have seen the look on Miss Bennett's face that first night when I asked if she'd have the maid fetch and clean my skirt and boots."

Charlie joined the laughter as he guided the rig into the cemetery and up the hill. When he'd helped Izzy down, she unfurled a blanket beneath the burr oak tree and sat down to organize her supplies. He tended the horse, and soon they were ready to record information from the first stone on the list.

"*1855?*" Izzy's voice sounded wonder as she echoed the date. She looked toward town. "What did they see when they crossed the river? What changes did they witness before passing?"

"You haven't gotten your fill of Nebraska City history yet?"

"Not even close," Izzy said. "Transcribing all these stones has raised countless questions. In fact, yesterday Jennie and I—"

"Uh-oh," Charlie interrupted.

"Uh-oh what?"

"I know that tone. Here comes a Busy Izzy idea."

Izzy glared at him. "*Jennie* called it 'brilliant.' She said I should talk with Birdie about it right away, but since it might affect you, I thought I should talk to you about it first."

"What do you mean, 'it *might* affect me?'" If he wasn't worrying about her, he was wishing she'd leave—or stay. Nearly every decision he'd made since Izzy arrived was affected by her presence. Never mind the telegrams Mother Manning sent every few days demanding he do something to "bring your sister to her senses." Izzy was talking. He'd better pay attention. It *might affect him.* And Jennie thought the idea *brilliant.* He'd been so distracted he had to ask Izzy to repeat what she'd just said.

"You weren't listening," she accused.

There was no point in denying that. She knew him well. "I'm sorry." He shuffled the stack of papers he'd been using as a guide, pressing them to his chest with crossed arms. "There. I'll do better. Tell me your brilliant idea."

Izzy glowered at him. "Don't make light of it."

"Since I don't know what *it* is, I can hardly be making light of it. Please. Go on."

Izzy spoke of collecting early settler's stories and using a resulting book to raise money for cemetery improvements. "We could sell subscriptions," she said as she concluded. When Charlie didn't respond right away, she cocked her head. "Well? What do *you* think? Is it a good idea? Would you print it?"

Ah. So that's how it might affect him. "I'd be willing to consider it—assuming you don't want a hard binding. Even then, I'll probably need to purchase at least one piece of equipment. But that discussion can wait. There's another more important question to be answered first." This was going to be easier than he'd anticipated.

"What's that?"

"It's a big undertaking. Are you prepared to see it through?"

She fidgeted as she had as a child when a topic made her uncomfortable. And, as she had then, she didn't answer the question directly. "I didn't say I wanted to *do* it myself. I'm supposed to be leaving as soon as this cemetery survey is completed. It's only something for the committee to consider. If they think it's worthwhile, someone will step forward to oversee it."

He nodded. "I see." She might not realize it, but the two of them had just taken a few steps down the same path. He was surprisingly happy about that. "But if you stay in Nebraska, they won't need someone else. You could take it on. In fact, I'd say you're the perfect person to do it."

Izzy looked doubtful. "I'm not trying to convince you to change your mind about wanting me in Nebraska."

"There's no need to convince me. No need at all. In fact, I want you to stay. You may not realize it, but you have a knack for the newspaper business. I'd welcome your help with the *Register*." He grinned. "Assuming, of course, that you can squeeze me in between society business and writing a book."

"But—you didn't want me to come at all. And you certainly didn't want me to *stay*."

Charlie nodded. "True. But having you back in my life has been very good for me. I'd like to think Nebraska's been good for you, too." Her eyes filled with tears. She gulped. Nodded. He produced a handkerchief, which she took.

Dabbing at her tears, she croaked, "Y-you really want me to stay?"

Charlie nodded. "Much to my amazement, I do."

"Then I will," she croaked.

He cleared his throat. "Talk to Birdie about your book idea when we get back to town. If she's as enthusiastic as I think she will be—it really is brilliant, by the way—I'll introduce you to some of the old settler's tomorrow after the ceremony. I imagine they'll be thrilled to meet someone interested in their stories. Especially someone in the newspaper business."

※

On Decoration Day Isobel rose before dawn. She dressed by lamplight—the blue plaid today—and pinned on the red, white, and blue rosette Sarah Carter had made for the members of the Ladies Cemetery Improvement Society. She smiled at herself in the mirror. *I'll be a bona fide member. A citizen of Nebraska. Charlie asked me to stay. He asked.* Happy tears threatened.

Looking out the window toward the east, she wondered what the citizens of St. Louis were planning for Decoration Day. Would Mother Manning participate? Would Alfred? *Alfred. And little Mary Halifax.* She pondered the names with the dawning realization that the pain once associated with them had transformed. That transformation made her willing to extend something like what Jennie had called *grace* when she'd talked about dealing with her mother-in-law. In fact, Isobel thought, instead of sending an abrupt telegram about her decision to remain in Nebraska City, she would write a letter. Mother Manning would not welcome the news that she could no longer command her stepdaughter's life, however said news arrived. But a letter would be a sign of respect. An attempt to give grace.

Her toilette accomplished, Isobel descended to the lobby and strode out of the hotel with confidence. By the time she neared the Bishop manse, dawn was lighting the sky and Ezra Carter was leading Jezebel up to Jennie's kitchen door. Together, the women nestled an impressive array of baked goods into straw. Mr. Carter led Jezebel toward Tanner Mercantile, with Jennie and Isobel following on foot. As they walked, Isobel told her friend about Charlie's invitation to stay in Nebraska and work at the newspaper.

"Tell me you said *yes*," Jennie pleaded.

"I said yes."

Jennie gave a whoop of joy and pulled Isobel into a hug. A few moments later at the mercantile, Birdie introduced Isobel as the newest permanent member of the Ladies Cemetery Improvement Society. Spontaneous applause welcomed her.

Charlie arrived with the day's special edition of the *Register*. On the front page a two-column-wide schedule outlined the day's festivities. As expected, he'd eschewed donning his uniform. He'd already told Isobel not to expect it, that he'd be too busy in the newspaper office that morning to participate as a veteran. Almost as an afterthought, he'd said that he had yet to join the local G.A.R. post. Isobel hadn't pressed the matter. Whatever Charlie's reasons, she would respect his decision.

Placing copies of the *Register* on a counter, Charlie hastened to help Henry set up two long tables beneath the awning outside. Jennie took charge of arranging cakes and pies, sandwiches and biscuits, while others worked out the details of serving.

Isobel did more observing than helping at first, and yet she did not feel like an outsider. Charlie had been right about the ladies' reaction to the news that Isobel was staying in Nebraska.

More importantly he seemed genuinely pleased. It was as if a weight had been lifted. No longer would she live beneath the cloud of Mother Manning's disapproval. No longer would she be *the jilted spinster, poor thing.* Life was good.

Nebraska City had dressed for the day. Flags flew. Windows sported bunting. Red, white, and blue ribbons spilled out of flowerpots. After the wagon trains lining Main Street departed for the west, a team of citizens cleared steaming piles of manure, loading hand carts and wheeling them out of sight. Little by little, the streets filled again with all manner of conveyances, many decorated with bunting and ribbons, wildflowers and prairie grasses.

At mid-morning, the Nebraska City cornet band took up a position on a hastily constructed bandstand not far from the mercantile. Business at the luncheon counter picked up. Music filled the air, and to the tune of the "Battle Hymn of the Republic" over a dozen uniformed men marched up Main. Once they reached the bandstand and finished a rousing version of "Battle Cry of Freedom," they broke ranks. Most ended up at the society lunch counter, consuming vast amounts of cake and pie in the name of supporting a good cause.

By noon the once heavily laden table was nearly bare. Jennie and Isobel carried the few remaining items inside while Henry and Charlie took down the tables. Birdie was hanging a sign on the door that read *Attending ceremony at Wyuka Cemetery. Back at 2:00 p.m.* when a wagon pulled up to the front door. The ladies offered appreciative *oohs* and *aahs.* Someone had outdone themselves, draping bunting about the wagon sides and wiring flowers along every wheel spoke. Isobel didn't recognize the driver, but the Bishops' rig followed. When Jennie went out to greet them, Mrs. Bishop leaned down to say something as she gestured at the wagon. Jennie's face beamed with joy as she announced that her in-laws had hired a conveyance to transport the Ladies Cemetery Improvement Society to Wyuka in style.

With the cornet band's wagon in the lead, a stream of conveyances proceeded to the cemetery. The Ladies Cemetery Improvement Society came third. Someone had draped bunting on the tombstones marking graves where wreaths would be laid. By the time everyone was parked, wagons and buggies lined the cemetery paths and spilled out onto the road. A speaker's stand consisting of an upturned box had been placed at the base of the burr oak tree.

As the ceremony began, Isobel took Charlie's arm, grateful for his presence and his willingness to murmur names as various citizens took part in the ceremony. When Mayor Dickey introduced the speaker, Isobel got her first glimpse of the Honorable J. Sterling Morton, his wife, Caroline, and their young sons. When Isobel murmured a request that Charlie introduce her to Mrs. Morton as soon as the ceremony concluded, he nodded assent.

Applause for Mr. Morton's speech had not entirely died down when the cornet band struck up a solemn version of "Battle Hymn of the Republic." After a prayer offered by Reverend Huber of the First Evangelical Lutheran Church, it was time for the laying of the wreaths. The members of the G.A.R. had obviously practiced for this event, for they marched smartly to the grave closest to the speaker's dais and formed a circle around the grave. The Post Commander gave the order and the men snapped to attention, holding a smart salute as the Officer of the Day announced in brisk tones, "Private John W. Dorsey, Indiana Militia, War of 1812." A couple walked slowly forward and placed a wreath at the foot of the marker.

The solemn ritual was repeated at each veteran's grave. Mrs. Oliver and her sister placed the wreath honoring Chaplain Oliver. Mr. Bishop did the honors at Freddie Wilcox's grave, with Jennie and her mother-in-law looking on. Tears welled up as Isobel thought about Jennie's loss—and her victory over consuming grief. Whatever information Jennie wanted preserved about Freddie Wilcox, Isobel would see that it was done.

Everything went smoothly—until it didn't, at the grave of Private Gideon Long.

Chapter 26

...I have learned, in whatsoever state I am, therewith to be content.
Philippians 4:11

The solemn ritual at Private Gideon Long's grave began with the veterans forming a circle and standing at attention, as had been done at every other grave in the cemetery. But when Private Long's name was read aloud, every single man took a step back and clasped his hands behind him, refusing to salute.

What on earth? Isobel looked over at a frowning Charlie. An obviously upset Birdie stepped forward and placed a wreath at the grave. She glared at each of the veterans. Most dropped their gaze, but one stared back at her with what Isobel could only interpret as thinly veiled animosity. Goosebumps prickled. She tightened her grip on Charlie's arm, taking comfort in his presence, thankful that Henry had quickly moved to Birdie's side. As they stepped away from the grave, one of the veterans reached over, ripped the bunting off the marker, wadded it up, and threw it in the grass.

Furious, Birdie moved to pick it up, but Henry stayed her, his hand on her arm. She obviously wanted to pull away, but then Henry murmured something, and she relented. When the bugler began to play "Taps," she marched away, past the decorated wagons, down the hill, and toward the road.

A wave of unease rippled across the crowd. Murmurs circulated. As Isobel and Charlie walked back to the society's decorated wagon, Mrs. Oliver bemoaned the veterans' behavior. After all, she said, one couldn't be certain the rumors were true. Mrs. Bishop opined that Birdie should have known something like this would happen.

Henry waited quietly for the ladies to gather at the wagon before saying, "Birdie and I are going to walk back to town. Don't forget, we have refreshments waiting at the mercantile."

"Perhaps we shouldn't intrude," Jennie said.

"She'll be glad for the company once she's walked off her anger. Please come. It'll do her good to have friends about." He hurried to catch up with his wife.

Awkward silence reigned for much of the ride back to town. Keeping his voice low, Charlie said, "That was Wade Inskeep tearing the bunting off the stone. He came into the newspaper office the day you and Edgar handed out the flyers about the cemetery project. Claimed to have seen Long run off during a battle. Called him a *deserting coward*. He ended with a threat about what might happen if someone tried to put a wreath at the grave."

Isobel met his gaze. "Did you tell Birdie about that?"

"Of course."

"And she went ahead with it anyway?"

"Birdie said she would do right by her friend Grace Long and Grace's son, no matter what anyone thought."

The wagon had clattered across the bridge before Isobel spoke again. When she did, it was to ask a question. "Wouldn't there be official reports of something like that—of the desertion, I mean?"

"Probably."

"Is Birdie the only one who doesn't believe it?"

"It would appear so—after what happened today. No one rose to Long's defense."

"What would it take to learn the truth?"

"I'm not sure."

"We should look into it."

Charlie didn't answer right away. "And what if we learn that Inskeep is right?"

"What if he's wrong and a man's name has been slandered for no good reason? Whatever happened, the community—and especially Birdie—deserve to know."

By early evening on Decoration Day, Trouble was pacing about the cabin like a caged tiger. Gideon was calmer, having spent the day with Ma's Bible and a leather-bound notebook he'd procured from the mercantile. Like many Union soldiers, he'd kept a journal while serving. But his journal, along with everything else in his haversack, including the Bible gifted him by the Christian Commission, was lost when he was wounded.

Recently, Gideon had taken up writing again. This time, though, he wasn't recording daily events. Instead, he'd plunged into God's Word in a desperate search to understand why God had allowed him to think he'd been called to preach and then taken away the possibility. His writing had become a kind of conversation with God. He hadn't discovered answers to his questions yet, but time in the Bible calmed him, and so he kept at it. He'd even taken to tucking the notebook in his coat pocket so that, wherever he was, he could ruminate, pencil in hand, Trouble at his side.

Trouble. Insistent. Whining. Pacing. Panting. Finally, the dog's restlessness won out. Closing the notebook and laying down his pen, Gideon scooted back and slapped his thigh to summon the dog. He responded, and Gideon took the dog's battered head between his hands. "Sorry, boy. I know it's hard, but

I can't have you wandering until I'm sure they're all finished at the cemetery." He glanced out the window, judging the time by the length of shadows. "It won't be long, now."

The dog grew still, listening, watching Gideon's face. Gideon chuckled. If it were possible for a dog to understand human speech, this one did. "You're a good dog," he said, stroking the broad head. When Trouble lowered his head, Gideon smiled at the unspoken request, digging his fingers into the animal's fur and scrubbing his way down the topline all the way to the feathery tail. Motionless, Trouble soaked in the attention, but the moment Gideon stopped the massage, the dog thrust its snout into his palm and whined, then looked at the cabin door and back again.

"Not yet," he said. "Soon, but not yet."

With a deep sigh, the dog retreated to the door and sank down, head resting on his paws, watching. Waiting.

Gideon shook his head. "You're a stubborn son-of-a-gun, aren't you." He sat back, remembering that day in Missouri when he'd encountered what he thought was a carcass covered with mud, a deep gash across its head, part of an ear missing. He didn't want a dog, but the thing wasn't dead yet, and he couldn't leave it to suffer.

Before touching the suffering creature, Gideon crouched down and muttered, "Just my luck to come across a blue-eyed, long-haired, tail-thumping ball of trouble. You'll probably bite me the minute I put my hand on you. I'll get rabies and die."

As it happened, the dog didn't bite. Instead, it licked Gideon's hand. Of course, that was all it took. And now, the man who hadn't wanted a dog not only had a dog but a good one. Trouble had proven easy to train, even when it came to basic hand signals. He was a good companion, with simple basic needs and—

Gideon frowned. *Basic needs.* Was that it? Did the dog need to answer nature's call? "Sorry boy," he said aloud. "Guess it's been a good long while since we came inside." The moment he rose from the chair, the dog leaped to his feet, bouncing up and down, one front paw, then the other, back and forth. The second Gideon opened the door, Trouble darted out of sight. A moment later, he raced back into view from around the corner of the cabin, planted his paws, and let out a sharp, insistent bark.

"Sssst! No!" He knew better than to do that. *No barking* was one of the first things they'd worked on—the first thing that had convinced Gideon he had a smart, tractable animal who would be a good companion.

Intending to repeat the hiss and sweep his arms toward the door to signal Trouble into the cabin, Gideon hesitated. *Smoke?* He inhaled again, wondering about the source. Trouble whirled about, danced in Gideon's direction and then returned to the west corner of the cabin. Back and forth, back and forth, he moved, not barking, but letting out odd little yips.

When the dog once again disappeared around the corner of the cabin, Gideon followed. Trouble stopped halfway up the wooded hillside and repeated the odd little dance. "All right, boy, all right." Judging by the light, things were probably finished up at the cemetery.

Fetching his notebook and a pencil—he might check the snares but didn't plan on hunting—Gideon went after the dog, quickly aware that Trouble was leading him straight for the cemetery. Not a good idea. And yet—surely anyone who'd so much as lingered after the ceremony would be long gone by now. As it happened, he was a little curious about the wreaths Birdie had mentioned as part of her society's contribution to the day.

At the cemetery Trouble loped up the hill and disappeared from sight. Gideon followed, surprised when his path led into a swath of blackened grass. He stopped short at Gideon Long's grave. There was no bunting atop the stone as he'd seen on other veterans' markers. What had been a wreath was little more than blackened vines and ash. A low cry of emotion threatened to escape his lips. He cut if off by raising the back of his hand to his mouth. He stood motionless for a moment, surprised by the unexpected swell of emotion. Wondering why he cared about a pile of ashes and some burned grass.

Trouble was growling at something down in the creek bed. When Gideon ordered the dog to *leave it* and the dog obeyed, he slid to the earth and sat, thinking. *Someone was angry enough to burn that wreath. Likely Wade Inskeep. Why do I care?* Trouble trotted over and reclined next to him, and Gideon raked through the dog's thick fur. *It doesn't matter what people think happened. You're helping Tom's family.*

Wade Inskeep. The name launched Gideon into the past. Inskeep had been next to him in the grass, waiting for dawn to break over the battlefield near Shiloh Church, staring across the hollow where rebels were lined up. Inskeep on his right, Tom on his left. When the sun came up, they could see light glinting off the fieldpieces. Inskeep muttered against the expected order that would send them across that hollow in the face of those guns. But then General Wallace surprised them by ordering up two of his batteries instead of sending them into the fray. The cannon put on a good show, and the rebels retreated before the Nebraska boys were ordered forward. Down the slope before them and up again, they passed a disabled cannon that had taken a direct hit from Thompson's battery. A dead cannoneer lay there, too. Inskeep went pale as they passed by. In fact, he froze in place. Gideon and Tom moved forward into the fight. It was the last Gideon saw of Inskeep. Now, staring at the blackened grass and ruined wreath, he wondered how the rest of the war had treated the man who harbored hate enough to burn a memorial wreath.

It doesn't matter. Let it be. A passage of scripture came to mind. *I have learned, in whatsoever state I am, therewith to be content.*

Knowing what he did about the man who'd written those words—well.

He remembered the phrase *I know how to be abased.* Looking at the remains of a wreath was nothing compared to what the Apostle Paul had endured *for the cause of Christ.* Gideon took a deep breath. *You've suffered <u>nothing</u> for the cause of Christ. Stop feeling sorry for yourself. Learn to be content.*

Unbidden came the memory of the woman in blue. Miss Manning had nothing to do with what it seemed God had set before Gideon. She was, however, a distraction, thanks to two notes that had painted over his life with a sheen that emphasized how lonely he was. Whatever Miss Manning had intended, those notes had raised the notion that maybe he would, at some far distant moment, have a conversation with a human being about—anything, really. A human, not named *Tanner.* He realized now that the possibility had hovered at the edge of his consciousness, never taking a definite form and yet glimmering like a jewel in the distance. Now, confronted with what happened at the very mention of his name, the glimmer faded.

Learn to be content. Do the work God has provided. Help Tom's family.

Gideon spoke to Trouble. "Come on, boy. Let's go home." The dog knew the word *home.* As Gideon rose from the earth, Trouble bounded away, guided by instinct as shadows lengthened and darkness fell.

Gideon followed with new determination to embrace the night. To keep to the path God had ordained. To forget the woman in blue and to abandon any notion of contact with anyone beyond the owners of Tanner Mercantile. He would learn to be content. After writing one last missive.

Chapter 27

*...he that wavereth is like a wave of the sea
driven with the wind and tossed.*
James 1:6

Isobel and Jennie returned to the cemetery the Monday morning after Decoration Day, intent on making good progress in the transcribing of tombstones. As Elsie plodded up the hill and the scorched grass around a grave came into view, Isobel frowned. "That's Private Long's grave, isn't it?" Pulling Elsie to a halt, she hurried over, barely managing to suppress the profanity that sprung to her lips when she saw what had happened.

Jennie crouched down and began to brush ash off the stone. "Birdie will be heartbroken."

"And furious." Isobel grabbed the ruined wreath. Marching to the western edge of the grounds, she launched it onto the prairie, then led Elsie to the usual spot to be hitched. When she saw the red bandana tied to a branch, Isobel cast a guarded look in Jennie's direction, but Jennie was still working at Private Long's grave.

The moment she touched the bandana, Isobel realized it held a note. Her heart thumped, but there was no chance to read it now. Tucking it into a pocket, she hurried to retrieve her travel desk and the papers needed to guide their work. For the rest of the day, she thought of little else. Later in the day, when Charlie suggested they dine at Lila's, Isobel feigned a headache and retired without supper. The moment she'd closed her hotel room door, she hurried to a window to read.

> *Miss Manning,*
>
> *As there is no absolute necessity for me to frequent the countryside either around or near the cemetery, please do not feel it necessary to signal the conclusion of your project with another bandana. I am well practiced in avoiding unwelcome encounters. Moreover, thanks to Birdie and Henry Tanner, I have been well informed regarding the ladies' plans for the cemetery. I applaud said plans with the greatest enthusiasm.*
>
> *You are mistaken in your assumption that I was unaware of your presence when I exited the mercantile some days ago. I regret having startled you. I shall not repeat the error of seeking an exchange of goods in the early morning hours. It was reckless of me.*
>
> *I suppose it is understandable that the nature of our encounters would pique your curiosity. However, your knowing my name would serve no purpose, and therefore I respectfully decline the veiled request contained in the post script of your letter.*
>
> *I wish you well in your endeavors, even as I bid you goodbye.*
>
> *A Soldier*
>
> *P. S. Thank you for your part in Decoration Day. It is a sad truth that hostilities born during the rebellion may never die in the hearts and minds of some. I saw evidence of such when leaving this missive. I hope the ladies will not be discouraged by the vandalism but will continue their good work.*

Isobel sat back, note in hand. Disappointment surged. The soldier might have intended to bid her farewell, but the note only increased her curiosity about him. Expecting barely legible scratches, she'd encountered beautiful handwriting. Instead of simplistic syntax, she'd read flowing language hinting at his being well read—perhaps even educated. He was most certainly more than "a soldier."

What was the real reason behind his self-imposed isolation?

At the second meeting of The Ladies Cemetery Improvement Society, Isobel noted a studied avoidance on the part of everyone present when it came to the veterans' behavior at Private Long's grave. Nor was there any mention of the destruction of one of their wreaths. Isobel thought it possible that everyone present was ignorant of the latter travesty, although she doubted it. Still, instead of gossiping about what had happened, the ladies proceeded with the meeting concentrating on things like the resounding success of the luncheon counter.

In response to America Payne's glowing report, the ladies determined to repeat the event for Independence Day. As promised, the members who had volunteered to research costs reported on their findings. There was a general murmur of dismay when Mrs. Oliver presented the estimate for the cost of fencing.

Birdie wasted no time focusing attention on a solution to that problem. "I'd really hoped we could accomplish it this year without seeking a generous donor." She paused. "Perhaps we still can." She looked at Isobel. "I believe you have a proposal to consider."

When Isobel rose and explained her idea for a book preserving a record of the early days in Nebraska City, Mrs. Bishop raised an immediate objection.

"Nebraska City already has an organization dedicated to the preservation of its history. There is no need to duplicate the efforts of the Old Settlers Association. I daresay said membership would be affronted by our presumption. Beyond that, we've all just heard Mrs. Oliver's news about the high cost of fencing the grounds. Surely we must question the wisdom of taking on yet another expensive endeavor. Producing a book would be expensive."

Isobel smiled. Birdie had been so right about how this would go. Thank goodness she'd anticipated it and suggested solutions. "You raise two excellent points, Mrs. Bishop. Happily, I believe I can allay your concerns about both. Regarding the Old Settlers Association, Birdie facilitated contact. The gentlemen I spoke with earlier today were quite pleased with the idea—especially when I mentioned an intent to publish. The recording secretary even offered their meeting minutes as possible source material."

"How wonderful," Mrs. Bishop said—in anything but a pleased tone of voice.

"As to the expense," Isobel continued, "Rather than being a drain on society funds, I believe there is excellent potential for the project to add a good deal of money to society coffers."

Mrs. Bishop scoffed at the idea, cautioning that, while their newest member's enthusiasm was admirable, they must all take into consideration the fact that inexperience could often give rise to unrealistic expectations.

When Mrs. Bishop finally quit talking, Isobel spoke directly to her. "As to inexperience, while it's true I'm newly arrived here in Nebraska, I am far from inexperienced in the matter of fundraising. As an active member of a Ladies Aid Society in St. Louis, I was very involved with the Sanitary Fair that raised $550,000 for the care of the brave men in the Union army." She paused to let the figure sink in before continuing. "Of course, I cannot guarantee success, but as I said, I think this project has great potential. To minimize the risk—after all, there will be production costs—I'd suggest we sell subscriptions to the finished product. That will give us an idea of the kind of support we can expect. Another measure of the potential will be initial response to this." She lifted the piece of paper she'd been holding and read her draft of a newspaper announcement.

> The Ladies Cemetery Improvement Society announces the expansion of their project, to be a printed record of the early days of Nebraska City, intended to preserve an accurate history of our community for future generations. Citizens are invited to submit historical accounts at the offices of the *Register*. Sales of the resulting work will fund improvements and the ongoing maintenance of the cemetery grounds. The ladies gratefully acknowledge the support of the Old Settlers Association and of this newspaper. The former has offered to open its written records for those compiling the work. The latter has agreed to donate editorial and other services toward the completion of this worthy project. Direct inquiries to Miss Isobel Manning at the offices located on Main Street.

Once she'd read it, she said quickly, "I affixed my name, because as some of you know, I'll be working at the newspaper office every day, now that I've decided to stay in Nebraska." Again, she looked at Mrs. Bishop, lest the irascible woman hint once again at *Charlie's troubles*. "I can therefore assure the society that during regular business hours, someone will always be on hand to accept submissions."

During the lively discussion that followed, a motion was made and passed for Isobel to oversee production of a book to be titled *Early Days in Nebraska City*. Publication would depend upon a satisfactory number of submissions and society approval of the manuscript. Any member wishing to read the completed manuscript before publication would be able to do so at the offices of the *Register*.

When Mrs. Bishop raised an alternate idea of financing, demanding a donation for each entry submitted and a sliding scale offering more space to those who could pay more, Teddy Hall objected. "This should be a democratic project enabling everyone to participate."

Mrs. Bishop relented, but she was not finished making proposals. "I move that Miss Manning's announcement be placed in other newspapers beyond the *Register*." She was certain she could convince Mr. Morton of the *News* to follow the *Register's* example and publish it free of charge. "After all, we want to reach as *wide* an audience as possible."

Mrs. Bishop's motion passed unanimously, and the meeting concluded. While the ladies enjoyed refreshments, Isobel escaped into Teddy's display area to admire Sarah Carter's latest creations. Only when she saw Jennie and her mother-in-law depart did she return to Teddy's parlor and accept a cup of tea. As Isobel took her first sip, Birdie crossed the room to speak with her.

"You did well this evening."

Isobel looked doubtful. "Why does it always have to be a battle? Don't we want the same thing? It's exhausting."

Birdie gave a low chuckle. "You held your own. Many—perhaps most women—would have raised the white flag and surrendered to the indomitable will in the room."

Later that evening, as Isobel thought back, she remembered Birdie's comment about waving a white flag. She'd had her fill of surrendering. She didn't want to wave any more white flags. As far as it depended on Isobel Victoria Manning, Mrs. Julian Bishop was about to discover that she had met her match.

Chapter 28

And whatsoever ye do, do it heartily, as to the Lord, and not unto men.
Colossians 3:23

Nebraska City embraced the Ladies Cemetery Improvement Society history project with enthusiasm. Isobel kept busy either perusing anecdotes and stories dropped into the office mail slot or taking notes as someone reminisced.

A steamboat captain strode up from the river to regale her with the tale of a packet impaled on a snag downriver, from which the Presbyterians had rescued a church bell and chandeliers. A former freighter kept her spellbound as he described rumbling across the open prairie to Fort Kearney—at a top speed of about twelve miles a day. All sorts of people submitted claims of "firsts"—the first white child born, the first burial at Wyuka, the first house, the first ferry across the river.

Isobel wrote and sorted and took notes from her new desk positioned inside the back door. The work of *Early Days* alternated with selecting articles for the *Register* and, on occasion, tracing down Nebraska City news in person. Charlie had yet to add her name to the newspaper banner, but Isobel hoped that would happen in due time.

One sunny day in mid-June, she was at her desk when the sound of hoofbeats and creaking harness drew her attention. With a low murmur of joy, she summoned Edgar to join her. Outside, Levi Brown, owner of the livery where Elsie boarded, alit from a new buggy. *Her* new buggy. Delight sounded in Isobel's voice as she looked the rig over and proclaimed it *wonderful*.

Brown smiled. "Just arrived down at the landing. Took your old gal down and hitched her up soon as I could. Now, if you decide it isn't right for you, I'll have no trouble selling it. More than one lady cast admiring glances as I drove it here. Seems as if red spokes and fancy leather seat covers are just the thing these days."

Isobel smiled, remembering the man's reaction when she first told him what she wanted. He'd tapped the catalog page with his pencil.

"You *sure*? Costs more. Doesn't add a thing to the soundness of the rig."

Isobel had begged his indulgence. She'd wanted a buggy with red spokes since she was a little girl. Looking at it now, she was glad she'd stood her ground and didn't hesitate to say so.

Brown nodded. "You'll be keeping it, then."

"Definitely."

He pointed at Elsie. "I'm thinking you'll be wanting a flashy new horse, too. Something more in keeping with the stylish new rig." He paused. "You want me to keep an eye out?"

Isobel patted Elsie's bony haunch. "Certainly not. Elsie and I were made for each other."

"Well, if you change your mind, let me know. The horse market over on Seventh is mostly Texas mustangs, but once in a while there's better offerings." Brown gave the buggy an admiring glance. "Imagine a chestnut with white socks flashing, mane and tail flying. I'd make you a deal, seeing as how you already bought the rig." After taking a quick breath, Brown concluded, "I appreciate your business, Miss Manning. Hope to keep it for a good long while."

Isobel smiled. "All you need do to keep my business, Mr. Brown, is continue to treat my horse well."

"She'll think she died and went to horse heaven." Brown prepared to climb back up to the driver's seat.

On a whim, Isobel said, "I think I'd like to take it for a test drive. If you can wait a moment, I'll drop you back at the livery."

"No need for that," Brown said quickly. With a tug on his battered hat, he wished Isobel a nice drive and shuffled off.

Edgar laughed. "Guess he didn't like the idea of being driven by a lady." He motioned to the buggy. "That's a fine rig. You enjoy your drive. Charlie'll be back from his meeting before long. I don't imagine there'll be any newspaper emergencies in the interim."

Isobel thanked him. Moments later, as she drove onto Main Street, she felt a distinctly childish glee. *If only Mother Manning could see me now.* She chuckled to herself. Mother didn't think a true lady drove herself anywhere. Mother would never ride in a conveyance pulled by a *nag*, for that is what she would label poor Elsie. Mother had once pronounced a black buggy with red spokes and wheel rims *gauche*. Isobel called out to her horse. "What Mother Manning would think or say doesn't really matter anymore, does it, old girl?" Elsie's ears flicked back. When the mare snorted and gave a toss of her head, Isobel laughed.

As she passed the Bishop manse, Isobel acted on yet another whim. Pulling up, she hitched the buggy and strode to the front door. The housekeeper directed her around to the rear of the house to the kitchen, where Jennie was taking a pie out of the oven. Rapping on the door frame, Isobel called *hello* through the screen. "My buggy's arrived! Come with me for the inaugural drive."

Jennie set the pie on the counter and came to the door. "I can't. Lila Ritchie ordered five pies for first thing tomorrow morning, and I'm just now taking the third out of the oven.

I've two more to bake before I have to turn the kitchen over to Cook."

Not to be deterred, Isobel said, "What if we deliver the three you have? If Lila has those for the morning, that'll give you extra time to bake the other two tomorrow—won't it?" When Jennie still hesitated, Isobel pleaded. "Please come. It's not every day a lady editor with her very own desk in a newspaper office takes the inaugural drive in her very own rig."

Smiling, Jennie said, "You have a point." She untied her apron. "Give me a moment to change."

"You won't see a soul beyond Lila Ritchie. After taking the pies in, we'll head out of town. I still haven't seen the Morton property. Are there really *hundreds* of fruit trees?"

Jennie unlatched the screen door and motioned Isobel inside. "Yes. Hundreds. It's a pity you missed seeing them in bloom." She hung up her apron and reached for a straw-lined shallow wooden box on the far counter. Carefully, she settled the newly baked pie into the straw. Adding the two cooled pies, she covered them with a clean cloth.

While Jennie told her mother-in-law that Cook could have the kitchen, Isobel transferred the box to the buggy. She was waiting when Jennie exited the front door of the Bishop home. Mrs. Bishop loomed behind her in the doorway, scowling. As Jennie made her way toward Isobel's rig, the older woman slammed the door shut.

Isobel waited until she'd pulled away from the house to speak. "I didn't mean to cause you trouble."

Jennie sighed. "*I'm* the one who decided to go 'gallivanting about the countryside without a proper escort. Dressed like someone's kitchen help.'"

"My stepmother would have reacted the same way," Isobel said. She mimicked Mother Manning. "What will people *think*? Worse yet, what will they *say*? You simply must take heed. After all, being a member of this family carries with it certain responsibilities. I know you resent them, but you simply must learn to acquiesce. We may not have created the rules by which society operates, but we disobey them at our peril."

Jennie looked over. "You have much better hearing than I realized. Some of that was almost verbatim."

Isobel chuckled. "I'm very well-schooled in matters concerning societal expectations and how short I fall of meeting them—on nearly every level." She tensed a bit as she executed the sharp turn into the alley behind Lila's café, but Elsie responded beautifully. Tying off the reins, she climbed down to help Jennie extract the pie box from beneath the buggy seat. Together, the two stepped into Lila's kitchen, welcomed by the aromas of fresh coffee and frying bacon.

Lila brushed a blond curl off her forehead as she looked up from a massive stove atop which sat a large cast iron stew pot and two deep skillets. She greeted the ladies without stepping away from the stove, directing Jennie to set the pies on the counter by the door.

"I still owe you two," Jennie said. "Can Sam pick them up first thing in the morning?"

"That'll be fine," Lila replied, just as her son, Sam, jerked open the kitchen door. In his hurry to get inside, he nearly knocked Isobel over.

"Gosh, ma'am, I'm so sorry," he blustered, brandishing a telegram at his mother. "They want us to come. Can you believe it? They want us!"

"Samuel!" Lila scolded. "It's a *possibility*. That is all. We'll talk about it later." She looked over at Isobel and Jennie. "Please don't say anything about this."

"About what?" Isobel asked.

Sam explained. "About our going to Denver to open a café there—with family to help. Ma's brother and my cousins." Sam glanced at his mother. "And of *course* we're going. Why wouldn't we?"

"Because it's not that simple," Lila snapped. The bell on the front door rang, signaling the arrival of their first customers of the day. She pointed at the telegram. "Now put that thing in your pocket and get to work. There's coffee to pour and food to serve." Sam obeyed his mother, donning an apron and, coffee pot in hand, hurrying toward the two men who'd already seated themselves at a table.

"Sam thinks it'll be a great adventure," Lila said. "There's the draw of cousins, of course, but—I just don't know." She repeated her plea that Jennie and Isobel keep her confidence. "I don't want rumors started that I might be closing. Sam and I need business to stay strong."

"We won't breathe a word to anyone," Jennie said.

Isobel nodded agreement. "That's a promise." Lila thanked them and Isobel led the way back outside. She was about to climb aboard the buggy when a familiar voice called a hello. As Charlie approached from the direction of the newspaper office, he made a show of looking over Isobel's new buggy. "It's a beauty. I see you aren't wasting any time to try it out."

Jennie had skittered to the opposite side of the buggy. Charlie greeted her before nodding toward the café door. "Making a delivery?"

"Pie." Jennie reached up to smooth her hair.

"Peach?"

"Tomorrow." She adjusted her collar.

Isobel looked from Jennie to Charlie and back again. *Was Jennie blushing?*

Charlie smiled. "I'll be sure to arrive early for lunch, so I don't miss out." He nodded at Isobel, although he continued to address Jennie. "You might want to keep an eye on my sister. When we were young, she had a certain reputation for reckless driving." He lowered his voice as if sharing a confidence. "Ask her about the coasting incident."

Isobel shook a finger at him in mock anger. "Charles Victor Manning, that's quite enough. You're scaring my friend." She looked over at Jennie. "I was eight years old."

Charlie laughed and sauntered away.

Jennie was quiet as Isobel drove them toward the western edge of town. Interpreting it as renewed concern over Mrs. Bishop's disapproval, Isobel said, "I should have asked Charlie to come with us. You could have allayed your mother-in-law's concerns—at least in the matter of an escort."

Jennie's cheeks reddened again. "Charlie? Goodness! I'm glad you didn't. That would have been—I mean, I would have been so embarrassed." She fidgeted with her collar again. "Now that I think about it, Mother Bishop had a point. What was I thinking, flitting off dressed like a housemaid?"

"It was only Charlie." Again, Isobel glanced at Jennie, and the truth came clear. "Except he isn't 'only Charlie' to you, is he?"

Jennie looked horrified. "Don't be absurd. Charlie's mourning the loss of his wife and baby. What do you think of me?"

Isobel drove along for a few moments, thinking carefully as she formulated a response. Finally, she said, "I think you, Jennie Wilcox, are kind, intelligent, patient, and uniquely able to understand Charlie's—challenges. As for Charlie, I hope that, in time, he realizes that you have far more to offer than the best pie he's ever eaten." She glanced over at her friend, taking note of Jennie's deepening blush before focusing again on the road ahead. "I know he's earned a certain reputation here in Nebraska City, but he can be quite charming. You haven't had much of a chance to see that side of him." Isobel paused. "I might add that he's not exactly unattractive. A girl could do worse."

"We'll be turning south at the first road," Jennie said abruptly, "then make a big loop that will take us back into town."

Isobel looked over at her. "That's it, then? You have nothing more to say about my brother?"

"Only that I hope he was teasing about your driving." Jennie nodded toward the west. "I don't like the look of those clouds."

Chapter 29

*...he made a decree for the rain, and a way
for the lightning of the thunder.*
Job 28:26

Isobel forgot all about the storm clouds when, about a mile outside of town, a monstrous contraption came into view. Stationed alongside the trail, the thing boasted giant wheels and flaking red paint. It would surely terrify Elsie. Isobel tightened her grip on the reins and braced one foot against the dash. "What on earth is that?"

Jennie chuckled. "The inventor called it a 'prairie motor' and claimed it would revolutionize freighting. The first few days after it arrived, he drove it up and down the streets of Nebraska City—even across Table Creek. It was powered by a steam engine and pulled three passenger wagons."

Isobel glanced over at her. "Did *you* take a ride?"

Jennie nodded. "Up Main Street, over ruts and ditches, and all the way out here to the Morton's. Then a big circle back to town. It was quite thrilling."

"But it's here. And obviously not in working order."

"It departed for Denver with three loaded freight wagons in tow, but it only made it a few miles before it broke down. The inventor left it right where it was and departed, promising to return with new parts. He never came back. Someone detached the wagons and returned the freight to town. Then they hauled the behemoth back to this spot, and that was that."

As a wary Isobel drove toward the contraption, a boy climbed into what had to be the driver's seat. A second young man clamored up and over from the opposite side, sitting atop one of the giant wheels, his legs dangling. Isobel reined Elsie into the turn, all the while expecting the mare to at least snort and toss her head. Good old Elsie remained calm.

The boy in the driver's seat stood up and called to the other, "Hey, Paul. It's Mrs. Wilcox." When the two jumped down, Isobel pulled up.

Jennie introduced Isobel to Masters Paul and Mark Morton, who bowed formally. The younger boy had just expressed a hope that Jennie would contribute ginger snaps to an upcoming ice cream social at the Episcopal Church, when a woman exited the front door of the house in the distance and headed toward them.

"That's Mrs. Morton," Jennie muttered and reached up to smooth her hair.

So taken had Isobel been with the prairie motor that she hadn't really looked at the Mortons' home. She did so now, admiring the sweeping front porch, the gingerbread trim, and the elegant balance three gables gave to the overall architecture.

As soon as Mrs. Morton was near, she called to the boys. "Do you see those clouds? You scoot on home. And your little brother's napping, so don't slam any doors. Get a book from Father's office and join Joy. He's reading in the parlor."

The boys trotted toward the house, and Jennie introduced Isobel.

Mrs. Morton smiled up at Isobel. "I meant to speak with you at the Decoration Day ceremony, but people weren't inclined to circulate after that—unfortunate—display at one of the graves."

235

"I am very pleased to meet you," Isobel replied. "—and your sons, who seem quite the young gentlemen."

Mrs. Morton's smile broadened. "I am pleased to hear they comported themselves well." She paused. "Had we had the opportunity to converse on Decoration Day, I would have promised support for the society's improvement efforts at the cemetery."

"That's very kind."

"The decision isn't entirely lacking in self-interest. My mother was laid to rest at Wyuka. It's been nearly ten years now, although in many ways that doesn't seem possible." She paused. "It is a bit disconcerting to find cattle grazing on the grounds, freely depositing what cattle do. If the society would proceed with an estimate for the fence, Mr. Morton and I wish to see it accomplished."

They would pay for the fence? All of it? Isobel thanked her. "I shall bring the matter before the society at our Thursday evening meeting. Unless, of course, you'd care to attend and make the announcement yourself?"

Mrs. Morton shook her head. "Thank you, but no. Once an estimate is prepared, simply present it to Mr. Frey at Merchants Bank. Mr. Morton will see that he is prepared to supply the funds." A gust of wind ruffled her dark hair. She glanced over her shoulder and then looked up at Isobel. "You might want to take shelter at the house until we're certain those clouds aren't brewing a storm. I can have my man unhitch the horse and take her into a stall."

"Thank you," Isobel said, glancing over at Jennie, "but we both have obligations in town. I really don't want to cause either my brother or Mrs. Bishop undue concern. We can trust Elsie to get us home safely."

Mrs. Morton looked doubtful, but she didn't argue. "Then I'll wish you both a good day." She took a few steps and then turned back, speaking to Jennie. "You know how quickly weather can change here. Don't let Miss Manning delay in getting you both back to town and shelter."

Mrs. Morton's warning had been timely. The rain hit about halfway back to town, and *hit* was a good word for the heavy drops that sounded like pellets pounding the buggy top. Elsie didn't seem particularly upset about the thunder, but she did move out at a brisk trot. Isobel was surprised at how quickly hard-packed earth transformed to mud. Every few feet, the buggy wheels lost their grip and slipped sideways. Every time, Jennie gasped. Isobel kept a firm grip on the reins and encouraged Elsie forward. Bless the mare, she remained steady.

The strangest thing about the storm itself was that while dark clouds hung low, a band of blue sky remained visible on the eastern horizon. Isobel kept thinking the rain would let up, but it didn't, and traction became more and more of a problem. Puddles began to collect in low spots. When Isobel glanced behind them, she could see where the buggy wheels had carved deep ruts in treacherous mud. She raised her voice to be heard above the storm. "What should we do?"

Jennie shouted back, "Keep going! We'd be mad to leave the road now."

With a grim nod, Isobel drove on until, with a jolt, the left buggy wheel dropped into a deep rut. Elsie snorted and struggled to move forward, but the buggy didn't budge.

Jennie leaned out enough to spy the mired wheel. She ducked back beneath the buggy top and brushed a sodden fringe of curls off her forehead. "It's in too deep. We need help." When lightning flashed, she screeched and allowed a burst of nervous laughter. "That was too close for comfort."

Isobel tensed. She hadn't considered the danger from lightning. What a way to end her first outing by herself. Charlie would never let her hear the end of it. She didn't even want to think about Electa Bishop's reaction. The downpour let up a bit, but thunder still rumbled.

Isobel handed the reins to Jennie. "I'm going to see if there's anything I can do." She climbed down to inspect the wheel. She couldn't discern how much of it was truly lodged in mud and how much was simply immersed in a puddle of water. As quickly as it had begun, the downpour stopped. Straddling the wheel from the front and grasping the rim with both hands, Isobel called up to Jennie. "Slide over and take the reins. When I say *go*, slap them across Elsie's back side."

Jennie refused. "If it works, you'll get run over."

Isobel moved to the back of the wheel, planted her feet in ankle-deep water and mud, and prepared to push. "Go!" she yelled.

Elsie did her best, but the wheel barely budged. It did, however, turn far enough for Isobel to lose her grip at the same moment her feet lost purchase. She shouted a very unladylike word as she slid, slid, slid, and ended up flat in the muck, the wind knocked out of her.

Jennie cried out, but Isobel was powerless to respond beyond raising a hand and waving it to signal she was all right. Jennie let out a startled screech.

Isobel swiped a sleeve across her face to clear the mud away. Blinking, she saw dark boots and the bottom hem of a long coat. A hand reached toward her, palm up. She took the hand and allowed herself to be hoisted up and out of the muck. A dog yipped. She looked toward it. One ear. Blue eyes. *My rescuer. Again.* Goosebumps prickled as she gazed upward, but he was looking at the wheel, not at her. He'd pulled his hat down and collar up, and she could see nothing of the man's face.

"You hurt?" he asked.

"N-no." Shrinking away from the dog, she stammered, "I-I was trying to budge the wheel."

He motioned for her to get back in the buggy. "Drive," he said, as he put his shoulder to the wheel. "Drive, and don't stop."

Jennie slid back over. Isobel scrambled aboard and took the reins. When she called out *Ready?* he didn't answer. Lightly, she slapped Elsie's rump with the reins and called out, "Giddap, Elsie! Let's go!" Elsie strained to obey. At first nothing happened.

The man groaned. "Again!" he bellowed.

Isobel slapped Elsie's flanks harder. "Come on, Elsie girl. Let's go!" Elsie leaned into the harness. For a long moment it seemed useless, but then the buggy moved.

"Don't stop!" the man roared. "Go on!"

Jennie looked behind them.

"Can you see him?" Isobel asked. "What's he look like?"

Jennie bobbed this way and that as she searched. Finally, she said, "He's just—gone. Him and the dog both." She looked behind them again. "Wait. He dropped something."

"He said not to stop," Isobel replied, but she eased up on the reins and Elsie slowed. "What is it?"

"I can't tell."

"Do you see him?"

"No. He—they—trotted off toward the south. Dropped down into the creek bed, I suppose." Jennie sighed. "He didn't even let us thank him."

Isobel dared a glance behind them and saw a small object lying in a clump of grass just off the road. *Don't stop.* He'd yelled it. Still, Isobel hesitated. The worst of the storm was past. They weren't that far from town. She was already soaked. She pulled up. "I'll fetch it," she said, "whatever it is."

Once again handing Jennie the reins, she climbed down and waded through wet prairie grass to the object. *A book.*

Leather-bound. She snatched it up, again looking south, searching in vain for any sign of man or dog. Her heart racing, Isobel returned to the buggy. Once again seated, she opened the book, looking inside, searching for a name.

"Who is he?" Jennie asked.

"There's no name that I can see." Isobel perused the first few pages. Her breath caught when she recognized the handwriting. *It really was him.* But she didn't tell Jennie. Whatever the reason, she didn't want to. Heart pounding, she flipped a page. "It's a journal—of sorts. Not a journal, really, though. I mean, it's—notes? Thoughts?" She paused. "He's copied a quotation from someone named D. L. Moody." She read aloud. "'If we are to be disciples of Jesus Christ, we must deny ourselves and take up our cross and follow Him.'" She looked over at Jennie. "Have you ever heard of a D. L. Moody?"

Jennie shook her head.

"Here's another one from the same person," Isobel continued. "'Don't be kept out of the kingdom of God or out of active Christian work by the scorn and laughter and ridicule of your godless neighbors and companions.'"

Jennie gazed in the direction the man had disappeared. "Do you think he's a minister? A circuit rider, maybe? But why would he run off like that? And where's his horse if he's a circuit rider?" She tapped the book. "Are you certain there's no name?"

Shaking her head, Isobel closed the book and tucked it into her waist. "I'll look more carefully later. Right now—we need to get back." She took up the reins and started for town, painfully aware of her sodden, mud-spattered clothing. And wondering if Jennie might be right. Was her rescuer a minister of some kind? What would turn a minister into a hermit?

Chapter 30

A friend loveth at all times, and a brother is born for adversity.
Proverbs 17:17

Back at his cabin, Gideon hung both hat and scarf on a peg by the door. Shrugging out of his coat, he hung it on a chair back. Once darkness fell, he'd drape it over a corral pole to dry. Intending to read, he reached into the inside pocket of the coat. *Empty.* He checked every pocket. Twice. Frowning, he stepped out on the porch. The storm clouds had moved on, and the air was crisp and clean, smelling of moist earth and blossoms—Ma's yellow roses rambling up the rickety trellis beside the porch. There was even the hint of a rainbow in the sky.

When had he lost the notebook? *Of course.* He spoke to the dog. "Bet it fell out when that wheel lurched free. I was in a hurry to get away. Didn't even notice." The dog cocked his head and gave a low whine. "You're right. If it landed in that puddle, it's ruined." Trouble thumped his tail. "I like your attitude. Maybe it's not that bad. It could be anywhere between here and there. Better see what we can find."

The coat was too wet to wear. He pulled on one of Pa's flannel shirts. He didn't really need it for warmth, but he was accustomed to—a shroud, he supposed he could call it. Going abroad in shirtsleeves was simply not something he did. The notebook didn't contain anything personal in regard to names or dates, but it still served a purpose, and he wanted it back. It had become a kind of conversation with himself—a way to think things through that didn't involve talking to a dog.

With the first flash of lightning, Charlie stopped the press, stepped out of the newspaper office, and stared up Main Street toward the west. A loud clap of thunder sent him back inside with a scowl on his face. How far did Izzy intend to drive that new buggy? Would Jennie convince her of the potential danger? A summer storm could transform a pleasant country drive into a life-threatening ordeal. High winds might blow a buggy over. It could be struck by lightning. If the horse bolted—

The skies opened. Rain poured down. Hurrying to the back door, Charlie stepped outside. Sheltered beneath the platform at the top of the stairs to his apartment, he watched the dusty alley turn to mire. At least he knew Edgar was safe at home. He'd asked for the afternoon off to help his two younger brothers repair the porch steps. He hoped the Simmonses were faring well in spite of the storm. He knew so many stories about lightning strikes. Had, in fact, reprinted article after article on the topic. Lightning wasn't the only danger. What if Izzy's new buggy slipped off the road? What if a wheel dropped into a rut? What if that wheel came off?

Hands on his hips, Charlie paced, back and forth, back and forth beneath the sheltering platform. Maybe they'd noticed the clouds gathering. Maybe they turned back. At this very moment they could be sitting in the Bishops' kitchen, drinking tea and savoring a piece of Jennie's peach pie. Maybe he was worrying for no reason.

Another flash of lightning and a crash of thunder sent him back inside. Still, he paced while horrible possibilities played out in his mind. When he envisioned visiting two fresh graves at the cemetery, he decided enough was enough. He had to do something. Flipping the *closed* sign into place, he locked the front door, grabbed his hat, and charged upstairs to retrieve an umbrella. Snapping it open, he hurried toward the Bishops'.

Let the buggy be there. Let them be inside. Let them make fun of me for worrying. But please, dear God, let them be safe.

It was raining hard. Wind gusts dampened his pants from the knees down. As he skirted the courthouse, mud collected on the soles of his shoes until, with each step, it was as though he carried weights. At last, the Bishops' two-story, brick house came into view. But there was no buggy in the drive. He charged across the lawn and ducked under the porch off the kitchen.

Mrs. Bishop came to the door and spoke through the screen. "Jennie was going to show the way out to the Mortons'." Her voice wavered. "Something about your sister seeing the orchards."

Mr. Bishop came up behind her and said, "Electa was just going to make us a cup of tea, weren't you, my pet?" He looked at Charlie. "Why don't you join us?"

Mrs. Bishop nodded. "Yes. Tea. You can wait with us."

Charlie lifted a mud-caked shoe. "Thank you, but I'll wait out here."

And that's where he and Mr. Bishop stood waiting—mugs of tea in hand—when the storm passed. At last, a red-spoked buggy drawn by an ugly mare came into view.

※

"Oh, dear," Isobel nodding up ahead. "That's Charlie standing on your porch."

"And Pa Bishop," Jennie said.

As one, the men set down the mugs they'd been holding and strode toward the buggy. They must have called out to Mrs. Bishop, for she exited the kitchen and hurried after them.

Charlie sputtered questions the moment he reached Isobel. "What happened? You look like you fell into a mud pit! Are you all right?" When Isobel nodded, he reached up and lifted her down, then wrapped her in a hug as he murmured *thank God.* The emotion in his voice brought tears to Isobel's eyes. But in the next moment he was scowling at her and scolding. "I don't know whether to throttle you or hug you again. What were you thinking, staying out in such a storm?"

Mr. Bishop's reaction as he helped Jennie down was gentler and significantly more tactful than Charlie's, although the essence of his questions was the same.

When Mrs. Bishop joined them, she had a great deal more to say than either of the men. Why hadn't they turned back when they saw the clouds in the west? What route did they take? What if the horse had bolted? Isobel's hands were red. Didn't she have a proper pair of driving gloves? And how on earth did one get mud on one's *collar* and *cuffs*?

Jennie spoke up as soon as her mother-in-law paused long enough to take a breath. "A buggy wheel dropped into a rut. We were mired down. Stranded."

"On the prairie," Mrs. Bishop blustered. "Surrounded by thunder and *lightning.* You could have been—"

"But we weren't," Jennie interrupted, "and here we are, none the worse for wear."

Mrs. Bishop gestured at Isobel's ensemble. "Do you call *that* 'none the worse for wear'?"

Isobel looked down at her skirt. What could she say?

Jennie stepped up, pointing at Isobel and sounding a dramatic huff. "*I* stayed in the buggy. *She* simply *had* to get out in the rain to see what she might do." She rolled her eyes. "If you can believe it, she straddled the wheel from the *front*."

Pretending to take offense, Isobel smirked. "Well at least *I* was trying."

"To do what? Get run over? It's a good thing I was there to tell you to *push*, not *pull*. You would have ended up flat on your back in the trail. Crunched beneath a wheel."

"At least I was *doing* something besides sitting with my hands folded, waiting to be rescued." Isobel glowered. "I would have crunched nobly."

Jennie lifted her nose in the air and sniffed, "There is nothing *noble* about getting crunched."

Something about that word *crunched* made Isobel want to laugh. She pressed the back of her hand to her lips and turned away. She might have succeeded in suppressing it, had she not stolen a glance at Jennie. Relief and exhaustion combined. Giddiness won over, and the two young women began to laugh.

Mrs. Bishop stomped her foot. "I fail to see what could possibly be funny about the situation."

Mr. Bishop interrupted. "Electa, my pet. Let us be thankful."

Mrs. Bishop scowled at him. "Thankful?" she clucked. "You expect me to be thankful our daughter-in-law—"

"Laughs?"

Mrs. Bishop's scowl faltered.

Mr. Bishop smiled warmly. "Think on that, Electa. When, in the last year, have we heard our Jennie laugh? I'd say we should be thankful our dear daughter-in-law has a new friend." He winked at Isobel. "With spunk enough to get herself out of trouble without getting 'crunched' and humility enough to laugh at herself."

A wave of fatigue swept in, and Isobel reached for Charlie to steady herself. He offered to drive her to the hotel and then see to Elsie and the rig, and she gladly accepted.

"But first—" She stepped over to hug Jennie, whispering as she did, "Thank you for being my friend. And for keeping me from being crunched."

Jennie chuckled. "Any time." She pressed a hand over the notebook tucked into Isobel's waist and murmured, "Please tell me if you learn who he is."

Charlie was quiet on the drive to the hotel, until Izzy asked a general question about his day. He decided to tell her about his early meeting with three G.A.R. members. "That's where I was headed when I caught up with you and Jennie delivering pies to the café this morning."

"Why would you want to spend time with the very men who publicly shamed someone Birdie deeply cares for?"

Uh oh. Izzy had a tendency to be cantankerous when she was tired. This was not a good sign. "Well," he said, "actually, I was hoping they could give me—us—some more ideas about locating Private Long's service record."

"Why would they care to do that?"

"To begin with, I didn't mention Private Long once. I reminisced about the war. Then I waxed loquacious about how difficult it is for friends and family to carry on when so many thousands were lost or missing. In the context of my talking about my Missouri regiment, they assumed I was trying to track down a buddy I'd lost track of. I did nothing to make them think otherwise."

Izzy shifted on the seat. "I'm sorry. You may not remember, but I can be cantankerous when I'm tired. Please continue."

Charlie barely managed to suppress a knowing smile. He cleared his throat. "You'll be interested to know that in the context of talking about missing friends, all three of the gentlemen were quick to say they don't 'hold with what happened at the cemetery.' They hadn't been part of the honor guard. Apparently, what happened was all Wade Inskeep's idea. The men I spoke with didn't know it was going to happen."

Izzy nodded. "Good to know—if it's true. Now tell me what they suggested."

"One, an inquiry to the War Department. Two, writing the commanding officers of the First Nebraska. Three, contacting General Lew Wallace. Dr. Hershey—he was a surgeon during the war—mentioned that General Wallace praised the Nebraska boys after both their major engagements, first at Fort Donelson and then at Shiloh."

"How will you find him?

"It won't be hard. He's running for Congress in Indiana."

"And how do you know that?"

Charlie grinned as he pulled up at the hotel. "I read the newspaper." When Isobel prepared to climb down, he tugged on her sleeve to keep her in the buggy. "Are you certain you didn't injure yourself wrestling that wheel out of the mud?"

"I'm certain," Izzy said as she climbed down. "I'll likely be a little sore, but that's to be expected after landing face first in the mud."

He nodded. "Do remind me to never take you on in an arm-wrestling match. Freeing a buggy wheel from the mud is one impressive feat."

She'd rounded the buggy and stepped up on the boardwalk when she lifted one arm and flexed it like a strong man. "Just you remember that, mister."

Suddenly serious, Charlie repeated how relieved he was to see "her jug-headed mare" pulling her fancy buggy into the Bishop's drive. "I don't think I'd be able to survive another loss. To think what might have happened to you and Jennie—"

Izzy reached up and gave his hand a squeeze. "I love you too, Charlie. Now let's not be maudlin about it. I'm fine. Jennie's fine. Everyone's fine. And my jug-headed horse may not *look* fine, but she *is* fine in what matters—dependability." She tilted her head from side to side and grimaced. "You might be right about my staying in for the rest of the day."

"Good plan. Molly Simmons would be more than happy to bring you a pot of tea. And perhaps your worthless brother could be coerced into delivering soup around supper time."

Izzy glowered at him as she touched two fingers to her lips. It was a gesture they'd devised as children, and it could signal an entire dictionary. *I care. You mean so much to me. Don't listen to her. You are loved.* Often it indicated an intent to sneak into the pantry and to indulge in several of Portia's almond cookies.

"Almond cookies?" Charlie said.

"If only we had some," Izzy laughed.

Chapter 31

*Let the words of my mouth, and the meditation of my heart,
be acceptable in thy sight, O Lord, my strength, and my redeemer.*
Psalm 19:14

Isobel opened the soldier's notebook. Rich hues of wine and burgundy, along with an occasional wave of gold, adorned the handmade paper that lined the leather cover. As Isobel admired the fine workmanship, her conscience accused her. *You have no business reading a man's private writings.*

She argued with herself. *I won't tell anyone a single thing about what I read. I only want to know more about him.* She would leave the notebook with Birdie tomorrow morning, to be handed over the next time the soldier came for supplies. *And no, she would not surprise him by being there to meet him in person.* That would be wrong—even if it was tempting.

She could write another note. A promise not to divulge anything she'd read to anyone. A promise that he could trust her. At some point, in some way, she would find a way to convince him of that. As soon as she returned the journal. Diary. Book. Whatever it proved to be now that she was going to read it. And so she began.

I began to journal when I enlisted. Having lost that first record of events and thoughts, I begin anew, this time for a higher purpose than the simple recording of events.

Isobel frowned. This wasn't the first record he'd created. Nor was it the first one he'd lost, poor man. What did he mean by a *higher purpose?*

I have it in mind that the exercise of writing might aid me in climbing out of the dark valley in which I am mired. Perhaps it will help me to claw my way into the light. Surely no harm can come from the exercise. And so I begin in the year of our Lord 1868.

Four words were written on the line below that introduction, centered on the page, in slightly larger script.

A Quest for Hope

Isobel turned the page. At the top, the soldier had copied a verse of Scripture.

My tears have been my meat day and night, while they continually say unto me, Where is thy God? Psalm 42:3

What sad words. Those that followed proved to be a kind of response to the Psalm. The content made Isobel wonder if Jennie were right about their rescuer being a minister. Had he been a chaplain in the war? If so, from what he'd written here, he'd struggled mightily with his faith.

I have been in the place of the psalmist for so long, I scarcely know how to find my way out. It is small comfort to think an ancient sage knew this hopelessness and, like me, dwelt in darkness. How long did he suffer? How long did God leave him to think himself deserted by the Almighty? All I know to do is continue on the road I now tread. I see no way of escape, and yet I cannot seem to accept the idea that I have been wrong about what God wants of me. He placed a calling upon my life and then allowed circumstances that make it impossible for me to answer that call. Was I wrong about the calling? How could that be? Everything seemed to fall into place—until the moment that tore everything apart. I do not understand and so, like the psalmist, I cry out, "Where are You, God?"

Isobel's heart went out to the man. She turned back to the quotation about scorn and ridicule keeping someone from "active Christian work." Was that what the soldier meant about God placing "a calling" on his life? Why would it be impossible to answer it? Whatever had happened, something had been taken away and left him floundering.

She looked out the window. She knew what it felt like to flounder when a sure future was ripped away. It had happened on her wedding day. When tears threatened, Isobel blinked them away, feeling a bit guilty for thinking she could understand. The man writing these thoughts had probably suffered something much worse than a ruined wedding day. She looked back down at the beautiful script. If she kept reading, would she learn that he'd found a measure of peace? Suddenly, she thought of Charlie, who certainly needed both hope and peace. Was there something in this book that might help Charlie? She sat back, thinking. She might not take it to Birdie tomorrow morning, after all. For Charlie's sake.

Storms had a way of leaving beautiful sunsets in their wake. At least it seemed that way to Gideon as he made his way back to the cabin. Pausing outside the door, he admired the orange and pink clouds reflecting the last rays of the setting sun. "Guess it's lost for good," he muttered to no one in particular. Trouble reacted with a sound low in his throat, as if the dog had something to say about the situation, too.

He'd been so certain he'd dropped it by the mired buggy. For a moment, he considered his second encounter with the woman in blue. He lifted his hand and studied his palm, remembering that brief moment when she'd put her soft, uncalloused hand in his. If she was going to be driving herself around town and country, the woman needed a decent pair of gloves. He wondered about the ugly mare pulling the elegant buggy. The two didn't go together. Maybe the livery owner who'd rented the wild gray had gone as far in the opposite direction as possible. Then why the fancy buggy?

Movement brought his attention back to the moment and a red bird, flitting up from the creek bed and settling on a high branch. Reflected against the blue sky, it sang out. Gideon listened, wondering if a female would answer. The male repeated the warble several times, apparently in vain. When it flew away, Gideon muttered, "I know exactly how you feel."

As he turned to go inside, he pondered the lost notebook, grateful he hadn't included names in what he'd come to think of as his *emotings*. If it wasn't ruined by the rain, it still couldn't be connected to him. A few moments later, as he fried up a venison steak, an odd thought struck. What if the whole point of that book was for someone else? He had no idea what he might have written that would help another soul, but it was a comfort to consider the possibility. Might he end up ministering to a lost soul, after all? He gave a low laugh. Wouldn't that be something. The man who'd pictured himself preaching to hundreds, finally helping someone. *Just one.* It wasn't much. Then again, it was enough for the shepherd in the parable.

Maybe one was enough.

<hr />

The soldier's notebook might be an inanimate object, but every time Isobel left it in the handkerchief drawer of her hotel room dresser, the thing seemed to call out. When she and Charlie took supper with the Tanners on Saturday evening, she was preoccupied. She almost resented having to attend church on Sunday, so fascinated was she with the man's writings. Almost every page either presented a new mystery or compelled her to think about religion in ways she never had. First of all, the man seemed to be struggling with the very concept of whether or not he could call himself a Christian. Why would someone doubt such a fundamental thing? Isobel had never doubted that she was a Christian. After all, she'd attended church faithfully her entire life. All civilized people did. But the soldier parsed sentences and pondered individual words and cross-examined himself as if his very sanity depended upon it.

Perhaps it did. She was only partway through the notebook when her initial thoughts resurfaced. After all, did a sane person wrestle with religion so vigorously? If a person had questions about religion, withdrawing from the world was hardly the way to see them answered. Might he be dangerous? *Surely not.* Birdie and Henry knew the man. Not once had they ever hinted that people might not be *safe* around him. He'd risked himself to save her once and inconvenienced himself a second time. No, the poor man might be strange, but he wasn't unbalanced. He was, however, uncertain about his own standing with the Almighty. He copied a verse from the Old Testament. *Blessed is the man that trusteth in the Lord, and whose hope the Lord is. Jeremiah 17:7* And then he wrote a question. *Have I failed to trust in Christ? Have I placed my hope in something false?*

And, finally, Isobel read the answer to her question about Moody's identity. D. L. Moody was a minister who'd organized a service for men in camp after a battle. Another quote seemed to summarize the minister's message, referred to as "the simple gospel." Isobel agreed that Moody's definition was, indeed, simple. "Christ died for our sins. We must know Christ at Calvary first, as our substitute, as our Redeemer. The moment we accept Him as our Savior and our Redeemer, then it is that we become partakers of the gospel." The soldier wrote about "making a decision for Christ" in a moment of time. He had "repented" and "placed his faith in Christ." He did "trust in the Lord." Tragically, none of that seemed to make him happy. He mourned that reality on the pages of the notebook. Why wasn't he experiencing the hope that—according to him—was the best of the many blessings available to true Christians? The more Isobel read, the more confused she became.

Perhaps there was, after all, an element of insanity in this man—a kind that didn't make him dangerous to others, but odd enough that he wouldn't be accepted in normal society. A religious insanity, perhaps, about his inability to answer some sort of *calling.*

Whatever the man's problems, it might be wise for Isobel to keep her distance. She would leave the notebook with Birdie to be returned to its author. Somehow, Isobel would explain how it had come into her possession and why she'd kept it. Somehow.

Chapter 32

But God, who is rich in mercy, for his great love wherewith he loved us,
Even when we were dead in sins,
Hath quickened us together with Christ, (by grace ye are saved).
Ephesians 2:4-5

The morning after Isobel had determined to return the notebook to its author and take a step away from her mysterious rescuer, Molly swept into the hotel room humming a familiar tune. Isobel couldn't have named it, but she was certain it was a hymn. When she mentioned it, Molly's face lit up with a bright smile.

"Ma and the rest of us are praising the Lord, Miss Manning. We've been praying for Edgar for a long time, and the Lord finally got him. We had revival this weekend and Edgar got saved. He's been real bitter since our daddy died and he had to quit school and go to work. He didn't want a thing to do with God. Ma tried to tell him God would be a comfort, but Edgar wouldn't have it. So we've just been loving him the best we can and, praise the Lord, our prayers got answered."

Molly's voice trembled with emotion as she rattled on. As Isobel listened, she realized that while the syntax was simpler than what the soldier employed in his writings, the essential message was the same.

She wanted to ask questions but hesitated. Molly's enthusiasm was more than a little daunting, especially when Isobel realized that the kind of questions she would ask might lead Molly to conclude that *saved* was not a term to be applied to Miss Isobel Manning. When Molly finally paused to take a breath, Isobel offered her congratulations on the good news. That seemed to confuse the girl.

"Did I say something wrong?" Isobel asked.

"Not exactly," Molly replied. She thought for a moment before brightening and saying, "I never heard anybody *congratulate* when it comes to salvation, but I guess that's how folks in St. Louis do it." She nodded. "It's nice." She collected the latest pile of laundry and hurried out.

Perhaps, Isobel thought, she'd been unfair in her judgments. The least she could do was to finish reading the soldier's own words. But then, she would definitely hand the notebook over to Birdie.

Monday morning. Early. Charlie stood inside the open back door of his apartment, sipping coffee as a fine rain sifted from the dark sky. Jennie Wilcox had advised him to walk when the itch to drink struck. While he hadn't needed to take that advice in a couple of weeks, on this rainy Monday he was thankful for it. There was something about rainy weather that brought everything back. It made no sense because Vera had died on a bright winter day when the sky was clear. It might not make sense, but it was real. He needed to walk.

Retreating inside, he set his coffee mug on the window ledge. Last night, he'd barely resisted the piano music drifting up from the saloon near the river. Earlier in the day he'd invited Izzy to dine with him, but she'd begged off. The last thing he wanted to do was to worry Izzy, so he hadn't said anything about really *needing* her company. In the middle of the night, he'd gone to the office, lit a lamp, and read through a couple of newspapers until, bleary-eyed, he trudged back up the stairs and fell into bed.

He'd made it through a very long night, and now he could walk toward a warm kitchen and someone who understood. Toward someone with whom he could be completely honest. Jennie had said he was welcome in her kitchen any time, but that he should be ready to help her bake. She was probably joking when she said that. He was about to find out.

※

When Isobel arrived at the newspaper office Monday morning, the place was still locked. She looked up toward Charlie's apartment door. Dread descended. Opening her umbrella, she hurried up the rain slick stairs. He wasn't there. She looked south. Had he walked all the way to Wyuka in the rain? Should she hurry to the livery and drive out there?

Edgar rounded the corner.

Isobel called a good morning and descended the stairs. Closing her umbrella, she unlocked the office door and led the way inside.

Edgar cleared his throat. "You—um—you were looking for Charlie?"

Isobel nodded.

"I saw him on my way in." He paused.

A knot formed in Isobel's stomach. "Now you have me worried, and I was already worried. Please, Edgar. Tell me."

"Oh, it's nothing bad," Edgar said. "It's just—maybe he wouldn't want it noised about that he's calling on Mrs. Wilcox."

"He's—what?!"

"I walk by the Bishops' on my way in from the farm, and as I passed, I saw Mr. Manning stepping inside the kitchen. Mrs. Wilcox was holding the door for him. She was smiling."

Isobel removed her bonnet and hung it by the door. "Well. Thank you for telling me. And you're right. We should keep that information to ourselves." She barely managed to suppress a smile.

"Yes, ma'am." Edgar circled the office, humming as he raised the blinds to admit all the light possible.

Isobel recognized it as the same tune she'd heard from Molly that morning when the girl had talked about Edgar's being "saved." She'd just sat down at her desk when Edgar brought her a few envelopes submitted via the mail slot in the front door. Donning an apron, he went to work setting type.

The first envelope contained two sheets of carefully printed copy beneath the heading *Thomas Franklin Simmons*. She glanced at Edgar. Why drop it in the mail slot?

> Thomas Franklin Simmons was born in 1835 to William Marmaduke and Rebecca Hermione Painter Simmons. Tom grew up in Evansville, Indiana, where his parents operated a boarding house and livery. The boarding house was known to offer shelter to slaves escaping from across the river in Kentucky. Before his marriage to Nettie Ann Hancock, Tom often helped his mother pack provisions for those escapees and once gave the whole of his own savings to further the journey of a family. When President Lincoln issued the call for volunteers to quell the rebellion, the same hardy pioneer spirit that led Tom across the Missouri in search of a better future for his family inspired him to volunteer as a private in the Union Army. He was determined to follow the example set by his parents, and even though it grieved him to leave his

large family behind, he followed what he believed to be God's will, entrusting his wife and children to the same God he had been taught to worship as a child. He served honorably in the First Nebraska until he succumbed on the Shiloh battlefield, Tennessee, on April 7, 1862. Tom was a hard worker, a loving husband and father, and a faithful friend to all who knew him. Accounts such as the one in which this will be published often emphasize firsts. Tom was not the first at much of anything, but among fathers, husbands, soldiers, and friends, he was among the finest. Men like Thomas Franklin Simmons are not only the reason Nebraska thrives today but will also be the foundation for its promising future.

Finished reading, Isobel held up the papers and called to Edgar. "It's a fine tribute. You didn't need to be shy about it. You could have given it directly to me."

Edgar looked up from his work. "Given you what?"

"This." Isobel waved the papers. "About your father."

Frowning, Edgar rose and crossed the room. He reached for the papers, perusing them carefully before saying, "I didn't write this. I didn't even *know* some of it. I've never heard my grandparents' full names." He shrugged. "Ma must have written it. But I don't know why she didn't have me bring it with me to work." He studied the text again. "And I don't know why she wouldn't have told us about Pa's helping runaway slaves. That's something a body would like to know about his own father."

"Do you want to hold onto it?" Isobel asked. "You can bring it back in once you've had a chance to talk to your mother about it."

Edgar thanked her, returned the two sheets to the envelope and tucked it into his pocket.

Isobel had read through the other two submissions for *Early Days* when Charlie arrived, a small basket over his arm. "Almond cookies, courtesy of Jennie Wilcox," he said as he set the basket on the corner of Isobel's desk. "And I know it's a scandalous thing to say, but they might be better than Portia's."

Tuesday morning, Isobel stood at her open hotel window, trying to catch even the faintest of breezes. If anything, yesterday's rain had made things even more miserable by adding humidity to the air. And yet, she suspected that by noon, any lingering mud in the street would be dried and the wagons trundling along Main would raise a cloud of dust.

She turned away from the window with a sigh. If it was this hot in June, what would summer be like? She hadn't been awake for even an hour, and she already felt in need of a bath. *If I could fly away home…* She cut the thought short. *You are home.* Still, she sighed. She might not have any desire to return to St. Louis, but she did have fond memories of the zinc tub at the manse and the long, luxuriating baths she'd enjoyed as frequently as she pleased.

She descended to the dining room for a quick breakfast before heading for the office. She would be alone for the first part of the day, as Charlie was interviewing a steamboat captain who'd witnessed a fire in Kansas City. Edgar was out trying his hand at collecting late subscription fees. Charlie said they'd reached the magic number of 1,500 subscribers, which was supposed to be the right number for a newspaper to begin to turn a profit. But if said subscribers didn't pay their bill, numbers didn't matter.

On the way to the office, Isobel stepped inside Tanner Mercantile to say good morning to Birdie. They chatted briefly about the upcoming July 4th celebration and the society luncheon table. Birdie said that Jennie had promised two cakes in addition to several pies. Isobel made a mental note to hold back two pieces for Charlie. A pang of guilt hovered over the chat, and as Isobel exited, she promised herself that tomorrow she would drop the soldier's notebook off with Birdie. No matter what.

No new submissions had been dropped in the mail slot for *Early Days*, and so Isobel took on the stack of newspapers that would provide content for the next edition of the *Register*. The Senate had passed a banking bill "by a large majority." The word *Antietam* in one heading drew her attention to an article about the burial of Confederate dead. A treaty with the Navajo had resulted in their being able to return to their homeland in Arizona and New Mexico. They were walking. Three *hundred* miles. Isobel shuddered at the thought.

When the bell on the front door rang announcing the arrival of a customer, Isobel looked up. A very small woman with a very large basket over her arm waited to be acknowledged.

Isobel rose from her chair. "Good morning. How can I help you?"

"You're Miss Manning?"

"I am," Isobel nodded.

The woman drew an envelope out of the basket as she introduced herself. "Nettie Simmons. You know my boy Edgar. And Molly, of course."

Smiling, Isobel hurried to extend a hand. "It's a pleasure to meet you, Mrs. Simmons. You've raised two very hard-working young people."

"Fast-talking ones, too," Mrs. Simmons said with a little laugh. "At least in the case of Molly. I hope she hasn't overstepped with you. She says a lot of nice things about you, but I imagine that means she's talked your ear off more than once."

"I don't mind the talking," Isobel said.

"You're very kind," Mrs. Simmons held up the envelope. "Edgar said someone left this in the mail slot. He thought it was me." She handed over the Tom Simmons submission for *Early Days*.

"It wasn't?"

Mrs. Simmons shook her head. "I planned to, of course. Had it all thought out as to what I would write. But there's hardly a spare minute these days. My two youngest have been poorly, so I hadn't written it yet." She pointed at the envelope. "Seems I won't have to now."

"Did you want to make changes or corrections?"

Mrs. Simmons shook her head. "That's part of the mystery. Who could have written that? As far as I know, the only other person who might have known some of that is thought to be dead."

Goosebumps prickled. Could she possibly be talking about Private Long?

"I wish I could thank whoever did write it."

"If the author reveals himself—or herself, I'll be certain to let you know."

"I'd be grateful," Mrs. Simmons said. "Now if you'll excuse me—" She indicated the basket on her arm, "I've eggs and butter to deliver next door."

"You don't happen to have any elderberry jam in that basket, do you?"

"I'm afraid not. Why?"

"Charlie mentioned that he'd dug the last spoonful out of his last jar. Actually, it was more than a mention. More of a mournful moan."

Mrs. Simmons chuckled. "Tell him I'll see if I have an errant jar in the larder at home. Elderberries won't be ready until late summer—August or September."

"He'd be very appreciative."

"And please tell him he doesn't have to *buy* jelly at the mercantile. After what he's done for my Edgar, he's due a lifetime supply. It's the least I can do."

Chapter 33

*A talebearer revealeth secrets:
but he that is of a faithful spirit concealeth the matter.
Proverbs 11:13*

Late in the day on Tuesday, Isobel declined when Charlie suggested they take supper at a newly opened café instead of Lila's. "I want to ready my presentation about *Early Days* for this week's society meeting. I'll probably grab a sandwich from Lila's and take it up to my room."

"Why shuffle papers back and forth?" Charlie said. "I'll stay, too. I can find plenty to do and be here to walk you home when you're ready."

Isobel scrambled for a reason why that wouldn't work. "I appreciate the offer but—" she lowered her voice and said, "there's a certain attraction to the freedom a lady feels when she can…um…unlace her boots and…things." For a moment, Charlie just stared at her, but then he seemed to realize her reference to "unlacing things" was more about her corset than her boots. He blushed.

"Ah. Well." He cleared his throat. "As you wish, then."

"You could ask Jennie to go with you," Isobel suggested. "Then the two of you could offer Lila a review of her new competition. She'd probably appreciate that. In fact, she's mentioned wanting to keep business strong. Knowing her regular customers' opinions could help her."

Charlie muttered something noncommittal as he bent over the page of the *Register* he was proofreading.

Back at the hotel Isobel did not bother to change before taking up the soldier's notebook—and the Bible she had purchased at the stationer's earlier in the day. As she read, street noise diminished. Shops began to close and quiet reigned in the brief pause between regular business on Main and saloon business closer to the river.

The evening wore on as Isobel pondered Bible verses and the man who so intrigued her. At last, and with no small amount of regret, she reached the soldier's final entry in the notebook, beyond which there were only blank pages.

Precious in the sight of the Lord is the death of his saints. Psalm 116:15

Lord God, forgive my raging against what is precious to You. The very thing that gave Ma everything she longed for as Your child. Seeing her Savior. Reunion with Gabe.

Gabe? Catching her breath, Isobel sat back. *Gabe.* Her heart lurched. *Short for Gabriel. Gabriel!* She read the rest of the entry, silently mouthing the words.

Joy. Rest. Unending peace. Only good things forevermore.

I repent of my stubborn rejection of Your will.
I bless You for taking her home.
Help me accept all of Your will for me.

Isobel's hand covered her open mouth. The soldier's mother had passed away. His brother's name was *Gabriel.* Memory took her down a row of tombstones at Wyuka. *Arden Herbert Long. Grace Evelyn Long. Gabriel Matthew Long. Gideon Mark Long.* Gabriel and Gideon, twin brothers, one deceased as a child, the other vilified as a coward. Missing?

The only other person who knew those things about Tom, Nettie Simmons had said, *is probably dead.* Isobel muttered the word *probably.* She shook her head in wonder. Not only was he not dead, Private Gideon Long had returned to Nebraska. He was living in the area, trading at Tanner Mercantile, and making regular visits to Birdie and Henry's. He'd rescued her the day of the runaway and freed her mired buggy wheel only last week. Isobel focused on the final words in the notebook.

> *I determine to do my best to reject bitterness and to embrace the blessed truth that, even in deep sorrow, I <u>know</u> whom I have believed and am persuaded that <u>He is able</u> to keep that which I've committed unto Him against that day.*
> *I don't understand how He will do that. But I must believe that He will.*
> *Lord, I believe.*
> *Help my unbelief.*

Isobel read the entry again and again. He'd endured so much loss—his brother, his parents, his best friend, his reputation, and something else she couldn't quite decipher that had to do with what he termed "a calling." Tears filled her eyes. Had he seen the ashes on his tombstone? Did he know how Wade Inskeep and the others had behaved on Decoration Day?

A thousand questions swirled. Why return to Nebraska and then hide? *Had* he done something in the war of which he was ashamed? From the way Birdie defended him, that didn't seem likely.

Rising, Isobel crossed the room and retrieved the note Private Long had written her. She studied it. *Your knowing my name would serve no purpose.* He was wrong about that. Now that she knew his name, she was more determined than ever to find answers to the growing mystery of Private Gideon Long.

Charlie had already written the War Department. There was no reason to wait for a response before contacting General Wallace and the First Nebraska's commanding officers. If there was proof that could exonerate Private Gideon Long, they needed to find it. Three years had passed since the end of the war. It was reasonable to think there might be information now that hadn't been available then. All they had to do was locate it.

After a blistering hot and fruitless day of hunting, Gideon and Trouble headed back to the cabin emptyhanded. As always, Gideon took advantage of the cover provided by the web of creek beds and low spots spread across the landscape southwest of Nebraska City. They were near the cemetery when Trouble tore off after a rabbit. Gideon let him go.

The rabbit bounded into a thicket of brambles. Trouble followed, shoving his way in until only a furry rear end and a wagging tail were visible. The wagging tail was odd, for when Trouble was after game, he was usually all business. This time, he backed out of the bramble with something red in his mouth. Bounding down the creekbank to where Gideon stood, the dog dropped his treasure at Gideon's feet. *A red bandana.* He picked it up. Apparently, the woman in blue didn't believe he was serious about not communicating further. Untying the knot, he opened the note.

I have your book. I know your name.

With a sharp intake of breath, Gideon took a step back. He looked up toward the cemetery, half expecting to see a flash of blue. So real was the fear that she was up there, waiting to see him, that he ducked and took another step away, nearly falling over a boulder protruding from the earth. He sat. Hard. His hand trembled as he read.

> *I have your book. I know your name. I should like to return the book in person, for I have news that might please you. Please meet me at sunset this Friday beneath the tree where you left your canteen after our first encounter. You will recognize my rig. I have had sole possession of the book since the incident in the rain. Neither I nor the person who was with me has spoken of it to others, nor will we. Please believe that I will keep my word to protect the privacy you have gone to great lengths to preserve. To that end, I do not sign this note. My assumption is that you already know my name. I hope that you will appreciate my efforts to preserve anonymity, should this missive go astray.*

When Trouble sounded a low, concerned whine and put a paw on Gideon's knee, he started. Clearing his throat, he folded the note and tucked it in his shirt pocket. *Friday. Sunset.* He glanced up toward the cemetery. *Day after tomorrow. Just up there.* She had no idea what she was asking. Was there any way to obey the summons and still preserve his memory of her unlined, peaceful visage? If he did as she demanded—he knew what would happen. He'd had his fill of horrified stares or, sometimes worse, people who pretended not to look. He did not want that to be his last memory of her. But he did want that notebook back. What might she do if he didn't come?

Rising to his feet, he tied the bandana about his scarred neck, imagining a fragrance—the same one he remembered from the day he'd carried her up the hill to the spot beneath the burr oak tree. He wondered what she meant about having "news that might please." Was she, indeed, trustworthy? *You can test that in a few days. Retrieve the notebook as demanded. Then visit the Tanners*

Sunday evening. If she's kept her word, they won't know a thing about any of this.

He was surprised at how the possibility of her *not* being trustworthy affected him. A proverb came to mind. *Hope deferred maketh the heart sick.* That was it exactly. If she didn't keep her promise, he would be heartsick.

Chapter 34

*For now we see in a glass, darkly, but then face to face:
now I know in part; but then shall I know even as also I am known.*
I Corinthians 13:12

Private Long's notebook in hand, Isobel paced along the edge of the smudge of shade beneath the burr oak tree, around and around and around. Pleading a headache, she'd escaped helping the society ladies prepare for tomorrow's July 4th fundraiser. After taking a circuitous route to avoid detection from curious eyes, she'd arrived at the cemetery over an hour ago. She felt guilty about the invented excuse and the subterfuge, but surely a woman could be forgiven for something as important as meeting Private Gideon Long. Charlie and Birdie would understand. Isobel hoped God would, too. But the matter gave her pause.

Would God understand her lying? Since reading Private Long's notebook, she'd thought more about God than in all the previous years of her life combined. She wasn't really certain how the remote Almighty who'd hovered over her life in St. Louis responded to individual sin. Perhaps a person could make up for small lapses. *How* that was accomplished and exactly *when* atonement was finally earned was anyone's guess. She'd never worried about it. Until now.

Private Long's God seemed acutely interested in a person's day-to-day activities. What's more, He didn't stack up lapses on a scale and then weigh a person's good works against them. If Private Long was correct, the Almighty offered forgiveness freely. All a person had to do was ask for it. Simple enough—except for the element of how one gained access to make the request. Private Long believed that only the cross of Jesus Christ made it possible to square accounts. Accumulating good works and hoping for the best were not only inferior but pointless. Forgiveness could not be *earned*. It could only be *accepted*.

The concept was simplistic compared to the homilies Isobel had heard every Sunday of her younger life. She couldn't quite embrace it. Was it really that simple? What would Private Long say if she asked him such a thing? Was such a conversation even plausible? She'd thought about asking Pastor Duncan about it, but it seemed only logical to ask the man whose writings had inspired her curiosity. Of course, before any such conversation could take place, Private Long would have to forgive her for reading his notebook. *And he'd have to show up.*

Elsie stomped a foot and whickered. Going to the mare, Isobel patted the scrawny neck. "Sorry, old girl. We need to wait a bit longer." As time wore on, the sun began to sink toward the western horizon. Hope dwindled. With a deep sigh and a last look around, Isobel walked to the buggy. Setting the notebook on the seat, she climbed up, gathered the reins, and guided the rig around until Elsie faced the trail that would lead down the hill and out onto the road to town.

She was about to urge Elsie forward, when a whistle sounded from the direction of the creek behind her. A dog barked. Elsie lifted her head and pricked her ears toward the far southeastern corner of the cemetery. The dog came into view, bounding up the hill toward the rig. Isobel's pulse surged. She recognized the animal, but there was no sign of the man.

The dog streaked past her rig. Isobel leaned out far enough to see it drop out of sight beyond the blackberry brambles. A deep voice sounded from the opposite side of the oak tree.

"You have my book?"

Isobel nearly dropped the reins. "I-I do. Right here beside me on the buggy seat." She tied off the reins and prepared to climb down.

"Stay where you are."

It was an order, not a request. Isobel settled back. She picked up the book. "I'm holding it in my hand. What do you want me to do with it?" The dog had come back up out of the creek bed and was now peering at her from beyond the tree. *One ear. Blue eyes. Hopefully more friendly than the human sounded.*

"Assuming it dropped out of my pocket the day of the storm, you've had it for some time. Did you read it?"

Wasn't he going to step out into the open? She'd planned an apology, but that was when she'd thought their written communications would have already overcome the man's reluctance for face-to-face encounters. Talking to the air felt ridiculous when she knew he was standing only a few feet away. Ah, well. "I told myself I shouldn't read it. I didn't really intend to do so. When I first opened it, I was simply scanning for a name. Hoping to learn more about you."

"Why?"

Was he being deliberately obtuse? Wouldn't anyone in her situation have wanted to know more? Wouldn't they have read the notebook? Whatever she'd hoped for, Private Long's remaining out of sight while he interrogated her with one-word questions wasn't it. Taking a deep breath, Isobel attempted to explain herself. "My curiosity has grown over time. It began after the runaway, when I wanted to thank you in person for what you did. It seemed reasonable to think Birdie and Henry would be able to identify you—especially when I mentioned a dog. But they couldn't—or wouldn't. Then I saw you come out of the mercantile storeroom the morning of our cemetery workday, and I realized you were the very person who'd helped me. They *did* know you. I couldn't understand why they wouldn't introduce us. But not only were they unwilling, they resisted talking about you at all. Henry said that you are something of a hermit, and they'd promised to protect your privacy."

"I am, and they did. But you've stubbornly persisted."

Stubborn. Isobel pondered the word for a moment. Was she stubborn? She certainly didn't see herself that way. With a little shake of her head, she defended herself. "I *didn't* persist. Not after Birdie offered to give you a note. I wrote one, and I gave up on the idea of ever knowing more."

He was quiet for a moment. Pondering what she'd said? Considering whether or not to believe her? Finally, he spoke again.

"And yet, here I am, weeks later, in answer to your summons."

A summons. Was that how he felt about it? She didn't like the idea of him thinking her some kind of threat. What was he afraid of? How could she reassure him? Was it even possible to gain trust enough to have a real conversation? "I didn't mean the note as a threat," she said.

"Then why are we here? You could have returned my notebook through Birdie."

Isobel sighed. "I suppose, in my own way, I was trying to keep your confidence. Returning the notebook through Birdie would have required me to reveal that I'm aware of your identity. I didn't think you'd want me to do that." When the private didn't respond, she continued. "I don't want to do that, either—at least not yet."

"What do you mean, 'not yet'"?

There was an edge to his voice. Again. Isobel tried to explain. "I assume you know what happened on Decoration Day. That had to be hard for you—but you aren't the only one. It was extremely upsetting for Birdie. The Tanners have been wonderful to both Charlie and me. After that incident, we determined to try and silence the spurious rumors about Private Gideon Long. The war's been over for years. There must be records that will put all of that to rest. We want to find them."

"Why would you care about any of that?"

"For Birdie. For the Simmons family. For the G.A.R. members who've never believed the rumor. For history." Isobel paused. "Wouldn't *you* like to have your name cleared? To be able to come and go as you please?" When the private didn't respond, Isobel continued. "At any rate, I don't want Birdie to know that I know—in case our efforts fall short. Charlie says it's possible, no matter how diligent our search, that we won't be able to find anything. I don't want to create false hope." When Private Long still said nothing, Isobel added, "But protecting Birdie isn't the only reason I asked you to meet me here."

"Do tell."

Sarcasm? Doubt? Isobel forged ahead. "It's because I read the notebook. Because of the way you write about religion. About *your* religion."

"What you call 'my religion' is hardly unique. It's shared by countless people."

"Maybe so," Isobel said, "but it's unique to me. I've always attended church, but I've never encountered someone like you."

"That I believe."

"I don't mean that," Isobel said with a frustrated shake of her head. "I've never encountered someone who questions faith with such—*desperation*, for lack of a better word."

"Then perhaps you haven't spoken with many veterans of what some call 'the recent unpleasantness.'"

Isobel ignored the comment, turning the conversation back toward Private Long and his experience. "You write about a transformation that occurred in a moment of time. A moment to which, after a season of struggle, you can point with great certainty."

After a moment, Private Long said, "Not everyone's conversion is as dramatic as mine."

"Understood. But everyone has moments when they feel desperate. Moments when hope eludes them."

"And?"

"That moment in time changed you in such a way that when you needed hope, you looked to the Bible for help. You saw it as a pathway to understanding."

"Ultimately, yes—but not instantly. And for all the time I've spent in the Bible, I still have unanswered questions. There are still plenty of things I don't understand."

Isobel nodded and then felt foolish, realizing the man couldn't see her response. The more pressed she felt to resolve her own questions, the more frustrated she was by the strangeness of this meeting. With a huff, she said, "As I said, I'm a Christian—at least I think I am. And yet, in *my* worst moment, I never considered my religion as a harbor from trouble. Not once did I think to open an ancient book seeking answers. Instead, I ran away. I came to Nebraska. Your quest for hope took you to the Bible. Mine brought me to my brother. But Charlie was mired in his own troubles. He didn't consider religion, either. In fact, he openly rejected it. Why? What's the difference between the religion we grew up with and yours? Why do some people trust God and others reject him? Not that I've rejected the Almighty, mind you. I haven't. But still—you have something Charlie and I don't."

"And yet, you are both finding your way," Private Long said.

"What makes you say that?" How would he know anything about either her or Charlie?

"First, your brother," Private Long replied. "I sometimes set rabbit snares south of here. I've heard curses and sobs. Seen the flask and wavering steps. I know despair, Miss Manning. The notebook is part of my attempt to find my way through it. Your brother seems to be finding his way since *your* arrival. Now when he visits, there is no flask. He leaves flowers, says a few words, and departs. At times, he even seems to pray. A man who can pray over the grave of his wife and child is a man on his way to finding hope. It's logical to assume at least part of that is the presence of his sister."

Isobel looked toward Vera's grave marker. *If only that were true.* She shook her head and once again reminded herself that he couldn't see her reaction. She would have to put the denial into words. And so she did. Bluntly. "That's kind of you to say, but the truth is I didn't come to Nebraska to help Charlie. I came to *be* helped. I didn't even know he'd married—or lost his wife and baby. And for quite some time after I arrived, Charlie made it very clear that he was counting the days until my departure. He insisted I should give up on him and go back to St. Louis."

"And yet," the private said, "here you are."

"I had nowhere else to go." After she'd blurted out that truth, Isobel felt her cheeks flaming with embarrassment. Why had she allowed an encounter with this man to wander into such personal matters? She glanced at the western sky. It was getting late. Private Long had no interest in having the conversation she wanted to have. It was time to give up and get back to town. She would gather her thoughts and speak with Pastor Duncan.

Whatever Gideon had expected when he answered Miss Manning's summons, this wasn't it. Her brother hadn't wanted her to stay? He knew what it felt like to be unwanted. He'd seen rejection in the eyes of everyone he'd dared to look at on the long trek home. She had nowhere else to go? Could that be true? He thought back to the night of her arrival. Given Charlie

Manning's frequent state of drunkenness combined with what she'd just admitted, the poor woman had not had an easy time of it.

After muttering something about the late hour, she'd stopped talking. Now, she was sitting quietly. Was she embarrassed by the personal turn the conversation had taken? Compassion swept over him. He looked toward the western horizon, where the sun was sinking fast. He'd come intending to snatch the notebook and retreat to the cabin. *The cabin you were in when you wondered if the notebook might help whoever found it.* He took a deep breath. He was still afraid of what this woman might do with what she'd learned about him, but now he wondered if something else might be at work. Was this of God or was loneliness tempting him to take a ridiculous risk? Abruptly, he asked, "What do you intend to do with the information you've acquired about me?"

"Are you asking if I'm going to tell the world that Private Gideon Long is alive?"

"Yes."

"No. Not unless you agree to it."

He would never agree to such a thing, but she didn't need to know that this evening.

Miss Manning spoke again. "I haven't breathed a word of what I know—not about your notebook, not about realizing who you are, not about any of it. To *anyone*. Not to Birdie or Henry or Nettie Simmons—not even to my own brother. I haven't and I won't without your permission. I promise."

A phrase from the Old Testament came to Gideon's mind. Had the notebook been lost *for such a time as this*? He looked down at Trouble. The dog was watching him with interest. The tail thumped. Swallowing, Gideon said, "It's growing late, but if you still wish to discuss some of the things I wrote about, I suppose we could meet here once more." She answered immediately.

"When?"

For such a time as this. He allowed a faint smile. "My social calendar is open. What say you?"

"I'd say tomorrow evening if it weren't Independence Day. Everyone says to expect throngs from every corner of the county. The cemetery society is sponsoring another luncheon counter. I should help."

"Birdie told me about that. I wish you great success."

"Sunday evening probably isn't advisable, either, what with people's penchant for Sunday drives."

"Monday, then?"

"Monday. And the notebook?"

"Do you need it to remind you of what you want to discuss?"

She allowed a low laugh. "Hardly."

"Then drop it on the grass. I'll retrieve it after you've gone." From the shadows he watched as she tossed the notebook toward Vera Manning's obelisk. "What will you ask first when we next meet?"

Again, she didn't hesitate. "You said not everyone experiences a conversion like yours. All right. But you are certain that you had one. I'm not. I'd like to understand what makes your religion so different from the one I grew up with."

Goosebumps prickled as Gideon realized that Miss Manning had just asked 'Preacher Long' to share the gospel. He cleared his throat. "I shall do my best to answer the question in a satisfactory manner."

"I shall look forward to it," Miss Manning said and signaled her ugly horse forward.

With Trouble at his side, Gideon watched the buggy until it had crossed Table Creek. He retrieved the notebook. All the way back to the cabin and for most of the night, he pondered the next conversation he would have with Miss Manning. He wrote and rewrote the story of his conversion. And he prayed for the woman who seemed to understand that, while she knew *about* God, she didn't *know* Him.

Chapter 35

Boast not thyself of tomorrow;
for thou knowest not what a day may bring forth.
Proverbs 27:1

Saturday's Independence Day fundraiser succeeded so completely that the membership spent the entire day rushing back and forth to replenish quickly emptying tables. Eventually, the ladies were forced to return to their homes to round up whatever they could find to replenish stock. Birdie even broke into her last few precious tins of English biscuits and parceled them out at a price that even she labeled ridiculous. Every biscuit sold.

After church, Isobel and Charlie joined society members at a celebratory picnic at the cemetery—the perfect setting for a lively discussion of how best to use their earnings. Enthusiasm ran high for more fundraisers. America Payne offered to piece a patriotic quilt. The design she had in mind was from a wartime ladies' magazine. It featured good-sized white stars on a striped red and blue ground. What if they collected signatures on the stars? All sorts of ideas rose up, from writing to former Union generals to soliciting local dignitaries. America was appointed to oversee it all. She even offered her parlor for the quilting. The finished quilt would be displayed at Tanner Mercantile for the month prior to next year's Decoration Day. Silent bids would be accepted to avoid ruffling the more conservative religious feathers in the city. When Isobel expressed confusion on that point, Jennie explained that some would consider a raffle akin to gambling. Isobel wondered what Private Long would think of that.

On Sunday evening a tired Isobel looked out her hotel room window toward Tanner Mercantile. Private Long might be there at this very moment, playing checkers with Henry. Eating a piece of the pie Birdie had purchased the moment Jennie delivered her contributions on Independence Day. Said pie had not been brought back down when the society luncheon counter needed it, and Isobel knew why. It was being saved back in the event Private Long made a Sunday evening visit.

You'd risk losing the small amount of trust he has in you. Be satisfied with that for now. She knew that was probably right. Still, she wondered why they couldn't have a normal conversation like two reasonable adults. Oh, it was thrilling—romantic, even—to know she was the only other person besides the Tanners who knew that Private Gideon Long was living in Nebraska. But, really—it felt childish to play what amounted to hide and seek.

In the end, caution won the argument. She would be content—for now. Remembering how guarded Birdie and Henry had been on the topic of "the hermit," she would be grateful for the progress she'd made. She would be patient and accept what she didn't understand. She would strive to *give grace* when it came to Private Long's war record and focus on the topic about which he was willing to speak.

When Isobel stepped into the newspaper office on Monday morning, Charlie pointed at the three stacks of envelopes atop her desk. "It would seem the populace is embracing your society's project."

Given the throngs who'd come to town for Independence Day, Isobel had expected a few extra submissions, but she wasn't prepared for an avalanche. She'd only read a few submissions when she called to Charlie. "Anonymity invites interesting commentary." She read aloud, "'Trees planted too close together. Maples won't last when a storm blows through. You need a well. Trees will die without regular watering. Especially maples. Plant oaks and hackberry.'" She smiled. "Perhaps we should put an announcement in the *Register* that the Simmons boys have been hired to water the trees."

Charlie joined her in a quiet laugh. He sorted through the calling cards he was printing, rejecting a few before pausing to say, "You know, the Honorable J. Sterling Morton is a great promoter of tree-planting. You might consider contacting the Mortons about a well."

"They're already paying for the fence," Isobel said. "It's best not to be too pushy with generous benefactors. It can be seen as presumption." She opened another envelope, which contained a short note—and a dollar bill. She held up the dollar. "All it says is 'Glad to see folks caring for the graveyard.'" She'd tucked the money back into the envelope when the front door opened. A telegraph messenger stepped in.

Charlie took the telegram, tipped the messenger, and crossed to his desk to open it. He frowned when he glanced down. "It's from St. Louis."

Since Edgar didn't usually come to work until noon on Mondays, Isobel felt free to emote. "Don't tell me Mother Manning's haranguing *you*, now. At some point she's going to have to accept reality. I am *not* going back."

"It's not from her," Charlie muttered. "It's from Mr. Wilder, the banker."

Mother Manning's penchant for overspending was no secret to her stepchildren. Isobel set the submission she'd been reading aside. "It can't be good if we're hearing directly from Mr. Wilder. What's she done now?"

Charlie looked up. Shock and disbelief sounded in his voice. "She's died, Isobel. Mother Manning *died*."

The words landed like a blow. When Charlie handed the telegram over, Isobel had to read it more than once. *Regret to inform you...expired suddenly...just home from a ball.* She looked up and met Charlie's gaze. "A fall." She sighed. Mother never allowed herself to become truly inebriated. But she had always imbibed a little too freely when it came to punch. Looking back down at the telegram, she reread the words *ascending the stairs.* She imagined the yards of silk in a ball gown, the several petticoats and hoops—and the dancing *slippers*, so aptly named because they enabled a lady to slide across the dance floor with grace. *To slip.* It wasn't difficult to imagine how an older woman might lose her balance and trip. But to fall to her death? Isobel shuddered. Once again, she looked at Charlie who'd pulled his desk chair out and sat, facing her. For a moment they stared at one another, speechless.

Charlie was the first to break the silence. "I'll respond so Mr. Wilder knows we've received the message." He grimaced. "We'll need to go back, of course. I'll check on passage downriver while I'm out." He looked about the office. Regret sounded in his voice as he said, "Just when we've gotten the *Register* back on an even keel." And then he apologized. "I'm sorry. That sounded unfeeling."

"We're both in shock," Isobel said. "My mind's racing, too." Like Charlie, she felt regret more than anything. For herself. She didn't want to go back to St. Louis. She wanted to work here at the *Register*. She wanted to compile more stories for *Early Days*. And go to the society meeting at Teddy Hall's on Thursday evening to hear the final Independence Day luncheon counter report. Most of all, she wanted to drive out to the cemetery this evening and hear Private Long's version of that sermon.

Finally, Charlie rose to his feet. He would send a simple, "Telegram received. More to come" reply. Before opening the door to leave, though, he hesitated.

"What is it?" Isobel asked.

"Think carefully before you answer this."

"Answer what?" Isobel frowned.

He spoke slowly. "Do you think you'll want to move back?"

"Never!" Isobel said immediately.

"I said you should think *carefully*, Izzy. Things would be very different without Mother Manning there. The manse would be yours. You'd be an independent lady of means. One of the matriarchs of society."

Isobel glowered at him. "I'm too young to be a matriarch."

"You know what I mean."

She did. And with the image of her living alone in the manse came another—Alfred Warfield with Mary Halifax on his arm. *Unless she's Mrs. Warfield by now.* Isobel shook her head. "Things wouldn't be different *enough*." She added, "*You* might want to consider it, though. I have no difficulty at all envisioning you in Papa's library. You always loved that room. And you know Portia and Caesar would stay on." She blinked. "Portia and Caesar! What will become of them?"

Charlie shrugged. "That's one of dozens—perhaps hundreds—of questions we're going to have to answer in coming days." He paused. "Like you, though, I already know the answer to one. I do not want to live in St. Louis."

"If you think it will facilitate Mr. Wilder's handling of things, you might want to mention that in the telegram."

Charlie hesitated. "Let's wait a bit." He gave a little smile. "You mentioned Papa's library. I might want his desk. Perhaps there are things you'd like to keep as well. Think on it. Perhaps begin a list while I'm out. After all, not all the memories are bad."

Isobel nodded. "If you're keeping the desk, consider the books. Teddy said the ladies' literary club has been touting the opening of a library. Perhaps they'd welcome a donation—assuming we don't wish to keep every volume." She looked up toward Charlie's apartment. "There's only so much space for shelving up there."

Charlie nodded. "That's an example of why we need time to ponder before traveling."

After Charlie left, Isobel sat, staring out the window for a few moments before finally taking up pen and paper to begin the list he'd suggested. But she didn't write anything. Instead, she thought more about what it was going to be like, returning to St. Louis. They were going to have to plan a funeral. *A funeral.* She had nothing suitable to wear. How quickly, she wondered, could Teddy Hall produce mourning garb.

Chapter 36

*The steps of a good man are ordered by the
Lord: and he delighteth in his way.
Though he fall, he shall not be utterly cast down:
for the Lord upholdeth him with his hand.
Psalm 37:23-24*

Charlie sent a telegram and checked on passage to St. Louis. As he stepped out of the telegraph office and looked east, uncertainty over the situation he and Izzy faced rained down, along with a jumble of unanswered questions. What would they do with the manse? What about the furnishings? What about Portia and Caesar? Who would officiate the funeral? What about an obituary? Did Mother Manning have a will? What laws would govern what happened next?

Blindsided by the longing for a drink, Charlie reached for the flask he'd always kept in his coat pocket. *Idiot. You threw it away.* Still, he cursed the old habit and the weakness that had resurrected it. *Forty-one days.* That's how long it had been since Jennie Wilcox had cleared his office of the hidden bottles. Had she missed any, he'd be thinking up an excuse to send Izzy off on an errand so he could unearth it. Forty-one days and he was still captive to amber liquid. Still a fraud, pretending to rise above past losses when, in truth, he was as vulnerable as ever.

He argued with himself as he walked along, head down, not caring in what direction he walked—as long as it was away from the newspaper office, away from questions, away from the idea that Izzy might look to him for guidance. Away from the undeniable truth that he wasn't merely unprepared for this responsibility; he was unfit.

His mind a troubled jumble of desire and muddled argument against satisfying said desire, Charlie trudged along, oblivious to his surroundings. When someone laid a hand on his arm, he jerked away. And then, when he realized who'd touched him, he felt ashamed. "I beg your pardon." He avoided looking Jennie in the eye.

"I'd stepped onto the kitchen porch for a breath of fresh air when I saw you march by," she said. "I hope you'll forgive the intrusion. I could see by the way you trudged along that you were deep in thought." She tucked her hand neatly beneath his arm in the manner of a lady being escorted by a gentleman. "Would talking to a friend help, perhaps? Over a cup of tea?"

Charlie looked past her, surprised to see that he had, indeed, walked far enough to pass by the Bishop manse. He looked at the house and then back in the direction from which he'd come. "I—um—I should get back to the office. I just—I needed to think."

Jennie squeezed his arm. "Do you also need to talk with someone who understands?" When he didn't reply, she continued. "I waged a frightful battle against my old nemesis after returning to Nebraska. Now that I think about it, it's been a similar length of time since we cleaned out your office." She paused. "I've a couple of gooseberry pies in the oven. I have to keep an eye on them, but if you'll come in for tea, I'll listen."

Paralyzed by indecision, Charlie stared at the house. He didn't pull away, but he didn't accept her invitation, either. Finally, he said, "I don't—know." Again, he muttered about needing to get back to the office. "Izzy's waiting. We've had news—bad news." Finally, he met Jennie's gaze. "It's our stepmother. There was an accident. She died. We'll have to go back to St. Louis."

Charlie didn't really listen to the exact words Jennie spoke in response. Her kind voice was little more than a hum sounding above the rumble of responsibility threatening to overwhelm him. Her kindness, however, did not erase the longing for a drink. She'd mentioned tea. A drop or two of whiskey in a cup of tea would fortify him.

"Come in, Charlie. Please." She tugged on his arm. "Cook has the day off. Mother Bishop's at a meeting, and Pa Bishop's at the office."

No one will hear a word. There's no one to eavesdrop. That was the message she was conveying. But if there was no one home—Charlie shook his head. "Your mother-in-law would have my head for stepping inside when there's no one else there."

"You let me worry about Mother Bishop," Jennie said. "If you stay long enough, the offer includes a warm piece of gooseberry pie."

Charlie looked into her blue eyes. He looked toward the manse and the kitchen. A friendly place, that kitchen. A good woman, this. He didn't really care for gooseberry pie. Still, he allowed Jennie to lead him inside.

※

Having spent over an hour talking to Jennie, Charlie returned to the office, only to find it closed. He grimaced as he read the note affixed to the door. *Inquire at Tanner Mercantile if you require assistance.*

He looked toward the mercantile storeroom door. At least he knew where to find Izzy. Still, he dreaded explaining why an errand that should have taken moments had taken over an hour. Jennie had advised him to simply tell the truth. *The entire truth.* From anyone else the idea would have made him laugh. But Jennie knew the risks of admitting that the same old nemesis had almost captured him in its grip. And still, she advised truth-telling.

Walking over to the mercantile storeroom door, he hesitated. He looked down at the pie nestled in the basket Jennie had insisted he bring back with him. He took a deep breath. When he'd left her kitchen, basket in hand, he'd had a plan of action in mind. Now, his mood plummeted. He'd very nearly plunged right back into old ways. Taking a deep breath, he stepped inside the storeroom.

"I take it you saw my note," Izzy said. She was seated at the small table at the base of the stairs, a teacup and saucer before her, Birdie's tea service pushed to one side.

"I'm sorry I was gone so long," Charlie said as he set the basket on a step. "I brought pie." *Lame. Stupid.* Apparently not, though, for when Izzy peered into the basket, temper and impatience faded from her expression.

"You went to see Jennie."

Still feeling on edge, Charlie removed his hat and dropped into the available chair. "Not intentionally. But I ended up there." He raked through his hair. "I sent the telegram, I checked on passage, and then—" *Tell the truth.* With a shrug, he explained what had happened.

"And talking to her helped."

Charlie nodded.

"Thank God for Jennie," Izzy said and smiled.

Taking a deep breath, Charlie explained that he'd booked Friday passage for them both on the *Zephyr*. "There were other packets coming through sooner. But once we disembark in St. Louis, we'll get swept along with the demands of attorneys, bankers, the undertaker, and who knows who else. I thought we needed a few days to talk—with each other and with people we trust here."

Izzy nodded. "I agree. After you left, I tried to start the list you suggested, but I couldn't think. Then Edgar came in and—"

"The calling cards!" Charlie huffed. "I forgot all about—"

Izzy held up a hand to stay his protest. "It's all right. Edgar printed them. Mrs. Taylor picked them up a little while ago. She was very pleased."

"Edgar," Charlie muttered. "I didn't think—"

"He said you'd shown him how to run the small press. It was already set up. I didn't think there was any harm in letting him try."

Charlie nodded. The idea he was about to propose to Izzy made even more sense in light of Edgar's willingness to run the press. "That's grand. Thank you. And I'm sorry I was gone so long."

"You needed to talk to a friend," Izzy gestured about her. "Which is why I came over here after Edgar left. So did I."

"I shouldn't have—"

She interrupted him. "Stop apologizing, Charlie. I'm not upset with you. You were feeling overwhelmed. You did the right thing in seeking out an understanding friend. We'll muddle through this together. Birdie's invited us for supper, and I accepted." She rose to her feet. "Right now, though, I'm going to take a short drive to clear my head." When Charlie leaped to his feet, she said, "A drive *alone*." As she opened the storeroom door to step outside, she said, "My list of things to keep from the manse is on my desk. The only thing on it is Papa's desk and his books. I'll probably have a few things to add when I get back."

❦

Miss Manning was waiting at the cemetery when Gideon arrived, but instead of hitching the buggy in its usual spot, she'd brought it around on the path so that she was facing the road. He called to her from his now customary spot at the oak tree. "You don't seem inclined to linger."

"We received a telegram from St. Louis a few hours ago. Our stepmother passed away suddenly. We're awash in estate matters and travel plans. I begged Charlie's indulgence to take a drive and clear my head, but I can't linger this evening."

"I am sorry for your loss," Gideon said, cringing even as he heard the words escape his lips. "I don't mean that as a cliché. I truly am sorry. Losing a parent can cause a deep wound."

For a moment Miss Manning said nothing. Finally, she offered her thanks for his kindness, but then she, too, got past the cliché. "Our relationship with Mother Manning was—difficult. Always difficult. She never—" She broke off. "Never mind. None of that matters anymore. I didn't want you to wonder—although I suppose you would have learned the news from Birdie." Again, she paused. "I wish we had more time to talk. I don't know how long I'll be gone. Charlie says it could take weeks to settle everything. There's a large house, the furnishings, servants—the usual financial muddle. At least I hope it's a *usual* muddle. Our father was very responsible, but he's been gone—and I'm rambling. I apologize. I should go." Abruptly, she bid him goodbye. She urged the horse forward without waiting for a reply.

Gideon watched her drive away. As he made his way back to the cabin, he asked God to provide the Mannings wisdom for the myriad decisions awaiting them and safe passage back to Nebraska. His heart stuttered a bit at mention of the return trip. He frowned. It sounded as though the Manning estate was consequential. What if she didn't come back? What if he never had the chance to share the gospel?

Chapter 37

Blessed are they that mourn: for they shall be comforted.
Matthew 5:4

Obviously, Izzy's drive had done her good. She was more relaxed during supper with the Tanners, teasing Charlie as Birdie set a huge slice of Jennie's pie before him.

"I didn't think you liked gooseberry pie."

"I like this one," Charlie said, pointedly ignoring his sister's knowing look. He wasn't about to explain the basis for his friendship with Jennie Wilcox—and it was merely a friendship. He would never explain it by betraying Jennie's past.

When Birdie had served pie and poured coffee, Charlie introduced his big idea. "I've something for you to consider," he said to Izzy. "The trip is ten days there and ten days back. It has to be made, but I hate the idea of closing down the *Register*, just when I—when *we* have finally gotten her up and running again."

Izzy looked both surprised and pleased that he'd use that word *we*. "I'm frustrated, too—although I feel guilty about that." She looked over at Birdie. "I can't seem to manage grief. Instead, I'm resenting taking time away from our committee work and from writing *Early Days*." She glanced at Charlie. "Not to mention the paper."

"From what little Henry and I know," Birdie said, "Mrs. Manning was a difficult woman. Doing your duty by her may be all that can reasonably be expected."

Taking a deep breath, Charlie launched his question. "What if you didn't have to leave? What if I took care of things in St. Louis and you stayed here?"

Izzy's expression was one of surprise, but she didn't seem closed to the idea. She looked from Henry to Birdie before asking, "Do you think the lawyers would allow it?"

Birdie spoke first. "Why wouldn't they? It's not as if they'd consider a woman's opinion about anything." She glanced at Henry. "A harsh truth, my dear, but truth, nevertheless."

Izzy looked at Charlie. "Birdie makes a good point. When I consulted Mr. Wilder about coming to Nebraska, he was kind and helpful, but he also made it clear he was uncomfortable with the situation. If Papa had still been alive, I doubt I'd have seen the inside of the man's office—unless I was on Papa's arm." She turned to Henry. "In this situation, I assume Charlie would need some kind of proof that he was authorized to speak for me,"

Henry nodded. "You'd want to send along an official document naming him your representative in matters of the estate."

"They could speak with Jethro about that," Birdie said and then looked from Charlie to Izzy and explained, "Jethro Titus, Attorney-at-Law. He's a deacon in our church. Well respected."

Izzy seemed to be considering the idea, but still she raised an objection. "What will people think if I'm not at the funeral? What will they say?"

"Does it matter?" Charlie asked.

Izzy tilted her head. "I don't suppose it does, as long as you don't mind the snide comments and odd looks."

Charlie spoke with more confidence than he felt. "I can handle snide comments and odd looks." He forced a smile. "The question is, can *you* handle the *Register* while I'm gone?"

Izzy's jaw dropped. Presently, she stammered, "I-I'm n-not qualified to run a newspaper."

"You know more than you think. You've already helped with nearly every aspect of it."

"I haven't run the press. Or sold advertising space. Or—"

Before she could list more objections, Charlie interrupted. "Edgar and I will print the next edition before I leave. That will give him a refresher at running the press. You're excellent at selecting articles from the other papers, and you'd have only three issues to produce while I'm gone. Four at most. You can always reach me by telegram if problems arise." He reached across the table and squeezed her hand. "You can do this, Izzy. I know you can."

"You'd really trust me with your newspaper?"

Charlie nodded, smiling with the realization that yes, he trusted Izzy. "Truth be told, *you'd* have to do more trusting than me."

She frowned. "How so?"

"You know what nearly happened this morning."

"But it didn't," Izzy said quickly.

"Granted, but there's precious little opportunity to escape freely pouring liquor on board a steamboat. Once in St. Louis, I'll encounter friends who remember the old Charlie Manning—always the first to suggest a drink and too often the last to recognize when he'd had enough. There's no reason for them to think I've changed."

"But you have," Izzy said firmly. "You've left that Charlie behind."

Lord knew he was trying. Tomorrow would be day forty-two. Not that he was counting.

※

A flurry of telegrams passed between Nebraska City and St. Louis during the few days before Charlie's departure aboard the *Zephyr*. With the help of the Missouri estate attorneys and Mr. Titus of Nebraska City, documents were drawn up and signed. Charles Victor Manning was authorized to speak for Isobel Victoria Manning in all matters pertaining to the estate of the late Lucinda Carothers Manning, widow of Edward Victor Manning. Edgar performed well as a pressman, and Izzy was well on her way to planning the first issue to be produced in Charlie's absence.

Only one thing remained for Charlie and Izzy to discuss. He broached that topic on Thursday evening after they'd dined at the hotel. As he brewed coffee in his apartment for a waiting Izzy, his excitement grew. Surely she would say yes. Surely she would see the logic in it. The timing couldn't be better. They were both ready for it.

As darkness fell, Izzy sat at the small table in Charlie's apartment while he brewed coffee. "Am I in trouble?" she asked.

"Why would you think that?"

"You didn't want to discuss this—whatever it is—until we came up here. That makes me nervous."

"It's nothing to be nervous about," Charlie said. "It's a good thing. I hope." He set mugs of steaming coffee on the table and then collected the notebook he'd used in recent days. Sitting opposite her, he began. "I've wandered a lot since leaving home—in more ways than one. From the war to gold mining to Nebraska. I've spent much of that time fighting some*thing* or some*one*—including myself." He paused. "Mother's death has made me realize that it's time I committed to putting down roots. Here. In Nebraska City." He opened the notebook and pushed it across the table. "With you—if you're interested."

Izzy looked down at what he'd sketched and then looked up again, waiting for him to explain.

Charlie indicated the two front doors at opposite ends of the expansive porch he'd drawn across the front of a modest house. "Separate entries. Inside each door, one either takes the stairs leading up to a private apartment or enters the shared living space on the main floor—parlor, library, dining room, and small kitchen." He pointed to the floor plan he'd sketched. We'd be able to furnish it without buying a thing—assuming we can abide the stuff we grew up with." He sat back. "Be honest if you don't think we can make it work."

Izzy studied the sketch before looking up at him. "Y-you're proposing we share a house?"

"Yes. A house we have built."

She was silent for a long few moments. "I don't know what to say."

Charlie teased her. "I know you find Molly Simmons endlessly entertaining, but surely you're tiring of hotel living by now."

"On that topic," Izzy said, "I meant to ask if I might move over here while you're gone."

"Of course you can. I'm ashamed I didn't think of it." He tapped the drawing. "It doesn't have to look like this. It's only an idea."

"I like it."

"Then say yes."

She swiped at a tear. "Yes."

He was surprised by the happiness that surged through him. Reaching for the notebook, he turned to a blank page. Dipping his fountain pen into the ink well, he began a new list, murmuring as he wrote, "Parlor chairs. Dining set. Shaving mirror."

"My bedstead and dressing mirror," Izzy said.

Charlie looked up and smiled. "I remember you doing a pirouette in front of that mirror the day Papa gave it to you. Ninth birthday, was it?"

"Tenth." Izzy thought for a moment and then said, "Portia will have to help with the kitchen. Are we certain she and Caesar won't want to come back with you?"

"I can't imagine it. Not with their entire family living there in St. Louis." Charlie thought for a moment. "Do you even know how old they are? I have no idea."

Izzy shook her head. "Even when we were young, I thought them ancient. I suppose they are by now."

"I'll speak with Mr. Wilder about what to do."

Izzy nodded. She told him about the day of the wedding. Mother Manning's reaction and the housekeeper's kindness. "Portia was always there for me. Always. I want to make sure they can have a comfortable old age."

Charlie nodded. "I'll see to it."

"I'm just beginning to realize how our lives could change," Izzy said. "Do you think we might be able to sponsor the well at the cemetery? And a flagpole?"

"I'll let you know as soon as I know," Charlie promised. "In the meantime, begin another list of causes you wish to support. I like the idea of Manning funds making good things happen here in Nebraska. Also, if you have time and want to do it, get some estimates for the house. Look at possible building sites."

"We'll want to hire help with cooking and cleaning." Izzy paused to think for a moment and then murmured, "I wonder if Molly Simmons would take us on."

"Can she cook?"

"I'll find out."

"Just don't make any promises," Charlie cautioned. "I have no idea what to expect financially. We both know how Mother Manning was with money. You and I could well end up having to foot the shipping bill for bringing furniture west."

They talked half the night, refining the list of things to be crated and shipped to Nebraska City. They laughed and reminisced and revised the house plan. They discussed costs. Finally, Charlie walked Izzy to the hotel. He returned to his apartment with a smile on his face. For the first time since Vera's passing, he was daring to look ahead. Daring to plan for the future.

Chapter 38

Man is born unto trouble, as the sparks fly upward.
Job 5:7

The Sunday after Charlie departed, Pastor Duncan preached on the topic of prayer. He encouraged the congregation to address the Almighty with a surety that He was listening and would respond. He referenced several verses of Scripture, and Isobel recognized one from Private Long's notebook. In his closing prayer, Pastor Duncan mentioned an ailing member of the congregation by name and asked God to heal the woman.

Hearing Pastor Duncan's petition, Isobel wondered if that meant she could appeal to God in the matter of Charlie's river passage. Might God help Charlie resist the temptation to imbibe? Beyond readings from the Book of Common Prayer, Isobel had no experience with this kind of praying. Would God hear and answer someone like her? Doubt niggled. She liked to think she was a good person, but the idea of the Almighty or Jesus listening carefully to anything she said seemed presumptuous. Perhaps she would ask Private Long about it the next time they spoke. But first—her duties as a lady newspaper editor. She headed home to the apartment above the office. *Her* office, until Charlie returned.

Isobel faced the week with hopeful confidence, only slightly daunted by Monday morning's harsh lesson. Watching someone else brew coffee or make tea—which she had done countless times—was not the same thing as being able to do it oneself. Defeated by Charlie's little stove, Isobel realized she would either have to humble herself and expose her complete ignorance or plan on eating breakfast at Lila's every morning. She chose the latter, at least for the next few days until life without Charlie settled into a routine.

Once downstairs in the office, she swept up the few submissions for *Early Days* that had been tucked into the mail slot. After raising the blinds around the room, she settled at her desk, a satisfied smile on her lips. The smile broadened with the reading of the first note. Private Long had been in town last evening.

> *Our mutual friend informs me that you remain in Nebraska with new responsibilities. Should you wish to continue conversation, I shall await you at the usual place this Friday. God grant you and yours wisdom for the tasks that lie ahead.*

Did that mean Private Long had mentioned her and Charlie in his prayers? She rather liked the notion. She tucked the note into a pocket just as Jennie Wilcox bustled past the window and ducked inside. The young widow was crying, and Isobel envisioned tragedy at the Bishops'. She sprang to her feet. "What's happened?"

Drawing a handkerchief from a pocket, Jennie dabbed at the tears trailing down her cheeks. "I–Is Edgar—?"

"Not expected until noon today. What's gotten you so upset?" When Jennie only shook her head, Isobel drew Charlie's desk chair over and compelled her to sit. Moving her own chair close, she leaned forward. "Tell me what's happened."

It was still a few moments before the young widow regained her composure. Finally, tucking her crumpled handkerchief back into its pocket, she began. "Do you remember that morning we took the drive with your new rig and delivered pies to Lila Richie?"

"Of course."

"And Sam mentioned their moving to Denver to be near family?"

"Yes."

"Well, Lila has decided to do it. She drew me aside after church yesterday to tell me. And she has it in her head that *I* should take over the café." Before Isobel could say a word, Jennie discounted the idea. "It's probably a ridiculous notion. I don't know the first thing about running a cafe."

"It isn't ridiculous," Isobel said. "It's a wonderful opportunity."

Jennie gave a little shrug. "Lila seems to think I can do it. She's even willing to stay long enough to show me how she handles ordering and such."

"Then you don't have to worry over what you don't know."

"I was so excited I brought it up right away over Sunday dinner. Without thinking." Again, tears flowed and Jennie pulled the handkerchief out.

Ah. Sunday dinner with the Bishops. Isobel didn't have to think long to know *who* had quashed Jennie's hopes. "I take it your mother-in-law doesn't share your enthusiasm."

"That would be putting it mildly," Jennie croaked.

Isobel reached over to cover her friend's hand with her own and give it a squeeze. "I'm sorry."

"She was so angry. Said she always knew I'd bring shame on the family. That I was brought up common and that's what I'd always be, no matter what advantages I was given. She said that if I wanted to be a cook on a 'dirty little corner of town,' that I could go right ahead—as long as I didn't expect to keep living in one of the finest homes in Nebraska City while I was doing it."

"She threatened to turn you out?" That seemed extreme, even for Electa Bishop.

Jennie sighed. "I thought I might—be *more*, you know? More than just the daughter-in-law they didn't want in the first place." She paused. "Freddie always said—" She broke off. "But he was wrong. Time hasn't changed a thing. They might be putting up with me for Freddie's sake, but they're still ashamed of me."

"I don't think that's quite true," Isobel countered. "Your father-in-law seems genuinely fond of you. He called you *our* Jennie that day we were out in that storm." She paused. "And by the way, where was he when Electa was throwing her tantrum?" Had the man really just sat there and allowed his wife to rage?

"Pa Bishop is very kind," Jennie said, "but that doesn't mean he'll go against Mother." She gave a low, sad laugh. "I can't believe I thought they might *help*. Lila needs payment soon to fund her move. I don't have the funds." Her voice wavered. "I don't have *any* funds."

Isobel stared out the window, her mind racing. Might she be able to finance a café? Papa had always said real estate could be a good investment, but that was about all Isobel knew about the matter. Was Lila selling the building or the business? If only Mr. Wilder—that was it! Exactly what Jennie needed. With a nod, Isobel said, "You need to speak with a banker who isn't beholden to your in-laws."

Jennie let out a little huff. "No bank is going to loan money to a penniless widow based on her pie baking."

Isobel pondered that for a moment, and then a flash of memory made her smile. "Wasn't it a *banker* having words with Charlie over the last piece of your lemon meringue on Independence Day?"

"Mr. Hill. Yes, but—"

Isobel interrupted. "Never underestimate the power of a man's stomach to sway his decisions. My stepmother always made certain Papa dined on his favorite dishes right before asking him to fund one of her projects. It worked every single time." It couldn't hurt for Jennie to try a lemon meringue version of Mother Manning's schemes. "How long would it take you to produce another prize-winning pie? Could you have one ready this afternoon?"

Jennie looked doubtful. "You seriously want me to stroll into a bank and apply for a loan based on a pie?"

"Why not? It can't hurt to present a tasty reminder of your sterling qualifications." Isobel paused before summarizing what she thought Mr. Hill would need to hear. "First, Lila's is already an established business in an excellent location. Second, most of her current customers know you and your talent. Come to think of it, the risk would be minimal. Why, Mr. Hill would be performing a community service to prevent the closing of a business that serves Nebraska City as well as Lila's."

Jennie allowed a sad little smile. "Even if it worked out, I'd be homeless. Mother *will* make good on her threat. There's not even a storeroom above the cafe, much less an apartment."

Isobel was not to be deterred. "Henry helped me move my things into Charlie's space yesterday after church. You can stay with me until we come up with a better solution."

"I could never ask—"

"—you didn't ask. I'm offering. I'm not trying to force you to do this. But if you want it, don't let anyone talk you out of it before you've even tried. Least of all a woman who is—to put it mildly—something of a bully."

Finally, Jennie nodded. "If Mr. Hill agrees to meet with me, would you go along?" She smiled. "That bit about it being a community service to keep the café open? That's brilliant."

Isobel rose to her feet. "Let's walk up there right now and ask for an appointment. How much time do you need to bake the pie?"

A few moments later, as the two women made their way toward the bank, Jennie raised new doubt. "I know how to *bake*, but I haven't had much chance to expand my repertoire. After all, the Bishops have Cook."

"Then you open *Jennie's Bakery*."

A few more steps, and Jennie said, "I could manage bacon and eggs. Flapjacks. Oatmeal. Toast."

"So you serve breakfast in the morning and baked goods in the afternoon. Close after lunch. Or when you run out. First come, first served."

"Do you think people would like breakfast served all day?"

"Try it. See what happens."

As they stepped into the bank, Jennie said, "I can't abide those green walls. Do you think folks would like yellow? I've always wanted a yellow kitchen."

Monday night, Isobel woke to a rustling sound. Sitting up in bed, she lit the lamp on the bedside table, sat up against the headboard, pulled the coverlet up to her chin, and peered across the room. She barely managed to keep from screaming when she caught sight of a terrifyingly large rat dragging a crust of bread out of sight behind the bookcase on the opposite wall. She made certain all bedding was tucked up away from the floor and lay awake the rest of the night. Since Mr. Hill had agreed to ponder the idea of backing Jennie's Café, Jennie might need a place to stay. What would she think when Isobel mentioned the rat?

At dawn Tuesday, Isobel stomped about vigorously as she performed her toilette, nearly fainting when the pebble in her shoe turned out to be another dried crust of bread, presumably deposited by—*shudder*. The rat she'd seen was too big to fit in a shoe. That meant—she wouldn't think about it. Except she thought about little else that day.

When she mentioned the matter to Edgar—as he schooled her in how to build a fire in Charlie's stove—the young man offered to set traps for her. She purchased half a dozen at the mercantile, somewhat disappointed that neither Birdie nor Henry seemed to consider the presence of vermin in Charlie's apartment an emergency. Edgar set the traps before leaving work for the day. There was no word on Jennie's Café. Isobel spent a second sleepless night at Charlie's.

Very early Wednesday morning, a bleary-eyed Isobel checked the traps. *Empty.* She kept an eye on Charlie's bookcase while she fumbled about to dress and brew a pot of tea. Dragging a chair onto the balcony, she sat sipping tea and watching for light to spill onto the windowsill of the Tanner's upstairs apartment window. The moment it did, Isobel hurried down and knocked on the storeroom door.

Henry answered and Isobel recounted the trap failures. He offered to be her exterminator. Relieved, Isobel went to the office, where her troubles multiplied. First, there was a note from Molly Simmons in the mail slot. Edgar was ill and wouldn't be coming in to work that day. Edgar and his brothers were key players in *Register* distribution, a reality that exacerbated Isobel's problems. A telegram to Charlie seeking advice couldn't be depended upon, since the *Zephyr* wouldn't reach St. Louis until early next week. She'd already asked Henry Tanner for help once today. She needed to solve this quandary on her own.

Another problem arose before lunch, when Isobel accepted a shipment of newsprint paper and ink, only to realize an hour later that the newsprint was water damaged. It required more than one trip to the telegraph office to elicit the promise of replacement. Heaven only knew if it would arrive in time for the next edition. Isobel determined to hope for the best and dove into planning that edition, interrupted when Electa Bishop sailed through the front door to submit an article for *Early Days.*

Isobel did her best to hide her frustrations over the woman's poor treatment of Jennie. After all, Mr. Hill had seemed favorably impressed and agreed to consider the idea of a small loan. But Mrs. Bishop's three pages of exaggerations and accolades were too much. Was Julian Bishop really a visionary without whom the State of Nebraska would quickly fall into obscurity? When she finally did speak, Isobel managed to address only the excessive length of the article. "Submissions were to be no longer than one page."

Electa arched an eyebrow. "Surely such limitations do not apply to men like my husband."

"Actually—"

Electa interrupted. "I'd venture to say you'll be affording the J. Sterling Mortons more than one page. Especially now that they've agreed to pay for the cemetery fence. But we can discuss that another time. There's another more pressing matter I wish to discuss."

Isobel plopped down at her desk with a weary sigh and waited.

"It's about this nonsense of my daughter-in-law taking on a café." The older woman pronounced the last word as if it were an obscenity.

Isobel didn't mince words. "I do hope you've relented in your threat to turn her out."

Electa looked surprised. "You know about that?" She dismissed the notion with a wave of one gloved hand. "Well of course I'd never do *that*. I was overwrought. After all, it's—"

"Nonsense?" Isobel repeated Electa's word.

"I am happy to hear you agree with me."

"You misunderstand," Isobel replied. "I do not agree. In truth, I believe it to be an excellent opportunity for which Jennie is perfectly suited. She will undoubtedly make a great success of it." Rising to her feet, Isobel crossed the office and opened the front door. "Now, if you'll excuse me—" Henry stepped in the back door. He was carrying two gigantic rat traps.

Mrs. Bishop had remained stubbornly rooted to the spot near Isobel's desk, but when she saw the traps, she let out a horrified *oh, my* and skittered past Isobel and out onto the boardwalk. "We shall continue another time." Isobel chuckled as she closed the door and turned toward Henry, who held up the two traps.

"I've already set three upstairs, but it wouldn't hurt to leave a couple down here as well."

That night, a loud snap jarred Isobel awake. Even in the low light from the two lamps she'd left burning, it was obvious the traps were empty. The two in the newspaper office were equally sprung and equally empty.

Thursday morning, Isobel checked back into the hotel. Her former room wasn't available, but she didn't care. That night she slept soundly in a room the size of her water closet in St. Louis. She woke feeling more hopeful about life in general, especially after Molly reported that Edgar was feeling better. Things were looking up.

Thursday afternoon Isobel decided to try her hand at filling a small print order. It wasn't due until Monday, but how difficult could it be to operate the small tabletop press? After a successful print run, Isobel tied the invitations with a lovely bit of ribbon and delivered them with a combined sense of accomplishment and pride. The customer was delighted—until she discovered the error.

"The name," she said crisply, "is Smith—spelled S-m-y-t-h-e."

Isobel vowed to never again assume how to spell a name when taking an order. *Smythe*? Really? She decided to try her hand at typesetting and managed to draw a type drawer out of its slot and dump hundreds of tiny letters on the floor. Sorting the resulting mess took over an hour. Enough was enough. She closed the office early, intent on walking to the Bishops' to convince Jennie to join her at Lila's Café for an afternoon treat. They would discuss paint colors and plans while indulging in the most decadent dessert on the menu.

The plan to distract herself from weightier matters failed. Isobel tossed and turned for much of Thursday night. She worried about Charlie on board the *Zephyr*. Was he resisting the rivers of strong drink? It would be four more days before the packet reached St. Louis—assuming the trip continued without incident. Everyone knew that delays were part and parcel of steamboat travel.

Please, God, let Charlie— With a low grunt, Isobel paused mid-thought. *What have you ever done to deserve the Almighty's favor? Why would He listen to you?* It was a fair question. She had nothing but unanswered questions when it came to religious matters. Worried, lonely, and miserable, she curled her body around the pillow clutched to her midsection and squeezed her eyes shut.

Chapter 39

By sorrow of the heart the spirit is broken.
Proverbs 15:13

Early Friday evening, Gideon left two dressed rabbits on the well curbing at Tom's place. Intending to hurry to the cemetery for his meeting with Miss Manning, he hesitated when he heard the strains of a hymn wafting out of the parlor windows—a clear soprano and a wavering boy's voice attempting to harmonize. He remembered Gabe singing with Ma. And he recognized the tune.

Jesus, my heart's dear refuge,
Jesus has died for me;
Firm on the Rock of Ages,
ever my trust shall be.

Here let me wait with patience,
wait till the night is o'er;
Wait till I see the morning
break on the golden shore.

The imagery was about being patient in suffering and fixing one's eyes on heaven. He grimaced. *I'm trying, Lord. You know I'm trying.*

"Hey, mister. We found the rabbits. Thank you."

Dropping to his knees as if shot, Gideon hunkered in the tall grass. That had to be Molly, but a much younger voice sounded next.

"Where'd he go? Was it a *ghost*?"

Grace, the youngest. Born after Tom's final visit home. About six years old, Gideon reckoned.

"There's no such thing as ghosts, silly," Molly scoffed. "Besides that, ghosts don't have dogs."

Trouble! He'd failed to grab the bandana the dog wore for a collar.

"It don't look like a dog. It looks like a *wolf*."

Gideon closed his eyes, listening for the slightest sound that might indicate the girls were walking toward him. If he heard footsteps, he'd be forced to run. *Please, God.* Again, Molly spoke.

"It's a *dog*, and he's just sitting there, pretty as you please. He don't mean us any harm. See that? He's wagging his tail." Molly spoke to Trouble. "Hey, boy. Where'd you come from?" After a pause, she spoke a little louder. "You could come say *hi*, mister."

Gideon's heart hammered in his chest. He didn't move.

After what felt like half a century, Molly said, "We took the rabbits in, and then we came out to gather up some blossoms for our Ma. You've been helping us for a good while. So I'm gonna set the flowers right here on the ground to say thank you." She waited in the silence, then added, "Grace and me'll be going now. I hope you take the flowers." She lowered her voice a bit, this time addressing Trouble. "You stay put, ya hear? *Stay.*"

Trouble's low whine indicated the dog was obeying, albeit reluctantly. When Gideon finally dared to peer in the direction of the house, he saw the two girls walking hand in hand. The moment they'd entered—by way of the front door—their mother stepped out on the porch. When Trouble returned to

Gideon's side and slurped at his cheek, Gideon snorted a low protest.

Across the way, Nettie Simmons took a few steps to the broken railing. Presently, she called out. "Is that you, Gideon? Molly only caught a glimpse. Your dog was a little braver." After a moment of silence, she continued. "What you wrote about Tom was beautiful. You're bringing us game. God bless you for that." Again, she waited a moment before continuing. "Please don't be afraid to show your face. I know you didn't leave Tom. The children and I all know it. You've no reason to hide from us."

If only that were true. Gideon's hand went to the scars. He waited until Nettie went back inside before rising to his feet and, with Trouble at his side, retreating across Tom's untilled fields. His mind churned once again with questions about the Simmons family. Had anyone tried to buy Tom's place? If Nettie had refused offers, why hadn't someone planted a crop? The twins and Ethan were old enough to plow and sow at least a few acres. He thought back to abundant harvests in years past, the shocks of wheat dotting the fields, the corn cribs full to the point of bursting. Regret descended. He and Tom would have done well as farmers.

I know you didn't leave Tom. The children and I all know it.
You've no reason to hide from us.

The Simmonses had guessed his identity. What did that mean for the future? Might he be able to step out of the shadows with Tom's family? There was so much more he could do for them beyond delivering game. He could mend the porch railing. Patch the roof. Paint the house. He might even figure a way to go back to farming with Tom's boys.

The glimmer of hope was immediately extinguished by memories of the trip home. *Exactly when will any of that happen? Before or after Tom's kids get one look at you and run shrieking into the house to hide under the bed?*

Turning up his collar and thrusting his hands into his pockets, Gideon trudged along. Ideas rose up only to be quashed stomped by harsh reality. He was a creature of the night who lived on the fringes. That didn't mean there was no purpose in his life. He would continue to help feed Tom's family. He would share the gospel with Miss Manning the next time they met—but that would have to wait. God forgive him, but he had no heart for the cemetery this evening. No heart for yet another reminder of how lonely his life would always be.

Isobel stood in the center of the cemetery and turned in a circle, searching the horizon in every direction. Shadows were lengthening and still there was no sign of Private Long. Looking past the blackberry bramble, she peered down the steep bank and all along Table Creek. Dare she call out? Surely it was safe to call the dog.

"Trouble? Here, boy! Where are you?"

After a few minutes, Isobel climbed back aboard her buggy. Still, she hesitated to leave. *It's been a terrible week. I have so many questions. Where ARE you?* Of all the possible explanations for Private Long's failure to rendezvous, one kept coming to the forefront. What if he was ill or injured? With a last look about her, Isobel signaled Elsie to *move on*. Night was falling fast. At the edge of town, she pulled up and sat for a moment. To the left, the livery and a sleepless night of wondering and worry. To the right, Tanner Mercantile and caring people who undoubtedly knew where Private Long lived and could check on him.

Isobel argued with herself. *You promised not to speak with anyone else about him.* She imagined a retort. *And if he'd shown up this evening, I would have kept that promise.* Surely the man couldn't expect her to ignore the possibility that he might be hurt. Or ill. He wasn't going to be happy about her going to the Tanners. *Then the feeling will be mutual, because I'm not very happy with him right now.* He would simply have to understand. And if he didn't—well. Isobel would deal with that when and if she had to. A few moments later, she was knocking on the storeroom door.

Birdie answered the summons, smiling when she saw Isobel. "I'm glad you stopped by. Henry's at a meeting to organize a work day out at the Simmons place. He thinks you need a mouser, and he's going to ask Nettie about—"

Isobel interrupted. "I'm not here about the rats. Someone needs to check on Private Long. He was supposed to meet me at the cemetery this evening, and he didn't come. I'm worried he's hurt. Or ill."

"Y-you what?" Birdie stammered. "W-why would you think—"

"Please, Birdie. I can explain it all later. I know who stepped into the path of that runaway this past spring. It was Gideon. Private Gideon Long. Please tell me you know where he lives."

Birdie gave a little shake of her head. "I can't. We promised—"

Isobel gave a little stomp of one foot. "I know. *You* promised to keep his secrets. *I* promised. But Birdie—" She put a hand on the older woman's arm and gave a little shake. "What if he's hurt or ill? What if he needs help? We have to do something!" She glanced up the stairs toward the apartment. "Where's Henry? Is he here?"

"I told you. He's at church. A meeting."

"At *our* church?" When Birdie nodded, Isobel retreated to her buggy and began to climb aboard.

"Wait," Birdie called. "I'll go with you. Just give me a moment to gather supplies. Bandages and alcohol—that sort of thing. In case you're right."

"Hurry," Isobel said. She gathered the reins. Elsie's head came up. An ear twitched. The mare gazed toward the south. A dog barked. Presently, Trouble bounded onto the rough board platform outside the storeroom door. He wheeled about and faced Isobel, tongue lolling, tail wagging. Isobel rose to her feet and looked south where a lone figure was coming into view. She called out. "Gideon!"

Birdie came to the storeroom door, a basket over one arm.

Gideon stopped in his tracks.

Isobel called out again and raised her hand in greeting. She expected a response. None came beyond a shrill whistle summoning the dog. Hearing it, Trouble hesitated, looking uncertainly from Birdie to Isobel and then back again. Gideon repeated the whistle. The dog obeyed, retreating southward and out of sight. Isobel sank onto the buggy seat, the reins still in her hands. With a sigh, she looked toward Birdie, who set down the basket of first aid supplies and crossed to the buggy.

"You know," Birdie said.

Isobel nodded.

"But—how?"

Isobel sighed. Weariness washed over her. Inexplicably, tears threatened. Why was she so upset? Was she really surprised at the man's response?

"Come inside. I can't send you off into the night like this."

Isobel swiped at a tear. "I thought we were becoming—" she gave a low, sad laugh. "Friends. As if it's possible to be friends with someone you've never actually seen."

"You haven't—*seen* him?"

Isobel shook her head.

"Then how—?"

"Do you remember the storm on the day I got this buggy?"

"Of course. You and Jennie had a lot of people worried about you that day."

"Yes. Well, we weren't only caught in the storm. The buggy mired down in a rut." Quickly, Isobel told Birdie about her second encounter with Gideon and about finding his notebook. "Even as I read it, I didn't realize who he was. I only knew it was the same man who'd rescued me the day of the runaway. I never would have made the connection were it not for the very last entry, which included a single mention of Gabriel." Isobel shrugged. "After that, I was determined to meet him. I tucked a note inside a red bandana and tied it to the blackberry bramble at the cemetery. I promised not to give his secret away, but when he came for the notebook, he still called it being *summoned*."

Summoned. That's how he must have really felt about being forced to speak with her. He'd only agreed to it because he felt threatened by what might happen if he didn't. Suddenly, Isobel felt ashamed for having insisted on having her own way. Ashamed and defeated. Looking in the direction of the cemetery, she muttered, "And I was so certain things were taking a turn for the better."

"They are," Birdie said. "He was shocked, that's all. He'll come around."

Even if Birdie was right in the matter of Private Gideon Long, it was little comfort. Isobel still had rats and ruined print runs to deal with. Edgar was still sick. She had encouraged Jennie to disobey her mother-in-law, and there was still no news from Mr. Hill. Who did she think she was, leading the way into that bank with a pie? And what about Charlie? What if he slid back into his old ways? Unable to stem the tide of tears, Isobel sank against the cushioned back of her fancy buggy and let the tears fall.

"That settles it," Birdie said. She reached up to take the reins from Isobel's hands. As she tied them off, she said, "We know that Gideon is unharmed. Henry will see to Elsie when he gets back. You, my dear, are coming inside with me. Now." She extended a finger before Isobel could respond. "Don't speak. Do as you're told."

Chapter 40

*Now faith is the substance of things hoped
for, the evidence of things not seen.*
Hebrews 11:1

Gideon ran until he could run no more. Sliding down an embankment, he landed on his backside, gasping for breath, his heart pounding. Feeling—what, exactly? He lifted one arm and brushed the sweat off his brow with the sleeve of his shirt. Trouble sidled close and nudged his arm. Gideon hugged the dog. "I'm all right. She surprised me, that's all."

No. You were more than surprised. You were terrified. He sat for a moment, thinking about that. Knowing it was true. *Terrified.* Of what was he afraid? Dare he even admit it to himself?

When Trouble nuzzled his hand, Gideon raked the dog's thick fur with his fingers, scratching all the spots he knew the animal liked best, smiling at the unfettered ability to relish attention and to show it. The dog flopped over onto his back, all four feet waving in the air. Gideon groused about the animal being spoiled, but he provided the requested belly rub. Trouble cocked his head to one side and looked up, tongue lolling, wagging tail brushing the dust.

"All right. That's enough."

At the words Trouble flipped over, rose to his feet, and shook himself. Sneezing, he leaned close and looked up at Gideon.

Gideon shrugged. "All right. I admit it. I was afraid." He put one palm to the scarred side of his face. Unwelcome memories rose up from the long walk home after the war. The expressions he'd glimpsed when people got a good look at him—especially the ladies. He imagined Isobel Manning's face contorting with fear. Horror. Revulsion. He sniffed and cleared his throat.

"I'd started to think maybe it would be possible," he said to the dog.

Trouble's ear came up. The tail waved a bit.

"Not a complete revelation, of course. Maybe a side view." He turned his head. "This side isn't so bad." He looked back at the dog. "Birdie and Henry don't even notice anymore."

Trouble gave a low yip.

Gideon sighed. "Yeah. I know. You're right of course. They've just gotten better at *pretending* not to notice." He rose to his feet. "Terrible idea. Never going to happen." He patted the dog on the head. "Still, we've got to make another trip back to town. Can't have Isobel thinking I've lost my mind—even if I did run off like an idiot."

Isobel? Again, he cleared his throat and spoke to the dog. "You're right about that, too. I've no right to refer to the lady by her given name. No right at all. Miss Manning it is."

But oh ... if only ...

⸺

Isobel sat at the Tanners' table mopping up the last of her tears while Birdie prepared tea. Once the older woman was seated opposite her, she blurted out, "He must have known I'd be worried when he didn't meet me. Why would he run off? Is he angry? Does he think I betrayed him?"

"We can't know what he's thinking unless he decides to tell us."

Isobel didn't want to hear logic. She wanted reassurance. "I haven't told *anyone* about him, exactly as I promised. Not you. Not Henry. Not even Charlie or Jennie—and she was there when—"

"Jennie Wilcox knows about Gideon?" Birdie looked horrified.

With a little shake of her head, Isobel explained. "She knows the two rescuers are the same person, because I told her I recognized him. It was she who noticed that he'd dropped something by the trail. It turned out to be a notebook, but there was no name in it."

"You said he mentioned Gabriel."

"I didn't read Gabriel's name until later. I'd asked Jennie to keep our adventure in confidence, and she was more than happy to comply. Her mother-in-law was very upset by the entire episode. Jennie said the less Mrs. Bishop knew, the better. Neither of us even mentioned having help freeing the buggy. Jennie hasn't mentioned the notebook since we found it." Isobel offered a weak smile and a little shrug. "It's not as if she doesn't have other matters to keep her mind occupied these days."

Birdie nodded.

"I knew I shouldn't read it. *After all,* I told myself, *it's the private thoughts of someone you don't know.* I intended only to scan it, looking for the owner's name. But then it drew me in." She paused. "It's a long story."

"I'd like to hear it. But only if you can tell it without betraying a confidence."

Isobel thought for a moment. What could she possibly know about Gideon Long that Birdie and Henry didn't? *Nothing.* Besides that, she needed—and wanted—Birdie's advice. And so she told her everything, including Charlie's efforts thus far to locate the man's service record. "He'll do more in St. Louis—assuming he's successful in meeting with the friend he mentioned."

"Does Gideon know about that?"

"Yes, although he didn't seem to care about it, and so I didn't go into the specifics." She wondered now if that was an accurate description of Gideon's reaction. *Gideon.* No longer *Private Long.* What did that mean?

When Birdie finally spoke, it wasn't about the search for service records. "You say the notebook *drew you in.* What do you mean by that?"

Isobel thought for a moment before answering. "It isn't a diary. It's a collection of essays, for lack of a better term. He copies a verse or two of Scripture and then writes what he's thinking about it. Sometimes there's another verse or a phrase within the written response, almost as if God's answering back with other scripture. Sometimes it's as if he's *arguing* with God." She took a sip of tea before continuing. "I grew up going to church, but there's something different about his kind of religion. I can't explain why, but I'd like to understand it. He promised we could talk about that last week, but then the telegram about Mother Manning arrived."

With a knowing smile, Birdie said, "I take it that drive you 'needed' was about more than clearing your head?"

Isobel felt her cheeks warm with a blush. "I assume he learned about my staying behind from you?"

"Yes, but—it would have been a passing comment. I don't want you to think—"

"I don't," Isobel interrupted with a weary wave of a hand. "You and Henry are about as far removed from being gossips as anyone I've ever known. In fact, I'd be relieved that you finally know about this—if only he hadn't run off that way." She paused. "After he heard I stayed here, he left a note in the *Register* mail slot. We were supposed to talk this evening. But then he didn't come. A recluse living alone? All sorts of horrible possibilities came to mind. And you know the rest." She shook her head. "I

Days and its role in Isobel's discoveries. "The Simmons children still call him Uncle Gideon. They don't believe the rumors, either." She sighed and shook her head. "I've told him that, but it hasn't made any difference. I want to be his friend, but based on what just happened downstairs, the feeling is far from mutual." She shook her head. "I don't understand why God lets it all go on."

For a moment, it seemed that Birdie was about to share some advice. In the end, though, all she said was, "Don't give up. You said the two of you were to speak about spiritual matters?"

Isobel nodded. "I hope that doesn't offend you. I know you'd be willing as well, but I thought it made sense to speak first with the person who wrote what inspired my questions."

"It doesn't offend me in the least. Perhaps it will draw Gideon out. As I said earlier, God works in mysterious ways. I think you'll hear from Gideon again. Try to be patient. Don't give up."

"I won't," Isobel replied.

"I'm not talking only about Gideon," Birdie said. "I know you've had a terrible week. Don't give up. Not on the newspaper or anything else to do with your life here in Nebraska." She reached across the table and squeezed Isobel's hand. "Most of all, my dear, don't give up on God. You said you don't understand why He allows Gideon's troubles to go on. I don't either. But one thing I've learned is that just when I think God isn't paying attention is often when He's doing His best work."

※

All throughout the weekend, Isobel hoped for evidence of God's doing what Birdie called "His best work." She saw none. There was no word from Gideon. Jennie had no news about her efforts to purchase Lila's Café. Pastor Duncan's Sunday sermon was adequate but referenced nothing Isobel could use to prop up her belief in herself. She had no plans to "give up," but she wouldn't have minded a revelation or two. Her unease spread to thoughts of Charlie. Was he all right? Tomorrow was day ten of his absence. If the trip had gone well, the *Zephyr* might pull up to the St. Louis landing by the end of the day. Might Caesar meet the packet? Would Charlie send a telegram right away to let her know he'd arrived? Where would he go first—to the manse or the lawyer's? The bank or—a saloon? Was he safe? Was he sober?

On Monday morning as she affixed a cameo to the dark jabot at the throat of her ivory shirtwaist, Isobel was still looking for evidence of God's mysterious ways. Her spirits lifted when Molly arrived with fresh water and the news that Edgar would not only return to work by noon but would also bring a solution to the rat problem—Gus, the mouser with the sterling reputation. Molly also hinted at another bit of good news, but said she had to keep that a secret. Whatever it might be, Isobel dared to hope that life in general was going to be better this week.

Might there be a note from Gideon waiting at the office? Doubt niggled. What if he never—*don't borrow tomorrow's worries.* Isobel wasn't certain if that was advice from Jesus or one of the great poets. Whoever had said it, it was good advice. But when she stopped by the office on her way to breakfast at Lila's, the floor below the mail slot was bare. Either Gideon hadn't visited the Tanners last evening or, if he had—*don't borrow worry.* Both rat traps had been sprung. Both were empty. Isobel pursed her lips. *Don't give up.* Leaving the *Closed* sign in place on the front door, she exited via the back and marched toward Lila's.

Isobel was savoring her first cup of coffee when a smiling Jennie Wilcox swept in the back door. She was dressed in Sunday finery and gripped an official-looking valise in one gloved hand. Her face was aglow with joy as she plopped into the chair opposite Isobel and perched the valise on her lap. "Molly said I just missed you at the hotel. She didn't give anything away, I hope."

Molly? Ah. Molly. "Now that you mention it, she did hint at good news. But she said she couldn't tell me about it yet."

"Excellent," Jennie said. "I'm glad she passed my little test regarding trust." She took a deep breath. "I wanted you—no, I *needed* you to be the first to know." She opened the valise, withdrew a document, and held it out to Isobel.

Wiping her fingers on her napkin, Isobel accepted what proved to be a real estate agreement. She glanced over the top of the paper at Jennie before scanning the page to capture the pertinent information. *Lila's Café ... to be reopened within ten days under new management of owner, Mrs. Jennie Blanche Wilcox.*

Jennie's eyes glittered with happy tears as she said, "You have no idea how hard it's been to keep this a secret."

Isobel waggled the contract. "Is this why you were so distant at church yesterday morning?"

Jennie nodded. "I didn't trust myself. Mr. Hill insisted I tell no one until the papers were all signed—which just now happened at the bank." She put the contract back into the valise and closed the lid. Setting it on the floor, she looked about her then back at Isobel. "I can hardly believe it."

Isobel raised her fork in a gesture of triumph. "The power of pie."

"Pie and Pa Bishop," Jennie said.

"Pa Bishop as in your father-in-law—husband of Electa?"

Jennie nodded. "Mother Bishop heard about our calling on Mr. Hill. When she told Pa Bishop about it—" She lowered her voice and leaned closer. "There was something of a row. I didn't hear every word, but—you can imagine. Isobel, the Lord used you and that pie. Pa Bishop escorted me back to the bank the very next day." She blinked away tears. "The things he said about me—I wish you could have heard him. At any rate, he convinced Mr. Hill to take me on. He even negotiated better terms!" She shook her head. "God works in mysterious ways. He is *so* good."

Isobel nodded agreement even as she wondered over the coincidence of Jennie's quoting the same phrase Birdie had about the Almighty. A moment passed before she realized Jennie had stopped talking. "Well? What do you think?"

"It's wonderful." Isobel nodded vaguely. "All of it."

"I think so, too. Yellow is such a cheerful color. White curtains will complement the newly painted tables. Fresh and clean, all of it. If breakfast all day isn't well received, I can always change the menu—or my hours, or both. As for Molly—"

"Molly?" Isobel barely managed to cover that lapse. *Molly's good news.* Of course. Molly was coming to work for Jennie. She nodded. "She works hard and she's very—um—sociable."

Jennie laughed. "I know what you're thinking. But she has a sunny disposition, and she can learn to be tactful. Don't you think?"

Isobel wasn't quite as certain as Jennie about Molly Simmons's aptitude for tact, but she wasn't about to squelch the girl's chance. What was it Molly had said on that first day of their meeting? Something about 'saving up.' As Isobel recalled, the girl didn't know what she was saving for, but she wanted to be ready for it. She was thinking ahead—beyond emptying chamber pots. Isobel smiled. "I think you're the perfect person to help Molly 'be more,' as you so succinctly put it about yourself not so very long ago." She paused. "Although, Miss Bennet's not going to be happy with you when Molly resigns."

"Miss Bennet," Jennie said briskly as she stirred cream into her coffee, "should have been kinder. And paid better."

Isobel barely stifled a surprised laugh. Clearly, there was a great deal more to Jennie Wilcox than the ability to bake. Perhaps God was working wonders, after all. By way of award-winning pie.

324

Chapter 41

Where is the way where light dwelleth?
Job 38:19

Isobel had returned to the newspaper office from Lila's-soon-to-be-Jennie's when Edgar stepped inside the back door. He was holding a burlap sack at arm's length from which erupted a low growl followed by a louder yowl. With an apologetic shrug, he said, "I brought Gus."

"Whatever you do," Isobel said, "don't let her out of that bag." She finished raising the blinds around the room before retrieving Charlie's apartment key from her desk. Sidling along the wall to the back door, she slipped outside.

Edgar followed with an apologetic, "As you can tell, Gus isn't—um—*cuddly.*"

Isobel called over her shoulder as she hurried up the stairs to Charlie's apartment. "I don't want to cuddle. I want dead rats." She unlocked the door and let it swing wide, stepping back.

"You'll get them," Edgar said as he crossed the threshold. When he set the bag on the floor, the cat yowled again. "Things might get a little loud until Gus has cleared them all out." He bent to release the animal, then hesitated and looked over at Isobel. "She can be a little—ornery—towards strangers."

325

"They key's in the door," Isobel said, pulling the door shut behind her. Curiosity won out, though, and she went to the window to catch a glimpse of the creature that sounded more like a wildcat than a mouser. She could hear Edgar murmuring to the animal as he released the knot holding the sack closed. Pink nose, huge head and, finally, lanky body emerged. The creature darted away, pausing beneath the front window, back arched, tail aloft, glaring at Edgar with bright gold eyes fixed in an angry scowl. A black mark beneath one eye made it look like the cat had lost a fight with a bully and gained a shiner. This was not a creature accustomed to losing battles—although, now that Isobel looked more closely, it did appear that the long-haired tail might be missing an inch or two of length. The cat's hide was a conglomeration of stripes and solids ranging from gray with black stripes to pale yellow, from gold with orange stripes to black.

Tail aloft, the animal strutted up to Edgar and extended its forepaws up his leg. Isobel thought it a show of affection—until Edgar shouted a protest and hoisted the cat bodily to shake it off. In actuality, Gus was lodging a clawed protest against the human responsible for hauling her into town. As the cat sailed across the apartment, Edgar made his escape, locking the door behind him. "I probably should have told you she might do a little damage," he said to Isobel. "She likes to keep her claws sharp. I'll—umm—haul in a couple pieces of firewood tomorrow to entice her away from Charlie's furniture."

Isobel smiled. "If Gus takes care of the rat problem, I won't complain about scratched furniture. There's not a stick of wood in the place that's worth much, anyway. I doubt Charlie will want to keep any of it once the house is ready." She led the way down to the office. Edgar reset both rat traps before departing to tend to Gus's needs, which included fresh water and a place to "do her business."

The afternoon of that first day of Gus's residency, a telegram arrived from Charlie containing the blessed words, "arrived without mishap." Isobel sighed with relief. No mishaps meant he was sober. Mother Manning's funeral would be on Friday. He promised "more news to follow."

Over the next few days, a stream of telegrams flew between sister and brother. Charlie had been right that Portia and Caesar didn't want to leave St. Louis. Isobel wrote the dear couple a letter of appreciation the very evening that news arrived. Charlie would follow Portia's advice as to the dissolution of kitchenwares and linens. Most of the formal parlor furniture would be sold off, while Papa's library would be shipped in its entirety. The Nebraska City literary society had begun to discuss opening a public library, and Charlie agreed it would be a good cause to support with any books they didn't care to keep.

By mid-week Isobel and Edgar had a plan for the first solo edition of the *Register,* including the necessary mention of the editor's temporary absence, since this edition would be somewhat abbreviated. Her favorite part of her first foray into solo editorship was the two-column wide, front page announcement set off by an elegant border.

A Fine Establishment
Try the Pie!

Those who hunger and thirst for excellent fare will be pleased to know that the closing of Lila's Café is only temporary. Mrs. Jennie Wilcox, widely known as the foremost pie baker in the region, will soon reopen the establishment offering fare sure to please all diners.

Watch this space for opening day specials.
Jennie's Café
6th *& Main*

*Anticipated hours 6 o'clock a.m. until 2 o'clock p.m. daily
Closed on the Lord's Day*

As the days went by, Isobel spent evenings studying Charlie's sketch of the house they hoped to build. First, she drafted more precise plans. With Charlie's approval, she spent hours consulting with Henry, considering windows and doors, railings and rooflines. By the closing days of July, she'd come up with what the Tanners both declared a pleasing design. When Henry opined that her carefully detailed drawings were adequate for any builder, Isobel blushed with pleasure.

She was busy, and yet Gideon was never far from her thoughts. She continued taking drives to clear her head. Elsie grew to anticipate the path they would take—south to the cemetery and to the top of the hill, around the oak tree, a brief pause, and then back to town. The familiar drive helped Isobel keep abreast of the improvements being made at the cemetery thanks to society efforts. But it was fruitless when it came to facilitating a chance meeting with Gideon. There was no welcoming bark from a one-eared dog. No deep voice calling a greeting from beyond the blackberry bramble. After every drive Isobel told herself it would be her last. She returned to town with new resolve to concentrate on her work and to expend her energies and creativity on the home she would share with Charlie.

Home. It was a beautiful word. Isobel had never had a home that reflected her own likes and dislikes. Mother Manning had reigned supreme at the manse. Becoming Mrs. Alfred Warfield III would not have presented any opportunity for independence when it came to wall coverings or drapes, furniture or carpets. As a couple, she and Alfred would have taken up residence in a wing of the Warfield manse. Isobel would have simply moved out of one older woman's realm and into another.

Remembering the domineering Mother Manning inspired a memory of the only time Isobel had attempted to express individuality when it came to furnishings. She'd purchased a raffle ticket at the Sanitary Fair, hardly looking at the item being raffled. Her ticket won. When she took the time to examine her prize, an exquisitely made quilt, she fell in love with the vibrant bouquets scattered across the surface, some arranged in elaborate wreaths, others springing from intricate vases and urns.

After she and Portia spread the quilt out on the four-poster bed in Isobel's room, Isobel stood back with a smile. Portia likened the effect to having a garden indoors, remarking especially on a blue bird with wings outstretched above a book labeled *Holy Bible*. Mother Manning, on the other hand, took one look at the quilt and ordered Portia to "take that thing away at once." What, Isobel wondered, had happened to it? She telegraphed Charlie.

> *Important! Ask Portia about quilt from Sanitary Fair. She will know. If located, bring with you. Treat with care.*

In the days following his panicked flight from Isobel Manning's sight, Gideon spent every moment of daylight either hunting, processing kills, or tanning hides. He was especially careful to leave his offerings for Tom's family at different places around the Simmons house. Being predictable would lead to being found out—most likely by Molly, whom he remembered as a little spitfire with boundless energy and endless curiosity. Gideon doubted that maturity would have changed the girl much. Nettie would respect his privacy, but children—especially children like Molly—were unpredictable.

He temporarily abandoned the rabbit snares south of the cemetery and stayed away from town. But he failed to stop thinking about Isobel Manning, who had presented a singular opportunity for Preacher Long to do more than jot down notes about faith. Isobel had wanted to *talk* about it. She hadn't understood his preoccupation with anonymity—after, all, who would—but she'd tolerated it. Whatever she might think of his idiosyncrasies, she must think him mad now. Who could blame her?

Loneliness rose up again, casting a dark pall over everything. It was as if singular contact with one person had somehow rent the veil Gideon had managed to draw over any expectation of a normal life. He went back to fighting for peace of mind and begging God for contentment.

Trouble sensed the turmoil. When Gideon studied, the dog did not sprawl on the floor and eventually fall asleep. Instead, he stayed alert, nose on paws, good ear erect. On occasion, he crossed to where Gideon sat and put a furry chin on his knee. Every time the two left the cabin, Trouble bounded ahead—toward town. When Gideon called him back and headed in the opposite direction, the dog's tail drooped with disappointment.

Evenings, Gideon once again sought out the Old Testament saint who, as far as he could tell, had suffered the most—the Bible character with whom he felt a special kinship. His initial studies led only to disappointment, for he was reminded that not only did God not answer Job's questions, He asked His own—and a very long string of them, at that. *Where were you when I laid the foundation of the earth? Have you ever in your life commanded the morning? Where is the way to the dwelling of light? Do you give the horse its might?*

The point seemed clear. *I am God and you are not.* At first the words reminded Gideon of his own father's penchant for giving orders and demanding obedience. *Who do you think you are, talking back to me? Don't ask me <u>why</u>. Do it because I said so.* The unfortunate reminder made Gideon resist the notion of submitting. After all, Pa's *because I said so* wasn't really much of an answer—was it? And then, in a flash of insight one rainy night, Gideon allowed a revolutionary thought. What if "no answer" was, in reality, the best answer possible—when God was the one speaking.

I am God and you are not. Of course you don't understand what I'm doing. I'm the One who laid the foundations of the earth. I do know the way to the light.

Gideon looked up from the Bible and sat back, staring through the window at the pouring rain. *I know the way to the light.* Presently, he returned to the passage and prayed his way through it, echoing Job's questions.

I cry unto thee, and thou dost not hear me…

"I believe that You hear, but I'm like Job, too. I don't always *feel* it."

I stand up, and thou regardest me not. Thou are become cruel to me: with thy strong hand thou opposest thyself against me.

"I still don't understand why You gave me a heart for the gospel and then made it impossible for me to preach."

With God all things are possible…

Startled when a phrase from the New Testament landed in his mind, Gideon sat back. D. L. Moody himself had remarked on Gideon's fine speaking voice. A wonderful tool for the gospel, Moody had called it. And here Gideon was, in a place where he might go for days without uttering more than a few words. He glanced back down at the text in Job.

When I looked for good, then evil came unto me: and when I waited for light, there came darkness.

He kept reading, all the way to the conclusion of the book. This time, though, something new jumped out at him. He read it more than once. Finally, raking his fingers through his shaggy hair, he rose from Ma's rocker and stepped outside to pace back and forth. His mind swirled from memory to regret, from hope

331

he first time since the end of the war, he wondered
reature of the night wasn't God's doing at all. After
g had happened to his voice. Nothing had changed
his belief in God or his love for the Almighty's Book. What did that mean?

Back inside, Gideon read again. *So the Lord blessed the latter end of Job more than his beginning.* After a terrible trial and after God reminded Job of his place in the cosmos, He gave Job's life back to him. Gideon sank back into Ma's rocker. Was it possible that God's call on his life hadn't changed? What if the reason he'd set it aside had nothing to do with God ordaining a change and everything to do with his own human weakness? What if God still expected him to preach the Word?

The moment the thought sprang up, so did another passage of Scripture. He sat forward and turned to it. *Humble yourselves therefore under the mighty hand of God, that he may exalt you in due time; casting all your care upon him; for he careth for you.* The next verse mentioned the devil. No acceptable excuse was mentioned for failing to resist, for failing to be *steadfast in the faith.* How could a man called to preach be steadfast if he hid himself away?

Isobel seemed to think the truth of his military service existed somewhere. What she didn't realize was that he knew exactly how to obtain it. All it would take was a telegram to Dr. David McKay in Washington City. He would have written records regarding a Private Gideon Long, wounded at Shiloh and transported to a series of field hospitals and, finally, into the care of a doctor gifted in reconstruction. As far as gifting went in 1862. But Gideon had more proof tucked away in this very cabin. The uniform he'd worn when he marched with the First Rhode Island at the grand review of the armies in Washington City. Not to mention the medals. Wade Inskeep might claim he'd stolen it all. Assuming Captain Brown could be located, another letter would settle that—if Inskeep still raised objections.

None of it would resolve the matter of his appearance, though, and Gideon realized that was at the heart of his quandary.

Over the next few days, conviction grew as Gideon read about other biblical examples of endurance. He read the eleventh chapter of Hebrews and thought about the Apostle Paul, who allowed neither weakness nor illness nor some unknown "thorn in the flesh" to keep him from serving Christ. It was at once humbling, challenging, and terrifying. In the end, Gideon knew the answer to the question as to whether it mattered if people cringed when they first saw him. Except, God forgive him, it did. And then he realized that it wasn't so much *people* he didn't want to face. It was one person.

Medals for bravery notwithstanding, when it came to Miss Isobel Manning, he was a coward of the first order.

Chapter 42

For by grace are ye saved through faith; and that not of yourselves:
it is a gift of God: not of works, lest any man should boast.
Ephesians 2:8-9

Jennie's Café opened without fanfare on Monday morning, July 27. At least that had been Jennie's intention. It was only reasonable to give both the new owner and her helpers—a cook's assistant, a dishwasher, and Molly Simmons—the benefit of time to learn and to correct mistakes. But as Isobel approached the café that Monday morning, it was obvious a quiet opening was not to be. Skittering past the line extending out the door and around the corner, Isobel went to the back door. The sizzle of frying bacon and a plethora of inviting aromas wafted through the screen door.

Isobel stepped inside expecting chaos, but Jennie was smiling happily as she handed a platter of flapjacks to Molly, who cradled the platter and a butter dish on her left arm, grabbed two small pitchers, and strode into the dining area. She set the platter, butter, and syrups on the large round table Jennie had positioned in the middle of the room, which boasted eight diners. Molly had returned to the kitchen and was pouring coffee for the eight men—Isobel recognized Mr. Hill—before it could be requested.

"It looks like you have everything in hand," Isobel called to Jennie, who was adding more bacon to a skillet while waiting to turn flapjacks. Jennie nodded and suggested Isobel pour herself a cup of coffee. "You're welcome to steal a corner here in the kitchen. That's all I can offer until well past time you're expected at the office." She waved a spatula in the direction of the dining room. "Who knew?"

"The line extends all the way down the block," Isobel said.

Jennie's eyes grew wide. "Down the block? Really?"

"Told you," Molly said as she picked up two plates sporting bacon, eggs, and toast, and hurried off.

"I thought she was exaggerating," Jennie said. "After all—"

"—it's Molly. I know." Isobel poured her own coffee. As Jennie took a huge pan of biscuits out of the oven, Isobel asked if she might have one.

Jennie slid the pan onto a worktable and used a spatula to take out the first biscuit. "Butter's in the ice box. Jelly—I don't know. We might be running short on jelly already."

"Want me to fetch some from Tanners?"

Jennie looked surprised. "Could you?"

Isobel nodded. "Happy to help. I'll duck in and ask Edgar to hold the fort. Need anything else?"

Molly had heard the question. "Everything," she said quickly. "Butter. Cream. Coffee beans." She looked over at Jennie. "We'll be out of them by end of today. Need more if you're going to open up tomorrow."

"I'll see to it," Isobel said quickly. "Expect to get resupplied before lunch."

"You're a lifesaver," Jennie said. "Ask Henry if I can submit an order after I close, too." She nodded toward the bags lining the far wall. "I'll need to take stock of everything. I had no idea—" She brushed her bangs off her forehead with the back of one hand. "I hope it doesn't kill me."

"You need to hire more help," Isobel said.

"I know. Another cook. Maybe another server, too. Molly's doing very well, but it's too much for all of us. And I need to find someone besides Nettie Simmons to supply eggs by this time tomorrow."

"I'll ask Henry for suggestions," Isobel promised.

A male voice sounded from the opposite side of the counter. "You're doing fine," Mr. Hill said. He'd brought his own table service up to the counter and waved away Molly's apology when she realized what he'd done. "No apology, young lady. Least I could do." He smiled at her. "And you're doing fine, too." He addressed Jennie again. "Folks will either wait or they won't. But those who don't wait today will be back. Congratulations." He looked about him. "Nebraska City has itself a first-rate café."

Mid-morning of the crazed, not quiet opening of Jennie's Café, Charlie telegraphed a return date. *Slight delay. Library crated. Furniture almost ready. Quilt located. Open letter that follows at once. Good news. Depart St. Louis August 7.* Isobel wrote a short reply—including mention of Jennie's success—and handed it to the waiting messenger. Did Charlie's good news have to do with estate finances? Or had his friend learned something about Gideon's war record? Either topic would necessitate a more private communique.

Gideon. Would she ever have an opportunity to speak with him again? Weren't their conversations about faith important enough for him to continue them? Birdie seemed convinced the man would communicate with her again. She needed to be patient while he dealt with whatever was keeping him away. There really was nothing she could do about Gideon Long but wait. It wasn't as if she had nothing to occupy her time. She turned her attention back to Charlie's telegram.

Quilt located. She imagined the beautiful quilt on *her* bed in *her* room in the house she and Charlie would soon build... and smiled.

And then she started, looking first up at the ceiling and then over at Edgar as a yowl and a thump from above were followed by a bump and a crash. Without comment, Isobel reached into her desk drawer and held out Charlie's apartment key to Edgar.

Edgar slid off his stool and walked over to take the key, but he didn't leave right away. Instead, he said, "Best to be certain it's done before I go up there."

Isobel nodded. The noise intensified, and she gave a little shudder. "I thought you said Gus worked at night." Indeed, since being unceremoniously dumped in Charlie's apartment a few days previously, the cat hadn't made a sound. Sleeping, Edgar said. Until now.

At last, the battle seemed to end. Isobel surprised herself by following Edgar up the stairs and peering through the window while he dealt with the aftermath of Gus's encounter. She'd seen nothing yet when Birdie's voice sounded from below.

"Everything all right?"

Isobel moved to the top of the stairs and looked down at her. "You heard?"

Birdie nodded. "I was upstairs checking on our supper—stew simmering on the stove. That was quite a ruckus."

"Edgar's checking on things now."

Birdie held up an envelope. "A visitor last evening requested that I deliver this."

Isobel's heart lurched. She was halfway down the stairs to where Birdie waited when Edgar opened the apartment door and stepped outside.

"Charlie's going to want new bedding," he called down. "It's—um—probably beyond even Ma's considerable talents with laundry challenges."

"A small price to pay," Isobel replied, "if Gus gets results."

"She did," Edgar said. "Three in the night. Looks like two more just now. Probably the final battle, but to be certain, I'd suggest you keep her two or three days more."

337

Even as she gave a little shudder, Isobel said, "Were she a cat that cuddled, I'd want to give her a big hug."

"You'll be a friend for life if you open up a tin of sardines for her."

With a nod, Isobel said, "Back soon, sardines at the ready."

"No hurry," Edgar said and nodded toward the apartment. "It'll take me a while to dispose of the evidence."

"Dispose of the bedding too, if you think it best."

"Might wait a couple days to do that," Edgar said.

"I'll trust your judgment." At the base of the stairs, Isobel took the envelope from Birdie and then hesitated, torn between rushing to the newspaper office to read the note in privacy or winning Gus the cat's friendship. Holding up the envelope, she asked Birdie, "Am I going to be happy or heartbroken after I read this?"

"I haven't any idea," Birdie replied. "He made no mention of running off to avoid you last week and didn't hand over that envelope until he was preparing to leave." She paused. "I will, however, say that there seems to have been a shift of some kind in his demeanor. Exactly what that might mean remains to be seen. Henry says I'm imagining it—conjuring up evidence of something I've been praying for since Gideon returned from the war." Birdie continued. "I will allow that the evening was normal enough. The men played chess. I organized some of the reports for our next society meeting—which reminds me—oh, never mind. Another time." She looked up toward Charlie's apartment. "If you're going to escape seeing the ugly part of Gus's work, we need to skedaddle."

They skedaddled.

Isobel was forced to set Gideon's envelope aside when she got back to the newspaper office, for a family arrived with an obituary they wanted placed in the next issue of the *Register*. She immediately recognized the name of the deceased—the very woman Pastor Duncan had asked his congregation to remember in prayer. She offered sincere condolences even as she wondered yet anew about the role prayer should play in a person's life.

She remembered Birdie using the words *praying* and *conjuring* in the same sentence only moments ago. The way some people spoke about prayer, it almost seemed that it was a kind of conjuring that spoke wishes into the ether with the goal of adjusting outcomes. Isobel's experience with prayer began and ended with the pages of the *Common Book of Prayer*. Did Christians in Nebraska not offer rote prayer? Why or why not?

With a sigh, she realized how woefully short she fell when it came to understanding even the most basic tenets of the Christian faith—at least the faith she'd encountered in the lives of her friends here in Nebraska City. Not to mention Private Gideon Long, to whom she wasn't certain she could ascribe the term *friend*.

Not understanding prayer was yet another example of what was beginning to be at best an embarrassing lack of conviction and at worst a symptom of what Molly Simmons would undoubtedly label "being lost." She would have resented the very idea back in May. Now, though, Isobel accepted that *being lost* might be an apt moniker for the way she'd begun to feel of late. She might be *at home* in Nebraska City. But she was *lost* when it came to religious faith. As she opened Gideon's note, she realized that he was responsible for drawing her along a path that had at least the potential to close the distance she sensed between herself and the Almighty. Unfolding the note, she began to read.

Esteemed Miss Manning,
 I offer two apologies and a plea for forgiveness. First, for failing to meet you. Could I provide a satisfactory explanation, I would

do so. Second, for my boorish behavior when you called out to me from near Tanner Mercantile. Again, I cannot explain. And yet, I dare to hope for forgiveness.

Long ago, I relinquished any expectation of an ordinary life and embraced a solitary existence in the shadows. In His grace, God yet sends glimmers of light to pierce those shadows. You, Miss Manning, have been one such glimmer, shining the light of friendship into the gloom.

Should you find it possible to forgive my odd behavior, please know that I shall await you in the usual place this coming Friday. I will understand if you deem it best not to continue our discussions. Anticipating that that may well be the case—and that is a reasonable reaction for which you owe me no explanation—I wish to share a brief response. In part of our very first discussion, you expressed doubt in regard to matters of what you called "religious faith." When we talked, you had deduced from reading my notebook that I had had a singular encounter that changed my life. As I have recalled that brief conversation, it seems that I failed to adequately explain that moment. Put succinctly, "my conversion" cancelled once and for all my debt of sin before the holy and sinless Almighty God. The chasm sin had riven between us was closed forever.

I imagine you asking how, exactly, such a transaction took place. As the preacher God used to open my eyes was neither theologian nor scholar, I dare to use the simple terms he employed to explain this matter of eternal significance.

First, I recognized my sinful state and accepted that there was nothing I could humanly do to earn God's favor. I repented of the sin of which I had conscious knowledge. The preacher explained that this was more than "being sorry" for my mistakes. It involved a willingness to turn my back on sinful behaviors and to walk in a different direction—the way Christ would have me go. While

I did repent, I continue to struggle in finding the way Christ would have me go. You have read evidence of that struggle in my notebook.

Next, I accepted that Jesus Christ had done everything required to obtain forgiveness for my sin by dying on the cross. Its efficacy was demonstrated by His resurrection.

That is my best description of the elements necessary for authentic conversion. Repentance and acceptance. For me, that transaction took place in a moment in time—as you and I have discussed.

You expressed doubt as to whether you had experienced a similar transaction. If that is still the case, I bring you great good news, for anyone can do so at any moment.

I look forward to our discussion this Friday, should you deem me worthy of your time. In spite of my recent behavior, I have come to highly value our unusual acquaintance. Should you be unwilling to continue in conversation with me, others in your circle of friends would undoubtedly count it a privilege to discuss these matters. Your Pastor Duncan would most certainly delight in it.

Whatever your decision regarding meeting with me, please know that you have changed my life for the better and I will always be in your debt.

Regarding the all-important decision for Christ, I beg you not to delay.

Respectfully,
GJL

P.S. I have found the second chapter of Ephesians in the New Testament particularly relevant to the matters discussed above. Perhaps you would, as well. I shall make Ephesians 1:18 my prayer for you, asking that "the eyes of your understanding" will be enlightened and that you will know the hope of his calling.

The hope of his calling. Isobel read the note again and again. If what Gideon said about religious conversion was correct, she had her answer about that. Of course she was a sinner, but she'd been raised to believe different things about how God dealt with sin. If her upbringing was right, she only needed to continue to be a good person and all would be well. If what Gideon said was right, there was no denying that she, Isobel Manning, was *lost*. She needed to think about that. And she would. She would read the passage of Scripture he recommended as soon as she got back to the hotel.

Other things about the letter were more hopeful, especially his referencing *glimmers of light* and her role in introducing some into his life. She'd spoken to Birdie about finding a way to draw Gideon *out of the shadows*. He'd used that same phrase to describe his life, although he seemed to indicate he'd chosen those shadows instead of having them forced upon him. Birdie had quoted a poem about God working in mysterious ways. Could that be happening? Was God at work? Unbidden, her mind went back to the notion that she was *lost*. Was there more at play here than Private Gideon Long's isolation?

Tucking the note back into its envelope, Isobel slowly spun her chair toward the window and gazed south. Gideon wanted to meet with her again. A wave of relief washed over her. She hadn't lost him, after all. Far from it. And yet... *I'm* lost. What if that were true?

Chapter 43

The Lord is my light and my salvation; whom shall I fear?
The Lord is the strength of my life; of whom shall I be afraid?
Psalm 27:1

When Gideon first saw her on Friday evening, Isobel was standing at Gabe's grave. She must have arrived early, for her rig was already hitched at the edge of the grounds. *Call out to her. You don't have to walk right up to her, but it would be a good first step.* He probably should. But he couldn't. Not yet. Her reaction to his gospel letter was more important than whether or not he took a first step back into the light.

Trouble did what Gideon could not and bounded up the hill toward her. When Isobel backed away from the oncoming dog, Gideon called out, "He won't hurt you."

"I know that," she called back, shading her eyes with one hand as she looked in his direction. "But he might jump up and bowl me over."

Trouble wouldn't do that either, but Gideon didn't respond. He was in a hurry to get down into the creek bed and out of sight. For now, from a distance would have to be enough. Trouble continued up the hill, stopping a few feet away from Isobel, tail wagging. As Gideon dropped down into the creek bed, he heard Isobel laugh. Trouble had probably shoved his snout into her palm and given her hand a little nudge. Using the blackberry bramble as a shield, Gideon ascended to the cemetery and ducked past Isobel's ugly horse. Once in position by the oak tree, he called Trouble. The dog refused to obey and remained at Isobel's side.

"You go on," she scolded, "neither of us needs a reputation for causing trouble—even if that *is* your name."

With a whine of protest, Trouble padded to where Gideon waited by the tree. He hooked a hand through the red bandana to keep him close and commanded a *sit*. Trouble sat. The swish of a skirt hem brushing through long grass signaled Isobel's approach. Gideon tensed and took a step back.

As if she sensed his reaction, she paused. "It's so hot," she said. "I'd like to sit in the shade while we talk. I'll keep Vera Manning's marker between us and turn my back to you."

It was a reasonable request, and Gideon assented. Steadying himself with one palm against the rough bark of the tree, he tilted his head just enough to see the edge of the Manning obelisk from beneath the brim of his hat. Isobel took a seat. He saw the back of her straw bonnet and a barely visible gathering of russet curls. He'd have preferred she return to the buggy, which creaked when she moved. But if anything was going to change for him, he was going to have to learn to trust someone besides Henry and Birdie. Isobel seemed a good candidate. He would sit, too instead of staying on his feet, poised to flee. It was a beginning. As he settled on the grass, Trouble wrested free and returned to Isobel's side.

"You really *are* trouble, aren't you?" Isobel said to the dog, before calling out, "He's plopped down next to me. Seems fairly comfortable. Can he stay?"

Gideon dared a second look. Trouble had rolled onto his back, paws in the air. "He wants—"

"Oh, I know what he wants," she said. Presently, she spoke to the dog. "Belly rubbed. Now mind your manners."

After a moment, Gideon asked, "Is he? Minding his manners?"

"Perfectly. Although those blue eyes have the distinct look of an unspoken plea."

"He likes to be scratched behind the good ear. Avoid the other one."

"What happened to it?"

"I don't know. Probably a tussle with a wild animal. I found him not long after it happened."

"Poor thing," Isobel murmured.

Gideon surprised himself by launching into the entire story, ending it with, "I didn't want a dog and certainly didn't think I needed one. Turns out, we make a good team." When Trouble yipped as if agreeing, Gideon and Isobel both laughed. Finally, after a few quiet moments—not awkward, Gideon realized, just quiet—Isobel spoke.

"I hope you believe that I didn't intentionally betray your confidence with Birdie and Henry."

"I do."

"I truly was concerned you might be ill or hurt."

"If it's any comfort, Birdie roundly scolded me for worrying the two of you."

"Thank you for the letter. I've reread it several times since Birdie delivered it."

At last. The real reason they were once again conversing in a cemetery. "And?"

"Was the minister you mentioned the same one you quote in your notebook?"

"Yes. Reverend D. L. Moody."

"And you met him after a battle?"

"Fort Donelson in Tennessee."

"Was he a chaplain in the army?"

"No. He was serving with an organization called the Christian Commission."

"My experience during the war was with the Sanitary Commission. I believe the Christian Commission was pointed more toward religion, distributing tracts and the like."

"Yes. Reverend Moody distributed Bibles when he visited the wounded. In fact, he gave me one, although I lost it later on."

"You were wounded?"

New interest sounded in her voice. He could almost sense her sitting up straighter, perhaps even leaning forward, tempted to look around. "No," he said quickly. "I attended one of his services, mostly because I was bored. February 20, 1862. The day God reached into the kingdom of darkness and snatched me into His light."

"Kingdom of darkness?" Isobel echoed. "Surely you weren't so bad as that."

"Badness depends on who's doing the measuring. I remember Reverend Moody quoting Romans 3:23. 'For all have sinned, and come short of the glory of God.' Plain enough, although I didn't need a Bible verse to know I was a sinner. The part I didn't understand was why that was such a problem. After all, I saw myself as a fairly good person. But then Moody quoted another verse about God's standard being far more than my doing my best. 'Be ye holy; for I am holy.'"

"That's hardly a fair expectation," Isobel said. "After all, no one's perfect." She paused. "I have no quarrel with the pronouncement that 'all have sinned.' Feeling that reality is undoubtedly a motivation for much of the good people do. Everyone who believes in God has a vague sense of their need to settle accounts with Him. What gives me pause is the notion that everything I've believed all my life about that part of it is in error."

"What have you believed?" Gideon asked.

"That I'm expected to do good to atone for my sins."

"At what point does the scale balance? When has a person done enough?"

"That's the problem," Isobel said. "It's impossible to know for certain."

"There is another way," Gideon said. "The apostle John wrote, 'These things have I written unto you that believe on the name of the Son of God; that ye may *know* that ye have eternal life, and that ye may believe on the name of the Son of God.' The chapter goes on to use that word *know* several times." He gentled his voice. "We don't have to wonder. We can *know* our account is settled. Everyone can."

"Thanks to Jesus," Isobel murmured.

"Jesus," Gideon echoed. "Always and only Jesus."

"Is that the message you heard from Reverend Moody?"

"It is."

"And yet, only a few years later, you were writing about a 'quest for hope.' What happened?"

It was a very good question. Gideon thought for a moment about how to frame a truthful answer without revealing too much about himself.

"Private Long? Your quest for hope?"

"I never doubted I was forgiven," Gideon said. "The notebook isn't about that."

"Then explain why, at the outset, you express grave doubts about your standing with God."

She had a good memory, and she was right. He'd questioned everything once he got a look in a mirror. Once he realized the inevitable reaction when people saw him. "All right. Yes. I had some doubts. But the foundational ones about salvation were settled very quickly. My real struggle is with other questions. I still don't have answers to all of those."

"The ones that have to do with your calling."

Goodness but the woman was perceptive. And persistent—*stubborn*, as he had accused in the past. Remembering made him smile. Faintly. What could it hurt to reveal a part of what had happened? "After my conversion, Reverend Moody said some things that made me think I might become a preacher." He hurried ahead. "Sometime later, when I thought I'd been wrong, the quandary plunged me into a dark valley."

"You fell back into the kingdom of darkness?"

She'd picked up on the notion of darkness and light, which he'd used to illustrate spiritual realities. "No," he said firmly. "God never takes back the gift of salvation. Jesus Himself promised that no one can snatch us out of His hand."

"So your 'quest for hope' wasn't about finding God. It was, rather, about people believing lies about you. Making you feel the need to hide."

He swallowed. "That's part of it."

"Why would God let that happen?"

Another good question. Why *had* God allowed his face to be ruined? Up until a few days ago, he'd assumed that meant preaching was out of the question. But was it? Was it really? *Only if he didn't have the courage to face people as he was—scarred and disfigured.* The rumors about his military service were nothing compared to that. Clearing his throat, he answered honestly. "I don't know why."

"And yet you believe."

"With all my heart."

After a moment, Isobel said, "I want that."

"You want—?"

"The kind of faith that holds on, even when life takes me to a place I don't want to go. Even when I don't have answers to every question. I want to be able to *weather* life, not run away from it."

Weather life, not run away from it. The words made him cringe. He hadn't weathered life. For all his supposed knowledge of God and the Bible, he'd run away. Was still running.

"I've always believed in God," Isobel continued, her tone thoughtful. "But I thought of Him as some remote being not particularly involved in the everyday lives of those who believed in Him." She paused. "The God you talk about—the one you wrestled with in your notebook—that's a God who cares. Who listens. Who doesn't necessarily explain everything, but still—He listens." She paused. "That caring is consistent with the Jesus who died—" Her voice wavered. "For *me*." She cleared her throat. "The Jesus who died to give me the gift of salvation." Her voice took on a sense of wonder. "I've attended church all my life. I never understood the basic truth that being a Christian—a real Christian—isn't about what I do for God. It's about what God did for me." Again, she paused, and then croaked, "Do I have that right?"

"You have it exactly right," Gideon said. She was quiet. He thought he heard soft weeping and then a low laugh as she murmured to Trouble. "It's all right, boy. These are good tears." She cleared her throat. "Is there a prayer I should pray?"

Dumbfounded, his throat aching with his own emotion, Gideon didn't trust himself to answer. After all his doubting, all his rejecting God's call, it seemed that God had still trusted him to be the one to lead Isobel Manning into the kingdom of light. *Forgive me, Lord. The doubting. The hiding. Help me go forward.*

"You mentioned *repentance* in your letter," Isobel said. "Isn't there something I should say to God about that?"

I repent, heavenly Father. Forgive my bitterness.

"Hello? Private Long? Are you—did I say something wrong?"

He heard a rustling as Isobel rose to her feet. She was looking this way. She had to be. He sprang up, ready to run. "You said everything right. I was—" He sighed. "I was doing my own repenting. For doubting. And yes. Of course we can pray."

"Not like this," she said. "Not with my back to you."

The day was hot, but suddenly it felt like someone had built a fire nearby—a raging fire emitting waves of heat that made it difficult to breathe. He swiped at the sweat on his forehead. "You don't have to see me to pray with me."

"You called me your friend in that letter," she said. "You said I'd brought light back into your life. Won't you trust me? Please?"

Weather life. Stop running from the light. You were not meant to be of the kingdom of darkness. Repent. Step into the light. It would mean the end of an unusual relationship he'd come to cherish. He hadn't known that until this very moment, when he was on the brink of losing it. But God had used him to draw Isobel to Himself. In despair, he surrendered. *All right.*

Shifting his weight, he put a trembling hand on the tree trunk, but he still didn't step into view. First, he tried to prepare her. "You asked if I'd been wounded when I met Reverend Moody. I wasn't. This came later." He cupped his open palm over the worst of the scars. Spreading his fingers, he did what he could to hide the worst of it as he took a step away from the tree trunk. One step. He kept his eyes closed. He didn't want to see her expression transform from expectation to curiosity to—whatever it would become. Finally, though, he dropped his hand. He heard a sharp intake of breath. "This happened at Shiloh. Tom Simmons had been shot in the leg. High up. There was so much blood. I applied a tourniquet and ran for help. Never got any because—" He swept the air next to his face. Feeling a little dizzy, he opened his eyes but kept his gaze on Trouble, now seated at his side and looking up at him, head cocked, one ear pricked, blue eyes intense.

The grass rustled as Isobel approached. Taking a deep breath, he waited for the inevitable. He would hear the creak as she clamored up to the buggy seat. He kept his eyes fixed on the earth at his feet. But there was no creak. There was, instead, the hem of a brown calico skirt as Isobel came near. He frowned. Took a nervous breath. Looked up enough to see her remove a glove. And then... a miracle. She laid the palm of her ungloved hand against the scars, her fingertips just below the place where a normal man would have an earlobe, her hand resting along his jaw.

"You beautiful man," she said, her voice wavering. "What did they do to you." Unbelievably, she traced the scars with her fingertips, up the ridge of his nose, across what was left of the eyebrow, along his temple and down to the collar of his sweat-stained shirt. It was as if a butterfly had flitted across the hideous landscape of his face and come to rest on his shoulder. "Look at me," she said gently. "Don't be afraid."

Taking a deep, shuddering breath, he managed to obey. Couldn't believe what he *didn't* see in her warm brown eyes. He frowned and cocked his head. "Why aren't you running away?"

Her gaze widened, almost as if the question surprised her. "*No one* should ever be rejected because of the way they look."

They stood that way for a long moment. Thinking back on it, Gideon would have sworn the universe shifted, because certainly something shifted inside of him. He reached up to cover her hand with his as tears spilled down his cheeks.

Finally, after a few moments, Isobel said quietly, "You were going to help me pray."

He nodded. She surprised him when she bowed her head and reached for his hands. His voice trembled as he led Isobel through what Reverend Moody had once called *the sinner's prayer*.

Chapter 44

A man's heart deviseth his way: but the Lord directeth his steps.
Proverbs 16:9

Isobel stood beneath the cemetery oak tree, slowly turning in a circle as she scanned the new fence that had been erected this past week. All save the new gate, which America Payne said would be in place in the next couple of weeks. She smiled, remembering Mrs. Oliver's somewhat indelicate exclamation when Mrs. Payne reported on the fence at last evening's society meeting. When Chaplain Oliver's widow exclaimed *hallelujah and good riddance to cow pies,* the rest of the ladies burst out laughing at the uncharacteristic show of emotion. They'd moved on to other matters of business, entrusting Isobel with the task of publishing an official notice "expressing the society's gratitude for the generous support of the citizenry in regard to recent improvements, not the least of which was the fence that would heretofore protect new plantings from depredations by animals both wild and domestic." The notice would appear in the next issue of the *Register*.

It had been a long seven days since the moment, standing right here beneath the oak tree with Gideon, that Isobel's world had shifted. Looking back on the week, she contemplated the absolute ordinariness of the days and nights insofar as her duties were concerned. And yet, in some way she could not quite fathom, her life had changed.

She hadn't slept well that Friday evening, wondering over the full impact of what had happened in the cemetery, both for herself and for Gideon. Unable to sort through the emotions, she'd lain awake for much of the night, finally abandoning the notion of sleep and heeding Gideon's recommendation that she begin her new spiritual journey by reading Paul's letter to the Ephesians.

It was not a passage of the Bible with which Isobel was particularly familiar. Surprisingly, the words resonated. By flickering lamplight, she devoured the letter not once but several times, particularly grateful for the passage that reassured her that what had happened in the cemetery was real. She had been saved by grace. It was a gift of God. Nothing more had happened in recent days that was particularly earth-shattering, but a lightness of spirit blanketed her life with a strange peace. She almost said something to Edgar about "being saved," but her upbringing won out and she decided against it. People simply did not make their private devotional lives—or lack thereof—a topic of conversation. But she could talk to Gideon about it.

Her heart lurched when he first came into view in the distance. She raised her free hand in a silent greeting. Trouble dashed toward her. Gideon, on the other hand, paused at the bottom of the hill. For a brief moment, her breath caught. He reached up to tug on the brim of his hat and pull it lower on his forehead. *You don't have to do that.* She longed to somehow reach into his life and sweep away every unkind memory. Tears stung her eyes and she crouched down to greet Trouble, grateful for the distraction the dog provided, laughing when, quick as a flash, the dog licked her cheek.

"Trouble!" Gideon scolded as he strode up the hill. "No!"

"It's all right," Isobel said as she rose back to her feet. *Why am I blushing?* She felt awkward, standing there, here gloved hands clasped, waiting for him.

"Have you had a good week?"

Isobel nodded.

"Would you like to retreat into the shade?"

She blinked and looked around. She hadn't even realized she'd moved out of the shade, striding toward Gideon as he walked up the hill to meet her. "I—yes. Thank you." She followed him into the shade, then remembered the two newspapers she'd brought with her. "I've something to share with you," she said, and hurried toward the buggy to retrieve the papers.

She rattled on about Charlie's adding a subscription to the *Chicago Evening Post*. He'd done it while away, and the first edition had arrived only last Saturday. "The day after I was—after you and I—the day after," she finally said, not quite knowing how to characterize their last meeting. Gideon smiled. Had she ever seen him smile? One side of his mouth curved upward. The other remained inert. When he reached up with a lightly clenched hand to press bare knuckles against that side, Isobel realized that he was a very long way from feeling comfortable in her presence.

She held out one of the papers. "There's a familiar name in both editions. Third column on the left, half-way down." She watched as Gideon opened the paper. "I underlined it." When he saw the name *D. L. Moody*, the smile broadened. "It gave me an idea," Isobel said and gestured toward the tree. "Shall we sit?"

Charlie had been awake since long before dawn, partly because of the August heat and partly because of the emotions attached to going home. *Home.* A good word representing a long journey that had turned out to be less about death and estates and more about a shift within himself. Lord willing, the change would carry him into a future no longer tangled up in bitterness and loss. He'd dressed and exited his cabin as soon as daylight enabled him to see the shoreline. Now, standing at the railing on the hurricane deck as the *Octavia* churned her way upriver toward Nebraska City, he thought back to a brief conversation he'd had with Jennie Wilcox the last Sunday before he'd departed for St. Louis. When he walked Jennie home from church that day, she'd taken the opportunity once again to offer her condolences about Mother Manning's death.

"I know you and Isobel had a—difficult—relationship with Mrs. Manning," Jennie said. "I'm sorry you weren't able to resolve it before she passed on."

At first, Charlie didn't know how to respond. He'd never expected to resolve anything with Lucinda Manning. In truth, he'd hoped to never see her again. Thinking back on it now, he realized how well things had gone in St. Louis. He'd done his best to honor Mother Manning's life in spite of his personal feelings. Not only had he arranged for a suitable funeral, he'd also intentionally avoided criticizing the woman along the way to settling her estate. He was especially grateful for his circumspection, once he met with the attorneys and bankers.

Amazingly enough, Mother Manning's propensity for outlandish spending hadn't been a barrier to E. L. Manning's plans for his children. Only a few minutes into the first of several meetings about the matter, it became obvious that Papa had a realistic understanding of his second wife's failings—at least when it came to money. Many of his holdings had been managed by proxy, their very existence hidden. Papa had left clear instruction that they were to benefit his second wife only in case of an emergency defined as the threat of Mother Manning losing everything, including the manse. As a result, Charlie and Izzy had inherited an astonishing amount of money.

How, he wondered, would that change the future? He'd cautioned Izzy about expecting to donate generously to cemetery improvements. After all, he'd said, it was entirely possible they'd have to pay out of their own funds to ship the things they wished to keep. Expecting little, he'd sketched a modest home for them to share. How would Izzy respond when she learned that a cemetery flagpole was only the beginning of things she could donate to the causes she cared about? Charlie had made his own list of possibilities, but he didn't intend to mention them until he and Izzy met with their Nebraska City banker. The biggest question in his mind was what to do about the house. Would Izzy want to expand the current plan or scrap it entirely?

Already, Charlie had decided to make improvements at the *Register*. He'd ordered a second press. As soon as the house was complete enough for him to move out of his apartment, he and Izzy would move their desks into that space. Interior stairs added inside the front door would facilitate access. The main floor would become a dedicated press room. At some point, Charlie envisioned expanding both levels.

Would Edgar want to purchase an expanded set of print drawers? Would they need to hire help? Only the Lord knew what the future might bring. Thinking about it all was both invigorating and terrifying—an unsettling reminder of how quickly life could change—and not always for the better. Vera and the baby's names on that obelisk out at Wyuka Cemetery would always remind him of that. With a low grunt, Charlie stared down at the brown waters of the Missouri. Would it always be like this? Just when he was happy, just when he was looking forward to something, would memory rise up, snag hope, and yank it away?

Pushing back from the railing, he started yet another walk around the hurricane deck. It was never quite as effective as seeking out Jennie's kitchen but—*Jennie's kitchen.* Now there was a pleasant way to pull himself out of murky waters regarding the future. Izzy had written about Jennie's taking over Lila Ritchie's café. As he trudged along, Charlie imagined the mingled aromas of fresh coffee, baking bread, and something called *breakfast pie*. Whatever that was, he would have his first chance to taste it early tomorrow morning.

Sweet Jennie Wilcox. She'd blushed and said she was pleased to learn that both Charlie and Izzy were staying in Nebraska City, when Mrs. Manning's demise might have enticed them both back to St. Louis. She'd promised to pray for him. Charlie rather liked the idea of Jennie Wilcox praying for him, although he wrestled with the fact that he thought about her often. Perhaps too often. Was it disloyal to Vera and the baby to befriend another woman? Most often he thought Vera wouldn't mind—especially in light of its being Jennie who'd helped him take steps toward sobriety. Then again, he never should have needed that kind of help. *Enough.* Enough warring thoughts. Enough conflicting emotions. Would he ever get it all sorted? Perhaps. Perhaps not. But he could face Izzy and Jennie both with a clear conscience when it came to alcohol. That felt good. As for the rest—it would take time to get it all sorted.

When the levee came into view, three other steamboats waited there, glistening white in the morning sun, each packet's twin black smokestacks towering above their decks. The landing teemed with travelers—miners and soldiers, settlers and businessmen, each group distinctly set apart by both dress and decorum. A long line of wagons and carts crowded the levee, ready to retrieve the freight piled high on the *Octavia's* main deck.

Charlie retreated to his cabin for his satchel and a large package wrapped in brown paper. The moment he'd descended to the main deck, he caught sight of Izzy's red-wheeled buggy. Teamster Ezra Carter was there, too, driving a huge wagon drawn by a handsome team of draft horses. If their gleaming coats and braided manes were any indication, Carter was taking fine care of the team the Mannings had helped him buy, on the understanding that he would give them priority when it came to hauling—at least until the new cottage was completed.

Izzy had alit from her buggy before Charlie reached her and offered a welcoming hug. "It's so *good* to have you home," she said, then stepped back to look him up and down. "You look hale, hearty, and—" she tapped his bearded chin, "hairy."

"I believe *debonair* is the word you were seeking." Charlie teased as he brandished the package. "Your all-important quilt."

Izzy pointed at the small box tucked beneath the twine securing the wrapping in place. "And that?"

"Almond cookies, courtesy of Portia. I told her they'd get stale before you and I could enjoy them, but she insisted. Said to dunk them in coffee if need be." He patted his breast pocket. "She even wrote out the recipe for us." He tucked his satchel beneath the buggy seat and set the package atop it, then walked to the wagon to greet Ezra Carter, who introduced the young man sitting next to him as Lawson Tally, a recent arrival in Nebraska.

Charlie patted the tawny rump of one of the giant horses as he said, "I'm glad to see you're prepared to handle some serious weight." He motioned toward the freight being transferred to the landing. "That's only about half of it—not to mention the piano, which I hope Izzy mentioned?"

Carter nodded. "Lawson here seems to think he's Samson reborn. We'll handle it." With a tug on the brim of his hat to take his leave, Carter urged the team forward, and the empty wagon rattled away.

"The piano's going straight out to the Simmons farm," Izzy said.

"Really?"

Quickly, she explained. "I was bemoaning all the decisions we were having to make one day at the office. When I mentioned the piano, Edgar spoke up. Said his mother was church pianist before they moved west. Edgar and I agreed to surprise her."

"I hope it's a good surprise," Charlie said doubtfully. "From what I know of the Simmons place, there's a good chance a piano would fall through the parlor floor."

"Henry had the same thought."

Charlie grinned. "But Busy Izzy was not to be deterred."

"Indeed not," she retorted. "The last time Nettie brought eggs and butter in to the mercantile, Henry sneaked out to the house and checked the floor. Not to worry. Finding someone to tune the thing after it's in place might be a challenge, though."

"Somehow," Charlie said, "I think you'll solve that, too."

"Somehow I will," Izzy agreed. As she drove them up the trail toward town, Izzy told Charlie about improvements at the Simmons house, courtesy of a group of men from the church. "The roof's been patched, the porch railing repaired, and all the cracked windowpanes replaced. There's even a porch swing." She glanced over at him. "And you are formally invited to help apply a fresh coat of paint to the exterior tomorrow. Molly campaigned for bright yellow, but Nettie chose blue."

Charlie allowed a little frown. "Is my participation voluntary or expected?"

"You'll want to be there. Lunch is being provided on site by Jennie's Café."

Charlie felt his cheeks warming at the mention of Jennie's name. Good thing he'd let the beard grow. "Is that meant to be some kind of bribe to get me to help?"

"Only if a bribe is required."

"And how is the café faring now that the stellar opening day has passed?" Izzy had telegraphed about that first day and the long line extending out the door and around the corner of the building.

Izzy glanced over. "Not to read too much into it, but I find it intriguing that you asked about Jennie before inquiring after the *Register*."

"The only thing to read into that," Charlie said, "is context. You're the one who launched the topic of Mrs. Wilcox by saying she'll be serving lunch at the Simmons farm. As to the *Register*, I wasn't really worried. I knew you and Edgar could handle it."

Izzy's voice was warm with emotion when she said, "You have no idea what it means to hear you say that, but there were a few sputters that first week." She recounted a list of mistakes and missteps, ending with, "Apparently the good Lord thought I needed a fresh lesson in humility." She gave a low chuckle. "Sorting all that type certainly gave me one. And a new appreciation for Edgar's job. I hope to *never ever* have to do it." She paused. "I do wish we'd managed longer editions, though. Fortunately, subscribers didn't complain."

They chatted about the newspaper as Izzy drove them down a bustling Main Street. When they passed a closed Jennie's Café, Charlie took note. "I hope there's nothing wrong."

"On the contrary," Izzy said. "It means she's sold out of much of the day's offerings. Her regulars know not to dawdle about coming in. For now, it's meant to help her mind the budget. It eliminates waste almost entirely. Once she has a better sense of how it all works, she plans to maintain regular hours."

Finally, they pulled up at the base of the stairs leading up to Charlie's apartment. "Welcome home to your rat-free quarters." Briefly, she recounted a story of the nocturnal terror that had sent her fleeing back to the hotel. She scowled in mock anger. "You might have warned me when I asked about moving over."

"I would have," Charlie said. "They must have come in from the mercantile the very day I left. Encouraged by the lack of occupancy, I suppose." He paused. "I'd conducted a very successful round of trapping. Honest."

"Not to worry," Izzy said. "Nettie loaned me a demon-cat named Gus. I've reserved two of her very next litter—and yes, Gus is a female. Hopefully the timing works so that about the time we move into the cottage, we'll have felines prepared to terrorize anything that dares a foray into our pantry—or any other part of our new home."

Home, Charlie thought. Beautiful word, that.

Chapter 45

Trust in the Lord with all thine heart;
and lean not unto thine own understanding.
Proverbs 3:5

Morning light finally did the work of burning off the mist that had shrouded the tombstones when Charlie first arrived at the cemetery Saturday morning. As he stood at Vera's marker, he apologized for not coming as soon as he'd disembarked from the *Octavia*.

"Izzy met me. She'd just pulled up at the back of the office, and I'd jumped down when Birdie and Henry emerged from the mercantile. I meant to walk out here, but—you know how Birdie is. Before I knew it, she'd swept Izzy and me inside and herded us up the stairs for supper—which wasn't quite ready. I lost track of time. Then the sun had gone down and it started to rain." He paused. Took a deep breath. "I'm sorry." He raised both hands in a gesture of surrender. "And I didn't bring flowers, either. I will tomorrow. I promise."

What was it about rambling to a strip of earth that appealed to those left behind when someone died? He'd always thought mourning garb and funeral biscuits and all the trappings of death ridiculous. He didn't understand the point of visiting a grave. Until Vera and the baby died. But here he was, as if a trip to the cemetery would somehow reconnect him with what he'd lost seven months ago. Feeling foolish but not wanting to leave yet, Charlie turned in a circle, taking note of the new fence Izzy had told him about.

Izzy. She still didn't know the truth of their shared financial situation. He'd wait until their meeting with Mr. Hill on Monday afternoon to give her the news. By then, telegrams would have arrived verifying what he still couldn't quite believe. He had, however, let Izzy and Birdie know that the Mannings could donate a flagpole for the cemetery.

Thankfully, his mentioning the cemetery apparently inspired Izzy to mention the society's next fundraiser. America Payne was making a quilt, mailing off cloth stars for dignitaries to sign, their autographs intended to enhance the value of said quilt. Mention of America's project reminded Izzy of the package waiting beneath the buggy seat downstairs. She retrieved her quilt to show Birdie, and that led to the opening of the box of Portia's almond cookies and a second round of coffee. In the end, Charlie and Izzy told stories all evening about growing up as the mostly unwelcome inhabitants of a St. Louis mansion.

"I wish I'd told you more about those days," Charlie said aloud to the grave. "I packed up my father's library. The entire thing. Ezra Carter's going to haul a few crates at a time up to my—to *our*—rooms so Izzy and I can sort through them. We'll probably donate some to the new public library."

The screech of a steamboat drew Charlie's attention toward town. He was meeting Izzy for breakfast at Jennie's Café. His stomach growled. "I wish I knew how you'd feel about—" He broke off. He couldn't say those words aloud, but he thought them. *I wish I knew you'd be all right with—*. Apparently, he wasn't ready to think the words yet, either. With a deep sigh, he cast the beginning of a prayer toward the heavens, more emotion than conscious thought.

"Well, then. I'll be back tomorrow after church." He grimaced. Tomorrow after church he and Izzy were taking a drive to look at building sites. For a cottage Charlie wasn't sure he still wanted to build. He jammed his hat back on his head and thrust his hands in his pockets. Back less than a day and he was already fumbling life.

A beam of light broke through the branches of the oak tree and illuminated the tip of Vera's obelisk, where a delicately carved hand pointed heavenward. The stonecutter had thought it a nice addition, but what was intended as a kindness had only made Charlie angry, fraying the raw edges of his grief every time he looked at it. As he regarded it now, he realized something had changed. Instead of fueling bitterness, the carving reminded him that Vera and the baby were safe. *Safe in the Arms of Jesus* ... a new hymn Portia had sung as she packed kitchenwares and linens for transport to Nebraska. Charlie wished he'd asked her to write out the lyrics for him.

By the time Charlie stepped inside Jennie's Café, the place was bustling with activity. He took in the cheerful yellow walls, the scrubbed floor, the crisp white curtains, the counter separating the dining area from the kitchen. Izzy had written about Jennie's changes to what had been Lila's Café, but his imagination hadn't done it justice. The place looked terrific. A tall chalkboard mounted behind the counter listed the day's specials. *Apple Pancakes. Cheesy Grits. Breakfast Pie.* From where she stood behind the counter, Izzy called his name, and he wove his way across the room.

"Coffee's coming," she said. "Do you know what you'd like to eat?"

"You're serving? Give me a piece of the breakfast pie, please." He was only teasing about Izzy's being a waitress, but she took it in stride, saying he'd made a good choice and retrieving two plates from a tall stack.

Jennie pulled a pie—obviously a mix of eggs and crispy bacon—from the oven. Setting it on the worktable to the left of the stove, she slipped two more in to bake before moving on to a second oven. From the second oven she retrieved two huge pans of biscuits, which she shoved toward Izzy. Taking up a towel to keep from burning her hands, Izzy inverted the pans, dumping the biscuits onto the table while Jennie rolled out more dough. The two friends had obviously worked together in the café kitchen before. Charlie was about to joke about his fellow editor taking a second job when Molly Simmons burst in the back door.

Setting a huge basket on the worktable, Molly grabbed an apron, even as she blustered an apology for being late. "Some varmint pried a board loose, and the girls all escaped. It took all of us to round those up." She nodded at the basket brimming with an assortment of brown, white, pale green, and blue eggs.

Jennie smiled. "The eggs are much needed, and you're forgiven." Once Molly was circling the dining room refilling coffee cups, Jennie looked over at Izzy. "That chicken coop is my nemesis. It's either hens escaping or varmints on the prowl. Either way, between Tanner Mercantile and my café, Nettie's egg production can't keep up. If she doesn't want to grow her flock, I'm going to have to find a second supplier. Either way, Nettie needs a new chicken coop."

Izzy looked meaningfully at Charlie. He almost laughed aloud. The moment the two of them were seated, he said, "The answer is yes."

"I didn't ask a question."

"Ah, but you did." He leaned close and lowered his voice. "I'll add the chicken coop to the list."

"You have a list? Does that mean—" Izzy broke off as Molly arrived with two plates heaped with food—a generous wedge of breakfast pie, two biscuits with butter, and honey.

Charlie pointed at one of the condiment bowls and looked up at Molly. "Dare I hope that's your mother's elderberry jelly?"

Molly smiled. As if sharing a secret, she said in a low voice, "Mrs. Wilcox said not to noise it about. She's been saving it back special just for you."

Once Molly had retreated to serve other diners, Izzy launched into the itinerary she'd planned for Charlie's first weekend home. "I assume you'll want to visit the cemetery on our way out to the Simmons farm?"

"I was there at sunrise this morning," Charlie said. "It was especially peaceful. A misty morning until the sun rose. And then a beam of light shone on that hand pointing upwards."

"I thought you hated that hand."

"I did. Now I don't."

Izzy smiled. "I'm glad."

After a moment, Izzy once again brought up the subject of their need to select a building site.

"About that," Charlie said. He gazed toward the kitchen. *The building sites can wait. I want to take Jennie for a drive after church tomorrow.* It was true, but he probably shouldn't be that blunt about it. "I wouldn't think—since we haven't yet finalized the house plan—that selecting a building site needs to be done the first weekend I'm back."

"*You* might not think so," Izzy said, "but when we head out to the Simmons farm this morning and you see all the construction south of Main Street, you'll understand why we shouldn't delay. As it happens, only a couple of days ago, Mr. Blevins hinted at interest in two of the four sites on my list."

Charlie was not convinced. "I suspect land agents always hint at prospective buyers—whether said buyers exist or not."

Izzy set her coffee mug down. "*Henry* introduced me to Mr. Blevins. I don't think he'd recommend someone inclined to invent imaginary buyers."

"I didn't mean that the way you took it," Charlie hastened to say. "You've spent a lot of time on this, and I appreciate it." He shrugged. "Not the weekend I was contemplating. That's all."

"If it's any comfort, I've asked Jennie to accompany us."

"You—what?"

Izzy leaned forward and lowered her voice. "She's missed you as much as you've missed her. Everyone knows she and I have become fast friends. Our taking a Sunday drive with my recently-returned-home brother won't invite gossip. It's a perfectly innocent way for the two of you to spend some time together."

Charlie nodded as Izzy rambled on. He hadn't been concerned about what others might think. What if people did assume that he was courting Mrs. Jennie Wilcox? Maybe he was—a jolting realization that distinctly complicated the idea of sharing a house with a spinster sister. But Izzy didn't seem in the least concerned with the obvious ramifications to Charlie and Jennie. Was she dabbling in matchmaking? Didn't she realize—

"And you aren't listening to me."

Charlie stopped mid-chew and looked across the table at Izzy. She was staring at him questioningly. Washing down the last bit of biscuit with a gulp of coffee, he apologized as he glanced toward the kitchen. "Let's just agree that we'll wait a bit before committing to a land purchase."

Izzy followed his gaze. When she turned back toward him, she was smiling. "It's all right. It'll work out." She reached across the table and gave his hand a squeeze. "Have a little faith, Charlie."

Have faith? Izzy never talked about faith. Taking a deep breath, Charlie determined to set aside his premature worries and simply enjoy being home. In due time he would find a way to avoid repeating the scenario from earlier this year. Izzy must never again be made to feel like an uninvited, unwanted appendage to his life. Somehow, the future would work out. He would take Izzy's advice. He would have faith.

Chapter 46

Rest in the Lord, and wait patiently for him.
Psalm 37:7

From where she sat at her desk in the newspaper office, Isobel stole a furtive glance in Charlie's direction. What would he think of her plans for the next edition of the *Register*? She was fairly confident that she'd selected good material to reprint, but she'd also selected some religious content as a way of testing the potential for publishing Gideon Long's work—anonymously, of course. To test the waters, she'd made selections from a sermon originally titled *An Ode to the Bible*.

"What's this?" Charlie held up the edition of *Arthur's Home Magazine*, the source for the sermon.

"Something I found enlightening," Isobel replied. "Cheering, even." She pointed at the periodical in Charlie's hand. "You'll note I shortened it significantly. But I think I retained the best parts. And I feel that our readers will benefit from it."

"It's not the kind of thing people expect to read in a newspaper," Charlie said.

"Which is exactly why I think we should try it," Isobel countered. Still, Charlie said nothing. Instead, he turned back to his desk, the periodical in hand, and began to reread. Presently he began to circle passages and mark out others. It was unusual for him to show an interest in religious material. Then again, there had been many unusual moments since Charlie's return. While yesterday's Sunday drive with Jennie had resulted in a decision about which of the four building sites was best, he had resisted the notion of contacting the land agent first thing this morning to make the purchase. Even Jennie had sided with her.

"Don't risk losing it," Jennie said before pointing back at the cottage they'd passed on the opposite end of the block. "It's a lovely part of town. I've always loved that little house. Look at that garden! That's a sign of rich soil. You'll have a lovely place in no time at all. And those mature elms! Can't you just see a row on both sides of the drive up to your home? In time, you'd have a canopy of shade to welcome visitors." For the remainder of the drive, Charlie and Jennie engaged in a lively discussion about, of all things, the best flowers to plant in a Nebraska garden.

Isobel sat back, smiling. *Charlie and Jennie.* The way he'd looked at her. Not only yesterday, but Saturday when she was serving lunch to the workers painting the Simmons place. And yesterday morning in church.

Suddenly, Isobel understood. Charlie's reticence about buying property had very little to do with the Manning estate and everything to do with Jennie Wilcox. He was hesitating in the matter of building a house because Jennie liked a house that already existed. He might not have parsed that out in detail, but it was apparent to anyone who was paying attention. And Isobel was.

As Charlie continued his review of articles for the next edition, Isobel pretended to read through the most recent submissions for *Early Days*. But she wasn't really reading stories about Nebraska City's past. She was thinking about the future.

About what a pleasant prospect it had been to think about sharing a cottage with Charlie.

About how quickly things could change.

About the strangely-at-peace Charlie who'd returned from St. Louis.

About Jennie Wilcox.

And, Lord help her, about Gideon Long.

※

Late Monday afternoon, Isobel sat next to Charlie in one of two elegant armchairs positioned before a massive desk in the opulent office of Mr. Thomas Hill of Otoe County National Bank. It was not the same office where Isobel and Jennie had proposed Jennie's Café. Nor was this Mr. Hill the strutting Bantam rooster who'd sputtered polite but insincere vagaries over Jennie's lemon meringue pie.

This office, Isobel realized, was an inner sanctum. This version of Mr. Hill wanted the Mannings' business. Badly. Isobel had watched as the man perused the three letters of credit Charlie presented moments ago. She'd seen Hill's expression transformed from surprise to amazement to outright discombobulation. Now, as he set the papers before him, Hill placed his elbows at the edge of the desktop and steepled his hands. He addressed Charlie. "You can understand the need to await final verification from each institution before proceeding."

"Of course," Charlie said, "and it was to have been telegraphed first thing this morning. I assumed you would notify me if there was a delay." He rose to his feet. "If you'll send word once you've collected all the documents you require—"

Hill jumped to his feet, sputtering assurances that the Mannings had always been valued clients and would receive the very best that Otoe County National Bank had to offer. He proposed that the meeting continue. "Let me send a messenger to the telegraph office. In the meantime, we can set up your account."

"Or accounts," Charlie said. He took the papers from Hill's desk and handed them to Isobel. "Take a moment to consider how you'd like it sorted."

Isobel looked at the total on the top sheet. She'd always considered a woman's suffering *the vapors* a completely manufactured and somewhat pathetic ploy for attention. But at the moment, she was in very real danger of requiring smelling salts. She looked at Mr. Hill and croaked, "If I might request a drink of water."

"Right away," Hill said and bustled out of the office.

Charlie sat back down.

Isobel waved the papers at him. "You might have said something."

"I honestly didn't believe it," Charlie said. "I'm not entirely certain I do yet." He pointed at the papers. "Look more carefully. The top one isn't a total. There are three separate accounts at three separate St. Louis institutions."

Isobel looked at the other two pieces of paper, then stared, disbelieving, at Charlie. A man brought in a silver tray atop which rested a crystal pitcher of water and two glasses. Isobel drank deeply and had regained her composure when Mr. Hill returned.

"Good news," the banker said, producing the three telegrams they'd been awaiting and comparing them to the letters. Finally, he declared that all was in order. "Allow me to offer my congratulations." He looked at Charlie. "Will Miss Manning have full privileges?"

Isobel knew the banker intended no offense. He was simply operating as society believed: ladies had neither the mental acuity nor the fortitude to manage their own finances. Expecting such things of the weaker sex had the potential to do them great harm. She refilled her water glass and waited for Charlie's reply. When he suggested that they create one account with joint access and equal control, she could have hugged him.

To his credit Mr. Hill didn't question the decision. Instead, he began to talk about the need for them to establish goals and then make plans that would assure they attained those goals. Isobel knew it was good advice, but she was still in shock.

"Today," Charlie said, "we only require the opening of a single account." He smiled at Isobel. "Although you and I might wish to speak with the land agents about that property—if you're still sure we're making the right choice."

"If I may be so bold," Mr. Hill said, "when Mrs. Hill and I took our own drive yesterday afternoon, she pointed out a buggy with red wheels——a hint, I imagine, that she'd like a new buggy—" he cleared his throat. "I guessed that you must be considering the property on that block with the tidy little brick cottage. Mature elms and a lovely garden."

Charlie nodded. "We are."

"I assume from your mention of land agents just now, that you wish to build. However, should you be interested in the entire block, I happen to know that the cottage owner would be open to an offer."

Isobel looked at Charlie and shook her head. "We can't be pushing people out of their homes, just because we want—"

Mr. Hill interrupted. "Excuse me, Miss Manning. I would never suggest such a thing. Otoe County National doesn't do business that way. The situation is this: the property is owned by a widow who is moving back east to be closer to family. She discussed the matter with me a few days ago. In fact, I expect she'll be placing a property-for-sale ad in the *Register* soon. We're in the process of establishing a fair price." He looked over at Isobel. "Now that I think of it, you've probably met the owner's family. Isn't Mrs. Richard Payne on your cemetery improvement committee?"

Isobel nodded.

"That's the property owner's daughter-in-law. I'm sure the younger Mrs. Payne would agree that it's a lovely home and in excellent condition. But the elder Mrs. Payne says she has always been homesick for Indiana. Recently, a spinster sister wrote and asked her to come back. They'll share a domicile. It's all arranged—except for the sale of the house."

As Mr. Hill talked, Isobel's thoughts moved along a track of perchances and possibilities. "Charlie," she finally asked, "were you serious about expanding the newspaper office?"

Charlie nodded. "I've already ordered that new press. And the machine we'll need to stitch your book."

"You're still thinking we'll add interior stairs to the second floor and move our office upstairs?" When Charlie nodded again, Isobel said, "All of that could happen very quickly—regardless of what or where we build—if you moved out." She waited for him to follow her train of thought. "And wouldn't it be nice to avoid storing everything through the winter?" Inspiration struck. "We could use the offices to sort through all those crates of books."

It only took a moment for Charlie to catch up. He spoke to Mr. Hill. "We'd like to buy Mrs. Payne's house."

Hill sat back in surprise. "Sight unseen?"

Charlie shrugged. "We've seen the exterior. It's well kept. Lovely gardens. You said it's in good condition. In fact, it's undoubtedly much nicer than my current rooms."

"W-well," Mr. Hill stammered. "Do keep in mind it's much larger than—"

"I imagine so. As it happens, my sister and I have a lot of furniture. We'll take it." Charlie looked at Isobel. "We can always rent it out once *our* place is finished. This gives us time to redo the plans—if we want to. I mean—we don't have to build a modest cottage, Izzy. We can build anything you want."

Isobel nodded, murmuring, "I don't know what I want." She shrugged as she met Charlie's gaze. "You've had a couple of weeks to get used to the idea of being—" She hesitated to say the word, but finally did. "*Rich*. I've known for less than an hour.

Expanding the newspaper is a fine idea. I have no qualms about proceeding with that. After that—we'll see."

Charlie asked Mr. Hill to arrange the purchase of Mrs. Payne's house as soon as possible.

"Of course," Mr. Hill said, "and be assured I'll negotiate a fair price."

"Don't," Charlie said.

"Don't—what?"

"Don't negotiate. Give Mrs. Payne what she wants for the house, sentiment and all."

"It shall be accomplished by the end of business today," Hill promised.

"Please don't do or say anything that will make Mrs. Payne feel that she's being pushed out," Isobel said.

"You have my word on that," Mr. Hill said. "I'll facilitate the transaction and stop by personally to get your signatures on the documents."

As she and Charlie were leaving, Isobel paused to look back at the banker. "I've just remembered something I heard our father say once about investments." She glanced at Charlie. "You'll remember it, too, because Mother Manning was extremely unhappy when the dinner table conversation turned toward a topic she considered suitable only for the gentleman after they'd withdrawn." She looked back at Mr. Hill. "I don't remember the exact words, but it had to do with land in a growing city being one of the best investments a man can make. I wonder, Mr. Hill—would you say Nebraska City will continue to grow?"

Mr. Hill thought for a moment. "We didn't win the robust competition to become our new state's capitol city, but with river traffic enabling all kinds of growth, not to mention the new rail line to Lincoln, I'd say our prospects are bright."

"In that case—" Isobel spoke to Charlie. "Let's buy them all."

"All?"

"The building sites. All four. We can decide what to do with them later." Isobel nodded at the papers atop Mr. Hill's desk. "After we've had time to get used to those ridiculous figures. In the meantime, there's no reason for all that money to sit in an account doing nothing."

Charlie smiled. "Busy Izzy, tycoon extraordinaire."

Isobel allowed a little smile, but the truth of the matter was she didn't want to be a tycoon. Yes, she wanted to be respected as having a brain, but hadn't she already won that with the three men she most admired? She and Charlie took their leave of the banker and proceeded to the offices of Blevins and Black, land agents, to arrange for the property acquisitions. As they made their way along Main Street, Charlie covered Isobel's hand with his and give it a squeeze.

"Are you all right?"

Isobel sighed. "I will be. I just—" She allowed a low laugh. "I'm not certain what I want to be when I grow up. Now that I can be anything."

"I certainly hope *newspaper editor* is still in the running," Charlie said. "You have excellent instincts—for example, the idea of including some uplifting content in every edition. If the response to those sermon excerpts is as good as I anticipate, we might even consider asking local pastors to provide material."

Newspaper editor. He hadn't even added the word *lady* as a qualifier. Isobel smiled. "I don't want to change anything to do with the *Register*—especially now that you're willing to do things my way." The smile faded and she gave a deep sigh. "It's not the newspaper. It's everything else."

After they'd taken a few more steps, Charlie stopped and looked over at her. "You don't want to move into that house with me." It wasn't a question.

He was right. The moment Isobel heard the words, she realized it. "I don't think I do." She continued. "I *like* living at a hotel. Oh, I wouldn't mind a bigger room, but I can have a bigger room the moment one comes available. I like walking across the street and up a block to work. And I really like dining at Jennie's Café. I realize that once you've moved, you'll want to hire a housekeeper and a cook. I won't expect you to join me at the café every morning, but—I don't want to change where I live and eat. At least not right away."

"The best cook in town runs a café. Why would I hire a cook?"

Isobel chuckled. "Point taken."

Charlie's expression grew serious. "The other day when I was worried, you said 'it'll be all right.' Now I'm saying it to you. *It'll be all right.* You don't have to decide *anything* until you're ready. In the meantime, we'll follow your advice. We'll put sermon excerpts in the paper and we'll 'have a little faith.'"

Isobel squeezed his arm. She wanted to tell him what she'd discovered about faith. But she needed to wait until Gideon stepped forward. Then she would tell her brother the whole story, just as it had happened, without hiding anything.

Charlie nudged her arm. "And to clarify: you may not be moving into the Payne house, but that does not get you off the hook. We shipped furniture based on a house plan we might not be using. I'm going to need help knowing what to put where."

"It'll work out. It's only furniture."

"It's also your dressing mirror," Charlie said. "Your bed. Your writing desk. And your *quilt.*"

"All very suitable for one of your extra bedrooms. Besides, I won't live in a hotel forever." Isobel said it without thinking, but once the words were out, she wished she could take them back. What if she did live in a hotel forever? Her thoughts jumped to Gideon again. What if she never saw him again? What if—*stop.*

377

Phrases from Gideon's notebook tumbled into her mind. *Trust in the Lord...lean not on your own understanding...rest in the Lord...wait patiently...*

If only it wasn't so difficult.

If only Gideon would invite her to join him at the Tanners' some Sunday evening.

If only I weren't the richest lady in town.

Chapter 47

Be careful for nothing; but in every thing by prayer
and supplication with thanksgiving
let your requests be made known unto God.
And the peace of God, which passeth all understanding,
shall keep your hearts and minds through Christ Jesus.
Philippians 4:6-7

Gideon sat in Ma's rocking chair, her open Bible across his lap. Somewhere he'd learned of a helpful Bible study tool called a *concordance* that listed every verse in the Bible containing a given word. If he had access to one, he'd be searching out *wait* and *trust,* because it was becoming increasingly difficult to wait until God answered his prayers about what to do next in regard to—well, everything.

Should he tell Birdie and Henry about praying with Isobel? Should he ask her to come to the Tanners' next Sunday evening? Would she want to do that? Would she read too much into it? She didn't really *need* to talk with him. She'd prayed to receive Christ. Now she needed a pastor, a church, Christian friends, and her own Bible. She didn't need him for any of that. But it didn't matter how often he reminded himself of these truths, he still wanted to see Isobel again.

Trouble had been sprawled on the floor asleep when suddenly, he lifted his head and stared at the cabin door. A low growl rumbled in his throat. While the old quilt that served as a window curtain was drawn closed, Gideon knew it was possible for a flicker of light to leak out around the edges and betray his presence to a persistent snoop.

Slowly, taking care that the rocker not creak, Gideon set Ma's Bible aside and rose to his feet. As he took the rifle down from above the door, Trouble came close, ear alert, hackles raised. With painfully slow care, Gideon released the latch. Next, he opened the door for Trouble to slip outside. Expecting to hear a snarl, Gideon frowned when the dog only yipped. A young voice gave a surprised shriek. Weapon cradled with his right arm, Gideon used his left hand to fling open the door. In one swift motion he stepped across the threshold.

"I knew it!" Molly Simmons said. "I *knew* it was you."

Gideon lowered the rifle and stared, speechless. When the girl crouched down to pet Trouble, he said, "You shouldn't be here."

Molly looked up at him, defiance in her expression. "You shouldn't be hiding." Without rising to her feet, she said, "We know you didn't leave our Pa. We all know it. You don't have to hide from us."

He thought of the tattered uniform he'd laid away and the medals that bore silent witness to the truth. It was a comfort to think Tom's family didn't believe the rumors, but—he shook his head. "It's not about that."

Molly stood, frowning. "What, then?"

Taking a slow, ragged breath, Gideon reversed direction. One step backward across the threshold. The lamp was still burning bright, but what Molly needed to see would be in the shadows, and so Gideon slowly looked toward the light.

For a long moment, the girl was quiet. Finally, she asked, "Does it hurt?"

Gideon shook his head. "Not anymore." He returned the rifle to its place above the door before looking back at her.

The girl met his gaze. Finally, with a little nod, she said, "Ma made a big mess of ham and beans tonight. There's plenty left over. Cornbread, too. You hungry?"

Gideon frowned. He shook his head. "I—can't."

She insisted. "Sure you can, Uncle Gideon."

Have faith. Gideon took a deep breath. Was this it, then? Was Molly Simmons's curiosity God's way of leading him back? *Walk by faith. Weather life. Don't run from it.*

Molly extended her hand. "Please. It's just us."

It's just us. The girl had no idea. Gideon took a deep breath. Nodded. Turned down the lamp. Retrieved the rifle. Stepped back outside. Closed the door behind him. Took Molly's proffered hand. Started up the trail.

Simple gestures.

Small steps of faith toward the light.

❦

By the first week of September, Isobel considered the successful issuing of the *Register* a minor miracle in light of how much time it took to achieve Charlie's move out of the rooms above the newspaper office and into the house Jennie loved. As Charlie had noted, the rooms in the story-and-a-half cottage were small, while the furniture they'd brought from the manse was not. Still, when Isobel first stepped onto the polished entryway floor, she smiled. The house might be empty, but in the formal parlor to the right of the door, tasteful striped wall coverings in warm tones coupled with the tile-surround below a carved mantle exuded *welcome home.*

After learning that Ezra Carter had been a carpenter in another lifetime, Charlie engaged the man to line the walls of the room to the left of the entryway with bookshelves. This room would be his library, and while Papa's desk was far too large for the room's proportions, Charlie didn't care. Books and his father's desk and one comfortable chair were all that he required. When he said it, Isobel suppressed the urge to disagree. If things went as she hoped, Charlie would soon wish for *two* comfortable chairs in that room.

The house had one feature Isobel considered an oddity. At the back of the central hall, a sharply curving stairway led down to a lower level. Only half of the sturdy stone walls were sunk into the earth. It wasn't truly a basement, for large windows set into the part of the walls above the ground admitted cheerful morning light. This was the location for both kitchen and dining room. When Isobel commented on the somewhat odd arrangement, Charlie observed that the stone walls would not only retain heat in the winter but also facilitate cooling in the summer. Isobel supposed he was right, but it was still strange to think of descending into the earth to dine.

Once Charlie vacated the rooms above the newspaper office, Ezra Carter and Lawson Tally hauled crate after crate of books up the back stairs. Isobel and Charlie spent more than one enjoyable evening sorting them. The novels inspired long-ago memories of hours spent listening to Papa read aloud. After his passing, both Charlie and Isobel had often curled up in the library in a vain effort to read their sadness away. Charlie rejoiced when he rediscovered *Ivanhoe* and *The Last of the Mohicans*. Isobel claimed *Jane Eyre* and *Pride and Prejudice*. Both were surprised by the number of religious volumes.

"Do you remember these?" Charlie said one evening. He was standing in the midst of three open crates. "*Cruden's Concordance*," he read from an embossed leather spine. "Commentaries by Matthew Henry." He reached into another crate and withdrew a beautiful volume, opening the title page and reading aloud, "*Religious Affections: How Man's Will Affects His Character Before God.*"

Isobel picked up another volume. "*A Call to the Unconverted.* Richard Baxter." She studied the spines of the other books in the crate. "An impressive number of Baxter works."

"And more by Jonathan Edwards here," Charlie said. He looked across the room at her. "Our father was a good man and a wonderful parent, but I had no idea he was a student of the Christian faith."

"Nor did I," Isobel said. She set a few volumes of a commentary by an Alexander MacLaren on a table, arranging them in order as she said, "Once word gets out about the new library's recent acquisitions, every pastor in town will be flocking there." She paused. "We should consider setting up a reading room."

Charlie held up a hand in protest. "Don't assume we're donating them all." He opened a book and began to read.

"Charles Victor Manning," Isobel said with a smile. "What's become of you?"

Charlie looked up from the page and smiled back. "Something good." In simple terms, he told her about lunches in St. Louis with his old friend Dr. Wes Perry—lunches where the discussion was about a great deal more than a search for a missing soldier.

As Charlie described what had been a gradual awakening to truths that helped him overcome bitterness, Isobel's heart thrilled. But still, she did not speak of her own conversion. Not yet. She must wait until Charlie met Gideon. *Gideon,* who loved the Lord and had no idea the riches that could be available to him, thanks to the library of a man who'd died over a decade ago. But to access the wealth, he would need to step back into the light. It was getting more and more difficult to wait for that to happen. More and more difficult to think of the long winter ahead.

Early one October Saturday at the Simmons farm, Gideon crouched down beside Henry as the men cleaned paintbrushes "As chicken coops go," Gideon said, "it's not bad." He glanced over at the project the men had just completed. "Much better than I could have managed on my own. Although I can't say much for the paint job." He pointed at a swath over the coop door that was more board than blue. "I'll come back one day next week when the boys are in school and apply another coat. I don't want to hurt their feelings by re-doing their work."

Henry agreed. "They enjoyed helping. Especially when you told that story about you and Tom and that mule."

"It was good to hear them laugh," Gideon said. He gave a little nod toward the house. "Still watching?"

Henry looked toward the kitchen window. "Still watching." He finished cleaning the last paint brush and stood up. "She'll follow her siblings' example eventually. She just has to do it in her own time."

He was talking about six-year-old Grace, the lone Simmons holdout when it came to accepting Gideon's presence. Henry gathered up the paintbrushes and Gideon put the lid on the turpentine can and followed him to the wagon.

"Want me to talk to her?" Henry offered.

Gideon shook his head. "Nettie's offered, but I told her to let it be. There's no need to obsess on the one little stone in the river of blessing flowing through my life since Molly dragged me over here. Grace will find her way to abiding my presence or she won't. Forcing it isn't the way."

Henry nodded, pointing toward the pasture, where Grace's brothers were playing a version of *fetch* with Trouble. "I wouldn't have believed any of this possible even a month ago. God bless Molly."

"Amen," Gideon agreed, thinking back to that night when she'd accosted him just outside his cabin and then convinced him to follow her home. He'd refused to go inside, just in case Molly's siblings needed the security of shelter. It would be up to them, he said, whether they wanted to step out onto the porch and greet him or not. Apparently, seeing their sister walking alongside him helped. So did the sermonette he heard Molly deliver.

"Now, you got to know before you go out there," the girl said, "that's our Uncle Gideon for sure. But he don't look the same as we remember. 'Course, you three are too young to remember him, anyhow." She must have pointed at Earl, Ethan, and Grace before continuing. "What you need to know is that Uncle Gideon was our Pa's best friend. They used to farm together." She'd gone on to explain, "He was wounded and there's ugly scars. But they don't hurt, and there's nothing to be afraid of."

Dear Molly. Bad grammar, but blunt honesty and a heart of pure gold. By the time she led the string of children out onto the porch where Gideon waited, Nettie was standing at his side, her arms folded across her waist, an unspoken warning in her expression as she looked at her children. *You mind your manners.* Trouble did his part to break the ice. He was delirious with joy at the approach of each child in turn, wagging his tail, lifting a paw, rolling over on command, again and again and again.

At sixteen, Edgar merely shook Gideon's hand, said *hello, sir,* and that was that. Not to be bested by their older brother, twelve-year-old twins Elvin and Eben did the same. Earl and Ethan were shy at first, sidling onto the porch in a way that made Gideon think of boys entering a circus tent to see the freaks. He quashed the flicker of self-pity and before long, those two were sitting on the porch swing trying to convince six-year-old Grace to join them. Grace backed away, blurted out *you sure are ugly* and darted back inside. Nothing anyone said could convince her. And so, Gideon went about the business of building the chicken coop and ignoring the littlest Simmons. By about the fifth day of his working on the farm, the rest of the children seemed to take him for granted. Grace watched from inside.

The men had just stowed the last of Henry's tools in the wagon bed, when Nettie emerged from the kitchen, a basket over her arm, Grace at her side. The child was holding two small jars, one in each hand.

"Since you insisted you couldn't stay for supper," Nettie said, "Grace and I have something for you to take with you. As a thank you for all you've done." She spoke to the child. "Go ahead, now, Grace. Say thank you to Mister Henry and Uncle Gideon."

Grace kept her head down, but she did mutter the words.

"Tell them what you've helped me make today," Nettie urged.

"Apple butter," the child croaked and thrust the jar at Henry. With her free hand, she grabbed a corner of Nettie's apron. Slowly, she held out the other jar. Without looking his way, she mumbled, "Thank you, Uncle Giddy."

Gideon looked at Nettie, who nodded reassurance. Blinking back tears, he reached for the jar. The moment it left Grace's hand, the child hid her face in Nettie's apron. "Thank *you*," Gideon said. "Trouble and I love apple butter."

Grace turned her head just enough to scowl at him with one eye. "Dogs don't eat apple butter."

"Most don't," Gideon agreed. "But I'm fairly certain Trouble will love anything you've helped your Ma make. And the truth is, he'll have to be satisfied with just a taste of apple butter, because there's no chance Mr. Henry or I will share our apple pie." He nodded at the basket on Nettie's arm. "Assuming that's apple?"

Grace faced him. "'Course it's apple," she said. "Elvin and Eben and Ethan and me picked up two whole *bushels* off the ground yesterday." She made a face. "There's jars and jars and jars of pie filling and apple butter and Ma says we'll do jelly tomorrow. Maybe syrup, too." She paused before adding, "Our Pa planted them trees. It's our job to water 'em so they don't die. And now it's our job to pick up apples. Every day." She didn't sound all that pleased with the chore.

"I was there when your Pa planted those trees," Gideon said with a smile. "He made me dig the holes. And then I had to help water them, too, so I know that's hard work."

Nettie looked down at the child with a smile. "Uncle Gideon's right. Edgar and Molly were little back then, and the house was just a two-room log cabin with a loft." As she handed the basket on her arm to Henry, who retreated to set it beneath the wagon seat, she said, "It's not much of a thanks, but it includes lifetime access to fresh eggs." She pointed toward the enlarged coop and what amounted to a mobile chicken yard, a long, low cage on wheels that would enable a dozen or more hens to range the property without fear of predators. "When Elvin proposed that, I doubted it would ever come to be."

"And it wouldn't have," Gideon said, "if Henry hadn't come to the rescue." Gideon had no talent for the endless building and repairing and making-do required of a true farmer like Tom Simmons. Elvin, on the other hand, had obviously inherited his father's ingenuity. With Henry to help, they'd even devised a way to lift two opposite ends of the contraption so that, come next spring, it could be rolled down Nettie's garden rows without damaging the plants.

Nettie repeated the invitation for them to stay for supper, but Henry was already climbing up to the wagon seat. "Appreciate the invitation, but Birdie will be expecting us."

Gideon whistled for Trouble. The dog came running and jumped into the wagon bed. They'd only gone a short distance when Gideon looked back and waved.

Henry glanced over. "Did she wave back, *Uncle Giddy*?"

"She did."

Henry nodded. A moment later, he said, "If it's just the same to you, I'll drop you and the pie at the mercantile first thing so you can gather up whatever supplies you need while I take the wagon back to the livery. I don't care much for the idea of strolling down Main Street with one of Nettie's baskets over my arm." He cleared his throat. "A bit too school-marmish, if you know what I mean."

Gideon appreciated the subterfuge. Henry had probably realized it wouldn't be quite dark when they reached town. He was letting Gideon know that he could scoot inside the mercantile and out of the public eye. Gideon was grateful. Spending time on the Simmons farm was one thing. Sauntering into Nebraska City was another thing entirely. Scars aside, he didn't want to encounter one of the G.A.R. members. Not until he'd found a way for Wade Inskeep and the rest to know the truth. Strange how his attitude about all of that had changed. When Isobel first mentioned the inquiry to the War Department, he'd told her it wouldn't change anything. Now he wished he'd at least told her about Captain Brown.

As they trundled past the cemetery, Gideon cleared his throat. "I—um—wondered. What would you think—what would Birdie think—could we—might we ask Iso—I mean Miss Manning to join us some evening when I come in for supplies? Not tonight. Just—sometime. If Birdie wouldn't mind. If Miss Manning would accept an invitation." He could feel his face turning crimson. *Have you lost your mind? You sound like the turpentine ate a hole in your brain.* He jerked on the brim of his hat. Studied the road. Waited for Henry to say something. Anything.

Henry studied the road ahead for a good long while before responding. "Well, it's about time. I told Birdie it had to be your idea. You certainly took long enough."

Again, Gideon felt heat crawl up his neck. "That night when Molly snooped around the cabin, I told her I didn't think I could go with her. But then she said *it's just us*. She wouldn't give up. You know Molly."

Henry chuckled. "Indeed I do."

"It's getting more complicated to stay to myself."

"You can trust Nettie to keep the children in line," Henry said.

"It's not that," Gideon said. "It's me. Something's changed in here." He thumped his chest with a fist. "I'm just not sure what to do about it."

"You're already doing something about it," Henry countered. "Last week you built a chicken coop. Next week you'll invite Isobel to supper at our place. And when the Lord opens another door, we'll all be there to help you step through it."

Gideon was quiet for the rest of the trip back to town, pondering the miracle of God drawing him toward better things. Hope seemed to be hovering over much of his life these days. Even the impossible hope involving a woman who'd placed her palm against his scarred cheek and declared that no one should ever be rejected because of the way they looked. Gideon still imagined he could sense her fingertips flitting across the landscape of his ruined face. It didn't matter how many times he cautioned himself against reading too much into those moments, hope had begun to glimmer like the evening star rising in the night sky.

Chapter 48

To every thing there is a season, and a time
to every purpose under the heaven.
Ecclesiastes 3:1

Isobel stood at her hotel room window, looking down on Main Street. It was Saturday, and the dusty thoroughfare would soon be lined with wagons and buggies, as farmers from far and wide made their way into town for a day of bartering, buying, and socializing. As she watched, an early arrival pulled up outside Hobart General Store, one of Tanner Mercantile's many competitors in the growing city. The overall-clad driver hopped down and hitched the team before moving to the rear of the wagon and lowering the tail gate. *Apples. Red and green, blush pink and golden yellow.*

Isobel knew very little about the many varieties arriving daily from the Morton orchards, but between Nettie Simmons and Jennie Wilcox, Nebraska City was a veritable apple festival. Nettie's apple butter flew off the shelves at Tanner Mercantile and graced many a plate of apple pancakes at Jennie's Café. Apple kuchen, apple pie, apple crisp, apple dumplings all found their way onto Jennie's menu, producing mouth-watering aromas to greet diners, no matter the time of day.

Isobel turned from the window with a sigh. How could it be October? She'd been in Nebraska for five months. In some ways she felt that she'd lived here forever. Other things reminded her of her newcomer status—one of those, the changing season. Nebraska trees weren't nearly as colorful as those in St. Louis. Temperatures could drop precipitously and without warning. To hear her friends talk, Isobel had never actually lived through a winter.

At the last cemetery society meeting, America Payne had joked that it often snowed *sideways* in Nebraska. At least Isobel thought it was a joke. After consulting Teddy Hall about winter ensembles, Isobel wondered. Teddy had been adamant that yes, Isobel really did need three flannel petticoats and yes, every wool skirt needed a quilted lining. Similarly lined vests wouldn't be a bad idea, either. According to the dressmaker, the newspaper office stove would find it nearly impossible to keep the space heated, possibly for days at a time. That problem would only be exacerbated when the expansion meant a stairway and hole in the ceiling through which warm air would soar upwards, leaving the press room particularly frigid.

Birdie had ordered an array of knitted mitts—gloves with only the fingertips exposed. At the older woman's urging, Isobel purchased three pair. Every purchase, every visit, every conversation about the change in seasons drew Isobel toward regret. Gideon had left a note in the office mail slot about last evening. Something had "come up" and he wouldn't be able to meet her. What on earth could "come up" for a recluse? She supposed he would eventually tell her about it, but—still.

Before long, the weather would force an end to Friday evening rendezvous—unless he did something about it. Didn't he realize that? She now wore a shawl to their meetings. He seemed oblivious. And she was helpless to do a thing about it. Helpless, that is, as long as she minded her upbringing. If she'd learned anything at all from Miss Annabelle of Miss Annabelle Cumberpatch's School for Young Ladies, it was that "no well-bred lady" should "appear eager for the attentions of a gentleman, no matter how much she may admire him."

Blast the infernal rules of etiquette, anyway.

She'd purchased a coverlet from the mercantile—on the excuse that her hotel room was frigid. Which was true, but the truth was that she and Gideon had taken to sitting beneath the oak tree to talk. Trouble had begun to curl up between them, and the coverlet boasted an abundance of dog fur. Isobel didn't mind. Once, she'd reached over to stroke the dog's thick fur, unaware that Gideon had rested his hand on Trouble's back. When their hands touched, she felt as though a static shock had coursed through her. Of course, she'd snatched her hand away, but... what was that all about?

Every Friday, as she drove away from the cemetery, an unseen hand seemed to beckon her to look back at the lone figure watching from beneath the oak tree. What did that mean? Every departure began a new countdown until she could see him again. She wondered what he would think about this matter or that—and it wasn't only spiritual matters she wondered about. Not long ago she'd caught herself torn between which ensemble to wear to the cemetery based on which one might show her auburn hair to its best advantage. As if that mattered.

She scolded herself roundly and repeatedly. Hearts pounding and hands trembling and all that romantic nonsense were just that. Nonsense. Hadn't she agreed with Alfred when he'd said that? And then she wondered if Alfred still felt that way. Had a pounding heart and trembling hands figured into his attraction to Mary Halifax?

A knock on her hotel room door brought Isobel back to the moment. She admitted the chamber maid who had replaced Molly. The girl was the daughter of recent German immigrants, and she barely spoke English. She was efficient and responsive to any of Isobel's requests but given to silence. Isobel missed

Molly's constant chatter. It was strange how the things that one found annoying were often the very things one missed when absent.

As she dressed for the day, Isobel's thoughts lingered in the realm of things missed. Things about to be missed. People, in particular. Person. *Blast the infernal mysteries of*—pain interrupted the thought as she picked up her button hook and bent to fasten her shoes. She grunted softly. On the subject of missing, she would not miss the aches and pains earned from yesterday's adventures preparing the newspaper office for Ezra Carter and Lawson Tally's construction project. Charlie hadn't wanted her help. He and Edgar could handle it, he said. But Isobel didn't want to be left out. It was her newspaper, too—although she hadn't said it in quite those words.

The shoes buttoned, Isobel stood up. Wincing, she pressed her lower back with both palms. *Remember this moment when it comes time to haul your desk up the stairs to the new office. Some things are best left to the men in your life.* She grimaced. *The men in my life.* Despite every effort to distract herself, she pondered only one of those men all the way to the newspaper office. Popping in the back door just long enough to say hello to Ezra Carter and Lawson Tally, she greeted the two men who were already hard at work building interior stairs just inside the front door.

"Morning, Miss Manning," Carter said, with a nod and a tug on the brim of his hat. He gestured at the sawdust scattered across the floor. "We'll be sure there's not a speck of dust left once we finish up."

Isobel pointed to the tarps covering everything in the room. "Hopefully the tarps will keep it from being too terrible of a job."

Carter pointed toward the ceiling where a chalk outline indicated the part to be removed, creating access to the second story. "No telling what'll fall out when we tear into that."

Remembering her battle with rodents during Charlie's absence, Isobel shuddered. "I don't think I want to guess." When Carter and Tally chuckled, Isobel thanked them again for their work and departed.

As she approached Jennie's Café, Isobel forced her thoughts toward the future. Moving her and Charlie's offices upstairs would enable many positive changes at the *Register*, not the least of which was the production of the press's first book, *Early Days in Nebraska City*. The cemetery society would begin offering subscriptions by the end of the month. If all went well, the Ladies Cemetery Society would have sample copies in hand by the end of the year.

Isobel's next stop on her way to breakfast was for the mail. Her heart lurched when she saw the fat envelope from *Wesley Perry, M.D., The Willard Hotel, Washington City*. It was all Isobel could do not to rip the thing open right there. But it was not addressed to her. She resisted and hurried to Jennie's Café, where Charlie waited at their usual table in the corner.

When Isobel handed him the envelope and he saw the return address, Charlie asked, "Do you want to adjourn to my house?"

Isobel shook her head. "I don't want to wait." She plopped into a chair as Charlie opened the envelope and scanned the contents. Molly brought coffee, but Isobel didn't drink it. Instead, she watched Charlie read, her heart pounding. Finally, he held out a few pages so that she could begin reading.

"Fair warning," he said as Isobel took the papers. "It's not an easy read." Then, as he continued down the page, he muttered the word *lucky*.

Isobel removed her gloves and began to peruse the first page. *Lincoln Barracks... Emory General Hospital... catastrophic... facial wounds.* Tears threatened as she scanned the list of field hospitals, the names of doctors who'd cared for Private Gideon Long. For weeks. Months. She shuddered. *The poor man.* How had he managed to endure? Alone. Listed as *missing*. No one writing because no one knew where he was or how to contact him.

She looked up and out the window, bristling as she thought about Wade Inskeep's rumors.

"Ready to order?"

At the sound of Molly's voice, Isobel startled. Quickly, she lowered the papers to her lap, lest Molly read Gideon's name. Glancing toward the specials board, Isobel asked about new apple delights just as she noted the words *apple cinnamon coffee cake.*

"I'll have what she's having," Charlie murmured without looking up.

Isobel returned to reading. How long, she wondered, had it been before Gideon was able to communicate? How long before anyone so much as knew his name? And once they did know, where had he been? How far from the battlefield? She looked over at Charlie. "Did I hear you say he was *lucky*? How can you possibly think that?"

"Because he ended up at Emory."

"In a hospital," Isobel countered. "Unknown. Completely alone. With grievous wounds."

"But in the care of Dr. David McKay," Charlie said and pointed at the papers in Isobel's hand. "Scan to the bottom of those notes, and you'll see the name."

Isobel obeyed. While she read the pages Charlie's friend had paid someone to copy, Charlie told her what he knew about the renowned surgeon. "He pioneered new techniques. My friend, Wes, saw some of the photographs." He went on for a few moments, detailing work that, when successful, had given horribly disfigured men the courage to be seen in public again.

At one point, Isobel held up her hand to stop him. "Enough," she said as she imagined Gideon's dear, ravaged face. What, she wondered, had she not yet seen? What was hidden beneath the long hair and the hat?

"I'm sorry," Charlie said. "Dr. McKay's work—it's fascinating. Wes was able to get hold of some of McKay's notes about the Long case. You've got copies of that, too, if you want to read the details."

"I don't think I do," Isobel said. Molly returned, sliding generous squares of coffee cake onto the table.

"Your coffee's cold," she said. "I'll bring a fresh cup." She retreated without waiting for a response. Isobel handed the papers back to Charlie. She didn't need to read any more about Gideon's wounds. She'd seen the scars.

Charlie read while Molly served Isobel's hot coffee. Once she was out of earshot, he said, "The records show Long returning to duty in November of '63."

After over a year of hospitals and surgeries. Isobel shook her head. "If that's the case, why a tombstone that says he's missing?"

"It would have been all Mrs. Long knew at the time she ordered it. When he returned to service, it wasn't with the Nebraska regiment. He finished the war with the Rhode Island Light Artillery."

Isobel frowned. "Rhode Island? How on earth did that happen? And why?"

Charlie shrugged. "Since we can't talk to Long, we'll probably never know." He paused long enough to take a bite of coffee cake and then said, "Unless we can locate his commanding officer from the latter service. If we can do that, there's a good chance he'd remember Long."

"Because of the scars," Isobel said.

"Possibly, but there's more to Gideon Long than scars."

Indeed. Much more. Isobel tilted her head. "Go on."

"Long might have been a private when he enlisted, but he mustered out a sergeant—with a Medal of Honor."

"Wh-what?!!"

Charlie handed the papers over. "Look at the very last page." He sipped coffee.

Isobel read. *Corporal* Gideon Long had served with Battery B of the Rhode Island Light Artillery *with distinction*. Captain Thomas Frederick Brown had recommended him for the Medal of Honor, and it was awarded.

Charlie said, "Whatever Wade Inskeep and a few other local boys think, Gideon Long was no coward."

"He's a *hero*," Isobel said. And yet, still hiding. He might have allowed Isobel to see him, but thus far nothing else had changed. *Oh, Gideon...please.* A childhood memory flashed. *Something...someone...remember.*

Charlie folded Gideon's record and tucked it back in the envelope. Presently, he asked, "Remember Billy Olivet?"

The name brought it all back. A once beautiful boy horribly scarred after a kitchen fire. Before the injury, Billy had been part of the gaggle of neighborhood boys who played together. After, Isobel remembered seeing people cross the street to avoid speaking to Billy and his mother. Eventually, the family moved away from St. Louis. Isobel swiped at tears as she asked, "Do you have any idea what ever happened to him?"

Charlie shook his head.

Isobel lifted her fork and toyed with her coffee cake. She and Charlie were still sitting quietly when Jennie stepped out from behind the counter and crossed to the table to greet them.

"Something not quite right with my coffee cake?" she asked, nodding at Isobel's plate.

Isobel forced a smile. "Nothing's ever wrong with your baking, dear friend. I just don't have much of an appetite this morning." She and Charlie engaged in what Isobel interpreted—with delight—as almost-flirtation before Jennie excused herself to take breakfast pies out of the oven.

With Jennie's departure, Charlie returned to the subject of Gideon Long and Dr. David McKay's work. "Wes described some of the worst cases McKay tried to help. If Sergeant Long was one of those—and it seems likely he was—it would be understandable for the man to avoid returning home. Especially if he somehow knew his family was gone."

Isobel nodded. Finally, she looked across the table at Charlie and said, "Except he did come home." And she told Charlie everything.

Chapter 49

*Lead me in thy truth, and teach me: for thou
art the God of my salvation;
on thee do I wait all the day.
Psalm 25:5*

After more than a moment of stunned silence, during which Izzy pretended to taste Jennie's coffee cake, Charlie finally managed a response to the cannonball she'd just dropped into their lives. With a glance around them, he leaned in. Doing his best to avoid an accusatory tone, he said, "You've met the man. Been meeting with him out at the cemetery. But you said nothing."

Izzy nodded. "Birdie and Henry have known for a while now."

As if that made it all right? Then again, the Tanners had known the Long family for many years. If they'd done nothing to intervene—taking a deep breath, Charlie managed a nod.

Izzy pointed at the envelope beside him on the edge of the table. "I didn't know about the medal, but I'm not surprised." She put her hand to her cheek. "It's obvious he's endured a great deal. But when you get to know the man, you forget the scars. You see character. Honor. Wisdom. Loyalty."

Was she listening to herself? It didn't take a Pinkerton to realize Izzy felt more than admiration for Gideon Long—whether she wanted to admit it or not.

"That article I put in the paper," Izzy said, "the one that convinced you to feature more religious content?"

"What about it?"

"Gideon wrote it."

Gideon. Not Private Long. *Gideon.*

Izzy took a sip of coffee before carefully setting the cup back in its saucer. Sitting a little straighter, she said, "There's something else. Something I haven't told you about. I think it might reassure you when it comes to my friendship with Gideon."

Friendship. Didn't she realize it was more than that?

"He led me to Christ."

Charlie frowned. "He—what?" Not that she needed to define the terms. Or maybe she did—at least insofar as it applied to her.

Izzy related a remarkable series of events that had taken place while he was in St. Louis. In the end, it seemed to Charlie that she was describing a similar journey to the one on which Wes Perry had guided him. Certainly, it had had a profound impact on her. When she finally concluded the tale, he asked, "Is this at the root of your reluctance to build a house?"

"Is—what at the root of it?"

"What did you think I meant? Your faith, of course." When Izzy's cheeks colored, he realized she'd thought he might be asking about Gideon Long's role in that. It was true, then. She did have feelings for the man.

"My faith," she said quickly and nodded. "Yes. I think so. I hadn't realized it until just this moment, but I think you're right." She paused, then murmured, "I don't know yet what my life will be a year from now, but I've no desire for it to include a big house." She shrugged. "I've spoken about it with

Birdie—without sharing the details of our new reality, of course. We were discussing all the furniture you brought back—and Papa's books, when I asked her why she and Henry still live above the mercantile. She said they'd just never wanted more. That living simply makes it possible for them to 'have the blessing of giving more.' It's a rare approach to prosperity, but I might want to follow their example." She looked over at him. "It's a very personal choice, Charlie. I'm not in any way suggesting you should follow suit."

"I didn't think you were," Charlie said and smiled at her. "After all, buying all that land was your idea."

Izzy chuckled. "It was, wasn't it."

"It's wise to take our time about learning what God expects of us now." When Izzy nodded agreement, Charlie relaxed a little. Who was he to discount God's using unlikely, even bizarre circumstances to accomplish His purposes? Hadn't He done exactly that in the matter of the Manning estate? He would bide his time in the matter of passing judgment on Izzy's interest in her "friend," Gideon Long. At least until he'd had a chance to meet the man. Taking up the envelope containing Wes's report on Long's war record, Charlie suggested they proceed to the mercantile. Birdie and Henry would want to hear the news.

⚜

As Isobel took Charlie's arm for the walk to the Tanners, her mind raced. Charlie had connected her reluctance to proceed with building a house to her friendship with Gideon. Was there something to that? What would the arrival of Gideon's service record mean for his future? If it were up to Isobel, that news would run on the front page of the *Register*. Finally, all of Nebraska City would know that Wade Inskeep and those who believed him were wrong. But it was not up to her.

When Isobel and Charlie entered the mercantile, Birdie was at the cutting counter measuring a length of calico for a customer. At another counter two girls giggled and teased one another about someone named *George* as they considered a selection of hair ribbons. A gaggle of children stared longingly through the glass at the penny candies, and a young couple were busy evaluating the hats on a shelf near the door. Distracted, Birdie called out a greeting without looking up.

Isobel crossed to the cutting counter, and when Birdie looked her way, she said, "We've received an answer to that inquiry we talked about some time ago. The one Charlie's friend pursued for him in Washington City."

Birdie's eyebrows lifted in surprise. She looked at her customer. "Two yards, was it?"

The customer shook her head. "Not two, Mrs. Tanner. *Ten.*" She pointed at the girls pondering hair ribbons. "Enough to make a dress for both the girls, with plenty for the baby and Aunt Myrtle—and scraps for that quilt I was telling you about."

Birdie nodded. "My apologies, Mrs. Spenser. Ten yards it is." She glanced back at Isobel. "Henry's at the Simmons, helping paint the new chicken coop they built this past few days." She nodded at the envelope before proceeding to unwind cloth for measuring. "Good news, I hope."

"Very good."

Birdie stretched fabric along the yardstick imprinted at the edge of the counter, counting up to five before pausing long enough to say, "Much as I want to know, I should wait for Henry. Can you join us for supper? Henry should be back by then. Five o'clock?"

Back at the hotel—Charlie had decided to help Carter and Tally with the stairs—Isobel settled at the writing desk in her room.

Gideon's war record spread before her, fresh paper at the ready, she began to write. For the rest of the afternoon, she worked on the article she hoped Gideon would allow her and Charlie to print in the *Register*. After several drafts, she was finally satisfied.

> Subscribers to the *Register* will be pleased to learn that the efforts of our editors, assisted by those of Dr. Wesley Perry in Washington City, have combined to resolve issues surrounding the war service of Private Gideon Long, previously among those listed as missing after the 1862 battle near Shiloh, Tennessee. War Department records show that a severely wounded Private Long was near death when removed from the battlefield and subsequently transferred to a series of field hospitals. The nature of his wounds prevented Private Long's immediate identification, and he was eventually assigned to the Lincoln Barracks near Emory General Hospital in Washington City, where he remained under the care of Dr. David McKay. In November of 1863, as a result of the efforts of Captain Thomas Frederick Brown, Battery B, 1st Regiment, Rhode Island Volunteer Light Artillery, Long joined the Rhode Island First prior to the Mine Run Campaign. His service continued with distinction in several conflicts after that. In the Battles of the Wilderness, Corporal Long was awarded the Medal of Honor when he took command of two guns in his battery after their lieutenant was struck down. Corporal Long's actions prevented a flanking action designed to break Federal lines. Present at Appomattox Court House to witness the surrender of General Lee, Sergeant Long returned to Washington City with his adopted unit for the Grand Review of the Armies. He mustered out on June 13, 1865. It has come to the attention of your editors

that Sergeant Long has returned to the area. Citizens will soon have opportunity to welcome home a brave man.

Isobel read the summary several times. Would Gideon allow it to be printed or would the entire thing end up in the trash? If he allowed it to appear in the paper, might he insist she strike the last sentence? Would he finally brave the light or continue his life in the shadows? She had absolutely no control over any of it.

Rising to her feet, Isobel paced, back and forth, back and forth. She consulted the time. She waited. Paced. And stood at the window and stared, oblivious to the activity below. She opened her journal and read Scripture she'd copied and notes she'd written. She set it aside and paced some more. Finally, she stood before the dresser mirror and stared at herself. After a moment, she closed her eyes and prayed. "Almighty Father. I don't want him to say we can't tell people the truth." She paused. "And I don't want to spend the winter apart." She opened her eyes. Stared at her reflection. The red hair. The dark eyes. The unfortunate nose. She sighed. Birdie and Henry's example notwithstanding, there was more to her reluctance to build a house than she cared to admit. There was Gideon.

Lord, have mercy.

Good intentions aside, when he tried to help Carter and Tally at the newspaper office, Charlie quickly realized he wasn't much of a carpenter. Who knew there was more than one kind of hammer? Why did it matter if a measurement was off by an eighth of an inch? As the afternoon progressed, so did Charlie's appreciation for Carter and Tally. Before long, he contented himself with wielding broom and dustpan—the only part of the production for which he had even a modicum of competence. As he worked, he pondered the news about Gideon Long and what Izzy persisted in calling her *friendship* with the man.

The issue of Long's military record could easily be set to rights. All that would take was the publication of pertinent information in the *Register*. But that didn't mean Long would allow them to inform the public that he'd returned to the area. Given the man's injuries, Charlie could understand a desire to live in the shadows. It would be easy to honor such a decision—except for Izzy. What had she gotten herself into? She was a grown woman, but thanks to Mother Manning and Alfred Warfield, she was also vulnerable. How, Charlie wondered, would Gideon Long describe what Izzy insisted on calling friendship? What were his intentions? And, uncomfortable as it was to allow suspicion to rear its head, Charlie couldn't help wondering if Gideon Long knew about Izzy's recent inheritance. Did he know his *friend* was a very wealthy woman? Unanswered questions, doubts and concerns, swirled throughout the afternoon while Charlie swept and hauled trash.

Chapter 50

*Study to shew thyself approved unto God,
a workman that needeth not to be ashamed,
rightly dividing the word of truth.*
2 Timothy 2:15

Covered in grit and grime, Charlie hurried home to wash up and don a clean shirt before meeting Izzy at the Tanners'. Once at the mercantile he let himself in via the storeroom door. Mouth-watering aromas of beef stew and percolating coffee drew him up the stairs. Izzy had already arrived and was seated at the table chatting with Birdie while the older woman mixed up a double batch of biscuits. After putting the biscuits in the oven and pouring a fresh round of coffee, Birdie sat down and reached for the envelope Izzy had set atop the table.

"Henry will just have to forgive me," she said. "I can't wait." She began to read, and it wasn't long before she pulled a handkerchief from her apron pocket to dab at tears. Once finished, she beamed at Charlie. "You've given his life back to a good man."

"All I did was write a letter," Charlie said. "Wes is the one who spent hours slogging through records looking for Long's name. It's something of a miracle he found it. I doubt he would have, if he hadn't 'just happened' to attend a lecture given by Dr.

McKay. When Wes spoke with the good doctor afterwards, the mention of a badly wounded patient who was able to return to duty sparked just enough of a memory for McKay to set Wes on the right path."

Birdie set the papers down. "It's going to be wonderful to share this with Gideon."

"Not to mention silencing the Wade Inskeeps of the world, once and for all," Izzy interjected. She produced a sheet of paper from her handbag, unfolded it, and handed it to Charlie. "I worked on this all afternoon. We need to publish it. Front page, right below the banner."

Charlie was halfway through reading Izzy's newspaper announcement when he heard the storeroom door at the base of the stairs open.

Henry called, "Birdie? I convinced Gideon to join us."

A large dog bounded into the room, followed by Henry and a long-haired stranger who, at sight of Charlie, hesitated in the doorway, turning away just a bit. Hiding the worst of the scars, Charlie realized with a surge of sympathy. Quickly, he rose to his feet and crossed to where the man stood. As he offered a handshake, he introduced himself. "Charlie Manning. It's an honor to meet you, Sergeant Long."

Apparently surprised to be addressed as a sergeant, Long frowned a bit as he mechanically shook Charlie's proferred hand.

Birdie stepped into the awkward silence. "Gideon," she called, holding up the sheaf of papers relating the man's impressive war record. "Charlie's received an answer to his inquiry about your service. You need to see it." After a brief pause during which Long didn't move, she added, "Take your coat off, dear. You're staying. You can read while I serve up supper."

Still, no one moved.

Birdie waved her hands about. "Come along, boys and girls. The good Lord has opened a door. Let's walk through it." She began a running monologue. "Isobel, put the honey and that jar of jelly on the table, won't you? We'll need spoons, knives, and napkins. Henry, we need more butter brought up. Charlie—come set the bowls on the table after I've filled them."

At last, Long moved toward the table and the papers Birdie had set down. He hadn't taken his coat off yet, but he did sit and begin to read. Charlie and everyone else hurried to obey Birdie's directives. As Charlie retrieved soup bowls from the shelf above the stove, the dog approached, looking up at Birdie with a hopeful wag of its tail.

Birdie pulled a pan of biscuits from the oven before dishing up stew. She broke a biscuit atop the first bowl and as she set it on the floor for the dog, she looked a challenge at Charlie. "Don't say it."

Charlie stifled a laugh. "Far be it from me to challenge a woman wielding a ladle."

Birdie spoke to the dog. "And don't *you* expect this to become a habit."

Two days after meeting Isobel's brother, Gideon mounted the steps leading up to Charlie Manning's front door, quite literally quaking in the boots he'd polished before coming into town. Isobel's brother had been gracious at their first meeting, but he must have unasked questions and unsquelched doubts—things left unsaid at Birdie's crowded table. Tonight, Gideon would invite Manning to ask the questions, express the doubts, and leave nothing unsaid.

At the sound of a buggy's approach, Gideon jerked his head around and looked up the street. It appeared that Manning was about to welcome visitors. He sighed with relief. He had an excuse to fade back into the shadows for one more day. But the buggy turned a corner and continued toward Main Street. Gideon took a deep breath. *All right, Lord. Here I go.* He knocked on the door, then snatched the hat off his head.

Gideon launched his prepared speech the moment an obviously surprised Charlie Manning opened the door. "I don't have a sister, but if I did, and if I learned a man who looks like me had been spending time with her—unaccompanied and quite literally in the last place on earth one would expect the living to converse—I'd have serious doubts about that man." He paused. "You've probably heard plenty about me from your G.A.R. friends and must have questions best asked in private. So here I am. If tonight isn't convenient, I'll return whenever you say."

"Tonight's fine," Manning said and waved him inside. Taking Gideon's hat and coat, he hung them on a hall tree, then led the way into a finely appointed parlor where a low fire flickered in the fireplace. He waved Gideon into one of two chairs facing one another. "I'm afraid all I can offer by way of refreshment is water. I haven't so much as started a fire in the kitchen stove, and I'm a teetotaler."

Gideon shifted uncomfortably in the chair, wishing he'd taken time to brush himself off after shedding his coat. "Water's perfect." On the one hand, it was awkward to have Manning serving him. On the other, he hadn't been this cotton-mouthed since before his first battle with the First Nebraska. In Manning's absence, Gideon took note of the crystal candlesticks on the mantel, the gilt-framed oil landscapes hanging on the walls, the heavy formal drapes. He was as out of place as overalls at a ball.

Manning returned. Handing Gideon a glass of water, he took a seat in the opposite chair and set his own glass on the table at his side. Gideon took a sip before following suit. As he set the glass down, he said, "I have great respect for your sister, Mr. Manning."

"The name's Charlie. And I believe you."

"Thank you. Even so, I feel that I should apologize for allowing the unusual situation to develop."

Manning—Charlie—appeared to consider the apology, and then a slow smile emerged. "As to your 'allowing' things to develop, I'm fairly certain from what Izzy said when she told me about you yesterday, that you didn't have much choice in the matter of that first meeting." He paused. "She described a note. A 'veiled threat,' she said."

"She didn't mean it as a threat," Gideon said quickly, "but yes, at the time I took it that way. Later, after I came to realize she would not knowingly do me harm—even then, I allowed conversations to continue. In a most unconventional way."

"And because you did," Manning said, "Izzy's church attendance as a social exercise ended. What had been mere religion was transformed by personal knowledge of Christ." Manning leaned forward. "You have nothing to apologize for. I'm grateful for every moment the two of you have spent together." After a moment, Manning brushed the side of his face. "About this. I drove an ambulance after the Battle of Franklin. Do you know of it?"

Gideon stifled a shudder. "Enough. A disaster for the Army of Tennessee."

"To put it mildly. I was such a terrible driver, they shuttled me into service as a hospital steward." He leaned close and tilted his head, inspecting Gideon's scars. "I don't know a thing about what it's like to be inside your skin, but I do know that surviving whatever caused all of that should have killed you. And yet, you returned to duty." He sat back. "The Medal of Honor? You, Sergeant Long, are a walking miracle."

What did a man say to that? Gideon remained silent.

After a moment Manning said, "I suspect my sister has already told you she doesn't care about those scars."

Gideon nodded.

"You need to believe her."

That was all? He wasn't outraged by the clandestine meetings? Wasn't going to demand they cease? Gideon swallowed. "I am trying."

Manning nodded. "Good. Now, as to your concerns about what I might have heard from 'G.A.R. friends.' As it happens, I don't have any G.A.R. friends. When the chapter was forming, I was, shall we say, preoccupied. My wife and child had just died, and I was in no state to socialize. Since then, I haven't known quite how to feel about the outpouring of public sentiment directed at the men who lived through that horror." He paused. "I came across my old uniform when I was deciding what to keep from St. Louis and what to leave behind. It was hanging in a wardrobe. I snatched it up and told our housekeeper to burn it. 'The war was too much gore and very little glory,' I said.

"Well, Portia threw a fit. Snatched it out of my hands and gave quite a speech. 'You don't think there's *glory* in what you won for folks like me? You don't think there's *glory* in the fact there's no more children being sold away from their mothers like I was? How much *glory* would it take for you to look at this blue coat and be proud you wore it?'"

"And?" Gideon asked.

Manning pointed upwards. "In a trunk in the attic."

"Mine was so tattered it nearly fell off me on the walk home," Gideon said. "When I started mending the mending, I decided it was time to let it go." He shook his head. "But I couldn't quite manage it."

"And the medal?"

"In the box it came in."

Manning got up to tend the fire. His back to Gideon, he said, "I was hoping part of your mission tonight was to authorize us to print Izzy's article about you." He returned to his seat. "It could go a long way toward reintroducing you to Nebraska

City. Toward preparing folks for the many ways you've changed. Especially the Wade Inskeeps of the First Nebraska."

Gideon didn't hide his surprise. "You know Wade?"

"He made it a point to stop in the office not long after the cemetery project was first announced."

"With a story?"

Manning shrugged. "Not one Isobel would ever print."

Gideon took a deep breath. "I'm going to have to face Wade one of these days."

"Wait until he's had a chance to read the article," Manning urged. "It'll soften the blow. And give him the chance to repent."

Repent. Would an Inskeep ever do such a thing? "I've tried to mend fences before, but there was animosity between our fathers before us, and it just kept going, even after we joined the First Nebraska. My conversion only made it worse. When the regiment started calling me Preacher Long, Wade wielded the moniker like a weapon. He literally sneered the words, every chance he got." He shrugged. "Isobel's article probably won't change any of that."

"But it could," Manning said. "As Birdie is wont to say, 'God works in mysterious ways.'" From somewhere else in the house, a clock sounded nine o'clock. Manning rose to his feet. "You've a long trek home, but if you'll indulge me, there's one more thing I'd like to talk about before you leave." He led the way into the room opposite the parlor. Bookshelves lined the walls. The only piece of furniture was an ornate desk centered on a fancy rug. "Part of our father's library," Manning said.

"Only part?" Gideon looked about the room in wonder.

Manning nodded. "There are still several unopened crates over at the newspaper office." At mention of the newspaper office, he launched into a lengthy description of recent changes. Interior stairs just inside the front door now led up to what had been Manning's apartment and would now serve as offices. A second press was expected any day. They would be hiring and training another typesetter and someone to help with the printing. "Now," Manning said, "I imagine you're wondering what the newspaper expansion and my father's library have to do with you."

Gideon nodded.

"All the expansion is with one goal in mind: increased circulation. Increased circulation means providing content our subscribers want to read. Response to your first article indicates they want to read what *Anonymous* has to say about matters of faith. To that end, Izzy and I hope to convince you to write more. A regular column, if you will."

A regular column. He couldn't be serious. "But I'm not ordained. All I know is what I've gleaned from reading my mother's Bible."

Manning gestured about them. "Our father's library can help you with that." As Gideon perused the titles on a shelf near him, Manning continued. "I know you like your privacy, and you'd have it here. It's the only house on an undeveloped block, and it's closer to the edge of town than the mercantile. For the next few weeks, I'll be keeping long hours at the *Register*. You can come and go as you please. I'll give you a key."

All Gideon could do was stare at the man in stunned silence.

"Try it for the month of November. Or until the snow flies, whichever comes first."

"Wh-why would you do all that? For me?"

"Because I sincerely like the way you write. Because our readers do, too. Because you're a local hero. Because I empathize with what you've been through, and I'd like to see you step out of the shadows. Because you're my brother in Christ. Because you're a man of character. Because it will make my sister happy, and Isobel's had enough heartbreak in her life. She deserves to be happy. And, frankly, so do you." Manning grinned. "Would it help if I say I'd expect you to bring the dog?"

Gideon looked about the room. He shook his head. "He sheds. A lot."

"I own a broom," Manning said. "We'll work it out."

Chapter 51

What time I am afraid, I will trust in thee.
Psalm 56:3

At dusk on the first Monday in November, Gideon packed Ma's Bible, a notebook, and a pencil into a canvas bag and trudged up the trail toward town. Birdie had said something about stepping through doors the Lord opened. Tonight he would take her advice.

The western sky was still streaked with orange when Gideon let himself in the back door at Charlie Manning's cottage. The drapes were closed in the library, and it was dark enough that once he reached the room, Gideon had to feel his way across the desktop, looking for the matches Charlie had promised to leave out. Matches in hand, he dropped his pack and moved quickly to light the lamps about the room. Next, he built a fire in the fireplace. Trouble curled up in a corner and fell asleep.

Gideon set Ma's Bible and his notebook and pencil on the desk. He took a few moments to peruse individual titles in Charlie's library. As he made his way around the room, his wonder at the extent of Mr. Manning senior's collection grew. What might God do through a man with such a library? What would the Lord who said *unto whomsoever much is given, of him shall be much required* expect of Gideon Long? The possibilities were at once thrilling and terrifying.

Opening his notebook to the first page, Gideon pondered the words *A Quest for Hope.* If ever a journey could prove Birdie Tanner's claim that God worked in mysterious ways, Gideon's quest for hope could. Who would ever have expected God to use a runaway to yank a "creature of the night" out of hiding and launch him toward an encounter with a lone woman in a cemetery? Runaways and cemeteries, mired buggies and lost notebooks. Hardly the heroic elements of such high-minded things as *quests.* And yet, hope had been reborn. Now, Gideon thought, if only he could conquer fear.

Turning past the final page of his quest for hope, Gideon took up his pencil and wrote a new heading. *A Quest for Courage.* Retrieving *Cruden's Concordance to the Holy Scriptures* from a shelf, he opened the leather-bound book to page 852. The first Scripture he would seek was listed beneath bold type. *Fear, subjunctive.* He reached for Ma's Bible.

※

Much to Isobel's dismay, November raced by without her seeing much of Gideon. Oh, she was welcome to join him at the Tanners' on Sunday evenings, and she did. But to her mind he maintained a guarded distance. How she missed their tête-à-têtes at the cemetery.

According to Charlie, Gideon was making good use of the library at the cottage. But he had yet to take advantage of the books in the crates stacked in a corner not far from Isobel's desk. Was he avoiding her? That was not something she would voice—not even to Jennie, who had sensed an underlying current of unhappiness in her friend. *It's nothing,* Isobel said to

Jennie's query. Jennie said that a listening ear was at hand when *nothing* became *something*.

According to Molly, Gideon was bringing the Simmons family an impressive amount of game. Helping them stock up for the winter. He was apparently doing some trapping as well. The subject had come up one Sunday evening at the Tanners', and it served to remind Isobel of the wide valley between his childhood and hers, not to mention his life here in Nebraska and hers.

When Isobel finally sought Birdie's advice, the older woman was sympathetic but unhelpful. "Just because we love Gideon doesn't mean it's going to be easy for him to rejoin the community. We must be patient."

We love him. We.

Birdie smiled at Isobel. "Yes, dear. Of course I know."

Isobel turned away lest Birdie see the tears gathering in her eyes. "It's impossible," she croaked.

"Nothing is impossible with God."

"We have nothing in common."

"You have the most important thing. A God who has brought you together."

"What if that's not enough? Alfred and I had *everything* in common, but it wasn't enough. As for God bringing Gideon and me together—we aren't together."

"Be patient."

"I'm trying, but nothing's happening. He hasn't opened the crates in the office. He hasn't said we can print his service record. He hasn't brought Charlie another article." She took a deep breath. "I should stop coming on Sunday evenings. Gideon shouldn't be forced to tolerate my presence."

There was a slight edge to her tone when Birdie said, "Don't be so dramatic." She paused, and her voice was gentler when she continued. "Do you remember that evening this past summer when Gideon failed to meet you at the cemetery? You hurried back into town to ask Henry to check on him."

Isobel nodded. "And he turned tail and ran when he saw me. It was a horrible ending to a terrible week."

"I told you then that just when we think God isn't paying attention—"

"Yes, I know," Isobel retorted and sang out, "Just when we think God isn't paying attention, He's often doing some of His best work." She swiped at more tears. "Patience isn't easy."

"Especially when you've been hurt by someone you expected to build a life with." Birdie tilted her head and waited until Isobel looked at her before saying, "Gideon Long is not some high society dandy doing what his mama expects."

Isobel grimaced. "I know."

"Then keep joining us on Sunday evenings. And pray your heart out."

***

Powerless to effect any of the changes she longed to see in the matter of Gideon Long, Isobel buried herself in work. Happily, there was plenty of it. *Early Days* moved closer to publication every day. The Ladies Cemetery Improvement Society began to meet at America Payne's to quilt the red, white, and blue quilt they would raffle off in the spring. Isobel attended, but she soon realized she would never manage the tiny, even stitches characteristic of a true quilter. She appointed herself chief needle-threader and spent quiltings in happy conversation with her friends.

With the help of an attorney, Isobel established the Tabitha Fund, a trust named after a New Testament woman "full of good works and almsdeeds." The fund would enable discreet philanthropy based, for now, on Birdie Tanner's vast knowledge of events and needs in Nebraska City. By the end of November, the Tabitha Fund had sponsored a scholarship to Talbot Hall boys' school and promised an impressive budget for a memorial garden the cemetery society would create at Wyuka Cemetery in the spring. The latest in firefighting equipment arrived for Otoe Hook and Ladder #1. Birdie took delight in informing customers who, through no fault of their own, had fallen seriously behind in their accounts at the mercantile, that she'd made an embarrassing mistake. As it happened, the family account had a small credit balance. Schoolteachers received books for their classrooms they didn't remember ordering, and doctors informed patients their accounts had been taken care of by a benefactor who insisted on anonymity.

As Thanksgiving approached—the *Register* had printed President Johnson's October 12 proclamation affirming the celebration for Thursday, November 26—Isobel did her best to heed Birdie's counsel. She reminded herself of the many blessings God had bestowed upon both Charlie and her. She gave thanks in her prayers.

Jennie stopped in at the newspaper one morning and huddled with Charlie, the result being fifteen printed invitations.

Please join friends and family
at Jennie's Café
For a private celebration
Thursday, November 26, at 6 o'clock in the evening.

The Menu

Oyster Soup
Fish with Egg Sauce
Roast Turkey, Boiled Ham, Chicken Pie
Mashed Potatoes, Canned Corn, Sweet
Potatoes, Fried Green Tomatoes

French Rolls, Cream Biscuit
Cranberry Sauce, Chokecherry Jelly, Elderberry Jelly
Mixed Pickles, Pickled Peaches, Cold Slaw, Celery
Mince or Pumpkin Pie, Indian Pudding, Apple Tarts

Perusing the lavish menu, Isobel asked, "Just how many extra cooks did you hire?"

Jennie laughed. "The sauces and jellies and such are already made up. I'll prepare the desserts ahead, and I'll have all evening Wednesday and most of the day Thursday to cook." She paused. "I've so much to be thankful for. I can't think of a better way than preparing good food for all the special people in my life." She looked over at Charlie. "I want to invite Private Long. Do you think he'll come?" Before Charlie could answer, she spoke to Isobel. "It's my considered opinion we can stop pretending I don't know who pushed your buggy out of the mud that day."

With a low laugh, Charlie said, "There's no way to know if he'll come, but I think it's safe to assume, he'll appreciate the invitation. I'll leave it atop my desk in case he comes to study before visiting the Tanners Sunday evening."

It began to snow the Monday before Thanksgiving. At first, Isobel was thrilled by the beautiful puffs of white that floated down from the pale sky, transforming the landscape into a nostalgic scene worthy of Currier & Ives. Even after the temperature dropped, the citizens of Nebraska City seemed unaffected. Collars turned up, mufflers wrapped about their necks and heads, they tramped to work and shoveled the boardwalks, and life went on with a surprising dearth of complaints. Until, that is, when it was still snowing two days later.

"Hope this isn't a harbinger of the winter to come."

"When the clouds hang low like that, we're in for it."

"Folks farther west are going to be tying a rope between the house and the barn so they don't get lost feeding the livestock."

"Our neighbors lost their best laying hen last night. Blasted coyotes."

Isobel donned all three wool petticoats and soldiered on. She was thankful she was only a block away from the office. Poor Charlie had a longer walk through ever-deepening snow. Isobel could only imagine Gideon trying to get to town. He probably wouldn't even try. But he did, for on Tuesday, Jennie's supper invitation was back atop Charlie's desk along with a note expressing both Gideon's thanks and his regrets.

There was also an envelope for Isobel, containing a longer note and an article for the *Register*.

> *I enclose an article to be considered for the Register. It grew out of my recent studies, which have been enriched by Charlie's generous sharing of your father's impressive library. As I can think of nothing with which to repay his kindness, generosity, and trust, I will simply offer my sincere thanks when next I see him.*
>
> *You will remember the notebook in which I conducted what I called A Quest for Hope. There is a second part now, which I've titled A Quest for Courage. This recent search began as did the one for hope—in God's Word and with prayer. Finding hope enabled me to step out from behind an oak tree in a cemetery. Now, as courage flickers, I take three more steps, no less difficult, but with more specific goals in mind.*
>
> *First, I have signed G. Long to the enclosed and will continue such with all future writings.*
>
> *Second, I request that you proceed with printing my service record at such time as fits your editorial needs.*

Third, I take a necessary journey too complex to be shared in this missive. Sadly, this third step makes my attendance at Mrs. Wilcox's Thanksgiving gala impossible.

Please pray for me. While I am mindful of God's promises that I need not fear, for He is with me, I remain fearful and yet, now that the path is before me, I am determined to walk it.

May our dear Lord bless your Thanksgiving with abundant joy.

Your friend
Gideon

Very nearly blinded by the snow, Gideon slogged toward the cabin in the distance. Passing a series of empty hog pens, he stepped up onto the porch. His heart pounded as he knocked on the door. When no one responded, he retreated to the edge of the porch and looked about the farmyard. The place had never looked better.

Outbuildings he remembered as bare boards were now painted rust red. No discarded implements protruded from the deepening snow. The corral fence was straight, and the gate hung true. It was not what he remembered. Not what he expected. Encouraged, he retreated to the door and knocked again. This time, there was a response, albeit a profane one. The door opened just a crack. "Wade? Is that you? It's Gideon Long. It's been a long time coming, but I owe you an apology." After a moment, the door opened a little further. Gideon took off his hat and unwrapped the muffler.

Inskeep's jaw dropped. "Y-you!" He staggered backwards, looking at Gideon with horror. "What happened to you? You're supposed to be dead."

Inskeep didn't object when Gideon stepped inside, crossed to the fireplace, removed his snow-encrusted mittens, and held his hands out toward the flames.

"I saw you run."

Gideon turned to face him. "The line was advancing. Tom fell. I couldn't just leave him. I did my best to tie a tourniquet, put his hand to the spot and told him to press. Hard. I ran for help." He paused. "Next thing I knew, there was a flash of light. I woke up at a field hospital. They didn't know who I was." He shrugged. "Charlie Manning's going to print the whole story. I finished out the war with the Rhode Island Artillery."

"Do tell," Inskeep said.

Silence loomed large. Gideon gestured about him. "The place looks better than it ever did when we were growing up. You should be proud."

Inskeep grunted. "And you should be ashamed. Your place looks like there might be raccoons in the loft."

"I didn't want anyone to know I came back."

Inskeep scowled at him. "Why did you?"

"To take care of Ma. She wrote me about Pa dying long before Shiloh. After I mustered out, it seemed right. I could stay out of sight—mostly. Farm the place and see that she was taken care of."

"As I recall, you had plans to be famous." Bitterness dripped off the words as Inskeep continued, "Pretty boy Preacher Long with the deep voice, standing at the pull-pit telling everybody how they ought to live." He paused. "You always did like to lord it over everybody. Even before you got religion."

"You're right," Gideon said. "I was arrogant. I should have kept my mouth shut about that prank. You didn't mean for anyone to get hurt. But I made it sound like you plotted it down to the last detail, and the lieutenant believed me."

"Put me on guard duty every night, rain or shine," Inskeep said. He raised his voice a bit. "Cancelled my furlough." Spittle spewed as he shouted the next few words. "And Becky *died*. I never got to see her again." He slumped into a chair by the fire, but his rage was spent. He ground out the rest. "She's up on that hill under the sod." He glared at Gideon. "And don't you dare try to feed me that slop about her enjoying the glories of heaven." He looked away. "I know she is. But I'm not going there, so what good does that do me?" He sounded weary as he stared at the fire and muttered, "Why'd you come here?"

"To beg forgiveness."

Inskeep grunted. "Don't you preachers say God's the one who doles out forgiveness?"

"Yes. But if our brother has something against us, we're supposed to be the one to go to that brother and try to resolve it. I'm sorry, Wade. Sorry and hoping you can find a way to forgive me."

Inskeep looked at him in disbelief. His eyes glittered with malevolence as he spat out the words, "I'm not your brother." He rose to his feet. "There's no forgiveness for you here." He flung a hand in the direction of the door. "Now get off my place. And don't ever come back."

Chapter 52

*For thou wilt light my candle: the Lord my
God will enlighten my darkness.
Psalm 18:28*

Isobel turned up her collar before stepping out of the hotel and into the frigid morning. Winter was living up to every dire prediction made by the ladies of the Cemetery Improvement Society. A ridge of snow over which she could barely see lined the ice and snow-encrusted boardwalk. Most days, Isobel wore all three of her flannel petticoats beneath a lined wool skirt. With a vest. She wore knitted mitts at the office to keep her hands warm, and she'd become expert at building and tending fires at the office. She had seen it snow sideways. More than once.

Despite the cold on this December morning, Isobel slowed as she passed the windows at Tanner Mercantile where Birdie and Henry had arranged an enticing array of toys. Two dark-headed and one blond doll rode in a little wagon positioned beside a doll-sized perambulator, rocking chair, and bedstead. Henry had erected one of several log cabin playhouses, complete with a door, windows, chimney, and roof. While the varnished logs boasted a dark red hue, the rails of the fence marking off a little yard were red, white, and blue. Rolling hoops and sleds created a backdrop to the entire display, with books positioned throughout.

Isobel envisioned little Grace Simmons settling the blond-haired doll into the perambulator. Or towing books and toys about in a wagon. Did the children have sleds? Perhaps Saint Nicholas could make a delivery for the Tabitha Fund in coming days. *If only it would stop snowing.*

Neither Molly nor Edgar had been to work since Thanksgiving. Birdie said there was nothing to worry about. Nettie's larder was full. Gideon and Henry had long ago made sure there was an ample supply of firewood. The repairs done over the summer meant the house was well equipped to weather wind, ice, and snow. But Isobel still worried.

She especially missed Edgar as she plodded along setting type in his absence. She was determined that all of Nebraska City would read the truth about Private Gideon Long in the very next issue of the *Register*. First, they would learn the truth about his war service. More importantly, they would see into the heart of the man through his excellent writing, which was more devotional than instructive.

The piece was beautifully written, and it broke Isobel's heart, for while the words were about the spiritual ideal of "a calling" and "the folly of an average life," she intuited another message. What could be more *average* than establishing a home? Here was the truth behind the subtle change she'd detected in recent weeks when she saw Gideon at the Tanners'. He was going to distance himself.

She'd been a fool. She should have known that allowing herself to fall in love was *folly*. There was nothing about her that would inspire a man to anything beyond cordial friendship. Hadn't she learned anything from that debacle in the spring?

✤

Christmas Eve morning graced the earth with clear skies and dazzling light that reflected off deep snow and weighed down tree branches. Deep drifts mimicked the waves of the sea—or at least what Gideon imagined waves looked like. He'd never actually seen the ocean, but he'd seen paintings of ships caught in a storm.

Caught in a storm. It was an apt term for the way he'd felt since leaving Wade Inskeep's place and making his way home. He'd made slow progress, sometimes floundering in drifts up to his waist, praying to God that he wouldn't twist an ankle or worse.

When he finally staggered into the cabin, Trouble charged past him with a sense of urgency. It was all Gideon could do to build a fire in the stove. As the air warmed, he slumped in Ma's rocking chair, steam rising from his clothes, sweat moistening the scarf that lay about his neck.

Finally thawed out, he donned a clean Union suit and dove beneath the pile of blankets and comforts on the bed. He slept until noon the next day, waking only when Trouble licked his nose and gave the characteristic half-yodel half-growl that meant the dog needed to go out.

The visit to Wade Inskeep hadn't accomplished what he'd hoped, but he'd been obedient to what he thought God expected of him. Now he would pray. And move forward. He was not quite certain what "moving forward" would look like, but in his mind, every version of it included Isobel.

Lord, have mercy. The prospect of speaking his mind to the woman terrified him. But he was determined to take his own advice as expressed in the article he'd written for the *Register*. He was not going to settle for an average life. He'd assumed that all he would ever have was a life in the shadows. But then... Isobel.

He loved her. It was time he told her.

Standing at the mercantile store door, Gideon remembered the terror he'd felt at the prospect of letting Henry and Birdie know that he'd survived the war. Letting them see his face. He was just as frightened now, but for a different reason. Oh, he wasn't exactly looking forward to the various reactions he'd get from the folks at church tonight, but Isobel's article had been published. Most, if not all the people would know he wasn't a coward responsible for Tom Simmons's death. Many would have read the short piece he'd written about faith. It wasn't the congregation. It was how things would change if things went as he hoped tonight.

Lord willing, tonight would be the end of what he'd called an "average life" in the article. With Isobel's help, he would put aside that folly. Uncertain as it was, fraught with unanswered questions as it was, tonight was the night his quest for courage would end. He would forsake life in the shadows and look to the future.

Trouble had been patient, but now the dog pawed at the door, then looked a question up at Gideon, who smiled in spite of himself. "You're pathetic, you know? All you care about is what Birdie's going to feed you tonight."

Hearing Birdie's name, Trouble gave a low *yip* and once again pawed the door.

Taking a deep breath, Gideon led the way inside.

Trouble raced up the stairs. Birdie descended to the landing with a bright smile. "I'm glad to see you. I know Charlie and Jennie included you in the invitation to a late supper. Please say you've decided to attend church, too."

"I have."

Birdie clasped her hands before her. "Praise God, from whom all blessings flow."

Gideon took a deep breath. "It took much of the day to get here." He brushed off his coat. "I'm not really presentable. Can you help me with that?" He nodded toward the store.

Birdie led the way beyond the curtain and lit two lamps to illuminate the shelves of menswear. "What you really need is a horse," she said.

"You're right. But first I need a new hat."

※

Isobel had reserved the nicest sleigh at the livery, especially for Christmas Eve. She was going to take Charlie and Jennie for a sleigh ride before the church service—if she could convince them that everything was perfect for the candlelight supper they would host later this evening. By now, things had probably been perfect for hours, knowing Jennie's abilities when it came to entertaining and Charlie's nerves, which had necessitated that they set the table fully twenty-four hours in advance.

It would be the first time the pocket doors between parlor and dining room stood open to create a bigger space for entertaining. The first time the china Portia had packed for transport into the West would be used. The first time Charlie Manning and Jennie Wilcox would declare their intentions in regard to one another—without saying a word. When Charlie opened the door later this evening to welcome guests, Jennie at his side, people would assume, and they would be right.

Isobel smiled as she hitched Elsie, stepped down onto the snow-packed street, and made her way to the front door. With temperatures expected to dip below zero before midnight, she wondered if the church service would be sparsely attended. She wondered if part of Charlie's nerves might be the stress of courting Jennie beneath Electa Bishop's critical eye.

Electa and Julian Bishop had made a brief appearance at the Thanksgiving dinner Jennie hosted at her cafe. Pa Bishop had beamed with happiness that night, clearly proud of Jennie and reveling in the presence of the Simmons children. Clearly, the man would have been a wonderful grandfather. Electa, on the other hand, had maintained an expression that reminded Isobel of someone trying not to notice the lingering aroma of a kitchen failure. Thankfully, things had changed.

Somehow, Electa had discovered that Charlie Manning was the owner of not one but four very prime pieces of property in Nebraska City. If the woman knew that Isobel's name was on those land deeds as well, she showed no knowledge of that, for which Isobel was glad. But land agents were now regular visitors at the newspaper office, and word was circulating that the editor of the *Register* was an up-and-coming developer. Isobel had no doubt that this evening, Electa would arrive swathed in fur. She would discreetly check the mark on the bottom of the china, test the stemware to see if it was crystal, and inspect the silver. Sterling or merely plate?

Jennie swung open the door before Isobel knocked.

"You look lovely," Isobel said as she tugged on an ear. "Beautiful earrings. Are they new?"

"You know they are," Jennie said, blushing. She took Isobel's coat and hung it on the hall tree.

"And where is the giver of the jewelry?"

"He's down in the kitchen making sure the house isn't going to burn down while we are at church. Or something." Jennie paused. "Does he always get this way before a party? I've told him over and over again there's nothing to worry about."

"I've no idea how he gets before a party," Isobel laughed. "As far as I know, he's never hosted one."

"Well, come into the dining room and see what a lovely table the Mannings's second-best china makes."

"Second best?" Isobel asked as she followed Jennie down the hall.

"I was not about to be responsible for breaking a piece of Meissen," Jennie said. "Besides, I like the Spode better."

Isobel followed Jennie down the hall. Standing in the doorway, she gasped with delight. A garland of pine adorned the mantle and ran down the center of the dining table. Every few inches an orange pierced with whole cloves wafted alluring aromas into the air. Small nosegays comprised of ribbon flowers had been placed at each place.

"Sarah Carter was kind enough to show me how to make the ribbon flowers," Jennie said. "Aren't they lovely?"

Charlie spoke from behind them. He'd come up the stairs from the kitchen. "We gathered the rest from the yard—except for the oranges and cloves."

"*Now* you boast about it," Jennie teased and looked at Isobel. "You should have heard him when I suggested we dig through the snow."

"I didn't know you could do this," Charlie said and swept a hand toward the mantle. "I promise never to grouse again about gathering anything you want from anywhere."

Isobel reached out to tug on one of the apron strings tied about Charlie's middle. "On the topic of gathering, can I convince you to gather a few bricks and warm them? I'm taking the two of you on a sleigh ride before the service."

Jennie's face lit up. "I *love* sleigh rides!" She hesitated with mock concern. "But I'm not certain about *you* driving. The last time you and I—"

"My skills are much improved," Isobel said. "Plus, there's no chance of rain. Now, tell me what I can do to help you finish getting ready for the party." She turned to Charlie. "Bricks?"

※

Isobel held up her gloved hands, palms facing and waggled them towards each other. "Move closer," she said to the couple now seated in the sleigh. "It's not going to get any warmer. And besides that, there's a rumor going around that you two like each other. No one will be scandalized if you aren't clinging to the far edges of that seat." She climbed up to the sleigh seat with a laugh and urged Elsie forward.

As the sleigh whooshed along the streets, Isobel regretted not bringing a comforter for herself. It was cold up here on the driver's seat. Tucking her nose deeper into the scarf about her neck, she concentrated on the road ahead, guiding Elsie toward the river and then turning north toward Main Street. As they drove past the mercantile, she glanced toward the toy display, which had been decimated earlier in the day when a representative of the Tabitha Fund stopped by. Said representative had also depleted the stock of candy when Isobel suggested the fund surprise all the children in attendance at the Christmas Eve service with a sack of candy. And an orange.

Birdie had hesitated. "I don't know if we have that many oranges." Then her smile returned. "I'll count, and if we don't have enough, I'll send Henry over to Hobart's for more."

The afternoon had been one of joy, and Isobel had barely thought of Gideon. For at least five minutes at a time. Progress. She was making progress.

Why does it have to be so difficult? The lamplit church was warm and surprisingly full when Isobel, Charlie, and Jennie made their way up the aisle to an empty pew. Birdie and Henry had already arrived, positioning the orange crate now filled with bags of candy beneath a rear pew.

Pastor Duncan's message began with the reminder that this night above all nights was a night of hope—a reminder that the God of all hope was worthy of trust, for He always kept His promises. Israel had long awaited the fulfillment of the greatest promise of all. They had long been tempted to lose hope. But God had not forgotten them. In his time He had kept His promise and sent the promised Messiah.

Isobel's throat constricted a bit when the repeated use of the word *hope* reminded her of Gideon's quest for hope. *I will trust the God of Hope. I will be all right.* The romantic fantasy that Gideon would slip into the pew beside her and perhaps even take her hand was just that. A romantic fantasy. *Oh, but if only*—she swallowed and bowed her head. *Charlie is here. Sober. Jennie is next to him. My dear friend. A better friend than any I've ever had. Henry and Birdie are here. Lord, have mercy. You have given me so much. I am thankful. <u>You</u> are my hope. In <u>You</u> will I trust.*

Yes, it would be hard. But she would find her way past disappointment. Again. God had brought her all the way to Nebraska and brought her to Himself. She would be all right.

Pastor Duncan concluded the service by focusing on, of all things, fear.

And the angel said unto him, Fear not, Zacharias.

And the angel said unto her, Fear Not, Mary.

And the angel said unto them ... the shepherds ... Fear not.

Again, Isobel's mind flew to Gideon's notebook. He'd been on A Quest for Courage. She'd hoped it would bring him to her. But whatever the quest, it wasn't about her. She would pray for him. She would be all right.

The closing hymn nearly did her in, for it was all about light, and again her thoughts flew to Gideon, who had told her he'd thought of himself as a "creature of the night," assigned to live in the shadows. He'd said she helped draw him toward the light. Isobel forced herself to think on the Father of Lights, wiping at tears as she sang.

> *Silent night! Holy night!*
> *All is calm, all is bright,*
> *Round yon Virgin Mother and Child.*

> *Holy Infant, so tender and mild,*
> *Sleep in heavenly peace!*
> *Sleep in heavenly peace!*
>
> *Silent night! Holy night!*
> *Shepherds quake at the sight!*
> *Glories stream from heaven afar,*
> *Heavenly Hosts sing Alleluia!*
> *Christ the Savior is born!*
> *Christ the Savior is born!*
>
> *Silent night! Holy night!*
> *Son of God, love's pure light*
> *Radiant beams from Thy Holy Face*
> *With the dawn of redeeming grace,*
> *Jesus, Lord, at Thy birth!*
> *Jesus, Lord, at Thy birth!*

The moment Pastor Duncan said *amen* at the conclusion of his prayer, Isobel was out of the pew and hurrying toward the back of the church. Pulling the orange crate out from its hiding place, she stationed herself just inside the back door. Birdie and Jennie joined her, and together, the three women distributed bags of candy—and an orange—along with Christmas Greetings from the Tabitha Fund.

As the crate emptied, Isobel grew a bit uneasy. What if they ran out? But they didn't, and as the last of the congregation disappeared into the night, Charlie picked up the crate and they all prepared to leave. He'd just made a joke about the seven of them having to fight over the remaining four bags of candy when he stopped in his tracks.

Isobel bumped into him, then followed his gaze toward the sleigh, where a stranger stood, stroking Elsie's thin neck.

A stranger with a dog at his side. He was speaking to Elsie, for the horse had turned her head and was listening intently, her ears pricked, the breath from her nostrils visible in the bright moonlight.

As Trouble bounded toward them, Charlie turned to Henry. "Mind if we ride with you?"

"Happy to oblige," Henry said and the four headed off toward the Tanners' rented sleigh.

Her heart pounding, Isobel took the time to pull on her driving gloves. She bent down to pet Trouble. It gave her the time she needed to manage a calmer approach. As she neared the sleigh, Gideon turned to face her. He took off his hat. Moonlight illuminated the scars.

"I'm sorry," he said, nodding toward the church. "I rode with Henry and Birdie. I had every intention of joining you. And then—" He sighed. "It would seem my quest for courage will continue for a while." He paused, then repeated, "I'm sorry."

"I won't pretend I didn't hope you'd be there," Isobel said. "Pastor Duncan actually began his message on the topic of hope."

"I heard it." Gideon pointed toward one of the windows. "I stood beneath that window. In the shadows. Yet again." He looked away from her. "I bought a new hat."

What did a new hat have to do with anything?

"I wanted—I thought—" He broke off. Shook his head. "The old one has that wide brim." He reached up and made the familiar motion Isobel recognized. Pulling the hat down on one side, trying to hide his scars. "One side of that brim is going to fall off in my hand one of these days." He turned the new hat in his hands as he said, "This one has a different shape. No wide brim."

Oh, Gideon. Isobel reached up and put her palm to the scars. "I told you I don't care about these."

"I remember," he said, reaching up to take her hand. "I have missed you." He kissed her gloved palm, then lowered her hand, but he didn't let go.

"But——you said you don't want an 'average life.' It was in the article."

"What did you think that meant?"

"Me."

He let out a frustrated breath. "My dear Isobel. There is no possibility that life with you could ever be *average*."

Life with her? Surely he didn't mean—did he? With her free hand, she swiped at the tears that had begun to fall. "But—you wrote about a higher calling. You said—"

He gave an audible sigh. "All that work, and I failed to say what I meant."

"I might have read too much into it. Made assumptions. Too many that were far too personal."

"Even so, one thing is clear, if I'm going to write for the *Register*, I'll need the help of a really good editor."

"I can arrange that," Isobel said. "Exclusive access, if you require it." She felt the blush rise even as she heard the words.

"I'll hold you to that." He leaned close just as Elsie broke the mood with a loud snort and a shudder. Gideon looked over at the horse. "Really? Am I that bad at this?" He put his hat back on and looked toward the cottage. "We're going to be scandalously late to your brother's."

Isobel laughed when Trouble hopped into the sleigh and snuggled down into comforters and lap robes. And then Gideon's hands were at her waist, lifting her onto the driver's seat.

"I want you beside me," he said.

As the sleigh glided along the moonlit street toward Charlie's, Isobel tucked her hands about Gideon's arm. At the cottage Trouble bounded out of the sleigh and made for the front door while Gideon hitched Elsie alongside two other sleighs. He lifted Isobel down before spreading a blanket over Elsie's bony frame and then, adjusting the hat on his head, offered his arm. He'd only taken a couple of steps toward Charlie's front door when he stopped. "The Bishops," he said. "Mrs. Wilcox. They haven't seen—"

"Birdie. Henry. Charlie," Isobel said. "Three good friends and a woman who loves you." She pointed toward the parlor windows. "Just walk toward the light, beloved. Walk toward the light."

The End

Now unto him that is able to do exceeding abundantly above all that we ask or think, according to the power that worketh in us, Unto him be glory in the church by Christ Jesus throughout all ages, world without end. Amen.
Ephesians 3:20-21

Dear Reader

From Stephanie
March 2023

Thank you for making the leap back in time to 1868. When I set out to write *Love at First Light*, I had a vague notion of creating a *Beauty and the Beast* story inspired by the hours I've spent learning Civil War medical history—especially one night when I came across an archive of "before and after" photographs taken to create a record of advances in what would become cosmetic surgery. I ended up weeping over all those beautiful boys who survived horrific wounds and lived on, unimaginably disfigured. Gideon Long is my way of paying them tribute. My unending fascination with historic cemeteries, old tombstones, and the stories they represent suggested a plot twist that changed the story to "Beauty and the Beast in a Cemetery."

Like you, I'm a fan of historical fiction, and when I read a novel, I often find myself wondering what's real and what the author created for the story. If you're wondering that about *Love at First Light,* check out the Pinterest page for this book (link below). You're also welcome to e-mail stephanie@stephaniewhitson.com. I'll do my best to answer in a timely manner.

What's Real?

Nebraska City. I've tried to remain true to the known history of Nebraska City, Nebraska. The oldest map I could locate was dated 1878, fully ten years after the setting for my story. The brick hotel, a house like the Bishops', the newspapers, the "prairie motor" parked on the Morton property, the Morton's' house and orchards and, of course, Wyuka Cemetery were all there in 1868. I was assisted in research by knowledgeable historians. Any errors are fully my responsibility.

Gideon's wounds, recovery, and military history are as accurate as the military researcher who assisted me and I could make them. I am indebted to his assistance in tracking the possible trajectory of a Nebraska private's journey toward a Medal of Honor.

Arbor Mansion, the home of the Mortons, is a well-preserved historic site, and I've spent countless fascinating hours prowling its rooms (including the attic, thanks to a behind-the-scenes tour) and reading archival materials.

D. L. Moody, a bold ambassador for the Gospel, really did serve with the Christian Commission during the Civil War. He was present after the Battle of Fort Donelson.

Wyuka Cemetery in Nebraska City was founded in 1855. At the time of *Love at First Light*, it would have been the final resting place of about 200 deceased pioneers and located well outside the city limits on a treeless hill characterized by prairie grass and the occasional cow pie, courtesy of livestock wandering onto the unfenced ground. The names and dates and epitaphs that Jennie reads off as Isobel is recording information off tombstones are all real. Only one is not from Wyuka. That one appears on my great-grandmother's obelisk in a small cemetery in southern Illinois and is from a poem written by John Newton. There is also a Wyuka Cemetery in Lincoln, Nebraska. That Wyuka has prepared a self-guided tour that I highly recommend. Civil War connections are not hard to find and include nurse Hettie Painter, German immigrant Captain Peter Karberg, who served with the U.S.C.T., and Ruth Wilcox, whom the great Frederick Douglass called his adopted sister.

The Gospel and the Christian faith. Jesus Christ really lived, really died for my sins and yours, and really does love you. Just as Isobel came to realize that, so have I. So can you. God does allow seemingly awful things to happen (like being jilted at the altar and facing profound physical disability). He can and does use trials to make us more like His Son. His plan and purposes are always executed for His children's eternal good and His eternal glory (Romans 8:28). Just as Gideon discovered, God never lets go of His children. If you are in a place where you are wondering *why,* you might be encouraged by something my first husband wrote for a Sunday School class he taught not long before he died of cancer in 2001. He updated the notes on January 12, 2001, and graduated to heaven on February 3. Find Bob's notes here: https://stephaniewhitson.com/why-cancer/

What's My Imagination?

The tree in the cemetery. I needed a tree for this story, and there is an ancient, towering burr oak tree that inspired mine. It wasn't there in 1868, and there are no trees evident in the single historic photograph I was able to locate of what is known as the "old ground." But I reasoned that there could have been a tree along Table Creek and so I planted one. Gideon needed a place to hide when he spoke with Isobel.

The characters, while drawn with all the authenticity I could muster regarding how ladies and gentlemen dressed and behaved in 1868, are figments of my overactive imagination. I have historic photos of real women who inspired Isobel and Jennie, Birdie, and poor, unhappy Electa Bishop. I don't imagine faces very well, but my collection of antique cabinet cards provides endless inspiration. It's odd that while I can't conjure up Isobel out of thin air, I recognize her when I see her. That's strange and I know it, but it's true. You can see some of the photos that have inspired my imaginary friends on my Pinterest page. https://www.pinterest.com/stephgwhitson/love-at-first-light/

Works Consulted

A Brief Sketch of the Development of Negro Education in St. Louis, Missouri, J. W. Evans, The Journal of Negro Education, October, 1938

Fort Donelson, Gateway to the Confederate Heartland, DVD produced by the National Park Service, U.S. Department of the Interior

Godey's Lady's Book, February, 1868

Historically Eventful Nebraska City, Glenn Noble

History of Nebraska, Andreas

The History of Nebraska City, Nebraska 1854-1890, Mary Borne (MA Thesis), Lincoln, NE, July, 1933.

Images of America, Nebraska City, Tammy Partsch.

J. Sterling Morton, Pioneer Statesman, Founder of Arbor Day, James C. Olson

John Henry Kagi and the Old Log Cabin Home, Edward D. Bartling

Mollie, the Journal of Mollie Dorsey Sanford in Nebraska and Colorado Territories 1857-1866

Nebraska City Centennial 1854-1954 booklet

Nebraska City History 1854-2004 Sequicentennial booklet published by Nebraska City News-Press, Inc.

Nebraska in the Civil War, NSHS Educational Leaflet No. 8

Nebraska History Magazine Summer 1992 Vol. 73, No. 2

Sketches of Early Days of Nebraska City, A.E. Harvey, St. Louis, 1871

Standing Firmly by the Flag, Nebraska Territory and the Civil War 1861-1867, James E. Potter

Sterling's Carrie, Mrs. J. Sterling Morton by Margaret V. Ott

The G.A.R. in Missouri, 1866-1870, James N. Prim, The Journal of Southern History, Vol. 20 No. 3.

Women in Nebraska City 1855-1860, Laurence L. Falk, Ph.D.

Wyuka: A Place of Rest, Nebraska City's Pioneer Cemetery, Donald R. Hegr

Sites Visited

Arbor Lodge State Historical Site, Nebraska City, NE
   https://www.arbordayfarm.org/activities/arbor-lodge.cfm
   https://history.nebraska.gov/becoming-arbor-lodge/
Dover Hotel, Dover, TN
   https://www.nps.gov/fodo/learn/photosmultimedia/tour-stop10.htm
Fort Donelson National Battlefield, Dover, TN
   https://www.nps.gov/fodo/index.htm
G.A.R. Museum, Nebraska City, NE
   https://civilwarmuseumnc.org/
J. Sterling Morton Memorial Library, Nebraska City, NE
   https://morton-jamespubliclibrary.com/index.php/about-us/history/
Nebraska State Historical Society Archives, Lincoln, NE
   https://history.nebraska.gov/collection_section/research-and-reference-services/
Nelson House, Nebraska City, Nebraska
   https://visitnebraska.com/nebraska-city/taylor-wessel-bickel-nelson-house
Old Freighters Museum, Nebraska City, NE
   https://visitnebraska.com/nebraska-city/old-freighters-museum

Shiloh National Military Park, TN
    https://www.nps.gov/shil/index.htm
Wildwood Historic Center, Nebraska City, NE
    https://www.wildwoodhistoriccenter.org/
Wyuka Cemetery, Nebraska City, NE
    https://nebraskacityne.gov/wyuka-cemetery/

Discussion Questions

To learn more about the writing of *Love at First Light,* go to the Pinterest page created specifically for this book. Find it here: https://www.pinterest.com/stephgwhitson/love-at-first-light/.

1. If Charlie Manning were your friend, how would you help him through his grief?
2. In what ways are Birdie and Henry Tanner good friends? In what ways could they have done better?
3. What kind of future do you see for Molly Simmons? If you were writing her story, how would it end?
4. Why do you think Electa Bishop is the way she is? What events or interactions might have made her more likable?
5. What event or situation do you think made the biggest difference in Isobel's growth as a person?
6. The Ladies Cemetery Improvement Society is a fictional example of women banding together to realize civic improvements—something that was common in the 19th century. Are you aware of a similar organization in your community? What kinds of things do they take on? Share a success story.
7. How does your community observe Memorial Day? Do you think such ceremonies are important? Why or why not?
8. Who was your favorite minor character in the book? Why?

9. What spiritual lesson would you say was most important for Charlie to learn? What about Gideon and Isobel?
10. Do you keep the kind of notebook Gideon used to think through spiritual truths? If so, how has it benefited your walk with the Lord?
11. What scriptures comfort you most when you are tempted to lose hope?

Coming Christmas 2023

A Prairie Christmas

Featuring three Christmas novellas

A Picture-Perfect Christmas

Lydia McCord is desperate to bring an end to the tumbleweed existence she and her father have always led. When the Stanford Photo Car arrives in North Platte, Nebraska, Lydia is the first customer. To her mind, giving a certain local rancher's son her portrait will solidify their relationship and open the way for her to have a real home in a community where she can make lasting friends. While she is drawn to Nate Stanford, she resists the idea of romance. After all, life on a traveling railcar is the last place she'd be happy. But then the rancher's son shows his true colors. A rejected Nate Stanford has already left town aboard his mobile photographic studio. Is it possible Lydia's been wrong about where to find true love? What does it really mean to be *at home*?

A Patchwork Love
originally published in the anthology
titled *A Patchwork Christmas*

Mended Hearts originally published in *Christmas Stitches*

To receive book news from Stephanie, sign up for her newsletters at www.stephaniewhitson.com or follow her on Facebook; https://www.facebook.com/StephanieGraceWhitsonofficial/
BookBub; https://www.bookbub.com/profile/stephanie-grace-whitson

Printed in Great Britain
by Amazon